THE LOST ELEMENTS

À ma belle
Laurence,

Je voudrais te remercier pour
toute l'amitié et tout le support
que tu m'as offert durant ces 5 ans
au secondaire. Te connaître fut ma plus
belle croisade. Je te promet que je vais faire
de tout mon possible pour que cette année soit
encore meilleure que l'année 2014. Ça va être
difficile à faire, mais tu sais à quel point je
suis entêtée! Je t'aime ma belle, et cette
année sera à nous!

Merci,
Ta Jora
xoxe

THE LOST ELEMENTS

Lara Rosechild

U.S. Copyright Registration Number 1-234-567-891
WGAW Registered 1234567

10 9 8 7 6 5 4 3 2 1

First Edition © 2014 by Lara Rosechild

Hardcover ISBN: 987-6-5432198-7-6
Softcover ISBN: 987-6-5432198-7-6
Ebook ISBN: 987-6-5432198-7-6
Library of Congress Control Number: 2014908943
CreateSpace Independent Publishing Platform
North Charleston, South Carolina
ISBN-13: 9781499539899
ISBN: 1499539894

CONTENTS

I dedicate this book to those who have made all of this possible. I couldn't have done this without the help of my Mom, who was one of my first readers, and the one who took the most time to bring it to conclusion. Proves to say, that no matter how hard things can get with her, I know she'll always be there for me, and I for her.

"Whether you believe you can, or believe you can't, you are right."
-Ford

I won't forget that, Dad. Thank you for pushing me through this, and for teaching me that discipline and perseverance are key to following through with anything.

ONE

The mall in Boston was huge. It had four stories and was three times as big as an average-sized park. Even then, I could navigate through it as if it were my own house. All my favorite stores were here, as well as all my favorite restaurants. I'd come here since I was six years old, whether to spend time with my best friends or do some before-school shopping with my mom. I also happened to have an incredible photographic memory, so I really had no trouble navigating to places where I'd only been once.

I wouldn't deny it; Abby Claire was someone who liked to shop. I liked shopping but mostly for jeans, cute tops and books. It wasn't something I would do every week but once in a while, it felt good to cut loose and act like the typical teenage girl. I wasn't that different really, but I had to admit that I'd been through a *bit* more than other girls had.

If you asked any of the people I knew to describe me in one word, some would say bitch, self-absorbed, snob... Of course, those who called me that were, in my opinion, the worst people to ask. My friends, those who really knew me, would say things like kind, caring, selfless, loved, nice, sweet ... I could be all of those things and that included being a bitch. I guess it all depended on my mood and the situation but I was *mostly* what my friends said I was. I was myself.

1

Kaithlyn Porter and Brittany Hart were walking beside me, as they always did, as loyal and caring as any faithful friend in a story. There had never been once when they hadn't had my back. In some ways, we were a small family, always looking out for each other. There were no words that could describe how grateful I was for having them as trusting friends.

We walked alongside each other, head high and confident. How many years had we done the same, our friendship only growing stronger and stronger throughout the years?

We came to a stop in front of Kaithlyn's store. It wasn't actually Kaithlyn's store; it was her father's shop, Mr. Porter. Even then, the three of us referred to it as Kaithlyn's.

It was an antique store, full of rusty chains, dried up books and replicas of Princess Diana's jewelry. I just loved coming in there. It made me travel back in time, made me feel like the princess knight I had always wanted to be.

"If you guys don't mind," said Kaithlyn, "I would like to go see my father for a while." She fidgeted with the ring she had attached to a chain around her neck, a nervous tick I had noticed not even a year ago.

I looked at my redheaded friend. Her jade green eyes were shining with eagerness. We all knew Kaithlyn's father worked until very late at night and he would leave early. Kaithlyn only got to see him on Sundays but even then, he took that entire day to relax, crashing on the couch, drinking tea. Kaithlyn never said anything but I knew she was hurting inside. It was even harder for her because she had no other parent figure to look up to—her mom had died from breast cancer when Kaithlyn was three years old.

Mr. Porter wasn't a work-fanatic, but he was the only one who could pay the rent at the end of the month. Kaithlyn was working on the weekends, so she could actually help him with that, but a job at the local library didn't bring much and most of the time, Mr. Porter didn't even consider taking the money, probably because it was against his morals to do so.

"Why not?" I said, smiling. "It's been a long time since I've seen your dad."

"We can also ask him if he could use some extra hands," suggested Brittany. "I would also like to see the new stock he just got. Last time, I found a grimoire that was over five hundred years old!"

I smiled. Brittany was *the* princess in shining armor. Not only did she look like one, but she also had the character of one. Her black hair was pulled back in a ponytail, the angles of her face beautiful. The chestnut eyes were, maybe too big for Brittany's head, in my opinion, but that small fact made her look even more beautiful. She also had light freckles that ran along the top of her nose and a little bit under her eyes. Her face was free of imperfections and as fair as porcelain. When she didn't speak, she looked as fragile as a leaf in autumn; a strong wind and she would fly away. I knew her well enough not to think of her that way.

Kaithlyn pushed the door of the store open as if entering it like a fairytale. The store wasn't stuck on one, boring theme, like most antique stores. It had several themes. In one corner, there were ancient Asian artifacts and in another, were some things from the French Renaissance. Of course, most of these things had no real value to museums, so it hadn't been hard for Mr. Porter to get his hands on them.

I caught myself staring at *the* cream-white Greek gown. Ever since I could remember, the dress had always been there, an imaginary light dancing around it, making it shine of a thousand colors. How could this beautiful dress stay untouched? I didn't know. If I had the money and the occasion to wear it, I would have jumped at the opportunity to buy it. Mr. Porter had offered it to me several times but I had always declined. I wasn't fit to wear such a dress, even though I spent hours fantasying about wearing it, the satin smooth on my skin, its trail swiping the floor where I walked ...

This was a magical place and that was exactly where Mr. Porter fit. He looked up at the sound of the door's puny bell ring. That too was something that had always been there.

Mr. Porter smiled when he spotted Kaithlyn. He got up from his seat and hugged her warmly. Even a blind person could sense love pouring from every pore of Mr. Porter. His love for Kaithlyn was pure, and I admired that about him. He wasn't afraid to express his feelings, unlike most of our modern human society.

"Hi Dad," whispered Kaithlyn into her father's shoulder. I often wondered when the last time she had seen him was. I presumed it couldn't be more recent than three days ago.

"Hi Kate," said Mr. Porter.

One of the things I liked the most about Kaithlyn was that she wasn't embarrassed about hugging her family in front of others, even though others consisted of Brittany and myself. She didn't care if people made fun of it later. Kaithlyn was just being herself. Unlike many people who wanted to be cool, Kaithlyn didn't lie about her true self, just like her father, and that's how people got to respect her.

Mr. Porter turned to Brittany and me and released his daughter, only to hug us both. I hugged him back. Kaithlyn's father was like a father to me. I had known him since I was only six. Eleven years later, I still had the same love toward him. Even though I rarely got to see him, it was good once in a while to get some fatherly affection.

"Uncle John," choked out Brittany, "you're killing us!"

He let go of us both, laughing. "Choke me back when I do so," he exclaimed, patting both of our heads, his hands warm and big.

I went to lean against the desk next to Kaithlyn and smiled at her. "Your dad hasn't changed a bit since the last time I saw him," I said, grinning at Kaithlyn.

Kaithlyn frowned at me. I couldn't help but look at her perfectly plucked eyebrows, fine and graceful. "When was the last time you saw him?"

"Last April, at Easter," I answered, shrugging. "I haven't seen him since then."

"You haven't seen many people since then, Abby," said Kaithlyn, sourly, her nose slightly wrinkling.

"I won't deny that." I shrugged and hooked my thumbs into my pockets. I had my own reasons, reasons I didn't want to think about at the moment.

"Uncle John?" said Brittany.

"Yes, Brittany?"

"Since we're here, why don't we help you with your work?" I said instead of waiting for Brittany to answer.

"Thank you for answering, *Brittany*," said Mr. Porter. He turned to me and said, "I can always use a hand in a shop like this."

"Why don't you hire helpers?" I asked. "I know some people who could work for real cheap."

"Like who? The local drug dealers at your school?"

"Ha ha ha." I rolled my eyes. Another thing I liked about Mr. Porter, he and I had the same type of humor—ironic. "I meant me. I need some money but I won't ask for too much and you can really use the help."

"Thank you for your confidence in my business, Abby but I'm fine," Mr. Porter looked around and sighed heavily, "but if you girls don't mind helping me for free for an hour or so, that would be great. I just got new stock coming from Eastern Europe. You girls can unpack the boxes while I go to a meeting."

Kaithlyn frowned. "I didn't know you had meetings, since, you know, you're the only one who works here."

Kaithlyn's father shrugged. "You know I can't afford to hire someone, Kate. I have a meeting with the shopping center owners because I have a score to settle down in this mall. Coop, the owner of the store next door, complains about the differences between our stores, a modern *Calltext* phone store next to a medieval and ancient boutique. Pathetic, isn't it?"

I went to him and put a hand on his shoulder. "Go and show them what you're made of Mr. Porter."

Mr. Porter smiled at me and pushed up the glasses that had been falling off his nose. "I've never really liked Coop; he's always trying to sabotage my business. Last week, he came into the store and chased two customers away. Let me tell you, that was the last straw." He shook his head as if the next-door owner was a complete moron, a kid with no experience. "Anyway, there's a list on the counter of the objects you're supposed to find in the boxes. If there's any missing, circle them in red."

Brittany stood straight, a neutral expression on her face. She fisted her hand on her heart and said, "We won't disappoint you, Uncle John." There was a moment of silence; then we all burst out in laughter.

"I know you won't, Lieutenant Brittany. I have faith in you," he looked at Kaithlyn and me as well, "in all of you. Now, if you'll excuse me …" Mr. Porter put the jacket that had been resting on his chair "… I have some serious *Calltext* business to worry about."

Before he could step out of the store, I exclaimed, "Where are the boxes?"

Mr. Porter only turned his head, not looking in my direction and answered, "In the back." Then he left.

"Oh, this is great," exclaimed Kaithlyn, swinging her arms in the air. "I want to spend time with him and work rips him away—*again*."

I went to her and put an arm around Kaithlyn's shoulders, tightening when she slightly drew away. She didn't want my sympathy; that I could tell. However, for the good of her own subconscious, she needed to be comforted. "It's okay, Kate. You know there's nothing he can do about it. I know your dad and he's not the type to *love* work. He just … *needs* it to make a living for the both of you."

Brittany came to lean on the other side of Kaithlyn and put an arm around her waist. "He's doing this for you, you know? He loves you so much," she said calmly, her voice sounding like millions of bells to my ears. I sometimes envied her for her voice but it was nothing I couldn't handle.

"He's never there. I never get a 'Good night Kate' when I go to bed at night. I never get a 'Good morning Kate' when I wake up. He wasn't there for my birthday. I feel all alone in that apartment. I can even hear my echo!"

Kaithlyn shut her eyes and let out the breath she had been holding. "I know he's doing this for me, and I never said any of this to him because I know it would hurt him. I just wish there was something I could do to help."

Understanding what she meant by that, I shrugged. Jane, my adoptive mother was as hard working as Mr. Porter was, maybe even more.

She worked in some kind of social security company; that's what she had once told me when I had asked her about it. She hadn't given me any more details so I hadn't pressed the issue. I rarely saw her for more than twenty minutes in the morning and she came back very late at night or very early in the morning. I had once tried waiting for her but had failed, falling asleep on the couch.

I walked across the boutique and opened the back door. I turned to look at my friends, who were still leaning against the counter. "The more work we finish for your dad, the sooner he'll come back tonight." When they only stared at me, I sighed and went in the storage room, not waiting for them to follow.

The room was much colder than in front. It wasn't heated, for one and I could see my every breath hanging lazily in the air. I let out a long, smoky puff of air and looked around me. I had been in here many times before but I had never seen it like this. There were many boxes piled up on each other, every one of them had the sign 'Fragile' on it, marked in bright red. The boxes were in different shapes and sizes and they went as high as eight, maybe nine, feet, I wasn't really sure.

I was going to need a stool for that, considering I was only five four. I took my jacket off and tossed it on a stash of empty, folded boxes. I rubbed my hands and blew hot air on them. God, it was cold, and I wasn't even going to think about how cold it was outside. If I wanted to do my work, well, I was going to have to be able to move with complete ease—no matter what the weather. Sadly, that meant I had to take off my freaking coat.

It was only fifteen minutes later that I was sitting on the dark boutique floor with a ten kilogram box in front of me. I hadn't been able to reach the top of the pile, so Kaithlyn, who was only two and a half inches taller, got it for me. I felt so awkward, just standing there waiting for her to get the box for me, that I actually looked away. She just laughed at me teasingly.

Brittany, small and fragile Brittany, hadn't really done anything physical. She had fetched all three of us a pocketknife from Mr. Porter's desk and lists of the inventory.

I tightened my grip on the knife handle and tested its sharpness. *It was sharp enough*, I thought when the blade cut easily through the tape. I opened the box with one, swift movement of the hand.

"I'm sorry our *'girls' night out'* had to end this way," said Kaithlyn apologetically. "I just—"

"No need to explain," I assured her before peering into the box.

You know, there are those weird times, when you think the world comes to a stop. I often had those moments when I was with Luke or when I was reading a book or maybe even watching a movie. The world stops, just waiting for something to happen, as if the world depended on it. The weirdest part was that I was having a moment like that right now. Everything seemed to glow of a million colors. What I found in it was more interesting than what most antique stores usually offered. I had expected to find a portrait or maybe a porcelain plate but not a dagger with diamonds on the handle. I wondered how Mr. Porter could get, or even afford, these kinds of things. Maybe he got them from a drug dealer or maybe a pirate ... When I got bored, the only way out was with imagination; that was my only reply for thinking like that. Imagination was powerful and sometimes ridiculous. Anyway, all of these were probably replicas.

I scanned the list for *'Sarajevo diamond dagger'*. I checked it off the list and continued looking in my box. By the time I was done unpacking, I had found a king's emerald ring, a crystal vase from France, a pearl necklace from Finland ... anything you would usually find in a museum.

"Where do you put them once they're out of the boxes?" I asked Kaithlyn. Mr. Porter couldn't possibly want us to have the precious objects scattered on the floor. They were much too valuable for that kind of treatment.

Kaithlyn passed a hand through her hair and sighed. "He left a note saying that we have to place them *carefully*—in the safe. He knows I know the code."

"Wait," said Brittany. "Did you say, 'He left a *note*'?"

"Yeah. Why?"

"He didn't write anything while we were here."

"He must have written it before we came in. I guess he knew that we were going to come," answered Kaithlyn, coolly, not looking up from the box she was gradually unpacking.

"We didn't even tell him we were coming," I continued, obstinately. "He couldn't have known we were coming."

This time, Kaithlyn did look up from her work. "Abby, my father knows things. I don't know how but he just ... *does*."

"I guess ..." Letting it go, I got up to go get another box.

Once I was back on the floor, Kaithlyn had already taken the objects away, in the safe.

"Are you sure all this is going to fit into the safe?" I asked to Kaithlyn, slicing open the box I had in front of me.

"I'm sure there'll be enough space for at least eight people. It's like Alibaba's cave," said Kaithlyn looking impressed, "with shelved categories, of course."

"No kidding," added Brittany. "I didn't even know they made big ones like that."

"So ... how's Mary?" said Kaithlyn, trying an attempt at conversation.

The image of my little stepsister brought me a small burst of pure joy. "She's great. It's her first year in kindergarten, so she hasn't made many friends yet. I guess it'll come with time."

"Is she still as much trouble as she used to be?" asked Brittany, grinning at me. I knew why she did so. Last time Brittany had seen Mary was two months ago. Mary had poured her orange juice all over Brittany's *Juicy* shirt. Ironic, right?

"No, not really. She doesn't wake up very often at night. It's chaos when she's sick though."

Kaithlyn giggled and so did Brittany. I frowned at them. "What's so funny?"

After several seconds of hesitation, Brittany said, "No offense but you sound like a mother hen worrying about her child, or should I say chick."

"Ha ha, very funny. Laugh all you want mother hen's annoying chicken friends." That only made them laugh louder.

Once calm was restored from both of my friends, I said, "So, Britt ... how're things with Blake?"

Brittany lowered her head; then raised it up, her face almost expressionless. I could see a hint of pain in her dark brown eyes and I knew right then that something was up.

"We broke up."

What I first felt was pure shock. We all had known how much Blake Parker had meant to Brittany. They had been dating for at least six months. Brittany had only said good things about him. I didn't know—and didn't want to know—how far their relationship had gotten but I hadn't known things had gotten bad between them. Blake had had a playboy reputation before they had started dating, so I shouldn't have been that surprised about this. I hadn't been very approving in the beginning but after seeing how well Blake acted with Brittany, I had eased up. My first instinct had apparently been right.

"Why?" asked Kaithlyn, clearly as shaken as I had been. "You said things were great between the two of you."

"I did—before I found out he was cheating on me. I saw him making out with Victoria in the 'deserted' hallways. Not so deserted apparently ..."

"Oh, honey," murmured Kaithlyn, getting up from her place, kneeling next to Brittany and putting an arm around her shoulder. "I'm sorry."

"Don't be," muttered Brittany. With a higher voice, she added, "It was meant to happen sooner or later. Things haven't been that stable lately. I think it's better that I ended it before he did. I prefer dumping—not being dumped."

"You're right," I nodded at her encouragingly. "That's how Brittany Hart has to think—positively not negatively."

"Thanks, Abby. You're making the matter much more simple," said Kaithlyn sourly, her arm still around Brittany's shoulder.

"No," exclaimed Brittany. "Abby's right. I shouldn't let myself feel bad for something I didn't do. To tell you the truth, I feel free now that I've broken up with Blake. I feel free and powerful."

If only I could believe her like Kaithlyn … She was mourning over her lost relationship, and she was a pro at hiding it.

"How many boxes have we unpacked until now?" I asked, crossing 'fairy dust' off the list. Of course, I knew it wasn't real, because then … well, I wasn't really sure. Yeah, it would be strange if it were real … but then again, that would be impossible. "I just finished my second package." Although I had to admit that my fingers were getting sore from all that cutting, opening and writing.

"I'm still on my first," grumbled Kaithlyn.

"I just started my third one," answered Brittany.

"In total, we had fourteen boxes—minus six … we still have eight to unpack," I declared before getting up to get another one. "Seven with the one I'm about to get."

That's how we worked for the next half hour. Brittany and I (being the two fastest unpackers of the three) unpacked the boxes, while Kaithlyn placed them all in the safe. We worked easily around each other, talking about diverse things. Like the geography exam we all had tomorrow or maybe planning another attempt at a girls' night out.

"I don't know …" I said. "I don't think I'll be able to come this Thursday. I don't think Mrs. Wildfire will be able to take care of Mary that day. She agreed for today … but I wouldn't want to tire her. She's getting old."

"How are you even related to her?" asked Kaithlyn, taking a vase in her hand and bringing it in the safe. "Sorry. I don't have a good memory for other people's families."

"She's Jane's mother's friend," I said, opening the last box. "I've known her since I was five, since I was adopted. She's like the grandma I never had."

"I see …" Brittany had already finished unpacking, so she was walking around the store, stretching her legs. "Mrs. Wildfire is like the grandma you never had; Mary is like the sister you never had; Uncle John is like the father you never had and Jane is like the mother you never had. I'd say that's enough to live happily ever after."

"No Brittany," put in Kaithlyn. "You forgot two important things."

Brittany frowned. "The faithful steed and friends?"

"The valiant friends part and …"

"Prince charming?"

"Yes!" exclaimed Kaithlyn, grinning at Brittany. "Who wouldn't want a Prince Charming?"

I cleared my throat. "You guys quickly forget that I already have a boyfriend."

"Oh, right, how could anyone forget the perfectly sculptured body of Luke Rush? Six pack, broad shoulders, *fine* legs …" Brittany rolled her eyes at me. "C'mon. Finish this box so that maybe we can go get a raspberry gelato at *Ben and Jerry's.*"

"Why don't you guys go on ahead," I said. "I'm almost finished here … and anyway, we can't leave the store open and unsupervised."

Kaithlyn shifted in what seemed unease. "It's my father's shop, Abby. I'm the one who should be staying, not you."

"Mr. Porter is like the father I never had. Now go! I don't want frozen yogurt for seven bucks anyway."

It was only after they had both hesitated for several seconds that Kaithlyn said, "All right, we'll go. We won't be long."

Before the door closed behind them, I exclaimed, "Take all your time!"

Once I was alone, I sighed. I was so lucky to have friends like them. They had never let me down when I had needed them most—when I had had my first heartbreak, all the times I had skinned myself trying to climb the tree in Brittany's backyard …

I got back to work. I was fantasying about wearing that Greek silk dress at a ball and dancing with Luke when Mr. Porter barged into the store. I jumped up. It had been so quiet and I hadn't been expecting to be surprised.

He spotted me without any scanning of the room. He walked to where I was and sat, crossed-leg, in front of the box and me. For a minute, I just stared at him and he stared back at me, waiting for something.

"I hope you girls didn't have too much trouble?" he said after a while, taking the box from my hands and looking inside.

"It was just fine. Brittany and Kaithlyn went to *Ben and Jerry's.*" I took the list of the objects and handed it to him. "There's nothing missing but I haven't finished unpacking this one." I gestured at the box on my lap.

"Did you put the things in the safe?"

"Yes, sir."

"Did any customers come?"

"No, sir."

He pushed up his glasses and said, "Did you check the '*wind talisman*'?"

I took the list from his hands and nodded. "Yes, it's in the safe with the rest."

He put the box to the side and got up. He walked into the back-room, where the safe was located.

I frowned. Mr. Porter was no ordinary man—not at all. I knew better than to question him.

I got up and stretched my arms and legs. They were numb from all that sitting. I checked my watch. It was eight o'clock. Jane wanted me home by 8:30.

Mr. Porter came back with my jacket and a black velvet pouch in hand. He handed me my jacket and opened the pouch he had also given me.

What happened next, I could never forget. It was weird, very unnatural. The kind of feeling you would get from fairytales. Things like this couldn't happen, not in this time and age. I felt the air change. It moved around me, ruffling my hair and filling my ears with the sound of wind blowing through leaves. It was sweet yet mysterious. I closed my eyes and inhaled its imprinting fragrance. I could hear the whispering of the wind through carillons …

It was only when the magic was gone that I opened my eyes. I blinked several times before the little bursts of lights faded from my vision and was able to bring the room back into focus. Mr. Porter was smiling at me, as if he knew what I had just felt.

"What … was *that*?" I asked, my eyes wide with confusion and fear. Confusion was explainable but fear wasn't. How could I be afraid of something that had felt so good?

Instead of directly answering me, Mr. Porter slipped the pouch's content into his hand. "I present you the Wind Talisman."

I stared at it, compelled. The talisman was maybe as big as a pebble. The ornate was in what looked like real silver, but what deranged me most was the stone. It seemed to be blown glass; maybe it was but I knew this was no ordinary stone. It seemed to be liquid inside, moving and doing things beyond mere understanding or maybe I had stayed up too late last night.

It was Mr. Porter's firm voice that pushed me out of my reverie. "I want you to keep it."

I looked up from the stone and shook my head. "I can't accept." Yeah right, I couldn't. "It's way too—"

"Think of it as an early birthday present," he said interrupting me mid-sentence. He unclasped the chain and held it in a gesture that made me turn around. I lifted my hair and let him put the talisman in place.

"Now that this is settled," said Mr. Porter, (I turned around to look at him) "I'll finish the rest of this box. You can wait at the counter and take the candy bar. The girls should be coming soon. If there are any customers, please take care of them."

I nodded. "All right."

He took the box from the floor and went in the backroom, closing the door behind him.

I brought a hand to my throat, where the strange talisman was resting. I felt the fresh wind coming back to me, bringing me the slightest feeling of wellbeing.

I sighed and went to sit at the counter. From the looks of his working area, Mr. Porter seemed to be a well-organized man. There were no loose papers or any sign of dust on his desk. All of his tax books were neatly placed, as well as his cash register. There were no personal objects, though—no pictures, no nothing.

I took the only thing that seemed out of place—a chocolate bar. The *Kit Kat* Mr. Porter had told me to take. Instead of opening it and eating it, I slid it in my purse. Mary would surely like it.

I closed my eyes, allowing my fatigue to get the best of me. I hadn't really slept in the last few days. I had had nightmares—not the-monsters-in-the-closets type of nightmares, the *real* kind of nightmares. I repressed a shudder. I vaguely remember seeing the dream a long time ago, giving me the feeling of déjà vu. Not even two nights ago, I had awakened, sweat tickling down my forehead and back. I knew I had had a nightmare but the second my eyes opened, I forgot what it had been about but the fear stayed, unmoving.

My eyes fluttered open when I heard the light ringing of the bell. Two guys stepped into the shop. Both were elegant and dressed in black and white.

The first one to step inside was completely dressed in black. His hair, his leather jacket and jeans, even his shoes were black. According to the shape of his face and the way he was built, I estimated he was about seventeen, maybe eighteen years old. He had smoked glasses on, so I couldn't see his eyes. I wouldn't have been surprised, if they too, had been black.

The second one was much less dark. For one, he didn't wear glasses, so I had a clear view of his eyes—beautiful green eyes, almond shaped—brown hair with a tint of gold, a straight nose and prominent features. His elven face reminded me of Orlando Bloom in Lord of the Rings, which, I grudgingly admit I had watched not long ago. He was about the same height as the other boy, this time leaner and lankier.

The first one walked directly to the counter, not bothering to look around. Once he was right in front of me, he took off his glasses. What I saw was maybe as sweet and mysterious as the talisman I was wearing, vivid royal blue eyes, with the same liquid-y feeling.

I could have stared at them endlessly but then I remembered that I had to take care of customers, no matter how good they looked. I said, "Can I help you?" I wasn't accustomed to working behind the counter but I had been to enough stores to know how to treat a customer.

I wrinkled my nose. Was that cologne I smelled?

"Can I see the manager?" he asked, his voice firm.

"Hmm ..." I looked at the second man, who looked much more polite. Why hadn't he been the one to talk to me? "The manager is busy right now. Maybe I can help you ..."

"I had ordered a package," he said cutting me off. Did he even know what 'manners' meant? Probably not. "It's reserved in the name of Greenwhick."

"A minute, please," I said, walking away, toward the door to the backroom. I spotted Mr. Porter kneeling in front of the safe, placing the stock in.

He didn't looked up from his work when he handed me a small box. I looked at it and frowned. It was marked: *Greenwhick* and attached around it with a rubber elastic was a form.

"Thanks," I mumbled, my eyes reading the form. How had he known? Then again, it was Mr. Porter I was talking about.

The black headed boy was leaning against the counter when I came back carrying the pack with one hand. His hand was to his face, massaging his thick and stubborn-looking jaw. I could imagine it locked, unmoving as his will. I squinted and saw the tiniest hint of purple near his chin, running along to his nose. However, it was so faint, that I knew he couldn't have gotten it earlier than four days ago. Probably got into a brawl or ran into a post. Good-looking guys were always too good to be true. He was probably the jock type.

The guy looked up and smiled when he saw the package I was holding. It was actually more of a grin than a smile. I wondered if someone like him was even capable of giving a *real* smile. He looked like the type of guy you met at clubs and never saw elsewhere or he would look out of place. "There you go Mr. Greenwhick," I said handing him the package as well as pulling off the form that clung to it. I scanned it and found the customer's signature. "I suppose you've already paid."

"Actually, I haven't." He got his wallet out and slipped a hundred dollar bill on the counter, sliding it gently to me. I often did that … when I didn't feel comfortable touching the cashier's hand. "Keep the change and it's McKenna, not Greenwhick."

"I'm sorry," I said, taking the bill from his hand and putting it aside. I would give it to Mr. Porter later; I figured it wouldn't mater if I didn't right away. I took a pen from his pen box (a rather round metallic thingy people put pens and things of the sort into) and handed it to McKenna, which I thought was a pretty weird name. I know I wouldn't call my son that to save him future awkward humiliation or stupid things like that. "If you could just sign here …"

He took the pen from my hand and scribbled on the paper. Fast, dirty and unreadable, the type I just *loved*. He slid both the pen and the paper back to my side of the counter and studied my face. I almost blushed but I tried as hard as possible to keep my head cool. It wasn't often that I got this kind of personal attention except from my boyfriend. "I've never seen you here, have I?" When I shook my head, he grinned. "Who could forget a pretty face like that?"

Before I could blurt out something stupid like, "I have a boyfriend" or "You're not so bad yourself," the other boy behind him tensed and said, "*Dejarlo ir. Tenemos que ir.*"

McKenna ignored him and kept looking at me, as if … Heck, I didn't know as if what. His eyes lingered down my face and rested on the talisman. He squinted at it and then brought his eyes back to mine. "Nice necklace you got there."

I brought my hand to the wind talisman. I still didn't know why I felt so complexed by it and at the same time so good but the guy seemed to see it too, the difference. "Thanks."

"Where'd you get it?" he asked.

One of the few weird things about me you should know, when someone I didn't know asked me something, I never told the truth. For example, every time I had gone to Bath and Body Works, they always asked for my e-mail. I made one up, plastered a smile on my face and that was it. Strangers didn't need any help from me to get into my private life and somehow I felt as if this talisman was no different from my privacy.

"I got it somewhere downtown," I said, slightly inclining my head, trying to look as innocent as possible. For some strange reason, I loved acting in front of strangers. Sometimes, I took on a Jersey accent or something of the sort. Kaithlyn and Brittany always let out choked laughs but I always managed. "I doubt you know the place. It's called *Abigail's*." Oh yeah, and I also liked leaving false trails. Especially since *Abigail's* didn't even exist, as far as I knew.

"Thanks. My girlfriend would kill for one of these. Have a nice evening." McKenna winked at me and they left. I watched silently as they walked away through the glass door. The puny bell rang, and that was it.

TWO

I t was eight o'clock in the morning and everyone except me, myself and I was out of the house. Jane had already taken Mary to daycare and I, Abby Claire, was charged to lock up. After stuffing my lunch in my two-year-old backpack, I took out my keys from the front pocket and swung my bag over my shoulder.

The house was clean except for the occasional toy lying around somewhere. Our house was situated in a Boston suburb, not the most prestigious but not the most defaulted either. Everyone—Jane, Mary and myself (no pets)—had her own room, and no one was lacking space.

I took the book I was reading for school, *Pride and Prejudice.* I had been excited to read it at first but after fifty pages or so, the book had gotten long, really long. This was the first book I was *forcing* myself to read. I was a considerably good reader but I couldn't deal with slow, uneventful plots.

After locking the backdoor and checking that all windows were closed, I walked through the house, to the front door, where I stopped in the parlor. I looked at myself in the mirror, like I usually did before leaving the house. I wasn't being vain or self-conscious but I needed to look at least half-decent. I knew people who looked at themselves in the mirror for fifteen minutes, not taking their eyes off themselves. Now, that was being vain and really weird.

I had decided to wear gray leggings today, not something I usually opted for. I was more of a lay-low jeans kind of person but in times like this, when I felt bolder than other days, I cut myself loose, not completely but considerably. What did I have to lose anyway? Kaithlyn and Brittany had said I looked good in them, so why shouldn't I wear them? I had thrown on one of my favorite t-shirts and over it my cotton jacket, which I knew Kaithlyn would die for.

Walking out in the fresh autumn breeze was something I enjoyed most of all but this morning it was too cold and I could see my every breath hang in the air. I got right back inside and decided to ditch the cotton jacket for my leather one, and gloves and a scarf.

After finally locking up, I jogged to get my bus, making it just in time. I sat down at the back of the bus, opened my bag and pulled out my iPod Touch that I had paid for with my own money. The variety of songs I had was very diverse, which I was proud of for some strange reason.

I watched the drivers that passed by through the window, some angrier than others. When I saw someone interesting for a while (like waiting for the light to turn green), I made up all kinds of stupid and impossible stories about their lives. It was fun but sometimes I really got bored doing it, so I started reviewing last-minute concepts that I knew would be in my exams that same day.

Listening to Eminem, Nirvana and Elvis Presley and even some Vybz Kartel, made the ride to school pass quickly. Before I even knew it, I was standing in front of the huge, beige building a lot of people dreaded—high school, the apocalypse, same thing.

Students were pouring in, like tiny ants, pushing through the massive crowd. I did not look forward to getting in there.

It didn't take long for me to see Kaithlyn's bright red head of hair. Kaithlyn took even less time to spot me because she was already heading my way.

"Hey Abs!" Kaithlyn wrapped her arms around my neck, almost killing me. "What's up?"

"Not much more than yesterday," I said, slowly getting my friend's arms away from my neck. Kaithlyn was smiling brightly, beaming even.

Something was definitely going on. "What's up with you? You win the lottery?"

"Not exactly but I did win the jackpot!"

"What is it?"

Kaithlyn gripped my front arms and squeezed tightly, probably leaving red marks behind. "Wesley Shaw asked me out!"

My eyes widened. "Oh my gosh! That's great Kaithlyn! When did this happen?"

"Just now!" Kaithlyn was literally jumping on her tiptoes, jumpier than ever. I hadn't seen her this happy in a while, which made me kinda sad because it was kinda my duty to make my best friend happy. I didn't point it out because I knew how good it felt to be asked on a date. "He wants to go see a movie this Friday night."

"That's great, I'm really happy for you, Kate. Have you told Brittany?"

"No, but I'm gonna as soon as I see her." She let go of me and scanned the crowd. "Ah, there she is! Brittany!" Kaithlyn waved at our other friend and went to join her.

I took a step to follow her and was stopped. Hands snaked around my waist, pulling me back. I let out an *oof!* as my head knocked against a hard chest. Now who could that be? Smiling to myself, I turned around to see my captor—strong jawline, curly brown hair outlining a beautiful angular face. Light green eyes looked down at me and then appeared the cocky grin I loved so much.

This was Luke Rush, QB, hottie of the school and *my* boyfriend. We'd been together for at least four months now. I had received many sour glares from die-hard-for-Luke girls when the news first got out but I had just shrugged them away, not really caring what they thought because they weren't in my year. It was all over now, so I could enjoy him as much as I wanted without feeling creepy glances behind my back.

I wrapped my arms around his neck, leaning on his broad chest and pulling his face closer to mine. He brushed his nose against mine, grinning when I smiled more deeply.

"Good morning," he said, his breath washing over my face. It smelled of fresh mint. *Tic-Tac*, I thought. "I was thinking of you."

"Of course you were, Lulu," I replied, knowing that he hated it when I called him that. He growled deep in his throat and I didn't want to admit to him that it was sexy rather than scary.

Luke gathered me closer to him, resting his lips on my collarbone, making my heart race. He knew I was most ticklish there. He kissed me lightly there, sending little flutters—make that big flutters—all over my body. He worked his way up to my jaw and then my cheeks and eventually got to the corner of my lips.

Before he could kiss me decently, we both heard someone clearing his throat. Luke groaned and lazily lifted his head. The headmaster was standing next to us, his arms crossed tightly over his chest. He looked disapprovingly over his big, bulky glasses from the mid-eighties at Luke's arms around my waist.

"Mr. Rush, how kind of you to show your support and '*friendship*' to your fellow classmate." The headmaster was a heck of a crazy guy. He had a crown of hair over his oily head, with the thickest mustache I had ever seen. Trust me; that meant a lot. No one knew his name but he knew every single student's name, from oldie to newbie. For some strange and neurotic reason, Luke and I seemed to be the only ones getting caught. None of the other couples I knew had ever gotten caught doing far worse things than kissing. "Miss Claire, I believe I find you in this position more and more often. I believe a detention might be in order."

Luke's hands left my waist and I let him go. He went to stand in front of me, blocking the headmaster's view of me. Luke was a big guy, taller and much stronger than the average boy at our school. He crossed his arms over his chest.

The headmaster didn't seem at all impressed. "Would you want to join her, Mr. Rush? I believe there's a spot with your name on it."

I couldn't see Luke's face but I could tell it wasn't sending out happy waves. "No fraternizing with the opposite sex on school grounds. Is that why you feel in need of giving us detention?"

"I believe that is why," said the headmaster, squinting at Luke. "No exceptions."

"Well, I *believe* that you are in fault by giving us a detention."

"And, may I ask, why?"

"We aren't on school grounds."

I looked around. We were standing on the sidewalk, a foot away from what was the official school ground. Of course, the headmaster was standing within it.

The man raised his chin, his lip curling lightly at the corners. "You would make a fine lawyer, Mr. Rush, if it hadn't been for your lack of respect and good grades." He turned around and walked into the crowd, not completely blending in because everyone tried to stay as far away from him as possible.

"What a douche bag," muttered Luke under his breath; he turned to me and slowly leaned in, his cocky grin back. "Now … where were we?"

Before I could rise on my tiptoes to meet him halfway, I heard the squeaky voice of Victoria Porter. "*Hey*, Luke!"

Luke closed his eyes and forced himself to smile. Victoria was his ex-girlfriend but that didn't stop her from drooling all over him like a pink, bitchy poodle. She was like that small dog you just couldn't get rid of, yipping at your heels whenever she got the chance. He stood up straight and turned to face the tall, leggy blonde. Honestly, I didn't really know why Luke had chosen me over Victoria. The blonde was as thin as a pencil and had breasts the size of watermelons. She always had a boyfriend but for some reason, she was *really* hung up on Luke, probably because *he* had been the one to turn *her* down.

"Hi, Vicki," greeted Luke, tugging at my wrist for me to come stand next to him. He knew how much I hated Victoria and vice-versa. "What's up?"

"I'm having a party this Saturday for my birthday. My parents are out of town and everyone's invited." She glared at me, and then at the arm I kept around Luke's waist. "Well, almost everyone."

"It's nice to see you too, *Victoria*," I said, making my voice as bitter as possible. I smiled, showing off two-and-a-half years of braces. "Nice to know that you're *finally* growing up."

Luke faked coughed in his elbow, covering his smile.

Victoria glared even harder at me, making her pupils slightly smaller. She shook her head, making her blonde curls bounce around her face. "So, are you coming, or not, Luke?"

"I'll come but only if Abby's invited." He gripped tightened around my shoulders, making my insides feel all fuzzy.

Victoria rolled her eyes dramatically. "*Fine*, she can come but I'm warning you, Claire, don't think you'll be welcomed." She turned around and almost whipped my face with her hair.

When she was out of earshot, Luke scratched the air. "Meow. Tsss. Cat fight."

I lightly slapped him on the shoulder. "Guys and their cat fights. They always think it's going to end in some kind of kissing session or something. Let me tell you, if that were to happen between two guys, I wouldn't be looking forward to it."

"Do you want to start a kissing session?"

I ignored his tempting proposition and groaned lightly bringing my hand to my temple like all those mental cases do on TV. "That ... *person* is *sooo* infuriating!" Luke laughed aloud. He trailed a finger down my nose and to my lips, where he tapped them lightly. "I'm too nice for my own good, right? I can't insult someone properly."

"That's why I like you so much." The first bell rang and he gave me a quick peck on my brow. Luke took my bag from my shoulder and slugged it on his own. "You owe me one."

"For what?"

"For getting you a ticket to Victoria's party." We started walking toward the school and I fell into step with the other students, next to Luke.

"What if I don't want to go?"

Luke looked at me. "You don't want to go? It isn't like you to miss a good party."

"I'd love to go to a party where each and every room is used as a make out booth and where people get drunk." I rolled my eyes. "Of course I want to go. Would I ever pass up an opportunity to dance, even if it *was* at Victoria's place?"

"Then you still owe me."

"What is it you want?"

"I want—"

Before he could finish his sentence, I got tackled from behind, falling face first. I quickly deployed my arms to take the impact and closed my eyes. I never did feel the pain I had expected from my palms. Luke had caught me, my head only a few inches from the ground. He should never have been able to catch me in time. It couldn't be possible because he hadn't been looking at me and everything had gone so fast, probably because of football reflexes.

Once he was sure I was all right and on my two feet, he turned to who had hit me. It was Fletcher Right, a student from the school's soccer team—a nice tall build, dark skin, black hair and he was part of the soccer team, which counted for a lot.

One thing to know about our high school was that there was a cheerleading team, a badminton team, a track team, a soccer team and a football team. The cheerleaders shared the entire gym with the badminton team, the track team had the running tracks and the football and soccer teams had the football/soccer field. Only one team at a time could play, and let's just say both teams weren't on the best of terms …

So yeah, it only angered Luke more. Shouldn't it be me to be the angry one? "What the hell, man!" exclaimed Luke shoving at Fletcher hard, who didn't take one step back. Luke was a strong guy and it didn't surprise me that Fletcher stood his ground perfectly. "What's your freakin' problem, shoving her like that?"

Fletcher looked at me and grinned dirtily. "Hi, Abby. It's nice to have such a *fine* lady in my presence." Fletcher wasn't usually like this and I knew right away it was only to get on Luke's nerves. He was actually a sweet guy once you got to know him.

Luke didn't see the sweet side and mocking one that I saw almost every day on Fletcher. He was looking at him with what might have been hatred but lessened by a notch. It was hard to describe but I knew he wasn't very happy. "You know this guy?"

"We go to the same school, Luke. It's only normal for me to know who he is." When he didn't seem the least bit convinced, I added, exasperated, "Luke, I tutor him on Monday nights. It's okay; I'm sure it was just an accident." I looked at Fletcher, and he winked at me, which I knew he did only to be friendly and again, mocking but Luke misread it and actually *lunged* at Fletcher. I let out a small shriek, afraid of what was going to happen to Fletcher and my jealous boyfriend. Fletch stood his ground as well as any soccer player would—with strong, powerful legs. That didn't stop the two from falling on the ground and starting to go at it.

A crowd had gathered around us, already making bets on who would win. "Right," I heard a guy call next to me. It was another soccer player, talking with one of his friends. "My money's on Right."

"Rush's gonna make it," said another one. "You see the passes he throws at practice? He tha' man."

All I really felt like doing at the moment was slapping Luke and hugging him at the same time. Sometimes, I found that he could become too involved with my problems, which only brought on more problems when the principal of the school arrived. All of a sudden, the students who had been watching the fight now moved away until it was only the principal, Fletcher, Luke and me.

They were still rolling around when principal Mi put his foot right in between their heads, an inch from both their noses. Principal Mi wasn't physically an imposing man; he was short, partially bald and wore glasses. He was one of the scariest people I had ever met, not horror-movie type of scary but more of a don't-do-anything-you'll-regret-because-you-ain't-getting-it-easy type of scary.

"Rush! Right!" he barked out impatiently. His face morphed into what might've looked like a bulldog. The corner of his lips turned down and his eyebrows met to form almost a ninety-degree angle. "Get up!"

They both got up, mostly uninjured. Bruises were definitely expected but as far as I could tell, there wasn't any blood. Once they were both up and looking at each other with deadly stares, principal Mi pointed toward the door, meaning we should all go in.

The second bell had already rung and I was going to be late for class.

☙❧

Luke and Fletcher got a detention; meanwhile, I got a first notice, which wasn't too bad. I felt bad for Fletcher though, because he had only meant to tease and that was it. There was nothing going on between the two of us; that much I could tell but Luke had gotten easily frustrated, which frustrated me as well. We had to be able to trust each other and he had just showed me that he didn't fully trust me ... If we didn't have trust, then what would be left?

The first half of the day passed by pretty quickly considering it was the last day of the school week. I spent most of the time thinking of the discussion I would need to have with Luke about our trust issue, which I honestly thought was *his* issue because *he* was the one having doubts and not the other way around. At lunch, Kaithlyn and Brittany talked about Victoria's party and of plans on how they were going to crash it. Ideas like bringing a bomb and cutting her bra straps came up but they found that a bomb was maybe a bit too extravagant.

"But how the hell do we get ahold of her bra?" asked Brittany, munching on her peanut butter sandwich. She had taken off the crusts of her bread with her hands and had made small, airtight balls out of them. She threw one straight into the garbage can and I saw the silent sentiment of pride flash through her eyes. I smiled to myself.

"We both got gym this afternoon. I guess I can come up behind her and figure something out," said Kaithlyn, who was toying with her fruit salad. She was nudging her grapes aside as well as her carrots.

"Did any of you think that it was possible that she won't be wearing a bra?" I was seated next to Kaithlyn and was looking around for Fletcher. I wanted to apologize to him on Luke's behalf because I knew my boyfriend wouldn't apologize for something like that. He had too much pride.

"Did I just hear that you weren't wearing a bra?" asked a husky voice from behind me.

I was still a bit pissed off at him for earlier but there was no point bringing it up now; it wouldn't lead to anything serious with all our friends around.

I turned and winked devilishly at Luke. I knew he thought it was cute when I did that because he had once admitted it to me. "I guess you'll never find out."

One of Luke's close friends, Wesley, slapped him on the shoulder and grinned foolishly at me. "Got yourself a fine one, Rush—feisty."

Luke almost snapped at him for saying the word *fine* and I glared at him. He closed his mouth and his jaw locked like it did whenever he was keeping himself from saying something.

Wesley Shaw was the running back of the school's football team. The typical baby face girls always fell for, blond hair, blue eyes, the whole kit. Heck, add muscle and you had it. That was Wesley Shaw. I once actually had a small (and when I say small, I mean really small) crush on him back in eighth grade but I had quickly forgotten about it when the other boys started producing more testosterone.

"That's why you better keep your distance, Shaw." Luke let himself fall on the seat next to me and looked at my meager lunch. "You really should eat more. Your diet wouldn't be able to sustain a bird, even if the bird sat all day and did nothing else."

"Unlike you, I don't sweat like a maniac."

"You should exercise more. You know," Luke gave me his cocky grin and raised his eyebrows teasingly, "get your muscles pumping."

Before I could reply, Brittany sighed dramatically. "Okay, if you guys are going to talk about this, please go away," she pleaded, throwing the last of her crust balls into the garbage can. "It makes me sick."

"Says the girl who dated *Blake Parker*," said Kaithlyn, rolling her eyes. "Seriously, I don't know why you even bothered with that guy. I know you thought he was nice and everything but ..." She shook her head, her locks bouncing around her head. She turned her attention to Wesley and her eyes widened. "Wesley, is that a scar on your face?" She reached out to touch his face, her fingers, lightly trailing along his cheek.

"Oh, *that* small thing?" Wesley shrugged and put his hand over Kaithlyn's. "It's nothing."

For as long as I could remember, Kaithlyn had had a crush on Wesley. They'd always been good friends, but it was only now that they openly acted the way they wanted to, as a couple. I looked away, not wanting to look too creepy. I didn't want anyone to intrude in my personal life, so I didn't invade the others' privacy.

"You working t'night?" asked Luke, before getting a bite off his first sandwich. Yeah, because he had two and sometimes three on PE days. I watched as he gobbled half of his turkey sandwich in one bite.

"I don't get any days off; you know that, right?"

"I was hoping you would want to grab a bite to eat at the Chinese takeout I just discovered. You'd love it."

"Thanks," I said, "but I can't; I need the money."

"For what? Shoes?"

I shrugged. This wasn't the most comfortable subject I liked to discuss. It wasn't that I was poor or anything of the sort, it was just that money wasn't … Well, I needed the money for something and that was all there was to it.

"Uh, Abby, I don't want to freak you out or anything but the Head-Disaster is staring at you," whispered Brittany. She was looking over my shoulder warily. Suddenly, she quickly looked away and took one of the carrots that lay in my plastic container.

The Head-Disaster was the nickname we all gave the headmaster—the creepy, bald headmaster. I felt my whole body tense. This couldn't bring any good. Mom already didn't have much faith in me lately, so I didn't think extra attention from that direction was going to help.

Luke put an arm around my shoulders, pulling me closer to him. I let my head fall back on his shoulder and felt slightly better.

"I'm tempted to give the guy a piece of my mind," said Luke. I could hear his voice perfectly and I could detect obvious anger. "He shouldn't look at any student that way and *especially* not my girlfriend."

I didn't know what look Luke was talking about and I honestly didn't *want* to know. Ignorance is bliss, right? "So Britt, have you seen Dally today? He wasn't there in Spanish."

Brittany didn't answer my question. She just completely ignored it and kept staring over my shoulder. "I heard he molests freshman girls."

"You should never believe what you '*hear*' and that is something I definitely do not want to believe," said Luke firmly.

He was protective and very fond of me, maybe even more than just *fond*. He had never invaded my privacy or gotten jealous when I talked to other guys (yeah, right). He was perfect that way. Not too protective (am I sweetening it a bit too much?) but not careless either. So, when he did get this protective, I knew something was definitely wrong.

"Are you going to go to Victoria's party?" asked Kaithlyn, oblivious of the small talk we just had about the Head-Disaster.

"I was going to go with Luke," I answered, taking a bite from my apparently puny lunch, "but I'm not sure; I might rather watch a rerun of Gossip Girls."

"But you hate Gossip Girls," noted Brittany, pointing at me with the carrot she had stolen from me.

"Exactly."

I saw Luke rolling his eyes at me. "We're going together, Kate. Are you and Wes going?"

Kaithlyn looked intently at Wesley, who shrugged and nodded. "Why not? It'll be fun."

She grinned at him and turned to Brittany. "Are you going?"

"Of course, what kind of question is that?" Brittany brought all of her hair to one side and combed through her dark curls with her hand. I wasn't the type to be jealous but seeing Brittany so beautiful was making me a bit envious. She was so unconscious of how pretty she was and that only made her ten times prettier.

"Are you sure?" I asked, "with him being with Victoria and all." I knew she knew who *him* was.

"Honestly? I don't really care if he's there or not, I just wanna have fun. Anyway," she leaned back in her chair and grinned at all of us, "who else is going to be the designated driver?"

"Are you kidding? If I get drunk, my mom's gonna kill me!" Yeah, if I got drunk, things were gonna be worse than that. It would be slow and painful.

"If I get drunk, my dad isn't gonna notice," said Kaithlyn slowly, shrugging. "He's gone till like, two."

When it was time to go back to class, as I got up, I looked behind me. I almost had a heart attack when I saw the Head-Disaster staring right at me.

ॐॐ

Kaithlyn and Brittany were sitting in my room, munching on chips. The type of chips you know you shouldn't eat and yet you still do. Brittany had sneaked them up into my room (my mom was very much against any sort of junk food) as well as makeup (yeah, she was against that too) while Jane, my mom, had given Mary her bath.

"What are you going to wear?" asked Kaithlyn, rolling on her stomach over my bed. She snatched a chip from the bag that lay on Brittany's lap.

"Uh, clothes?" I put my hair up in a ponytail.

Brittany rolled her eyes. "No shit." She threw a chip at me and I caught it in my mouth, twisting hard so I could get it just in time. "I am so good at this."

"It's frisky outside, Britt. It's not like she can wear short shorts," said Brittany. She jumped off my bed, hopped over to my closet, flung the double doors open and stepped in. "You know, Abby ... a closet is usually used to store clothes, not ... toys you had back when you were three."

"I wasn't here when I was three, remember?" I pointed out, joining her in the walk-in-closet. It truly wasn't full, maybe a quarter full of clothes. Two quarters contained old school projects and toys I had when I was six or seven. The last quarter was empty.

Kaithlyn barely nodded. "Right, but seriously Abby ... c'mon, even I have more clothes than you."

"Look," I said, crossing my hands over my chest, "it's not like I can spend every dime I have on clothes. I have other things that have ... well, priority."

"Let me guess," called out Brittany. She too came to join us and started flipping through my stuff. "You spend all your money on books."

"And other things," I protested. Yes, I had to admit, reading was a passion of mine but I hadn't told anyone what I really had in mind. It was something big, something that could make me feel free again but of course, they would be against that, so I kept my mouth shut.

"Why don't you just get an e-reader or something like that?" Kaithlyn pulled out the white cocktail dress I had gotten from Luke not even two months before. It was short and puffy at the end and there was a red ribbon attached at its waist. It had that mermaid thing going on and my mom wouldn't have me dead wearing it. The fabric was as smooth as silk and hadn't been used yet. "What the hell is this?"

"Oh my God, Abby!" exclaimed Brittany, clutching at the dress. "When did you get this?"

I blushed a bit. Why did I feel like I should have told them about this before? "Two months ago ..."

"Two months ago and we never saw it?" gaped Kaithlyn. "You bought this by yourself?"

"What do you mean? 'By myself'" I asked, my lips tight as I took the dress away from them and hung it back with the other stuff. "I am perfectly capable of buying myself whatever I want." *As long as it doesn't cost too much*, I added mentally.

Brittany rolled her eyes. "Who got this for you?"

"Uh ... Luke?" God, I was asking for it.

Both of their eyes went wide and I honestly thought they were going to pop out. Before they could lash out at me or something of the sort, I said, "I forgot to tell you guys. It just didn't seem *that*—"

"*Important!*" burst Brittany. "Ugh ... God, I hate that I love you so much or I would *kill* you."

It took me around two minutes to convince them I had actually and truly forgotten about the dress. Once that was behind us, we came back to the original question. What was I going to wear? The dress was out of the question even though I knew Kaithlyn was itching to have me wear it.

"It's not *that* cold out," said Kaithlyn finally, after having looked over and over again at my wardrobe. "And anyway," she raised her eyebrows at me, "I doubt Luke will even *let* you get cold."

I rolled my eyes at her, knowing that she was hoping Wesley would be like that with her. "It's getting late; we should leave."

"Not until we find you something to wear."

THREE

Around an hour later, we arrived at Victoria's party. Kaithlyn had actually been right; it wasn't as cold as it had been yesterday and there was maybe half the party that was going on outside.

I had once been to one of Victoria's birthday parties. Last time, she had two missing teeth and puny pigtails. Yeah, no matter how unbelievable it was, we actually used to be friends, once upon a time …

Luke had said we would meet in front of the gates (because they had gates and a great security system that Victoria had probably turned off) but he wasn't there. Kaithlyn didn't wait a second and hurried through the gates, dragging me with her as Brittany went to park her car.

Victoria's house wasn't subtle. It stuck out like a sore thumb, an expensive, beautiful sore thumb. It was a creamy white, modernized Greek structure. It had large columns that were there majorly just for show. There were long panel windows, which allowed us to see the partygoers dancing and screaming as if there was no tomorrow. There was a DJ with afro hair moving his head with the rhythm, changing from tune to tune. There was a large dandling disco ball, swaying wildly from left to right.

I was almost reluctant to step inside the mansion, but when I saw Luke standing at the other end of the living room, which could've easily passed for a hotel lobby, I gathered up my nerves and walked inside.

Kaithlyn was already gone, probably off with Wesley. I looked around for her but there were so many people moving up and down that it was impossible to spot one of the only redheads. I had a really tough time getting through the crowd to Luke. I was short of breath when I reached him and he looked in my direction.

He smiled when he saw my flushed face and put an arm around me. Luke kissed my brow. "I thought you would never come."

"Sorry," I said, my voice barely audible over the booming speakers and voices. "I kinda got caught up with Kate and Britt back at my house. You know, girl stuff."

Luke made a disgusted face. "Purses?" he asked. He said the word as if it were the most horrible word ever invented in English literature.

I laughed and mockingly hit his shoulder. "What's so wrong with purses?"

"Girls have ... *issues* when it comes to purses."

"I think *guys* have issues when it comes to girls' purses, actually."

Luke didn't say anything for a while. "Huh, you're right. I'm not scared of heights, the dark or spiders but I *do* get edgy when it comes to purses." He looked me up and down. "Thanks babe for not bringing it."

I smirked at him and wrapped my arms around his neck. I gave him a light peck on the lips, smelling the hint of alcohol. I looked more deeply into his eyes and to my satisfaction, saw that he was sober. "Want me to go get it? It's in the car."

His eyes widened and I laughed. "Please don't do that." He tightened his grip around my waist. "Don't let it get me."

"You're such a baby," I teased, trailing a finger down his nose.

He grinned foolishly at me. God, I really loved this guy. He could bring my mood up in only a matter of seconds. He wasn't only lovable of the heart; damn, did he have a hot body. I could have stayed all night right there in his arms, happy with merely secret looks and inside jokes ...

We danced for a bit, not hard rock songs or hip-hop songs but slower ones, such as Mario's "Let Me Love You," one of my favorites.

We might've danced for minutes or hours; I wasn't really sure but I was content with whatever time we spent together.

Now, I knew most people would think I was a completely love-struck girl. Truthfully, I was but I couldn't feel anything else when I was with Luke. I had read so many books about girls who were completely devoted to their boyfriends and would do absolutely *anything* for them. I had always rolled my eyes and sometimes even stopped reading the book altogether; it was so psychotic. Then, as I stood there encircled with Luke's arms, there was no eye rolling whatsoever.

We didn't dance as long as we would have, that I was sure of, but my head was spinning a bit from all the lights reflected by the disco ball and the booming seemed to get louder.

"Do you wanna go outside?" I asked, my head close enough to his so that he could hear me. "I'm feeling a little bit claustrophobic at the moment."

Seeing as I wasn't kidding, Luke nodded and frayed a path between the dancing crowd members. We were a bit pushed around by the mass of bodies but Luke held his ground and guided me to the exit, where I greeted the fresh air with a sigh. I had never felt the need to leave a party before but I really didn't feel like getting back in there for some strange reason. Maybe it was because of the sleep I *hadn't* gotten in the past few nights.

Luke and I made our way to a little white bench a bit farther from the terrace. We sat there; I rested my head on Luke's shoulder and closed my eyes. Maybe I shouldn't have stayed up all night reading …

We stayed silent for a few minutes, enjoying the silence as well as the other's presence. I couldn't have asked for more. I was here, alone with the guy I loved most in the world. I held his warm hand in mine and drew circles in his palm. He let me be, watching my slow movements. I loved doing this; it was simple, pure and there was no ulterior motive behind it.

A few minutes went by like this, in complete silence, until Luke stood straighter. "Abby," he said calmly. His face got serious and I frowned. I let go of his hand and turned to face him on the seat. There was no reason for him to be serious at a party, especially when we were

alone, unless it was really important. "There's something I've been wanting to tell you …"

"Abby!"

I turned around, freeing myself from Luke's intent look. Brittany was coming our way. "Have you seen Kaithlyn?" she asked, concerned.

I shook my head. "Not since we came in," I answered.

"Where d'you think she might have gone?"

"She was with Wes …"

"Oh right, she has a *boyfriend* now," said Brittany, slightly shaking her head. "This is just so weird."

"Why?" I asked, tilting my head a bit to look into her eyes better. There was no trace of jealousy or sadness in them, which made me wonder why she would say something like that.

"I need a drink," she said, not answering my question. She let her eyes wander into the house until she spotted the bar. "See ya' later."

Brittany was already gone before I could tell her this was a bad idea. She wasn't much of a drinker. Actually, she wasn't a drinker at all. I could tell something was wrong but I wasn't really sure what …

Before I could follow her, I felt fingers slide around my wrists, pulling me back. "Abby?"

I turned back to Luke. He too seemed worried for Brittany, because he was looking in her direction warily. "Do you think she'll be all right?"

"No," I said, looking back at Brittany. "I should go get her before things get out of hand …"

"Luke, how nice to see you!"

I closed my eyes and hoped for what seemed like a smile. I turned around to meet Victoria's glare. She obviously didn't want me here and made sure I was aware of it. Blake was at her side, holding her by the waist. I looked him straight in the eyes, making sure he knew I wasn't happy to see him. Blake didn't look away. It was Luke who stopped our staring contest when he greeted Victoria.

"I thought you wouldn't show when I didn't see you…" She pulled out her lower lip, fake pouting. She knew it made some guys crazy and so did I. Heck, it made me crazy … just not in the same way. She tilted her head just a bit so that her blonde curls moved away leaving her pale neck exposed.

Luke stiffened next to me and so did Blake. I rolled my eyes. *Guys.* Luke put his arms around my waist and got me closer to him. His grip was tight on me and I knew something wasn't right.

Blake tightened his grip around Victoria's waist so that she straightened. "Hey," she whined, gripping his hand that seemed to dig into her skin. "You're hurting m—"

She stopped when Blake silenced her with his mouth. Then they started making out and actually grinding. I thought I would get sick. Luke made us get up and walk away from them, making us walk toward the double doors, back to the party. I didn't really want to go back in just yet but I preferred that to witnessing a session of saliva swapping.

"We're leaving," he said in a tight voice, his arm leaving my waist but still holding my hand.

I stopped in my tracks, waiting for him to face me. "Luke, I know she used to be your girlfriend but you need to get over it."

"It has nothing to do with that …"

"Then what is it?" I asked, raising my voice just a tad higher. "She was openly flirting with you, Luke and you reacted. You think I didn't see that? Come on, Luke, admit it. You still have a thing for her."

His jaw tightened and I saw his brows crease. "Abby, I don't have a thing for Victoria anymore. It's over between us. Nothing is going on." When I only kept on staring at him, he sighed. "Abby, my eyes are for you and for you only. I think I've made that quite clear."

I thought about him getting all protective when Fletcher had accidentally tackled me. I guess he had made it clear… "Then if she doesn't affect you anymore, how come we're leaving right after they started humping in front of us?"

He looked away for a second, as if trying to find an answer. "I'm getting tired. I stayed up late last night. I'm sorry."

Luke was deliberately lying to me and that hurt. There was something in his eyes that told me so. "Well, you can go on ahead. I'll leave with Kate and Britt later. I don't want to leave them alone."

He considered that for a moment. "How about we all leave? I mean …" Luke looked around us, motioning to the party, "… this party is bound to go wrong."

"What do you mean?"

I could see the anxiety building up in Luke. He was getting anxious, and I could see that the more we spent time here, the more he would be on edge. I sighed. "All right, we can go." Relief spread over his face. "But I wanna tell Kaithlyn and Brittany." His face got a bit darker but he nodded.

"I'll come with you."

We headed for the bar where Brittany had said she would be. Luke didn't let go of my hand the entire time. We reached the table where all of the drinks were held. There was a girl on the other side, handing drinks to everyone. She had thin blonde hair and the largest breasts I had ever seen—real watermelons! She handed me a drink but I shook my head. The bubbling blue drink didn't look at all convincing. She then handed it to Luke, her smile still glued to her face. This time, for him, she leaned in closer, revealing more of her generous curves. He didn't seem to notice and declined the drink.

I looked around trying to spot Brittany. All I saw was a couple making out in the dark corner behind the bar. My jaw almost dropped when I saw it was Brittany who was half of that couple and she was well around the guy. When I say around, I meant she was literally straddling him. I couldn't tell who the guy was but I could tell he was enjoying himself. Before I could even reach them, Luke was there, pulling Brittany off.

"Hey!" she protested, trying to get out of Luke's steel grip. "Let go you big bully." Her voice was slurred and I saw her falter when she took a step away from him.

"What's up man?" said the guy who had been holding Brittany. It was Mitchel Ross, one of the defense from the soccer team. He too seemed pretty drunk. "Can't you see we were enjoying ourselves?"

Luke didn't pay him any attention. He made Brittany look into his eyes and seemed to have made a decision.

He came to me dragging Brittany with him. "We're leaving. Now." The decision in his voice was clear.

"What's wrong?" I asked warily. I knew something was wrong. I hated being left in the dark and Luke should know that. I knew he was on edge but he owed me some explanation since we were leaving earlier than we'd planned.

"The drinks are drugged," he said in a low voice, so that only I could hear. My eyes widened but I still kept up to step with him, getting slightly closer. "Do you know where Kaithlyn is?"

"I think she's with Wes—"

"Abby!" Brittany grabbed my wrist, surprising me. "Tell Luke I have to go back to ... that *guy*!"

I grabbed her shoulders and shook her. "Britt, you're drunk and in no position to get hot and heavy with a guy you've never talked to."

"Please, I *need* this. I need *him*." I saw her eyes water and an edge of madness in them. She tried to shake away from Luke's grip but he didn't let go of her. Brittany let out a low moan and she fell to the ground.

"Brittany!" I fell to my knees and put an arm around her. Luke didn't say anything; he simply picked her up and started walking again. "Get her outta here. I'll go look for Kaithlyn."

"We can look for her together," suggested Luke, but that was all it was, a suggestion.

"Luke, you're carrying an unconscious girl. Don't you think people will ask questions?"

"I don't think we should worry about what other people think at this point."

I frowned and looked around. There were people dancing, like in any other party and they all had drinks, that bubbly blue drink I had declined from the girl behind the bar. I watched as they sipped their drinks as thought it was a liquor you couldn't get enough of.

I looked at Becky, a girl in my algebra class. She was the type of girl teachers loved; she was never late for class, always did her homework, and aced just 'bout every exam, but now ... she was grinding (something she had always considered blasphemous) with a guy from the track team. She had a blue drink in her hand and an empty look in her eyes ... It was as though everyone was under some sort of spell ...

"Are they being drugged?" I blurted out to Luke. He had picked up Brittany, who was thrashing wildly over his shoulder; it didn't even faze him.

Luke quickly glanced behind my head and nodded. "They must've put something in the drinks," he said sharply.

"You think Victoria wants to drug people ... and do something with them?"

"I highly doubt it. It's not her type." He looked around one more time before resting his eyes on mine. "No, I think it was someone else, someone who doesn't have the best of intentions."

This was bad. This was *really* bad. If someone had slipped something into the drinks, something that made people lose their inhibitions, then we really had to leave. I had to get Kaithlyn.

"Luke, go put Brittany in the car and stay with her to make sure she doesn't do anything stupid."

He shook his head. "I can't leave you alone, Abby. It's out of the question."

I sighed. "Luke, if we don't get her out of here, something bad is bound to happen. I'm not strong enough to drag her out of here when she's like this." I motioned toward her. Luke had to grab her legs to keep her from kicking at his stomach. "I have to find Kate." He was about to say something but I quickly continued. "You'll only slow me down by coming with me. Please Luke, the quicker I get Kaithlyn, the quicker we can leave."

I knew he didn't want to leave me. His jaw was set and his eyes looked uncertain. "Are you sure?"

I gave him a smile. "Of course I'm sure Luke. I just want to get out of here as soon as possible."

Luke nodded slightly. He gave me a quick kiss on the lips and turned around to leave. Brittany made a grab for my arm but I quickly dodged it. She was going to be so embarrassed tomorrow, when she would be all sobered up.

I had to think of where Kaithlyn could be. I had been here once, so I didn't have a hard time placing myself in Victoria's house. I headed for the kitchen, making my way through the throbbing crowd. I spotted Blake and Victoria in the corner of the room, along with other couples. Blake was sucking on Victoria's neck, a look of ecstasy on her face. Her legs were wrapped around Blake's waist and I was just about sure they were dry humping. I turned around to leave when I heard Victoria cry out in pain. I looked back to see what had gotten to her. Blake had leaned back and was wiping at her neck and licking his lips. I stared at Victoria's neck. Wow, those were two huge hickeys …

I continued my search for Kaithlyn by going upstairs. I opened every door and saw things I would've rather not seen, but still no sign of Kaithlyn or Wesley. I went downstairs—still nothing. I was getting worried. Where the hell could they be?

I felt my phone vibrate in my back pocket and pulled it out. It was Luke. "What's up?" I skipped the greetings, knowing he wouldn't be giving me any, since he was worried.

"Wesley called me; he's taking Kaithlyn home."

"Oh, all right. I'm coming." I shut the phone and slipped it back in my pocket. I was in the living room. It would take me longer to go through the whole house than just go out the back door, so I opened it and slipped out. The whole party had gone inside, so I was alone with the humungous pool. I looked at the candles floating in it and stared at the million-dollar fountain in the center. Wow, was all I could say for myself.

After having gawked at her pool for thirty seconds, I walked away, toward the exit. I made a dry turn to try to get out of this endless maze and bumped someone. I looked up to apologize but no words came out. He looked equally surprised to see me here.

"What are you doing here?" McKenna asked me, frowning.

"I was invited … What about you? You don't go to our school."

"I'm here … on business." He looked behind me and then brought his eyes back to me. "You shouldn't be here. It's not safe."

"You know about the drugs?" I asked him, surprised. Was he a cop who was leading an investigation like on one of those cop shows? He really didn't look like a cop to me, too young and too good looking.

"Drugs?" Now he really looked surprised.

"I think someone slipped something in the drinks because every-one's acting ... strange." He looked at his watch. "Are you a cop?"

He glanced at me. "Are you really a cashier?" I stared at him, unable to answer. How the hell had he ... "You should leave."

Before I could tell him anything else, he was heading for the back door. He nodded in my direction and went in.

What a weird night ...

☙❧

I was sitting on one of the living room's leather couches. Jane was pacing in front of me, her eyes giving up the fact that she was deep in thought and I was in deep shit.

Jane Claire was a beautiful woman, a woman you would normally see on the cover of a mom's magazine. I was nothing like her. Her short brown hair ended right beneath her jaw, to be 'efficient' she said. Her dark brown eyes were the color of chestnut. She was about two inches taller than I was. I, on the other hand, had long black hair that I usually pulled back in a ponytail. My slender figure was just a little smaller than Jane's voluptuous form.

While Jane had the most common eye color, I had the most uncommon. I had strange eyes. The first thing people noticed when they saw me was the color of my eyes; that's why strangers tended to stare at me longer than they normally would. My eyes were purple. I'm not talking *almost* purple ... They were light purple, like you would normally see in anime characters' eyes. No one ever treated me as a freak of nature (although I often considered myself that); if anything, my purple eyes gave me a certain charm.

Jane had taken good care of me. I had a good education, a roof over my head, food on my plate, just the right amount of strictness and a lot of love. Now, I was about to get the amount of strictness I needed to balance everything out. I'd known all along it was coming. Jane was very patient —the most patient person I had ever known— but every-one had their limits.

"Where were you when I called you?" asked Jane, looking tensed.

I was planning on telling the truth—mostly. So, I said, "On my way home."

"Made any detours while you were at it?"

"No, Mom. I didn't make any detours. I was held back. That's all." I clenched my fist on the scarf I still hadn't taken off.

"Why were you held back?"

I tried to read Jane's expression but all I could see was frustration and something I couldn't quite put a finger on. "Brittany got sick from eating all that popcorn, so when we brought her home, I stayed a bit to make sure she was all right."

Oh yeah. Jane didn't really approve of parties, much less parties hosted by 'stupid and ignorant high-schoolers,' so I had said we would be going bowling and then we would go catch a movie, nothing she didn't approve of.

"You are two hours late, Abigail! I'm sure Brittany would've understood if you had told her that you had to come back before ten o'clock. You shouldn't have come back so late." Jane's expression was as hard as rock. It might be my dose of strictness but that didn't mean I had to like it.

Fight fire with fire, I said to myself. "So what if it did? Are you going to ground me because of that? I'm almost seventeen, not five."

"Does that mean that you have to act restlessly and carelessly?" asked Jane, her voice rising. "I did not raise you to be like this."

"What did you raise me to be, Mom?" I threw back. "To be a fine and polished statue? To be what every mother wishes? Well guess what, I'm not like that!"

"I didn't raised you to be perfect, Abigail. I raised you to be respectable and careful. What you have not been lately." Jane's voice had gone louder as well. I knew that I was provoking her. My upbringing was a touchy subject between the two of us.

"I am carefu—"

"No you are not," said Jane, cutting me off. "You think you're careful, but you are not."

"You know what," I exclaimed, getting up, "I don't want to talk about this anymore. I'm tired and I want to sleep."

Before I could hit the stairs, Jane stopped me. "Do not turn your back on me Abigail Claire!"

She had used my full name. Not a good sign. I balled my hands and turned around to face my adoptive mother. "What?"

"You are deprived of going out for the next two weeks," Jane said, firmly. "And that's my final word."

I stared at her, my mouth falling open. "You can't do that," I said worriedly.

"Why not? You have disobeyed me more than once in the past few weeks. Why shouldn't I?"

"You don't have that kind of power over me, Jane," I said, a little bit too bitterly.

"You're right," said Jane, her eyes locking with mine. "But I do own this house. You will therefore abide by these house rules. If you do not like it—"

My eyes widened. "You wouldn't," I murmured.

Jane smiled at me. The most lovely, evil smile she could've possibly mustered up. "Watch me."

In the end, I got kicked out of the house. Last time I had seen Jane, was when she was closing the door on my face. I felt more angry than insulted. I still couldn't believe my own mother had kicked me out. That was just sad.

There I was, standing on the sidewalk, broke, with nowhere to go. It was way past twelve now. I couldn't go to Kaithlyn's or Brittany's house. Their parents would most probably freak out. Maybe not Mr. Porter, but the apartment was going to be crowded, even for three.

I could always go to Luke's... But if Jane ever found out, she would never let me step into the house again.

I only had five bucks in my pockets, so I couldn't pay for a motel. Why had I left my purse inside the house? I didn't want to go back in. I would look stupid. It would feel like crawling back to Jane. And I didn't want to do that. Ever.

After several minutes in deep thought, I could only think of one person who would let me sleepover without any doubt. Someone Jane wouldn't disapprove of.

I woke up with the smell of frying bacon in my nostrils. My stomach gave a loud growl. I put my hand to it and opened my eyes. At first, I didn't know where I was. It was only when I saw my coat on the floor that I remembered.

I had gone to sleep at Mrs. Wildfire's house. I had been dead tired by the time I had arrived, having taken the bus and walking for a half hour, and Mrs. Wildfire welcomed me with open arms. I had fallen asleep the second my head had hit the pillow.

The canary yellow wallpaper looked golden under the rays of sun that passed the window's thin and light curtains. I could tell there had once been a kid living in this room. There were toys, mostly for boys, in boxes. The bed I had slept in had Spiderman bedsheets, as well as a Flash pillow case. I had to admit, the boy had a good taste when it came to superheroes.

I yawned and slid out of bed. I still had the top I had worn last night. I had taken off my jeans, so that left me with only underwear. I scanned for my jeans on the floor as well as my socks, but didn't find them. Mrs. Wildfire must've taken them to the washing machine.

I took my watch from the bedside table and looked at it. A quarter to seven. At least, I thought lamely, I got my five hours of sleep.

I expected to hear the door crack when I opened it, but it didn't. Mrs. Wildfire must've oiled it in the past few weeks. There was a short hallway extending in front of me. Mrs. Wildfire's room was on my right and the bathroom on my left. I took a left.

As I had thought, my clothes were there, piled up and clean. I slid on my jeans and left my socks there. It wasn't very cold in the tiny apartment, and I liked walking barefoot.

I soaked my face with cold water several times before feeling completely awake. I looked at myself in the mirror. I had purple bags under my eyes and my face looked all bloated. Ugh, I hated that first look in the mirror, it depressed me more than anything else.

It was only when I was drying my face that I heard voices coming from the kitchen. One of the voices was Mrs. Wildfire's. The others I couldn't identify. A man and a woman.

I didn't want to pry, but I was Abby for crying out loud. And I was always curious.

"...looking for the Elements," said the male voice. Husky, I noted.

"The Council is sending specialized Nightriders to look for them. They're trained Seekers," said the woman, her voice calm and sweet.

"And how is that of my business?" asked Mrs. Wildfire, her voice much lighter and yet firm at the same time.

"They need shelter," put in the man. "They're used to live in Eldoras, so they're not accustomed to our way of living."

"You know you don't have to ask me if they're aloud to stay at the academy, Kristen," said Mrs. Wildfire, calmly. "I gave you the permission to be the one to run the academy. You don't need to ask me for things like this."

"I know," said the woman named Kristen. "But it wasn't only for that that we came."

I had enough of it. What were Nightriders and Seekers? It wasn't my business, so I didn't have to know. Right?

I stepped into view. They were all sitting around the round table. I looked at the two strangers. What first caught my eye was the man. Well he wasn't exactly a man, but he definitely did not fall in the category of boy. I guessed he was about eighteen, maybe nineteen, I wasn't really sure. He had sandy-brown hair and emerald green eyes. He was imposing. He was big. I could even see how ripped he was through his shirt. He wasn't bulky. Not at all. He just had a lot of muscles. And he was tall. Even when he was sitting, I could see that.

The woman -Kristen- wasn't as imposing as her friend. She was delicate, small. Her long black hair was pulled up in a ponytail, just like mine. Her big gray eyes looked wise and knowing. Sharp. She looked like she was about eighteen, a bit younger than her friend.

"Ah, Abby," said Mrs. Wildfire, cracking me a smile. I looked in the elderly woman's eyes and smiled at her with all my teeth. Every time I saw her, I felt like giving her a hug. Her big bosom and stomach felt like home to me. I refrained myself from actually giving her a hug, wanting to be properly introduced to the strangers first. "You're awake. I made some bacon. Want some?"

I nodded. "Good morning, Mrs. Wildfire," I said, smiling. I turned to look at the strangers, who looked out of their environment. They would fit better in a James Bond movie. With guns and everything. No, not true. The guy would fit right in in one of the 'Expendables' movies, while Kristen would fit more in a movie like 'Sucker Punch'.

"Abby this is Kristen Wolfe, a friend of mine," said Mrs. Wildfire. "Kristen, this is Abigail Claire."

Kristen got up and offered me her hand. When I shook it, Kristen said, "It's a pleasure to meet you, Abigail. It's a nice name."

"Abby. I prefer you calling me Abby," I insisted.

"All right." Kristen let go of my hand. "Abby it is."

"And this," began Mrs. Wildfire, "is Damien Greenwhick." Now that definitely rung a bell. Greenwhick was the name McKenna had used on our first encounter.

"Hi Abby," called Damien, grinning. "Hope we didn't wake you up."

"Oh don't worry," I assured, while going to sit opposite to him. "You didn't wake me up."

"Claire..." observed Damien. "Are you Janine Claire's daughter?"

"Yes," I answered, frowning. "How did you know?"

"We once met her years ago through Mrs. Wildfire," said Kristen, regaining her seat. "She'd told us that she had adopted a girl named Abigail. I think that was before she had a child of her own. Mary-Anne, am I right?"

I nodded. "We call her Mary."

"How old is she. Mary, I mean."

"She just turned five this summer," I said.

I hadn't noticed that Mrs. Wildfire had gotten up and filled a plate with cantaloupes, bacon slices and eggs. She placed it in front of me.

"Thanks," I murmured, getting my knife and fork before digging in.

"How old are you?" asked Damien, trying an attempt at conversation.

"Sixteen," I said after swallowing what I had in my mouth. "Seventeen in three weeks."

"So you're a junior," noted Kristen. "What school?"

"Fenway High School. FHS," I answered.

"What university do you want to go to?" asked Damien.

"I'm not sure yet," I said. "But I do want to excel in medical care."

"You want to be a doctor?" said Damien, frowning.

"Yes, got a problem with that?" The minute I said that, I wanted to take it back. "Sorry. I didn't mean to..."

"Oh, don't worry about it," said Kristen, grinning at Damien. "He's not a morning person either. Trust me, you don't want to be next to him when he wakes up."

"You live together?" I asked.

"Yes, we kind of do. We live in an academy, here, in Boston," said Damien. "With several other people."

"What kind of academy is it?"

Damien and Kristen looked at each other. "Well, it's complicated," finally said Kristen. "We live there, we learn there... It's like campus, but this time, it's in one building."

"Cool. No parents?"

"No. But we are legal adults, so we can take care of ourselves," answered Damien cooly. "What are you doing here? Aren't you supposed to be at your proper house?"

Was he mocking me? At seven in the morning? "What about you? Aren't you supposed to be at your academy?"

He narrowed his eyes and then looked at Mrs. Wildfire. "I like this kid. She's fun."

"She's one of a kind, all right," said Mrs. Wildfire, smiling at me. "I've never seen anybody like her."

I didn't like it when other people talked about me, especially when I was being complimented, so I asked, clear and loudly, "Do you know anyone named McKenna?"

I could see how the question had taken all three adults off guard. Damien's eyes had widened, Kristen's jaw had locked and Mrs. Wildfire grimaced. Wow, that had hit a spot.

It was Kristen who was the first one to recover. "Yes. We do know him. How do you know him?"

"We met twice," I admitted, shrugging.

"How?" asked Damien, clearly fazed. I couldn't tell why.

"First time was at Mr. Porter's shop. He came to get your order," I said, directly to Damien. "It was in the name of Greenwhick. Second time was at a party I had gone to... yesterday, as a matter of fact. He was there because of some drug problem. It was a really weird situation. Everyone at the party wasn't acting like themselves..."

Both Kristen and Damien nodded. Kristen turned her attention to Mrs. Wildfire. "Sorry, Elizabeth. We have to leave." But her eyes said 'We'll talk about it another time'.

"Alright, Kristen," said Mrs. Wildfire as Damien and Kristen got up and walked towards the door. "Take good care. Both of you."

Damien looked back at me and grinned. "Have a nice day, Abs." And he closed the door behind him.

I smiled even when he was gone. I could feel that we would understand each other well. Even if we were most probably never to see each other again.

"They're nice people," said Mrs. Wildfire, sitting at Kristen's place. "I've known them since... they were little kids. They've always been nice."

"Yeah. Very nice."

FOUR

SHANE

I was watching the Celtics' basketball game on TV. They weren't doing as well as they had last game—15 to 49. Not so good. Worst that could happen (for the opposite team) would be a huge comeback, but I doubted that would happen today.

I stared blankly at the plasma screen. When I saw the L.A. Lakers score another one (five in a row), I clicked it off. I got up and walked down the hallway to the kitchen.

The academy was like a hotel, velvet floors, woodcrafts on the walls, long hallways, five star rooms. There were also communal rooms on every story. There was a level made especially for Nightrider students and a level for everything concerning weapons. It was all a Nightrider's paradise, except for the demons. Demons didn't dare come in here.

So, Kristen, Damien, Gabe and I had the whole place to ourselves—no one else, just us. There were usually more Nights over here but all of them had been called back to Eldoras for a special meeting concerning the Lost Elements. I could've gone but who in their right mind would go to one of those meetings? It was all talk and no action. They said they would send out troops to take care of a vampire problem on the East Coast and nothing had been done. We were still dealing with these filthy bloodsuckers every day ... So, I just tended to avoid Eldoras at all costs, because it just frustrated me more than anything else did.

I was sitting on a steel stool, finishing the glass of cold water I had poured myself (I didn't really like the way it hurt my teeth but freezing cold water was just too good to pass up), when Damien and Kristen bolted into the kitchen. Damien didn't have the foolish grin he wore half the time and Kristen shot a murderous glare in my direction. Neither seemed too happy. Great, what had I done now?

Kristen was fast—faster than I was on this one. She approached me smoothly and before I could stop her, she slapped me—*hard*, not a girl slap, a Kristen slap. I was sure it was going to leave a mark, like all the other bruises she had given me for all the times I had screwed up and hadn't been paying attention, which didn't happen very often.

"What the hell was that for?" I asked, innocently, putting a hand to my cheek. "Jesus Christ, Kristen! What was that for?"

"You know very well what that was for!" she yelled at me. Her face was red from anger, and Kristen rarely lost her temper. "Don't play dumb, Shane. *Think*."

Before I could think of the bad things that would affect Kristen (or anyone) Damien said, "Abigail Claire ring a bell?"

"Nope. None at all."

"Dammit, Shane," said Kristen, her voice cooler than it had been. "The girl you saw last night."

I looked at her blankly. "I saw plenty of girls last night." Was it possible that I had left a trace yesterday? I had made sure to erase everyone's memory at that party … except one … that black haired girl with the big, wide purple eyes. The one I had first seen at that antiques boutique. That girl who had made me waste an entire day at finding a store that didn't even exist … *Abigail's*, she had said. She had been playing with me, damn her. "Her name's Abigail Claire?"

"Yes, and she *remembers* you from a *party* with drugs?" said Damien, saying every word slowly.

Now I saw the mistake, my mistake, to be exact. "She was leaving when I arrived and I was in a bit of a rush to get inside, so I didn't get to erase her memory of me."

"And what were you doing at that party? It's not your type to go hang out with humans." Kristen sat down in the chair in front of me. She wanted answers and she knew she was going to get them.

"Word on the street had it that there was supposed to be this vampire party going on in one of the big time houses in Boston, with humans. So I went to make sure … they had faery drinks given to the humans."

"And you went alone?" asked Kristen.

"Of course he didn't," put in Damien. "Gabe went with him."

One thing I didn't like with Damien was that he was so damned good at reading minds and he had no problem getting into my head to get the answers he wanted. There was no point lying to him; he was a Greenwhick and the mind had no secrets to him.

"Did you guys catch any?"

"There weren't that many really. There were around ten high school buddies who wanted to have some." I winced, thinking of what we had found in one of the upstairs bedrooms. "A girl was raped by one of them bastards. I personally took care of him."

"What did you do?" asked Kristen. I knew Damien wasn't asking any questions, because he already knew the answers.

"What do you think I did?" I snorted. I hated any man who dared hurt a woman, whoever she was. So, I hadn't been really … *nice* to the guy in question. "I kicked his ass and got myself two new fangs to add to my collection." I wasn't kidding when I said I had a fang collection. I was up to four pairs now.

"What about the others?"

"We got them all locked up downstairs."

"All of them?"

"All except one. I think he was the one who had conducted this whole thing. He'd been biting the hostess for a while, so I figured that's how he was able to get his buddies in, as well as the drinks."

"What about the—"

"The humans were all taken care of. I gave them all the seru—"

"All except Abby," interjected Damien sourly.

"Speaking of which, there's something fishy about her, Damien. Don't you think?"

Damien looked into space, as though he was thinking about it. "Now that you mention it ..."

"I don't think she was human. For all I can tell, she *wasn't* human," I said. "She didn't smell like one." I hadn't really paid attention to it last night because I had been in too big of a rush and I also hadn't noticed on the first day because of all the magical stuff the vendor sold in his shop.

"Oh, now you're a smell expert?" asked Kristen.

"He's right, Kristen," said Damien. "She wasn't human."

"Doesn't mean because Janine's a Nightrider that Abby's one as well. She could have adopted a human," pointed out Kristen.

Damien got up and walked toward the fridge. "We know that. It's her mind. She doesn't think like a human. She doesn't smell like one and her brainwaves are—"

"What about her brainwaves?" asked Kristen, cutting Damien in mid-sentence.

"They're not like those of a regular human—much faster, like hybrids," explained Damien, opening the fridge and opening a container. He sniffed and wrinkled his nose. "I don't think this spaghetti is good. Smells like a rat died. How long has it been there?"

"Since yesterday," I said and grinned. "Kristen made it."

"Figures," mumbled Damien.

"You're saying she's a hybrid?" said Shane. "Half human and half ... nymph?"

"She's definitely human, but part nymph? They're super rare. Almost extinct, like dragons." Damien had finally decided to take a tangerine. He came to sit next to Kristen. "Since the vampires started killing them by the hundreds, there are only a few still living on earth. Maybe some in *Eldoras*, treated well. Most probably in *Tartarus* ... the chances are like ... one in a million."

"Werewolf?" suggested Kristen.

"No way. They smell like wet dog," I said, making a face of disgust. "What human would want to have a kid with ... *that*?"

"I think you're over-exaggerating. They don't smell that bad," said Kristen, frowning.

"That's because you're used to the smell, wolf-girl," I teased. "Your wolves don't always smell like roses, you know."

As if on cue, two large gray wolves stepped into the kitchen. I had to admit, they were imposing, even for me. Kristen had trained them to be killing machines as well as pets—a male and a female. The male was taller and larger than the female and much more territorial. His green eyes looked exactly like Damien's. His name was Genghis.

The female's name was Khan. She was smaller than Genghis but she was as strong. She was two months pregnant, so it was Genghis protecting Khan.

Khan laid on the floor next to Kristen's chair. Genghis sat next to her nuzzling his nose in her neck. Kristen didn't bother them and neither did I. It was amazing how much love I could see between the two of them, even if both were only animals. I knew Genghis would die for Khan. Same thing for Khan. That sort of devotion was rare, even in us.

"How many weeks left?" asked Damien, looking at the two wolves, who were obviously in love, if that was even possible for animals.

"Days," corrected Kristen. "Several days left before birth." She looked at me, all serious. No matter how much she could make you regret, she had that thing about her that made people respect her. The way she looked at someone when she was on duty. Damien also had that thing but he rarely used it because he was so easygoing most of the time. "We have to erase her memory."

"But we still don't know what she is," I objected.

"She'll be better off if we just leave her alone. Dragging her into our world would be a bad idea."

"But what if she is part nymph? We can use her to—"

"Shane, are you hearing yourself? We are not bringing her into this no matter how useful she might be. She still has human blood, so she has the right to be left ignorant and that is that." She looked at me sternly and I knew it was pointless to convince her otherwise. Her family was one of the stubborn ones, so it was only normal for her to be like that as well.

I nodded and left.

ﮩﮩﮩ

ABBY

I was sitting on the couch, reading the book, *Pride and Prejudice.* It was a very humid day. There was a lot of fog outside, so I couldn't go outside and enjoy the fresh November breeze. I smiled at the thought of sitting outside on the front porch with a hot chocolate in one hand and a book in the other.

I would have ... if it hadn't been for the five-year-old at my feet. Mary, my stepsister adored me, idolized me even.

I set my book down and passed a hand in Mary's silky brown curls. She looked up from her drawing and smiled radiantly at me, her chocolate eyes full of joy and wonder.

Of course, she was joyful. What five-year-old wouldn't be happy spending an entire night with her sister?

Jane had called me, saying that she wanted me to take care of Mary for the night. Neither of us had apologized or even asked for an apology. We had just done the transition with poker faces on. It pained me to do so, especially with one of the people I loved most in the entire world, but it was all part of the game we were playing. Give nothing and get nothing in return.

"Oh, come here you little daredevil!" I said, hauling a giggling Mary on my lap. "Want me to fix us some snacks? After, we could go take a bath—with bubbles." It was what Mary loved most in the world ... even more than her own mom sometimes—a bubble bath. Mary nodded eagerly, winding her arms around my neck. I got up and carried her all the way to the kitchen, sitting her down on the marble counter.

I opened the fridge and got a pack of carrots out. I handed it to Mary who easily took hold of it.

"Do you want Mom's number one dip?" I asked, showing Mary the pinkish mixture in a bowl.

Mary nodded and pointed at the tomatoes. I got them out as well and closed the door with my hip. I set the food on the counter next to Mary and popped the tomato box open. Instead of taking a knife to cut them in slices, I bit in one as if it were an apple.

"Where's Pinky, Abs?" asked Mary, pouting. "I can't find him anywhere."

Pinky was Mary's little pig. She took him wherever she went. It had once been mine but I had never felt like Mary felt about Pinky. To me, he had been just a toy. To Mary, he was her best friend.

"Let's look around," I suggested, putting the things down, "before we go upstairs, all right?"

Mary nodded and let herself fall off the counter, onto the stool. She jumped off the stool and said, "I'll go look in the playroom." She ran off.

I decided to prepare the snacks while Mary was looking for Pinky. I opened one of the drawers and pulled out a knife. Once I had a plate, a bunch of carrots and a knife in front of me, I got to work. Usually people liked eating baby carrots just like that, but Mary was very special. She wanted every carrot cut in four.

When I was done with that, I placed the carrot pieces halfway in the dip, so Mary could just get them like that. I took one and put it in my mouth. The creamy taste of the dip and the crunchy hardness of the sliced carrot brought back memories of hot summer evenings on the back porch. All in all, it tasted great.

"Mary!" I exclaimed. "Did you find him?"

"No!" replied the five-year-old. "Not yet!"

I checked the clock. I was going to have to give Mary a bath soon. "Three more minutes! Not more!"

I felt a whoosh of air on my right. I pivoted and saw nothing but the fridge and the window slightly opened. Why had Jane left it open when it was more than freezing outside? Closing the window, a whip of wind whistled through the gap and letters flew down the counter. I looked at the pile of mail that had fallen from the sudden rush of air and picked them up one by one, reading there labels.

Jane Claire—Dedham Institution for Savings. Jane Claire—Community. Jane Claire—Photos 2006.

Nothing interesting for me here, I thought. I was tempted to open the *Photos 2006* but decided against it when I remembered that it was considered illegal. Jane would no doubt sue me for just about anything at the moment …

I felt another whoosh of air. This time, when I turned, I almost screamed when I saw a dark figure. I shut my lips when I recognized McKenna. He was leaning and looking at his nails as if he'd been there the whole time. What *the heck* was he doing here?

He looked up from his nails and said, "Nice place."

I didn't say anything. I kept staring at him trying to convince myself that this was all just a bad dream. I wanted to pinch myself awake. How had he known I lived here?

"What are you doing here?" I asked, remembering all those horror movies I had watched. Mary, I thought wildly. Where's Mary?!

"You met Kristen and Damien, didn't you?" said McKenna. "What were you doing at Mrs. Wildfire's house though?"

Since he wasn't answering any of my questions, I decided to give him the same treatment. "They're nice people, Damien and Kristen, I mean. And how the hell did you know I was at Mrs. Wildfire?"

"I have connections." He gave me a cocky grin. This sucker was attractive and he knew it. I looked him up and down. No way did I stand a chance against this guy if he tried to attack me.

"Hey," said Shane, passing a hand in front of my eyes. "Are you still alive?"

"What do you want with me? And what the hell are you doing here, McKenna?" I asked, noticing that my voice was a little bit off, probably because I was scared that this guy would hurt me or even worse, hurt Mary.

"No need to be so formal, Abby. I won't fire you if you call me by my first name."

I frowned. "I thought McKenna was your first name."

"Who in his right mind would call his son McKenna? Then again, I guess I probably haven't introduced myself properly." He took a step toward me and I took one quick step back. "You wound me, Abby. I would never hurt you."

"How do you know my name? Who are you?" My voice was shaking a lot. I cleared my throat to tried to make it better.

"Damien and Kristen told me about you earlier today." He extended one of his big hands toward me. "I'm Shane McKenna."

Oh no. This was horrible … He was named Shane. I loved the name Shane! I mentally slapped myself. Focus girl! You still don't know why he's here.

Mary suddenly barged into the kitchen, squeezing her pig against her chest. "I found Pinky! I found—"

The five-year-old took in the stranger standing next to her older sister. Mary stared at Shane.

"Hello little girl," said Shane, going to crouch next to Mary, whose eyes were still wide with amazement. I was going to stop him but then didn't. Somehow, I knew he wouldn't try to hurt her. It was a strange feeling, to see a stranger approaching your younger sister and not feeling worried. My mind was screaming '*Charge him!*' but my … *instincts* told me not to. There was just something about the way he looked at her that made it seem all right for him to approach Mary. And that look in *her* eyes …

"What's your name?" asked Shane, passing a finger over her fluffy cheek.

Mary winked several times before answering. "Mary-Anne Claire."

"Mary-Anne …" he said thoughtfully. "What a nice name."

"Mommy and Abs call me Mary. Not Mary-Anne," said Mary. "I don't like Anne. Makes me sound old, like Mommy."

Shane clearly held himself back from laughing. "You sure sound like a grown up. Who taught you manners?"

"Mommy," mumbled Mary. "She gets very mad at Abs, sometimes. Like yester—"

"I'm sure Shane here has to leave," I said stopping Mary from saying more. "Don't you Shane?"

Shane got up and swung Mary in his arms. Being an older sister, I had the reflex of putting a hand out in case he was going to drop her. I didn't *expect* him to have any experience whatsoever with young children.

He didn't drop Mary. In fact, Shane was handling things pretty well. He managed to take care of Mary and look good at the same time. I didn't know how he pulled it off.

"Are we going to eat these snacks or what?" asked Shane. When I didn't respond, he rolled his eyes and put Mary on one hip. He took the bowl in one hand and walked out of the kitchen.

I followed. When I saw him settling in one of the couches, I asked, "What do you think you're doing?"

"What does it look like I'm doing?" Shane put Mary on his lap and handed her the bowl. "We're eating a snack."

"No way." I took Mary from his arms. "*We're* going to eat the snack. *You* are leaving."

"But—"

"No buts," I said firmly. I placed Mary on her feet and stood in front of her. "Shane, you are leaving—*now*."

"No. *We're* leaving." He got up. "Now."

"What?" I stared at him. "No way."

"Yes way. Kristen asked me to bring you back and I do what she says." His voice was thick and firm—very firm and so, was his will.

However, I wasn't spineless. I too, had a strong will. "Get out of the house. *Now*."

"What are you going to do?" he asked, mocking. "Make me?"

Before I could reply, something pricked me. It didn't hurt much but I still put my hand to my neck. I didn't feel anything, no blood, no nothing. Must have been a small cramp.

Shane's eyes suddenly widened. "Abby—"

Whatever he had been about to say was interrupted by the sound of shattering glass.

I only had time to pivot toward Mary and shield her from the hideous monster that was coming toward us at an incredible speed.

FIVE

ABBY

I didn't see Shane move. I only felt a rush of air to my right. I put a hand on the back of Mary's head so that her eyes could be covered by my shoulder. I looked up. At first, I saw nothing, but after I saw two figures on the wall.

Shane was one of them and the other was … a monster.

It had three eyes instead of two, hundreds of razor-sharp teeth, extremely sharp claws … Its skin looked slimy and was of a greenish gray color. The nose (or was it a nose, I couldn't say) was two holes. Except the ragged piece of cloth around its waist, it was completely naked, which made it ten times uglier. However, its physical aspect didn't seem to bother it. It wasn't made to look good or even bad. It was made to kill.

I was about to puke. This creature looked too much like last April's. I fought the envy to faint by holding Mary even harder.

I got up and kept Mary in my arms, doing my best to cover her eyes. I was *definitely* going to have nightmares. I sucked in air when the monster clawed at Shane's chest, but was relieved when Shane cut the thing's throat. I closed my eyes when Shane made the gesture to slit the thing's head off.

"Well," said Shane, a little breathless. He let the creature's body fall to the ground and cleaned his blade on the thing's arm. "That was close."

I opened my eyes, glad that Shane was blocking the view to the monster. Then I saw his chest and my eyes widened.

"You're hurt," I breathed.

"Yeah," admitted Shane, wincing as he moved to scratch his head. His shirt was torn open and there was blood everywhere. "I'm fine. Don't worry about it."

"Don't worry about it?" I yelled hysterically. "A monster just came in the house. It had claws and sharp teeth—"

"It wasn't a monster," interrupted Shane. "It was a type of demon, a ghoul."

"I don't care what it was. It was going to kill y—"

"But it didn't, did it? I'm still alive, and that's what we're not going to be if we stay here any longer."

At first I thought he was joking, but when I looked in his eyes, I knew he wasn't. He was serious. *This* was serious.

"Abs ..."

I let go of Mary's head and looked into her eyes. They were filled with fear and worry. I swallowed tightly; I didn't like that look on her sweet, innocent face. "Are you all right?" I asked, passing a hand through Mary's silky curls.

"Yeah ... I'm scared, Abs," whispered Mary.

"I'm also scared, Mary," I replied, putting my forehead against Mary's, "but don't worry." I looked at Shane and exhaled heavily. I had no other option but him. I wasn't someone who put their full trust into a person a few minutes after meeting them. It had taken me years to create a trustworthy bond with Kaithlyn and Brittany ... and here I was, putting my life—and Mary's—in the hands of a complete stranger ... but he was our only chance at getting out of this unscathed. He *had* just saved us from a monster. "What do we have to do?"

Shane fished a vial out of his pocket. The content was the color of amber. The vial seemed to be made out of pure crystal and real leather. There was an emblem at the center. It looked like a lion.

"Drink this," he said, opening the vial and handing it to me. "Not more than three drops."

I knew this was crazy, that I was going straight to hell by doing what this complete stranger told me to do but I knew I had no other choice. I couldn't call the police, because he was a cop, a monster-fighting cop but a cop still. I couldn't call Jane, because then she would also be in trouble. I had no other choice but to listen to Shane ...

I took the vial, put my lips to it and let a drop slide down my tongue. It was sweet and tasted like maple syrup and what could pass as roses. I took two others.

"Give three to Mary as well," instructed Shane. After I did as he said, I gave the vial back to Shane. He put it to his lips and let three drops fall into his mouth. "We should be good for about three hours."

"What does it do?" I asked, setting Mary down.

"Humans won't be able to see or hear us," answered Shane. He took Mary in his arms and before I could protest, said, "There'll be more of them; this was only a scout. We might need to run, so it would be easier for me to carry her."

"You're talking about humans as though you weren't one."

He gave me a look. "I'll explain everything to you later. Now, I need to get the two of you to safety."

I nodded. Answers could wait. "Where are we going?"

"The academy," said Shane pacing to the front door. "It's the only safe place I can think of." He put his hand on the handle and looked straight into my eyes. "You have to do whatever I say. You have to trust me on this."

"I will."

"Take this," added Shane, handing me the dagger he had used to kill the demon. I stared at its blade; there was still blood. Seeing the horror on my face, Shane sighed and wiped it on his jeans. "It might come in handy."

"I'd rather not ..." I said as I put shoes on Mary. I slipped mine on and grabbed our coats. I looked at Shane, who still had the dagger in hand. "No thank you Shane ..."

He nodded, slipped the dagger in his boot and opened the door.

When I saw nothing wrong in particular, I let out the breath I had been holding.

"We have about ten minutes before they start coming back," explained Shane. He got what looked like a cellphone out of his pocket. He dialed a number and put the device to his ear. "Damien ..." I heard a loud buzz at the other end of the line. "I know but look—" Shane looked impatient. "Look, bro. We're in trouble. There was a spy ghoul in her house ... There's a kid with us and I don't want her in my way." ... "Yes, we need a lift. Five minutes." He closed the phone and put it back in his pocket.

My throat was aching, more than before. I put my hand to my neck and felt a little bump. Not big but not small either. Was it possible that I had been bitten by a mosquito? At this time of year? I doubted it but I still let it go.

"We need to go," said Shane firmly, walking out of the house and into the night. I had no choice but to follow him. "Run actually."

We ran. It was surprising how well he could run, even with a forty-pound kid in his arms. Shane was actually holding back from running faster to stay close to me. I wasn't that good at running; my PE grades proved it. If only I had strength in my legs ... The aching was growing. It took a lot of will power not to put my hand to the bump.

It was only five painful minutes later that we came to a stop. We were at one of the corners of the park, of Boston Common.

"They should be here any minute now," said Shane, putting Mary to her feet.

As if on cue, two black motorcycles rushed toward us. When the drivers hit the brakes, one made a hundred and eighty before coming to a stop. I stared and could only think of one word—*showoff.* The woman took off her helmet—Kristen. She was grinning. "Need a ride?" she asked us.

The other driver, the one who'd executed the one eighty, was Damien. "Hello Mary," he said, kissing her on the forehead.

"You know her?" I asked Damien, surprised as hell.

"Sorry. No time for answers," said Damien, swinging Mary in front of him. He unzipped his leather jacket and put it around Mary. Damien looked a bit like a pregnant woman except for Mary's legs dangling at

LARA ROSECHILD

his sides. He closed the jacket, careful not to get Mary's hair stuck in the zipper and passed me his helmet. I caught it with ease.

"Kristen, Damien and Mary will ride on one," explained Shane. "We'll ride on the other."

"Why can't I go with Mary?" I asked, putting a hand on my waist.

"So we know who the demons are after," said Kristen, swinging a leg over the bike and putting her helmet on. "We have to separate you two."

"Fine," I grumbled. I slipped the helmet on.

Shane hopped on the other bike and roared the engine to life. I almost jumped out of my skin when he did. It had been awhile since I'd been so close to a bike. "Drive south," indicated Shane to Damien. "If you don't get followed for about a half hour, you should be good to go back to the academy."

Damien nodded and sped away with Kristen and Mary. I watched them go, still doubting if I should trust them too. Anyway, it was too late now. My little sister was riding away with complete strangers... Well, not *complete* strangers. Mrs. Wildfire had seemed to trust them, which meant I could *partially* trust them as well.

"Hop on," said Shane. When I didn't give any sign of moving, he rolled his eyes. "Are you doubting my riding skills?"

Ignoring what he had just said, I swung a leg on the other side of the bike and sat down behind him. "Jane would never approve of this," I muffled in my helmet.

"Trust me," I heard him say. "That's the least of your worries right now." He revved the engine and we went flying.

I hadn't felt so free and fast and bold in a long, long time. When he accelerated, my fingers dug in his skin. Of fright or excitement, I couldn't tell.

"Are you okay?" I heard him say.

"Yes," I answered, my voice shaking. How long had it been since I'd been on a motorcycle? Without almost getting killed? In April, that had been the last time.

"More than half an hour of this."

64

Okay, I thought to myself. I can live on a bike, especially if I'm not the one driving.

The aching came back, this time greater. It was becoming more of a burning than an aching. I made sure I had an arm around Shane's waist before putting a hand to my neck. The bump was definitely bigger than before. I swallowed or at least tried to. I tried to suck in air but couldn't.

"Oh shit!" shouted Shane. "They're after us."

I hadn't realized my eyes had been closed. I opened them and saw that he was right. There were half a dozen demons I had seen earlier. They were running on both their hands and feet. Some were running on the ground, and some on the walls. Rules of gravity didn't seem to apply to them.

"Hold on tight!"

I put both my arms around him and did as he said. The bike accelerated. I bit back a cry when the pain in my neck grew a bit more. My head was pounding; it felt like it was going to blow off.

The demons were now far behind but Shane didn't slow down one bit. I didn't know how fast we were going. I didn't care. The pain was just too much. This time, I didn't hold back the scream that had been building up in my throat. I let go of Shane and fell backward. I fell unconscious when my head (with the helmet on) hit the cement.

⋘⋙

Abby! Abby! Answer me! I know you're alive."

The voice was distant and at the same time annoying. I wanted some peace and quiet for once, just for once. Always somebody wanting something from me. Never left alone and now with all that was going on, I still couldn't have it.

I was burning, and I didn't want anybody to bother me when I was in major pain.

"Wake up, you idiot!"

No matter how hard I wanted to keep them closed, my eyelids opened. Shane was on his knees next to me. He seemed angry for some reason. I didn't know why. My helmet was on the ground, fractured.

"We don't have much time," he said, putting an arm around me so that he could help me up. "The poison will kill you if we don't bring you to a Healer. Can you walk?"

I managed to nod. He let go of me. I took a step forward and was glad not to fall down. It was only when I was several feet away from the bike that I did. Shane caught me from behind before I could fall face first on the ground.

"Looks like the side effects have already started," said Shane, carrying me to the motorcycle as if I weighed nothing. "Sorry but I'll have to …"

I never heard what he had wanted to say next. I was already out.

SIX

There was something damp on my forehead. I couldn't tell why but there was. It reminded me of the time I had caught a cold when I was six or seven. Jane had tucked me into bed and given me homemade chicken soup. I had loved the extra attention Jane had given me and the soup. What I also remembered was not liking the damp cloth on my forehead. After all these years, I still didn't like the feeling of dampness. It made me feel ... *icky*.

The cloth was removed from my forehead. The place where it had been now felt cool. I shivered. It was only then that I became more aware of my body.

It was aching all over. My legs and arms were numb and hot. I felt sweat roll down my neck and face. Even when I felt warm—sizzling hot—the thought of the recent events made me feel like an icicle.

I wanted to see Mary. I wanted to see my friends and my boyfriend. As crazy as it seemed, I wanted to see Shane. He was, after all, the one who had saved us from vicious monsters. He was maybe one himself, but he had still risked his own life for people he barely knew.

"You'd think she's dead," said a familiar voice. It was Damien, by the sounds of it.

"I have seen many corpses in my life." That was Kristen. "And none were sweating like she is."

"But look how pale she is," replied Damien. "How could she be so pale when she's sweating?"

"The poison's work," said Kristen. "It can have different symptoms for different people. If you were in her place, you could have had a blue tongue. Jeez, I don't know. You can ask the one who poisoned her."

"Why would anyone want to kill *her*?" asked Damien.

"I don't know," admitted Kristen. "For one, I can tell that she's not human. That's for sure. She's recovered much faster than a human."

"We've already established that," said Damien, his tone sounded a little impatient. "The ghouls must've seen that Shane was with her, protecting her and yet, they kept following them." He paused. "Ghouls don't usually prey on something they can't have ... unless they were ordered to."

"So you're saying that somebody wants her for a certain purpose," said Kristen. "Or maybe she has something that they want ..."

"We should talk about this later," cut in Damien. "I'm sure Abby doesn't want to wake up listening to such a conversation."

My eyes fluttered open. How the hell had he known I was awake? I looked at their faces as they hovered over me. Kristen looked a bit worried but Damien was just smiling.

I started to move my fingers and toes to make sure I could at least control several of my useful bones. I wet my lips and slowly got up to a sitting position.

Damien and Kristen were sitting on chairs next to my bed, or rather, my *hospital* bed. The room looked exactly like the ones in hospitals, or something like it. There were two rows of beds just like mine on each side of the room. Almost everything was white, the sheets on the beds, the curtains, the tiled floor, the walls. Now I remembered why I hated hospitals. They were completely lifeless.

I brought my attention back to Kristen and Damien, who were watching me intently. "Where am I?" I asked Kristen.

"The infirmary," she said.

"Are we at the academy?"

"Yeah." Before I could ask any more questions, Kristen added, "Are you feeling all right?"

I blinked. I put my hand to my neck and felt nothing but smooth flesh—no bump, no wound and most of all, no veins popping out.

"What happened?" I said.

"You were poisoned by a ghoul," answered Damien. "You'd be dead if it hadn't been for Mrs. Wildfire healing you."

I thought back but I couldn't remember seeing Mrs. Wildfire. "Mrs. Wildfire healed me? But how could she know ... *how* to heal me?"

Kristen glanced toward Damien. She was obviously uncomfortable with this. "Uh, how can I put this?" She looked at me and then back at Damien, as though she was seeking help.

"Abby, there are a lot of things you don't know..." Damien started slowly. "You unfortunately have no choice but to be part of it, because someone—we don't know who—wants you, for some reason."

"What you lived not long ago was no nightmare. Those were truly ghouls and they wanted you dead." Kristen eyes were as hard as stone, and I had this gut wrenching feeling in my stomach that everything she was saying was true.

"Just tell me, are you guys gonna turn into monsters anytime soon?" I blurted out.

Damien let out a laugh and Kristen smiled. "Of course not, Abby. On the contrary, we fight these ... monsters. We're part of a huge underworld called Nightrealm. We call ourselves Nightriders." She paused, and gave me a reassuring smile. "We're not that different from humans, really. We're just faster, stronger and we have ... *unique* abilities."

"And how come humans haven't figured out that you guys exist? I've seen so many monsters lately ... So, there must be a lot of you."

"We're around one million all around the world, but that's just Nightriders; there's plenty m—"

"Kristen, I think there's only so much information the girl can take in one day," interrupted Damien.

I ignored what he said. There was one more thing I had to ask. "So is that what you guys were talking about when you were at Mrs. Wildfire the other day? Is she a Nightrider too?"

"Yes, she is, and so is your mother, Janine," answered Kristen.

I stared at her as though she had just told me that the world was coming to an end tomorrow. Jane was a monster-fighting Nightrider? Oh my God … How was this even possible?

"Where did Shane run off to?" asked Damien, crossing his arms over his chest.

"I don't know," said Kristen, shrugging. "He left two hours ago. Said he had some business to take care of."

"Oh." I needed to thank him for helping Mary and I… My eyes widened "Where's Mary?"

"You don't have to worry about her, Abby," said Kristen, coolly. "She's with Mrs. Wildfire."

"How long have I … been *asleep?*" I asked.

"Two days," said Damien, matter-of-factly.

"Which reminds me …" Kristen got up and looked at Damien. "Gotta go get her something to eat and drink. You make sure she doesn't try to run away."

"Sure," agreed Damien, shrugging. "Why not?"

Kristen blurred out of the room. It took me several seconds to stop staring at the empty chair. Was it just my dizziness or was she really *that* fast—or was it both?

"Don't worry," assured Damien, smiling at me. It sounded like he could read my thoughts. "You'll get used to it soon enough."

"Yeah," I muttered. "I hope I will."

"So … you want to be a doctor?"

We talked—small talk. I had to admit, Damien knew how to talk to a lady. He never brought up heavy subjects like me being poisoned, or how I felt that two of my closest relatives were freaking *Nightriders*! He asked about school and interests.

"Bugs Bunny or Mickey Mouse fan?" he asked at one point. Damien sat back in his chair.

"Definitely Bugs Bunny fan," I said without hesitation. "I don't like listening to Mickey's squeaky voice. When I do, I feel like ripping my hair out."

"Daffy Duck or Donald Duck?" said Damien.

"That's a tough one," I admitted. "I like Daffy's and Donald's personalities, especially their way of talking. They're hilarious." Before he could ask anything else, I said, "My turn to ask questions."

"Fine," he grumbled.

"How is it that you know Mary?"

Damien seemed to think about it for a while. "We see each other every Friday and Saturday night. Sometimes Janine would bring her on Wednesday afternoon. I'm kind of like her nanny on Thursdays."

My jaw dropped. I closed it as fast as it had come down. I opened my mouth again to say something but no sound came out. I was, in some way, speechless.

Damien gave me an apologetic look. "I'm sorry you were in the dark for so long, but Janine was doing it to protect you."

"Protecting me from what?" I croaked. There was a bulge forming at the back of my throat and I hated it. "The truth?"

"Abby ..."

He never finished his sentence. Shane came in the room. He was carrying a tray of food in one hand and a bottle of beer in the other. He seemed to be much better than last time I'd seen him. His skin wasn't white anymore; it was alive. I was sure that if I were to touch him, he would be warm rather than cold as stone. He was wearing jeans and an unbuttoned shirt.

"Good," he said, putting the tray on the steel nightstand. "You're awake. How're you feeling?"

"Good," I said. "Thanks." The bulge in the back of my throat that had once been was no longer. I had swallowed my tears and looked at Shane straight in the eyes.

Neither of us said anything for a while. I started becoming aware of my body once again. I was wearing a too small tank top and mini shorts for night. I was there, sitting in a bed with thin white sheets, and in the company of two guys. I was sure I was bright red by now. I looked at both of them, to Damien, and then to Shane. I could almost hear my heart beating faster as it pumped more blood to my cells. Oh man, well this was embarrassing ...

I cleared my throat, to make sure I had their attention. "If you guys don't mind," I finally said. "I'd like to …"

I was glad Damien interrupted me when he said, "I have to talk to Kristen about something." He got up and walked to the door. He turned back and looked at Shane. "Shane, why don't you show Abby to her room? I'm sure she doesn't want to stay in here."

"Right," answered Shane tightly before taking a long drink from his beer.

Damien disappeared from my vision and I could swear he'd been there not even seconds before. My head was still pounding and sometimes, I thought I could see in doubles. I stared at the empty air where he had been and snapped out of it. I shifted my attention to Shane who was looking at me.

"Are you going to eat that?" he asked, inclining his head to the tray.

I gave the tray one look. My mouth started to water. I took the tray with two hands and put it on my lap. It was chicken soup and a piece of ciabatta bread. I ripped out a piece and dipped it in the soup. I propped the piece in my mouth and closed my eyes. I had never tasted something so good before. The bread was warm and delicious. As for the soup … I had no words to describe it.

Shane took the seat where Damien had been. "Like the soup?" he asked.

I nodded. I didn't want to be rude by talking with my mouth full but then again … "It's delicious," I said, covering my mouth with one hand. It truly was delicious. I don't think I'd ever tasted soup this good. Even Mrs. Wildfire's chicken soup didn't compare to Damien's.

"Damien made it." When he saw my eyebrows rise, he added, "He's a great cook. Much better than Kristen's cooking; that I can tell."

When I was done with the bread, I took the bowl in both hands and drank it in big gulps. The hot liquid slid down my throat, heating up every inch of my body. I put the bowl down on the tray and wiped at my mouth with my wrist like a first grader.

"That was good," I said, very satisfied with my meal. "Compliments to the chef."

Shane took the tray from my lap and put it on the table. He had finished his beer and put it next to the empty bowl. "Do you want to go see your room?" asked Shane.

I nodded. "If you don't mind, please."

"Abby," he said, sighing. "You don't have to be polite with me. I'm not that old."

"I'm sorry..."

Shane put a warning finger up before I could finish my sentence. "Don't. You're not sorry. It's just your manners."

"Oh ... I'm s—"

"You see," said Shane, making a gesture toward me. "Here you go again. Why are you sorry? You don't have to be. I just wanted you to understand that around here, we're not that polite with each other."

"All right," I agreed. "No more being polite with you." This was completely ridiculous. Who didn't like manners?

"Right." He took something that was laying on the arm of his chair and threw it at me. "We haven't put the heater on yet. So you might get cold in these clothes."

I looked down at myself. I unfolded the silk fabric. It was a white bathrobe; it was soft under my fingers. I had had one like this when I had been twelve but I had lost it. I slid my arms in the sleeves and got my hair out from under it. I stretched my legs and slid them out of the covers.

"This is Kristen's. Sorry if it doesn't cover much but that's all we had."

There were several bruises on my tibias as well as my thighs, and several small scars. They would most definitely heal in the next week or so.

My right leg started tingling, as if there were thousands of tiny ants on it. If I didn't walk soon, I was sure it would spread to my left leg. I put both my feet on the ground and got up. The bathrobe ended right bellow my knees.

Shane got up and pulled a pair of slippers from under the bed. He placed them in front of me so that I could slip my feet in. I didn't bother to tie the rope of the bathrobe. It wasn't that cold.

When I was sure my legs were capable (more than capable) of walking, I took the several steps it took to the infirmary door. Before I could put my hand on the handle, Shane had already swung the door open and was out of the infirmary, holding the door for me.

The first thing I saw from the academy, apart from the infirmary, was the hallway. The floor was originally smoothed oak but there was an endless burgundy velvet carpet covering its center. I wouldn't be surprised if people walked barefoot around here. I sure as hell would.

There were paintings, a lot of paintings. Most were of diverse battle scenes. One of them contained ghouls and other creatures. Actually, almost all of them contained ghouls and other creatures. They were all on different battlegrounds, painted by different artists, too. However, in all of them, I could see fierce passion. The colors were vivid and clear, no mistaking that.

I stopped when one of them caught my attention. I narrowed my eyes and looked carefully at the painting. It was a wolf, sitting on a big rock, howling at the moon high above. Its gray fur shone under the moonlight. I could just imagine how soft its fur would be or would it be rough and thick? Maybe it would be neither of the two. I couldn't tell.

I looked at the bottom of the painting and read, "Camellia DiCaprios," aloud. I turned my head toward Shane, who was standing a few steps behind me. "How come I haven't heard of her?"

"That's because she's a Nightrider like me," said Shane, taking several steps closer so that he could have a better view of the painting. "Most of the paintings here are her work."

"These paintings are beautiful. Can't you be a Nightrider and be famous?" I asked, not looking away from the wolf.

"It would be annoying and inconvenient," explained Shane, shrugging when I gave him a look. "Because you wouldn't be able to go out without being followed."

"It annoys most of the celebrities," I said. "Why would it be any different for a Nightrider?"

He sighed and walked away. I frowned and tagged along. "We Nightriders aren't just here for decoration. We work. Our job is to rid Earth of demons."

"So what you do is kill demons, not monsters."

"Yes. We kill as many as we can."

"The ghoul at my house … he was a demon. Right?"

Shane nodded. He stopped in front of a door and turned toward me. "Part demon. Wait here." He opened the door and closed it behind him. I stood there, motionless. It was going to take a while to find words to describe Shane McKenna. He was very hard to read.

I was leaning against the wall in front of the door when Shane finally got out. He was carrying a book. He handed it to me; I took it. The book was heavy and old in my hands. The cover was made of leather and its pages were ancient looking, *very* ancient looking.

"What is it?" I asked Shane. I looked up from the book. Shane had closed the door behind him and was looking at me intently. When he saw how puzzled I was, he sighed.

"It's a book," he said lamely. "What's it look like?"

"You got to be kidding," I exclaimed, raising and dropping my arms in exasperation. "What is it?"

"It's a NightBook. It's one of the originals," added Shane, taking it back from me. He opened it and went through several of the pages, letting his fingers trail over the writings. "It's handwritten by a famous Nightrider writer."

"What's his name?" I asked. I wouldn't be surprised if I had never heard his name before, which was pretty rare for me, since I spent most of my free time reading.

"Olivignetti. He called himself Olivignetti, anyway."

"What's written inside it?" I asked, putting on a face that could pass for interested. "Gory details of how to kill a demon?"

Shane looked amused. "Yeah, stuff like that."

My jaw dropped. I hadn't really thought there were such things in the book and how could Shane be *amused* about it? There was nothing funny about killing. The guy was probably nuts like everything that was happening to me right now.

"Don't look so surprised," exclaimed Shane, putting both his hands up at the sides of his face, as if proclaiming his innocence. "You wanted to know."

"I didn't actually think that you would find it funny," I replied, putting both hands on my hips. "What's wrong with you?"

"What's wrong with *me*?" he exclaimed. "More like what's wrong with *you*? You're supposed to know that I kill demons."

"I know that you do. I've seen you in action," I allowed. "But I didn't know you enjoyed killing!"

"I kill demons, not humans," said Shane.

"It's still killing."

"It's my job. That's what I do. That's what I am!"

"Do you like killing?" I said, my voice just above a whisper.

"No," answered Shane, lowering his voice to a normal level. "I don't."

"Just wanted to make sure. Sorry to have jumped to conclusions like that. It's a bad habit of mine."

Neither of us said anything for a while. Shane was still holding the book and I was still in my bathrobe.

"Wanna see your room?" he asked finally.

"Yeah, about that ..." I shifted my weight to my other leg and crossed my arms over my chest. "I don't think I'm going to stay here."

Shane frowned. "Where do you intend to go then?" he asked, closing the book in his hands.

"Um ... back to my house?"

"Are you serious?" said Shane, raising his eyebrows. I nodded, suddenly feeling very small. "Forget it."

He started walking and I followed him. "Why?" I asked. "I have every right to go to my house."

"No, you don't," applied Shane, his voice firm. "You can't go back there."

"Why not?"

"I know you're not the dumbest person ever but I didn't know you were *that* stupid."

"Are you saying I'm stupid?"

"Think, Abby," he said, coming to a stop. Shane turned to look at me. "You were attacked by ghouls, *in your house*. It doesn't really sound good if you go back there."

"It could have been a mistake," I protested, bringing the bathrobe even closer to my chest. It *was* getting cold. "They could have had the wrong address. They could have been attacking the neighbors."

"I doubt that," said Shane. "Ghouls don't usually make mistakes. They'd be killed if they did."

I frowned. "Why?"

"Ghouls aren't very smart. They can't make a battle strategy or plan an ambush. Somebody else plans it for them, another greater demon that promised them something in exchange for their loyalty."

"So you're saying that somebody wanted to attack us?"

Shane nodded. "Ghouls are disposable creatures, just like pawns in a chess game."

"Who would control them?" I asked.

"Vampires. Vampires tend to take advantage of people, and things."

"*Vampires?*" I cried out. What the hell was this guy talking about? Demons were believable enough, since I had seen them with my own two eyes—*twice*! But *vampires*? That was just something I couldn't swallow or this guy was *truly* too good to be true. He was nuts! I snorted. "What about *werewolves*? Would they do it?"

"No. It's not in their nature to work with demons, even though they *are* part demon themselves."

"Werewolves, vampires, demons ..." I said in a breath. I could barely wrap my mind around what I was saying or what I was hearing. Two possibilities occurred to me: the monsters Shane, Kristen and Damien were talking about really existed (if they did, I was in deep *shit*), or I was just losing my mind. Yeah, I was definitely losing my mind.

"Nymphs, dragons, ghouls, warlocks, shapeshifters ..." continued Shane for me. "Can't wrap your mind around it, can you?"

I slowly shook my head. "It doesn't seem real, not yet. I think I'm just going crazy, or this is a bad dream, and if I pinch myself, all of this will be gone."

"Spend a few more days with us and trust me, you'll get over it," said Shane. He stopped walking. "So this is it."

"This is what?" I asked, frowning at him.

"Your room."

"Oh."

I looked at the door in front of us. The door was exactly like Shane's. Well, not really. Shane's door handle had many fingerprints on the doorknob, and this one had none.

When I made no move to open it, Shane rolled his eyes and opened it for me. He stepped in and turned to look at me. "See?" he said, bringing his hands up and then letting them fall to his sides. "No monsters here to get you."

I stepped across the threshold and looked around. At first, all I saw was darkness but as my eyes grew accustomed to the dark, I could slowly make out the shape of the room. It was about twice the size of my old room. There was a large bay window on the right side of the room. I could also make out the shape of a closet door to my left. Right ahead, I could see the outline of another door. I guessed it to be a bathroom. Well, I hoped it was. I didn't want to open it and find things that weren't meant to be found and by that I meant skeletons. Yeah, skeletons in the closet ...

Suddenly, there was light. My eyes widened at the new sight of the room. The walls were light purple. The window curtains were of a darker shade of purple. The floor under our feet was, again, a *purple* rug. I wasn't at all surprised when I saw that the sheets on the bed were also purple and indigo. The decorator of this room sure must've loved the color.

"That over there's the bathroom," said Shane, pointing at the door in front of us. "That's the closet. That's a bed and that's a—"

"I know what a bedroom is, Sherlock," I said, interrupting him. "You don't need to explain to me such fundamental things, you know. I wasn't raised under a rock."

"So you know what a bedroom is. I have to admit, I hadn't expected that from you."

I turned around and stared at him. "Are you mocking me?" I asked, squinting my eyes.

Shane grinned and went to sit on a chair in front of a desk. "You sure are feisty," he said.

"I don't like being played around with, McKenna," I inquired, crossing my arms over my chest.

"And I don't like being bossed around, Claire," replied Shane, his cocky grin still on his face.

"Then I guess we're clear."

"I guess we are."

☙ ❧

I had changed out of my 'hospital clothes' and changed into a pair of skinny jeans and a red shirt. I had found them lying on my queen size bed. Why I had such a humungous bed all to myself, I didn't know. I even had my own freaking bathroom. Everything in the room was spotless, just like in luxury hotels. I wondered if I was the only one to have such a room and if I was, I wanted to move out immediately. It wouldn't feel fair if I were to keep it for my own.

By the time I was cleaned and ready to go, the clock on the bed-side table indicated that it was seven in the afternoon. My stomach started grumbling. It hadn't even been two hours since I had last ate and I was still hungry. What kind of girl was I? A hungry one, that was for sure.

After five minutes of considering what I should do next, I decided to go take a look around. It wouldn't hurt anybody if I got to take a look around, would it?

Still barefoot, I got out of my room and silently closed the door behind me. The hallway was empty by the looks of it. I looked before at my right and then my left. The left was where Shane and I had come from. Since I had already seen what there was on that side, I decided to turn right.

The pattern of the hallway was the same as it had been before, velvet carpet, wooden carvings and Nightrider paintings. I stopped to look at every single one of them. Most of them were from the same painter, Camellia DiCaprios. It was all so confusing to me. The way she used the canvas' relief to make the paintings look so real. There were at least ten different shades of different colors in each painting. I couldn't put the finger on why they all looked so familiar …

"They make you think don't they?"

I whirled around, only to come face-to-face with a boy, the other boy whom I had seen at Mr. Porter's boutique with Shane. His light eyes shone brightly under the soft dim of the lights overhead. His blondish hair reflected a thousand different hues of yellow and brown, and his skin seemed like that of a porcelain doll. He hadn't changed much since the last time I'd seen him but he seemed so much different in this new light. It was as if I was seeing him for the first time all over again.

"I've already seen you before. Let me guess, Nightrider, right?" I asked, looking at him straight in the eyes.

He smiled at me, a warm, welcoming smile. Well, he was a more affectionate character than Shane; that was for sure. "Gabriel Longshadow," answered the boy, not taking his eyes off me. "You must be the girl that's had everybody talking. Abigail, is it?"

He had a very fine British accent. I loved British accents! "Abby, actually," I corrected, smiling back at him "So Gabriel—"

"It's Gabe, actually."

I grinned. "Gabe. Do you live here?"

"Yeah. Right there," he said, pointing at a door behind him. Huh, weird. I hadn't heard him opening or closing the door … "Your house was attacked by ghouls, wasn't it?"

I nodded. "Did Shane tell you that?"

"No. It was Damien, really. Shane told me that you didn't work at that antique shop."

"He told you that?" I asked, frowning. Why would Shane say such a meaningless thing to Gabe? Or anyone, actually. There were much more important things than that … and how could he have known that I didn't work at Mr. Porter's? "How could he have known that?"

"Well, he was looking for that store you had indicated—Abigail's, I think—to look for who had sold you this." Gabe motioned to the necklace Mr. Porter had given me. I hadn't noticed I still had it. It was a miracle that it hadn't been lost in all of the events that had happened. "He looked all over downtown for that shop and never found it. I think that hinted him toward the fact that you didn't work at that antique shop."

My mind froze for a while. "He actually went all the way downtown and spent an entire day looking for a shop that doesn't even exist?"

Gabe nodded, a foolish grin appearing on his face. "That'll teach him to trust someone he barely knows."

I snorted. "You tell *me* ..."

"Yeah. He also said you were a reader."

"A reader?" I asked, surprised. "What do you mean?"

"A person who swims in books, as in, you love reading."

"But how can he tell that?"

Gabe shrugged. "Shane has his own ways. If he wants something, in this case, answers, he'll get them. He's very persistent."

"I guess you're right," I said, shrugging.

"Do you want me to show you around?" asked Gabe, taking a step back. "Although, I must admit, you don't seem very lost."

"Actually, I am lost. It's just that I know how to compose my face to look like I'm not."

Gabe grinned. "I guess it worked then."

The look on his face made me laugh. Something I hadn't done since I had awakened. "Show the way."

SEVEN

"This is where we store the weapons," said Gabe.

It looked like a place where you would find cars. The walls and the floor were all made of cement. There were table and hangers and both were covered with weapons. Blades, spears, lances, pistols, what looked like grenades and other mythical looking things.

"We call this the weapons' room."

I turned to look at Gabe, my eyebrows raised. "This isn't a room; this is an entire level."

"Well, we sure don't have a room like this to impress visitors. We use *all* of these, including those that aren't very useful."

"There are enough weapons for an army!" I exclaimed, gesturing at everything around us.

"You say that like it's a bad thing," pointed out Gabe, looking offended. "What do you think happens when demons decide to attack the city by thousands? That we just sit there and do nothing?"

"That's not what I meant," I said firmly. I sighed. *It just scares me... It scares me that the world is actually much darker than I thought it was.* I'd once thought that failing a math exam was the worst thing that could happen to me.

I looked around me, at the weapons. It was only after seeing several of them, that I said, "Why are there drawings on some of them?"

Gabe looked at where I was looking and said, "Let me show you."

We walked toward a row of swords I had been looking at. Gabe took one and held the handle firmly. "This is a *talwar*. It's an Indian type of sword. It's over eight hundred years old."

"How come it doesn't look that old?" I asked, letting my fingertips trail along the blade's sharp end.

"We clean every one of them once a week. Cleaning day's tomorrow, if I'm not mistaken."

"No actually, it's today," said a familiar voice behind us. I turned and saw Shane. He was in a white undershirt and had black cargo pants as well as gloves on. He looked like he had just finished repairing a car.

"It is?" asked Gabe, not at all surprised to see Shane in this state. He put the sword back in its place. "Well then I guess I better get changed."

"Yeah better get changed. 'Cause I ain't doing this all by myself," grumbled Shane, rubbing his hands together and then taking his gloves off.

When Shane turned around and walked away, Gabe looked at me and whispered, "Idiot can't raise a finger without me."

"I heard that," exclaimed Shane over his shoulder.

Gabe chuckled and said, "Well, I better get going. You can stay with Shane while I go and get ready."

"She was just fine before you entered her life, Gabe," said Shane from across the room.

I turned to look at Gabe but there was no one there. I only heard the click of the door closing behind him. Man, I was going to have to get used to having very *fast* people around me.

Instead of just standing there and looking like an idiot, I decided to go see what Shane was up to. Once I reached him, I could see that he was sharpening a special dagger. It was characterized by its H-shaped horizontal handgrip, which resulted in the blade of the sword sitting above Shane's knuckles. I could only imagine how sharp and deadly that was.

Shane looked up from the blade and grinned at me. "I see you've met the Englishman of the house."

"Gabe's a nice guy," I admitted. "I like him."

"Want to help me out with this? I need a second pair of hands."

"But isn't Gabe coming back?" I asked. "I don't want to mess up or anything..."

"Gabe takes about three minutes to change but he always finds something more important to do on the way back. So, he'll probably be back in half an hour. As for you messing up... Well, no one messes up on my watch."

"You're very confident. You know that?" I said pointedly.

"I know."

I was about to sit on the bench in front of him, when he said, "You can sit on the Ghost if you want."

"On the *what?*" I exclaimed, confused.

Shane rolled his eyes, placed the knife on the floor and got up. He walked up to me and not taking his eyes off me, pulled a white drape off a big lump that I hadn't paid any attention to. I shifted my eyes to what had been under the sheet.

I gaped at it. It was some kind of vehicle that looked like it belonged in space. There was a horizontal seat, as if made to lay on. There were what looked like a motorcycle's handlebars. The paint was black and purple. There was a glass covering what would be the driver's face. The whole vehicle itself was airborne, as if to go as fast as possible.

"I'd love to take you for a spin but I still have work to do," said Shane, looking enviably at the strange thing called a Ghost.

After hesitating several seconds, I sat on the Ghost. I let out a breath of relief when it didn't lurch forward and then looked as Shane went to take the bench and brought it closer to me, then as he went to get the knife and the tool he had been using to sharpen the blade. He sat down and looked up at me. Under the bright light of the room, his eyes looked even more like the night sky, with stars in it.

"I want you to do the same thing I do, all right?" When I nodded, Shane looked down at the blade. He put the H-shaped handle between his knees and held the lower part of it with one hand. With his other hand, he took the sharpening tool and passed it over the blade. Sparks flew when he did so.

"Do this at least fifteen times on each side," instructed Shane, giving me the knife and the tool. "Show me how you do it first; then I'll leave you alone."

I put the knife like Shane had put it and held it as he had. "What's it called? The knife, I mean."

He looked up from my hands and said, "It's a *katara*, and it's a dagger, not a knife."

"Do you like using the *katara*, then?" I said.

"I don't *like* using the *katara* but I find it practical. It's easier to pierce the flesh with it. The Indians used it for sacrificial rituals."

"Gabe didn't tell me why there were symbols on the weapons," I said. I pressed the tool against the side of the blade and pressed it along. It left a trail of sparks behind, like it had with Shane.

"The symbols ... they are holy marks, 'Marks of the Heavens.' That's what you can also call them. These marks burn demons' skin like pure acid, so no form of demon can lay hands on it."

"And these 'Marks of the Heavens,' do they have any particular meaning?" I asked, giving the sharpening maneuver another try. "Or are they just ..." My voice trailed off, waiting for him to answer.

"The one that you're holding has marks but they're so small, that human eyes can only see them with a magnifying glass. It's even hard for me to see them."

"Why did they make them so small?" I asked, pivoting the *katara* around in my hands. It was only then that I realized how light it was. I had always thought swords and weapons were heavy and hard to manipulate—but no. This one was as easy to manipulate as a pencil.

"I don't know; you should ask them, they'll answer you."

At first, I thought he was joking but when I saw the look on his face, I knew there was no mockery in his words.

Shane got up and went to pick up another weapon. This one was some kind of whip. Its razor ends looked like those that were used to catch fish, hooks, perfectly curved and sharp hooks. God, I did not want to be Shane's enemy at that moment.

As Shane regained his seat and started working on the whip, I said, "Are you serious?"

"About what?" he asked, a slight frown appearing on his face.

"That I can ask them ... the ones that marked the weapons."

Shane looked up from his work and right at me. "Sure I'm serious. Those who marked them, or those who *blessed* them, are old and experienced spellcasters, in other words, sorcerers. Some are as old as the sword you're holding. One thing you can envy from sorcerers; they live for a long, long time. Other than that and the spell-casting ... a lot of the older ones just can't wait to die."

"Oh..." Another mythical creature I had to add to the list. I shrugged. "I guess I just wanted to make sure you weren't making fun of me."

"I don't joke about things like this. Kristen could inform you much more than I can. So don't ask me to go into detail. I only know the basic stuff, what needs to be known."

"Speaking of what needs to be known, I would like to see Mary," I said, making my voice sound firm and unquestionable. "And I need to talk to my mother..."

"I don't know when all of that is going to happen, Abby. We haven't figured everything out yet. You'll just have to wait."

I gaped at him. Was he seriously going to make me wait to see my little sister? "Wait? You expect me to wait to see if the ones I love are alive and well?"

"Yup." He got up and went to set the whip he had been sharpening at its place. "That's exactly what I expect you to do."

"I'm not some dog you have the power to control. I'm going to go see Mary and Jane, whether you like it or not."

"You're not gonna' leave the academy until you're allowed to. It's as simple as that."

"What did I say about me not being a—"

"I don't care what you said!" exclaimed Shane, putting his hands up in exasperation. "You could get killed, or worse—"

"Good thing I came back; otherwise, you two would have beaten each other to a pulp."

I turned around and tried as best as I could to calm down. Gabe stood there, out of his clean jeans and into dirty ones. He already had a sharpening tool in his hands.

I got up and placed what I had in hand on the Ghost's seat. I walked out of the room. I knew the guys were watching me, so I kept my head high. Once I was out, I heard Gabe say, "What's up with her?"

I don't know, I thought to myself. I sincerely don't know…

❧

It didn't take long for me to find the way back to my room. It was actually pretty easy. All I had to do was run straight for the elevator, press the number seven, take a right, pass three doors on the left and there it was. I opened my door with a click and shut it once I was inside. The room was dark, depressing and I hated this place at the moment. Of course, it was beautifully designed and all but it was keeping me away from Jane, Mrs. Wildfire and most of all Mary, and Kaithlyn and Brittany and Luke… Oh Luke. He would know what to do in my situation.

It took a while for my eyes to make out the form of the bed. I let myself fall on it, putting my hands over my eyes where tears were threatening to erupt. I loved Jane and Mrs. Wildfire with all my heart, they were the ones who had raised me, taken care of me, but Mary was my little munchkin and being away from her was almost unbearable, especially knowing that there were dark things lurking around every corner, waiting patiently for a chance to strike.

Why was I always on edge when I was with Shane? I had talked to many boys, good-looking ones too but I had never been this edgy with anyone before. It was as if he knew how to pull the trigger, how to tick me off. That annoyed me more than anything else did. The worst part was that he had been telling the truth. Since I didn't know if it was the truth or him that bothered me most, I decided to blame it all on him. Somehow, it seemed better that way.

After lying down for several minutes, I decided that if I wanted answers, it wasn't by staying in here that I'd get them. I was sure Shane wouldn't agree to let me go out alone. It had been very clear in his tone that he had been set in charge not to let me go anywhere without him. Maybe he hadn't said it but I sure had understood it.

Not wanting to draw attention from anyone, I decided that a good old down-the-window-with-a-rope-trick might come in handier than going out by the front door. I couldn't risk getting caught. I just *had* to get out of here.

I opened my window to what I knew was nothing but darkness and calm silence. I heard the distant sound of old dried up leaves rustling along with the wind. The smell of autumn was overwhelming as well as a relief. No matter how much my life had drastically changed in less than three days, the Earth was still spinning and life was still going on.

Closing my eyes to enjoy the moment, I inhaled loudly by the nose and exhaled through my mouth. At exactly that moment, I felt alive and well. For the slightest of moments, I didn't feel as if my world was crashing down. I felt as if there was still a chance—just a small chance—to save it. I held on to that for as long as I could, until it was time to leave.

❧❦

I was standing on the academy's diagonal roof, my heart pounding. How the hell had I gotten myself in this mess?

I hadn't thought about *how* I was going to get down. I had just gotten out of my room by the window and had gone walking around the roof, looking for an easy way down. Of course, I had found none. Every time I had thought I had found a track leading down, it had only turned out to be a deadly fall.

After I had done the perimeter of the academy several times, I decided to go back to my room. There had to be something I could use to get down. The warmth of inside was wonderful as I got through the window frame. While I was at it, why not get an even heavier jacket?

The first thing that came to my mind were the bed sheets. I had seen many movies where the kids had tied their clothes and sheets together and had made a rope to get down their house, to run away, as I was doing. Well, not exactly but not far from it.

I was about to pull the cloth off the bed when I felt something hard against the tip of my foot. It was maybe just the bed's base but I just wanted to make sure. I got on my knees and pulled my hair back so that it didn't fall in my face.

What I found wasn't the base; it was a trunk, a big wooden trunk with complicated carvings on it. I pulled on the handle. It didn't bulge. Gripping the handle tighter, I pulled with all my strength. I was glad when I saw that it moved an inch or two. I was going to have to push myself harder, *much* harder.

❧◦❧

SHANE

I had already finished my side of the weapons' room before Gabe had even had the chance to finish half of his. Sharpening blades was one of my many specialties and it was one of Gabe's few defaults.

I got up and went to sit next to Gabe, deciding to help him, so that we could both finish at the same time. Things were kinda slow when Gabe wasn't there to lighten them up. Sure, there was Damien but it wasn't as much fun as when Gabe was there. He was my brother and no matter how much I denied it, I was dependent on him.

"She's a tough one, isn't she?" asked Gabe, not looking up from his working on a scimitar, which I'm sure would've scared the shit out of the person we were talking about.

"It's not as if she's the first one," I said. Sure, she had a tough facade but I was sure it would all go down when she had to work under pressure. "She just has a bad temper."

"Funny how she's not the only one," muttered Gabe under his breath. Knowing what Gabe meant, I elbowed him in the stomach.

"My point!" exclaimed Gabe, pointing at me with his blade, a cocky grin on his face. "We both know you have a bad temper, Shane, and so do a lot of other people." He sighed. "You guys are so alike, it's scary."

"You're gonna become scary if you don't shut up," I threatened, which didn't seem to bother Gabe one bit. I sliced harder at the sword I was supposed to polish, enjoying the look of sparks flying. "I don't look one bit like her. She's a self-concerned person, thinks she's royalty and knows nothing of the real world. Her world is nothing but mushy feelings and complex emotions. Our world is nothing like that."

"What is our world?" said Gabe, taking the voice of what might have been a damn psychiatrist.

"Dark, efficient, realistic." I was unblinking when I said it, my tone emotionless. "That's why her world and our world tend to clash. There can't be a perfect balance unless we stay away from each other. Everything is black and white. There isn't any gray. There never was; there never will be."

"Ah, so you're a black-and-white type of person, aren't you?"

"That's one way to look at it," I said and shrugged. "I don't really think of such mentally challenging questions, Gabe. And what the heck, you're not even my damn shrink!"

Gabe raised his eyebrows. "You have one?"

I threw him a deadly stare and he howled with laughter. "C'mon, man, admit it. You like her."

I didn't hesitate when I answered, because then he would think something was up … which obviously there wasn't. "Yep, and you're such a good matchmaker, Gabe. Remember last time?"

He seemed to think about it for a second and then cracked up again. "All right, all right, I'm in no position to talk."

"You're right. You're not."

After Gabe had calmed down and made a few funny-ass comments, he asked me, "How are those jumps coming up?"

"Fine," I answered. "Three feet higher than last time." I had been trying to surpass myself with jumping. I had (and still was) getting up early in the morning to practice. Being a Nightrider didn't require the extra training but I didn't care; I wanted to be a good jumper. It would strengthen me much more than the average.

"Cool. You gonna' show me how to do one of those spins?"

"All right, I'll show you for twenty bucks."

Gabe's eyebrows shot up. "You're kidding me, right?"

I grinned. "Take it or leave it, man. It's your choice." I threw my head back and laughed when Gabe cussed as he fished a twenty-dollar bill out of his pocket and handed it to me.

"You better make it good, bro.' If you don't, I'm asking for a refund," said Gabe, getting up and throwing his dirty cloth on the Ghost where he had been sitting. He wiped his hands on his jeans and gave me an expectant look. "You gonna' do it outside?" he asked.

I nodded. If I wanted to put up a good show for Gabe, I was going to have to use the academy as an obstacle course. Its multi-level roof was perfect to show off what I was capable of.

Once outside the academy's doors, Gabe and I climbed up the metal ladder that led to the top of the roof. Only those who knew where to look could actually find it.

Gabe perched himself on one of the chimneys and crossed his arms over his chest. "Show me what you got, bro'."

Without saying anything, I ran toward the nearest downhill part of the roof and easily slid down. I dove off the roof and turned on myself, so that I could catch the gutter with my hands before falling off. I heaved myself upward, using my hands to push me up. Going a little bit over the top, I did a pirouette before landing on my feet. Not stopping to catch my breath, I ran toward a wall and with my foot, kicked myself up, landing right in front of Gabe.

Just for a moment, I saw a glint of amazement in Gabe's eyes but it was gone as quickly as it had come.

"Nice," said Gabe, grinning and punching me on the shoulder. "I guess it was worth my twenty bucks!"

Still pumping with adrenaline, I didn't stand still. My eyes were flying everywhere, analyzing everything. It usually took several seconds for them to calm down completely. It was a very useful Nightrider instinct, in case there was any more danger. It was then that I saw an open window.

I was there in less than ten seconds. My eyes widened. This was Abby's bedroom. I was sure she wasn't in there; she would have come out to see what the ruckus had been about. I peeked inside and indeed, saw no one. Maybe she had wanted to let in fresh air and had gone to see us in the weapons room? I heavily doubted that.

I slid easily into the room and looked around. It was obvious that someone had been looking around. I was sure it was Abby who had

rummaged through all the closets and drawers she had found. The supply box under the bed had been discovered and opened.

I kneeled down next to it. The ropes were missing. I had learned the necessary contents of a supply box at a young age, so it was easy for me to see what was missing.

I got up and got out of the academy's window. She couldn't be that far away. Gabe was already down the building, already waiting for me. I knew how he got down when I looked to my left. There was a rope hanging on the edge of the roof. I walked to it and studied the knot; it was a stained with droplets of blood. For a while, my mind went blank with horror. Was she hurt? Had someone hurt her? I knew if I didn't stop having stupid premonitions soon, I was going to go berserk. Without further thought of Abby, I let myself slide down the rope, landing with a soft thud.

"Where do you think she went?" asked Gabe, flipping his phone on and pressing a number. Probably speed dialing Kristen or Damien, I thought.

"She might have gone back to her house," I said, somehow making my voice sound cool and under control. "But I doubt it. I don't know... Maybe to Mrs. Wildfire's?"

Gabe put the phone to his ear and said, "Abby with you guys?" There was a low buzz coming from the other end of the line. "All right. Yeah we can do that, or ..." Another buzz, this time louder than before. "No shit!" exclaimed Gabe, a look of astonishment on his face. "Really? Okay; yeah, we'll go."

He hung up the phone and slid it back in his pocket. Gabe looked at me. "Khan just gave birth! Five healthy pups."

I closed my eyes and suppressed the urge to punch him in the face. "Did he tell you anything about what might have happened to Abby?" I asked through clenched teeth. The damn pups could wait. If Abby got hurt, Kristen would have my head and something else I was deeply attached to.

"They're at the park. They were taking a walk with the wolves when ... well, you know ... And anyway, Abby wasn't with them. Damien

also said that she couldn't be near the park because he would have felt her. So we can count the park out."

"Call Mrs. Wildfire. See if she went there," I said, exhaling what breath I had left in me. While Gabe, who went farther away to make the phone call, I thought. Where would Abby go? Somewhere she'd feel safe... I didn't know Abby well enough to know where she would feel that safety. If only he had some kind of tracking device...

EIGHT

ABBY

Running wasn't my favorite thing to do. It was maybe the worst activity I could think of at the moment. Good thing I had worn sneakers; high heels would have given me splinters and I hated splinters. Actually, I disliked everything at the moment and Shane even more. He was the reason I was running in the freaking cold night! Everyone I passed looked at me, panicked, thinking I was being chased by a rabid dog. Which in a way, I was.

The night's chill was torrid. My body was fine with the cold, because it was sweating but my throat wasn't. This was one of the reasons why I hated running.

There was only two blocks left to run, I knew this was a crazy stunt I was pulling. If Shane got to me before I could get to my destination, he would *kill* me for running away. I could just imagine the blazing look in his eyes he would give me when he saw me. A chill ran up my spine. Getting Shane mad wasn't necessarily a good thing but I had to do it. Everything that was happening to me was insane, beyond insane, if that were possible. I needed to see someone who would make me feel normal again...

The rows of apartments around me looked as if they might jump on me at any moment but I was sure I was over-thinking the situation.

Exhaling heavily, I walked up the front steps of Luke's home. I couldn't remember the last time I had come here. I would have gone to Brittany's or Kaithlyn's but their houses were too far away by foot.

I hesitated before ringing the doorbell. Luke had always said that his parents were never there, so I guessed that he was alone. I took a deep breath and pressed the button.

Nothing happened at first. It was only half a minute later that the door opened before me. I let a breath out when I saw Luke standing at the threshold. He was wearing slack jeans and a grey undershirt; his eyes were half-closed, as if he had just been dragged out of bed but when he saw me, his eyes got round. Very round.

"Abby?" he exclaimed. "What the hell are you doing here?" Before I could answer, he put a hand around my shoulders and half-dragged, half-led me inside. "C'mon in here."

Luke's apartment was one of the darkest I had seen in all my life. The curtains were closed so that not even the streetlights could lighten the room. The brown couch was flipped over, as if somebody had used it as a barricade. There were dirty dishes piled up on the kitchen counter and empty bottles of beer spread everywhere. There was even a shattered bottle on the living room's ugly orange rug.

I looked at Luke and saw shame and sadness in his eyes. Something ripped inside me. I couldn't stand seeing him this way, all sad and not the cocky and cheerful way he usually was. I led him to his room, as if he didn't already know where it was. I had come here more than once, so I could orient myself pretty well.

The last time I had come here, the house had been cheerful and smelled good with cookie dough. However, since Luke's father died, nothing had been the same. His mother got remarried with this man, and she hadn't known he was an alcoholic. So, he slowly led her to what he was. She started drinking and doing drugs. Luke got some swings from his stepdad but the older man wasn't only using his fists; he used the broken glass bottles too.

This was a part of Luke only I knew. I had never really seen how bad it had been. Luke had told me about it but I had never seen it firsthand.

Luke's room was the cleanest room I had seen since stepping into the house (except his bed, which wasn't at all surprising for a boy). His room was as blank as a piece of paper. I didn't see anything personal hanging around anywhere. There was only a literature textbook lying open on his unmade bed.

"What are you doing here?" he asked when I flopped down on his bed. "And at this hour."

"I need your help with something," I said as he sat down next to me. "You were the only person I could think of and could trust..." I hesitated for a moment. *Could* I trust him? Of course I could, it was *Luke*, the boy I had known more than half of my life. He was my boy-friend, for crying aloud! We had shared everything, from favorite toys to deepest darkest secrets. This couldn't be *that* different, could it?

"You can tell me," said Luke, sensing my moment of hesitation. He put an arm around me, as if to prove his point. I cuddled up next to him and buried my face in the crook of his shoulder.

"I'm ..." How could I tell him that I had been almost killed by demons and had been abducted by not so bad Nightriders and had somehow escaped? Why had I escaped in the first place? To make myself feel normal again? Had I really done that? Had I really barged into Luke's worst nightmare and was about to inflict on him more problems? What kind of evil person was I? He didn't need more prob-lems on his shoulders. I had to get out of here before anything more could slip out of my mouth.

When I got up to leave, his fingers wrapped around my wrists and pulled me back down on top of him. I stood on my knees, my face merely inches from his. His breath on my face was warm and sent tick-les up my spine.

"Abby, why don't you tell me? You know you can tell me anything, right?" When I looked away, he took hold of my chin and made me look into his eyes. They were forest green and I really didn't want to look away.

This was turning out to be tougher than I thought it would be. He made it so easy to talk. I felt like I could tell him *everything* and yet... I couldn't impose the truth on him, as it had been done on me. It would be selfish in every sense of the word.

I kissed him smack on the mouth, jumped up and headed toward the door. I had to get out of here before I said anything else. When I opened the door, I thought I was going to faint.

"You shouldn't have done that, Angel," said Shane, his arms crossed over his chest. He had that wild look in his eyes, as if he was still pumping with adrenaline.

"What are you doing here?" I muttered. This was not good. This was horrible. What would I say to Luke? "How the hell did you find me?"

My questions didn't seem to reach Shane's ears. He was watching something behind me. I turned around and all I saw was Luke. He was standing, his fists clenched, a feral look on his face, as if he were holding back from striking.

"Abby," whispered Luke, almost like a moan, "get away from that ... *thing*."

I gaped at him. I had never seen Luke this way. He wasn't usually this rude with a total stranger. However, I guess he could be rude with total strangers who barged into his house unannounced. I hadn't told him what Shane was, had I? Of course not; I had probably been thinking it but I hadn't had the chance to tell him anything important.

Before I could say anything, Shane was standing in front of me in a defensive crouch. He was making some kind of noise... Was he ... *snarling*? If he was, it was nothing like movie-type snarling. It felt real and dangerous and kinda weird since there was no threat anywhere.

"Shane, what are you doing?" I asked, my voice uneven. What the hell was up with him? Oh right, I ran away on his watch.

"Abby get out!" snarled Luke, not taking his eyes off Shane. "Get out of the house and run!"

"I'm not leaving until someone tells me what's going on," I cried out. What was going on? Why were they both behaving the way they were? Why did both have a murderous look in their eyes?

Just then, Gabe appeared from behind me. His eyes widened when he saw Luke and at the same time Shane. He put a hand around my waist and started pulling me away. "Abby, stand b—"

Then, Luke lunged. He ran toward Gabe but got tackled by Shane. They fell on the floor, Shane hovering over Luke. Shane threw a fist toward Luke's face but he blocked it with his hand. I almost shrieked when Shane's fist threatened to break Luke's jaw and both of them kept getting at it.

"Stop! Both of you, stop!" After repeating it several times, I was getting desperate. Nobody was listening to me, dammit! All I really wanted to do at the moment was whack both of their heads off.

"Stay here," said Gabe, letting go of me. He headed toward the fight that occupied at least half of Luke's bedroom floor. He crouched down and with all his strength pulled Luke off Shane by the collar. He held him in a headlock. Shane, who was still high in the heat of the action didn't notice Gabe and punched Luke in the abdomen, who didn't even let out a whimper.

Before Shane could do anything else to Luke, I got myself between the two and put a hand up, as if alerting him not to do anything more stupid than he already had. "Shane," I said, making my voice ring with some kind of authority.

For the first time in three days, I looked in his eyes; *really* looked at them. For the first time, I noticed that they were completely black—black coal, but when his breathing got lighter, the color in his eyes came back, as if it had been set free.

Once I knew Shane wouldn't lunge at Luke another time, I turned to look at my boyfriend, the human one in all of this. When I looked at him, thought, he didn't look one bit human. The cut on the face was slowly but surely turning into a scar. He was bleeding from the mouth, where Shane had hit him hard but the blood was decreasing by the second. One of his eyes was of a vivid amber yellow; I had never seen such a color as an eye color... The other one was green.

I frowned. What the hell? "Luke, your eye..." I put a hand on his cheek, feeling his hot skin under my fingertips and said, "Are you all right?"

"Don't touch him!" spat Shane from behind me. I turned to look at him and saw that his fists and teeth were clenched.

Then I got mad. All the rage and the anguish that had built up inside of me was about to explode. "Who are *you* to tell me that?" I asked, my voice higher than necessary. "You have no power over me. Luke is my *boyfriend*, Shane, not some kind of animal you can beat up for no reason. Why'd you attack him, anyway? We were having a ... friendly talk; we weren't planning on killing somebody! You had no reason to act the way you did! And what the hell are you doing here?"

"Why are you defending that *thing*?" said Shane, his voice equaling mine. "He could have killed y—"

"Killed me?!" I raged. "We were *talking*, not playing Russian roulette!"

෨෧

In less than an hour, I was back in my prison cell, sitting on the bed, reading the book Shane had given me several hours before. It was 12:45 am. I *wasn't* tired.

Shane had forced a sleeping pill down Luke's throat when he had least expected it. Gabe had made it clear that he didn't approve of Shane's way of acting, but he hadn't said anything when Shane slugged Luke over his shoulder and carried him all the way back. After that, he had locked Luke into a room somewhere in the basement and had given me a mad look, as if I had done something wrong (which I guess I had by running away). Then he had said, "Look up the words *mutante figuram*."

The only reference I had was the old grimoire he had given me. So, I decided to use it, as any helpless person would do.

I saw many things in the old book. Stuff like, *forum, nympha, infernium, caelum, lupinotuum, daemones, lux, angeli, tenebrae, caede, reincarnation* and finally *mutante figuram*.

It said: "*Shapeshifters are known for their ability to change forms at will. Most are only capable of shifting into animals. In some rare cases, the shapeshifter can turn into something such as mist. This phenomenon only occurs when the shifter's family has had contact with one of the five Lost Elements. The shifters can be identified by their faster heartbeat and unusual heat radiation. Unlike werewolves, shapeshifters have yellow-like eye colors instead of grey eyes. They are also identified by the sun-like birthmark, usually on their neck, that mark them as 'Children of the Sun.' Their mortal enemies are the Children of the Dark, in other words, vampires. They may sometimes ally with ...*"

I shut the book and closed my eyes. I had read enough. Luke *couldn't* be a shapeshifter. He just couldn't, but everything the book said corresponded to Luke's ... Screw the book. Luke wasn't a shapeshifter and that was that. Although I kept repeating that to myself, I knew, deep down, that he was part of the world I had wanted to keep away from the ones I loved.

And yet, he had already been part of it. All the time I had known him, I had thought he had green eyes... I was apparently wrong. He had knowingly worn contact lenses to hide his true self. To hide his yellow eyes.

Then I was really mad at myself, because I had been the one who had gone to his house. I had wanted help and I had gotten nothing. I was still in the damn academy and Luke was being kept prisoner.

I wanted to kick something, or punch, whichever would help most. I kicked the wall and hit at the book several times. My knuckles were getting white and I was hating myself...

It was only after I had screamed into my pillow that there was a light knock on the door. "Abby, are you all right?" It was Gabe and even though he wasn't the culprit in this situation, I was also mad at him.

"As far as being held prisoner goes, I'm fine!"

I didn't hear anything else for the next two hours. I was still crushed against the pillow and my heart might have been bleeding. I wasn't pissed anymore. I was sad, which was worse. I was more than worried about Mary... I had to see her or at least talk to her...

I jumped from my bed and tripped out of my room. I remembered there had been a phone down in the kitchen. Before I knew it, I was facing the elevator and I was about to press the DOWN button when the doors slid open.

It was Kristen, wearing a bloodstained shirt. I stared at her, my mouth dropping open.

"Are you all right, Abby?" she asked me, frowning. "You look like you just saw a ghost."

"Your clothes… Oh my God, you're bleeding!"

Before I could get my hands on her, she walked by me, escaping my grip. "It's not my blood, Abby. D'you really think Damien would let me get in this shape?" She laughed when I kept on staring. "Khan just gave birth and I couldn't let the babies on the cold ground like that…"

Babies? Birth? Khan? "Uh, I'm not sure, I understand. …"

Kristen rolled her eyes and started walking. I followed her. "Khan, my wolf, she's downstairs now, if you wanna go see her. Just be careful; Genghis is there and he's very protective of her."

"You have wolves?" I asked, awestruck. There were wolves in the building and I didn't even know it?

"No one told you?" When I shook my head, she *tsk*ed. "Shane or Gabe, or even Damien should have. God knows what would've happened if you'd run into them!"

I swallowed hard. Yeah, that wouldn't have been good. We reached a door and Kristen opened it. She walked in and I stayed at the door, leaning on the frame.

Kristen's room was just like mine, except for the empty shelves and drawers. She had all kinds of makeup on the little table in front of the big mirror and clothes lying around.

"Sorry for the mess, I don't get the chance to clean up often." When she saw that I was still next to the door, she pressed me to come in.

I shook my head. "No thanks, Kristen, I was going to go downstairs to make a phone call."

"Where would you have gone downstairs?"

"In the kitchen?"

"Oh no, Abby, the guys are in the kitchen."

"So?"

"So…" She took off her bloodied shirt and walked to her drawers. "You won't have *any* privacy. These guys are like hawks. They hear everything and if they smell something fishy, then it's over."

"I don't have my cell phone. I left it at my house."

She passed me a black object after putting on a dark red blouse. "Here. Take mine; just bring it back to me when you're done. I'll be in the kitchen."

Before I left for my room, I asked, "Why are you wearing a blouse?"

Kristen grinned at me. "Damien is taking me to a nightclub—crawling with demons."

"Uh, good for you?"

She didn't seem to notice my hesitation and cheerfully thanked me. Kristen started rummaging through her little desk, pulling out a little makeup bag. "Abby, before you go, take this as well. We're about the same size. I hope you like it."

I walked to her bed, to where she had pointed. I picked up the fabric and stared at it. It was a white, strapless dress, plain except for several stray wrinkles, which would end at her mid-thighs.

"You don't have to give me this Kristen. I don't deserve it..."

"Maybe you don't but I'm sure it'll make you a helluva lot happier if you had it," she said, giving me a pearl white smile. "I know if I were you, I wouldn't like being kept here for purposes that I wasn't aware of..."

"Thanks, Kristen," I said truthfully, "for understanding."

She gave me an even wider smile and I walked away, clutching at the cell phone and the dress as if they were lifesavers.

෧ල

"She what?"

"See made me wahules!"

"She made you waffles! That's great, Sweetie!"

I heard the soft giggle from the other end of the receiver. "Damien came to thee me this morning."

"Oh did he?" She was talking about Damien and I felt a pang of anger. Another thing had been kept from me, but the feeling was quickly gone when Mary recited all the things they did together. She was maybe one of the only people in the world who made me smile by only speaking. "Nana let me wide with him on the goat."

"On the goat?" Did they actually go to the farm or was I losing my sense of good-ol'-sister-who-understands-everything-I-say touch?

"Yeah! It was sooo much fun!" She squealed delightfully and I couldn't help but smile. "And Damen show me Kan's babies! I want one, Abs. They were so cute and so smaaall and fuwy!"

I felt tears threatening to erupt from my eyes. I wasn't sad or anything of the sort (apart from the fact that I had been abducted but whatever). I was just happy hearing she was having so much fun. I wasn't very thrilled at the fact that she had been near wolves but I guess that if Mrs. Wildfire permitted it, then it was safe.

I had waited for it to be 8:00 o'clock in the morning before calling Mrs. Wildfire. I had gotten five hours of sleep.

"Okay, Sweetie. I'm glad you're having so much fun over there... Can you pass me Nana?"

"Yep! Bye bye," said Mary cheerfully.

"Bye, Mary. I love you bunches."

"Me too!"

I heard shuffling at the other end of the line until I heard Mrs. Wildfire's voice. "Hello, dear. How are you doing?"

I know I should've been mad at Mrs. Wildfire for lying to me all these years but I couldn't muster up bad feelings against this old woman whom I loved so much. "Hey, Nana. I'm fine, thank you."

I heard her sigh. "Child, I've known you for over ten years now and it's the first time you've called me that. Are you sick?"

I laughed aloud and I heard her chuckle. "No... I'm just a bit lost..."

"I'm so sorry, Abby, you had to find out this way. Your mother and I both knew it would eventually come but we'd hoped it would be later rather than sooner." She exhaled loudly. "But I guess everything happens for a reason, right?"

"Right." I laid back on my bed and stared at the ceiling. I was so tired about all of this and yet I knew I would never get a break since it was my life now, apparently. "Have you heard from Mom?"

"No, I haven't. When Damien came yesterday, I asked him to call every institute on the East Coast and none had anything concerning her… He also called several Nightrealmer nightclubs but they too didn't know anything."

I bit my lower lip. "Do you think she's all right?"

"Abby, maybe you haven't known your mother as a Nightrider but I have and let me tell you, almost nothing gets past her. She's strong and won't let herself be pushed around."

"I'm afraid for her … and I regret how I was last time I saw her. She didn't deserve it."

"Sometimes, we do things we regret but if we try hard enough, it could all go for the best."

"I guess you're right but I'm still afraid …" There were so many things I wanted to know, so many questions left unanswered and I knew Mrs. Wildfire would be the first one to answer them. "What's a Nightrealmer?"

"They haven't told you much, have they?"

"I know close to nothing and that makes things even worse, because I don't know *what* to look out for."

"Well, a Nightrider is what we are. While a Nightrealmer can be either a vampire, a werewolf, a fey, a Nightrider… am I missing anything else?"

"Shapeshifters," I grumbled.

"Yes, those too. Basically, all we have to do is keep the other Nightrealmers in check and slay demons."

"Demons aren't Nightrealmers?"

"God forbid, no. All they seek is flesh, blood and corruption; we cannot reason with them; therefore, we slay them."

"But vampires … isn't that what they seek as well?"

"Yes … in some way but they were once human, so we believe it immoral to slay them as we do with demons. Same goes for werewolves and shapeshifters, but if they ever endanger a human in any way, we act." She paused and cleared her throat. "You remember that party you had gone to the other night and you had seen Shane?"

"Of course."

"Well, he was there to prevent a possible bloodbath. A few vampires had decided they wanted a feast, so what better place than a party with intoxicated teenagers?"

"That's why he was there?"

"Yes. Speaking of which, are they treating you all right?"

"If by 'they' you mean Shane and Gabe, then I guess."

"You guess... ?"

I sighed. "You know how Shane gets... he ... has a strong character." What I really wanted to say was much more colorful but I bit back my tongue when I remembered whom I was speaking with.

"He is very handsome, isn't he... ?"

"I didn't mean it that way... I guess he is kinda ... good-looking but looks are only skin-deep..."

"I know dear; I know but that doesn't mean that he isn't eye-candy!"

I had never heard Mrs. Wildfire speaking this way and frankly, I didn't want her to continue. "Mrs. Wildfire..."

"Now don't 'Mrs. Wildfire' me, Abigail. Yes, I am old but I am not blind. I know a nice face when I see one."

I laughed. "I'm sorry..."

"If only you knew what kind of stories we tell each other, the old folks, your jaw would most certainly drop," she said before laughing. "Ahh... I have to go now Abby, but I'm looking forward to our next talk."

"So am I. Mrs. Wildfire..." I sighed heavily and smiled to myself, "Thanks for taking care of Mary. I really wish I could come see you..."

"I'm guessing it's for the best... All right then! I have a little girl I have to put to sleep now. She hasn't slept all night! Bye Abby. I love you."

"Bye Mrs. Wildfire. I love you too."

I waited to hear the click on the other end of the line before turning the cellphone off. I stared at the ceiling for what might have been five minutes. I didn't think of anything or anyone, I just stared...

NINE

It was now 9:36 am and I couldn't stand this moping around. I opened the door of my room and stepped out into the dim light of the hallway. I turned and saw Shane sitting on a stainless steel chair, reading a book, what book, I couldn't tell.

He folded the corner of the page he had been reading and put it down on the floor. "You shouldn't have done that," he said, not looking at me in the eye. "You dragged your friend into all of this."

"My *boyfriend*," I corrected. "Well you didn't have to follow me. I can take care of myself," I pressed. "And what are you doing here? Stalking me?"

"Damien read your shapeshifter. He had no real bad intentions, so they decided it was okay for him to have his own room."

"Luke's in there?" I asked, looking at the door in front of which Shane was sitting. "If you guys decided that he had no bad intentions, then why are you here guarding his door?"

"I said *they* decided that he wasn't a bad guy," corrected Shane. "*I* don't trust him."

"He's not a monster, Shane. Aren't you supposed to ally yourself with shapeshifters?"

"It's more complicated than that, Abby. You wouldn't understand. Even I have difficulties understanding." Shane got up and got right in front of me. His eyes seared into mine. "I don't want anything to happen to you Abby. You're too much of a mystery."

I didn't fully understand what he meant by mystery but I ignored it. I wanted to see Luke. Not backing or looking away, I asked, "Can I at least see him?"

When he didn't answer, I batted my eyelashes. "Please?" I used the sweetest voice I could muster but that didn't seem to affect him too much.

He clenched his jaw and looked at me with determined eyes. "No and that's my final answer."

"Ugh!" I threw my hands in the air. "You're impossible! *Please* let me see him. You can even *stay* in the room if you really don't trust him."

He rolled his eyes. "You are so *stubborn*." He looked down at me. "*Fine*."

I sighed and moved away so that he could open the door with a key he kept in his back pocket. He opened the door and gestured me in. The room was the same as mine but this time, there wasn't as much purple. Luke lay on the bed, eyes closed, a peaceful look on his face.

I couldn't remember the last time I had seen Luke sleep. Maybe when we had been fourteen or fifteen, I couldn't really tell. Now, as I watched him breathe softly, I couldn't help but feel sad. Why did things have to be like this?

Closing my eyes to hold back tears, I prayed; to whom, I didn't know but I just thought, *Let there be a way to make everything right…*

When I opened my eyes, Luke was sitting up, watching me, watching me as if I wasn't real, a dream that couldn't be true, but I *was* there and it *wasn't* a dream. I ran to him and jumped into his opened arms. I inhaled his scent deeply, enjoying the way it prickled my nostrils.

The tears I had been holding back now streamed down my cheeks. I wasn't one you would consider a *crier*. So, when it happened, it had to be for a damn good reason. Luke put a hand into my hair in a petting gesture. He curled his arms around me, almost rocking me back and forth. For the first time in the past few days, I felt safe.

༐

SHANE

I had left the parasite and Abby alone. I didn't want to watch her cry, much less see the intimate way the shapeshifter had held her. I shouldn't have left her with the dog but I knew that if I hadn't, I would have regretted it. She would have *made* me regret it.

I went down the hallway feeling a little weird. I knew I could leave them alone; the insect wasn't evil or anything of the sort. Well, it depended on your point of view. We had only taken him in because he was a *blessed* one.

"Blessed my ass," I muttered as I got down the stairs. In other words, the mutt's life had been intertwined with one of the five Lost Elements. I would have to ask him about that sometime.

When I was halfway through the remaining stairs, I decided to try something I hadn't done in a long time. I looked down the hole that extended down the circular staircase. Giving myself a boost, I jumped down the hole that was just a bit larger than my shoulders—one false movement and I could die. I was reckless at the moment and I didn't really care what happened to me, as long as it got the thought of Abby with the shapeshifter out of my head.

The air rushed past me; I felt like a cannon ball sailing toward enemy territory. It was only because I had had years of practice that I didn't die when I landed. A normal human would have died, an unexperienced Nightrider would have broken a leg and a dog like the shapeshifter upstairs would, I hoped, not have made it...

I pushed open the kitchen doors. Damien was sitting on one of the stools, filling out some paperwork. Genghis was at his feet, playing with the troublemaker of the pups. I walked to them and grabbed the pup by the collar. The little wolf started biting my hand, as if to pry it off. I let him down and nudged the younger wolf's hip with my foot.

"This one's going to get beaten up, man," I said, looking down at the wolves. "He's going to get into more fights than I'll be able to count."

"Right, I still can't count the number of fights *you* get in every week." Damien grinned and piled up his papers. "Kristen and I are going to Eldoras for a while. There's something we have to settle down over there."

"I think I might already have a lead with that shapeshifter concerning the Lost Elements."

"I know, I read him for you. Work on that. You and Gabe are in charge of keeping things in order around here. There's going to be Seekers and reinforcements coming in about two days from Eldoras."

"Why are they all coming?" I asked, while opening the refrigerator and pulling a beer out. "We don't need reinforcements."

"Searches of one of the Elements have led to Massachusetts. The others aren't *really* reinforcements; they're just in need of a place to stay for a while. It'll take a bit of time before they get placed, so don't count on getting rid of them after three days."

"And you expect Gabe and me to manage all of this on our own?" I asked, trying not to make my jaw drop.

"You can ask Mrs. Wildfire for help if you want," said Damien, raising both eyebrows.

"Be careful with what you say, Greenwhick, if you don't want me to ruin your ugly face even more…"

"Abby can help you," added Damien, shrugging.

I sighted. "I was afraid you would say that."

❮❯

ABBY

Luke and I were sitting on the bed, our backs pressed against the head of the bed. I was done crying; I wasn't going to cry for a while now. At least, I hoped so.

"Why didn't you tell me you were a shifter?"

"Why didn't you tell Kait and Britt what you were?" asked Luke, shoving my question right back in my face.

"That's because I don't *know* what I am. Shane and Damien keep on saying I'm not human but they're not even *sure*… And anyway, I was

109

just abducted three days ago," I said. It was true. All I knew was that I was a hybrid but a hybrid of what? Heck, I was maybe just a human...

"Didn't anyone take blood samples to check what you are?"

"No. Well, I don't really know, actually. I was unconscious for three days." Maybe one of them had taken a vial of blood when I had been asleep, recovering from the ghoul poison, but I doubted it. Then again, I was in a crazy academy...

"You were unconscious for three days?" exclaimed Luke. "What happened?"

I told him how I had met Shane and Gabe. Then I asked, "Weren't you supposed to smell him when we were at Victoria's party?"

"I left before he even came, Abby," answered Luke. "Go on." I continued where I had left off; I told him all the way to when I woke up. "You have to try Damien's chicken soup one day—it's to die for."

"I can't believe all of this," said Luke when I had finished.

"Me neither," I muttered under my breath. With a louder voice, I said, "But you know what? It's how things are and no matter how hard you try to change things, they'll always stay that way."

Luke nodded solemnly. "I get what you're trying to say."

"So ... who was the shapeshifter from your parents?"

"My father. He told me all about what I had to expect and what I had to do. That was before he got killed. And you know what? I don't believe any of the shit my mom told me about him dying in an auto wreck. I know he was murdered."

"Why would you think that?" I asked. I hadn't really talked about Mr. Rush's death with Luke. I hadn't felt comfortable bringing up a subject like that. Now that he was there, as a shapeshifter but mostly as Luke Rush, my boyfriend, I felt like talking would help, both for him and me.

"'Cause they never found his body, Abby," whispered Luke. "They only found his beat up car and blood. That's all. When there was the funeral, the casket was empty—no body. Up to this day, they haven't solved anything. No one cares of what happened to Benjamin Rush."

I didn't say anything, not because I wanted Luke to say something else but because I had nothing to say. I always hated it when I found myself in this kind of situation. I felt helpless and dumb. No matter how much I wanted to say everything was going to be all right, I didn't, because then I would be lying.

"So ..." said Luke, after half a minute of silence.

"So ..." I continued. "What?"

"Are you going back to school?"

I thought for a while and then said, "I don't think I can."

"Of course you can," insisted Luke. "I'm a shapeshifter but that doesn't stop me from having a life apart from that."

"I know but I don't think Shane would agree to it."

"Shane? You mean the bastard who shot me with a sleeping drug? Please Abby, don't tell me you listen to that jerk." The way he said it made him sound disappointed, as if I had done something I shouldn't have.

"All right, let's say Shane would let me go back to school, where would I live?" I considered asking Kaithlyn or Brittany if I could sleep at their houses but I doubted Shane would agree... Wait. Why was I thinking according to what Shane might do? He wasn't my boss. He didn't own me. He had saved Mary's life and mine ... but even then, he didn't *own* me.

I could go back to my house but I doubted it was safe, not after what had happened there. Truth was, I could only stay here. Kaithlyn's dad would ask why I couldn't just stay at my own home and so would Brittany's parents. I didn't want to consider sleeping at Luke's house, because I didn't want to sleep there with his parents around.

I could go to Mrs. Wildfire's place, but it was at the other side of town and it was a real pain to travel from there to my high school by subway and bus, which would most probably take me over an hour or two.

So yeah, the academy *was* the only place I could consider staying. Maybe I could stay here for a bit, while things got more into hand but when would that be? Tomorrow? In a week, a month, a year? Would things ever get back to normal?

Luke didn't answer. Apparently, he was thinking the same things I was.

"I guess I have no other choice than to stay here," I finally said. "Unless I could pay myself a motel room down the street with my pocket money…"

"Can't you just go to Mrs. Wildfire's?" asked Luke. "Or is it too far… ?"

"I could but then I'd always be running back and forth from there to school. I don't really want to deal with that."

"If you have to stay, then I will too."

I looked back at Luke, my eyes wide with shock. I knew how much staying here would affect him. He didn't seem to like Nightriders, much less the one who had knocked him out cold.

"You don't have to do that," I said, sitting back on the bedpost. "I can take care of myself."

"I know you can. I just don't trust *them*; that's all."

"You might think what I'm going to say is ridiculous but… the people here aren't as bad as you think they are."

"'Aren't as bad as you think they are'?" quoted Luke, with the heaviest tone of sarcasm I'd ever heard him use. "You got to be kidding me! You believe the crap they tell you?"

"If it weren't for them, I wouldn't be here right now!"

"That's right. You wouldn't be! You'd be hanging out with Kait and Britt, gossiping or something."

"I wouldn't be alive if it weren't for them," I insisted.

"Please don't tell me you're defending these … *people*." He said the last word as if it was the biggest insult. That's when I saw how much he *hated* Nightriders but if he hated them so much, why would he stay here with me? Right, it was his duty as a boyfriend or something.

"Why do you hate them so much?" I asked. There had to be a good reason. Right? Did he hate Nightriders in general or was it just Gabe and Shane? Or was it just Shane? I didn't know and that kind of questioning gave me a lower hand in the situation. Another thing I hated, damn freaking weaknesses.

Luke looked away from me, toward the bay window. He got up and looked out into the night. "It's nothing really."

I watched him for a little while and then slid off the bed. I walked to Luke's side of the bed and put a hand on his shoulder. His eyes moved to my hand and then to my arm, to my shoulder and finally his eyes bored into mine. Such a beautiful shade of yellow he had. They weren't the eyes I was accustomed to but they somehow looked very familiar.

"Abby…"

I looked at his birthmark near his neck; this was the first time I was seeing it. I had already seen Luke with his bare chest, but I had *never* seen the mark. Huh, weird. I moved my hand from his shoulder, brushing Luke's sun-shaped birthmark. My hand froze there. What happened next, I wasn't sure. I felt something that could be described as a lightning bolt shoot through my arm and then through my whole body. I stiffened and took my hand away from his neck only to stagger back. I was trembling, my breaths coming in as if I had just run the marathon. My head was swirling; everything seemed out of focus.

I barely heard Luke say, "Abby, are you okay?"

No, I wasn't. I was exactly the opposite of okay. I felt someone putting arms around me but they didn't stop me from falling.

TEN

Why did this always happen to me? I hated it. It was a sign of weakness and I hated to show it. Well, truthfully, I didn't really faint. I *blacked out.* My vision went black but I could still use my other senses. I knew that because I had very well heard Shane coming in the room, cursing at Luke.

"What did you do to her?" Weird how that question never got old. Funny how I knew the next sound was Shane punching Luke in the jaw, or was it the other way around?

I tried to open my eyes, which I was unsuccessful to do fully. All I could see was a fine line of light. I concentrated and saw two figures against the wall. Luke and Shane, I thought. Shane had an arm across Luke's throat and a fist against his chest. I strained my ears and listened.

"She touched my mark! You know what happens when someone touches a shapeshifter's mark! It's an automatic self-defense mechanism!"

"… Ought to kick you out," hissed Shane. "You don't belong here."

"Then why'd you drag me here, huh?" replied Luke. "I ain't done nothing to you. And ain't it against the law to bring in hybrids other than Nights in your damned sacred places?" Shane didn't answer, so

114

Luke continued, "I don't belong here and neither does Abby. And you sure as hell know that."

"There's also the law that says to give refugee to those who need it."

"I don't need refuge and neither does Abby," muttered Luke.

"I was put under orders to take in any one who might have a connection with the Lost Elements," said Shane, not loosening his grip on Luke.

"Don't start with that shit," spat Luke. "I have no connection to your stupid Elements."

"Your aura says otherwise."

Now it was Luke who stayed silent.

I had enough. I forced my eyelids open. It required a lot of facial strength on my part but I did it. I was lying on my back, on the seat of the bay window. Staring at Shane with pure anger, I got up and walked to the two guys.

Luke's eyes flickered to mine, a hint of surprise in them. Shane took in Luke's face and turned to look at me. What I did next surprised all of us; I slapped Shane on the face—hard.

Shane's eyes widened with shock. I wondered if it was the first time a girl had slapped him, because it sure looked like it.

I heard the door behind us click open. I turned around and saw Gabe leaning against the doorframe. He was grinning at me, as thought I had just achieved a great feat.

"I was wondering when this would happen," he said, still sporting a devilish grin on his face.

"It was bound to happen," I heard Shane say. He walked to Gabe and fished something out of his pocket. "Here you go asshole." Shane handed a five-dollar bill to Gabe and lightly punched him on the shoulder. He then left, as though nothing out of the usual had happened.

Gabe looked at the bill and put it under the light, looking if it was fake. Once he was sure it wasn't, he slipped it in his pocket. "You guys want some coffee?"

I looked at Luke. He shrugged, still confused about what had happened. I looked back at Gabe and said, "You made a bet?"

"Yeah. I bet him five bucks he was going to get slapped by you in less than four days." Gabe shrugged. "I always win. So … do you guys want coffee?"

I checked the clock on the bedside table. It was late in the morning and I was sure I wasn't going to get any sleep. "Sure. Maybe Luke, you would want to—"

"I'll take coffee," he said, cutting me off.

"Well then get ready; we're leaving in ten minutes," said Gabe, turning to leave.

"Aren't we staying here?" I asked.

"You kidding me? With Damien gone? I suck at making coffee, and Shane … Well, Shane might spit in Luke's."

"He really hates us, doesn't he?" I said, remembering how he had looked at me when I had slapped him. Well, maybe I *had* deserved that look.

"He doesn't *hate* you. He's just confused, that's all." Gabe shrugged. "He *hated* me when we first met. Don't worry; just let him cool off."

I nodded. Luke on the other hand, didn't say or do anything. He stayed frozen, looking at me. I quickly looked away.

"Ten minutes, in the garage," said Gabe before leaving the room, going in the same direction Shane had gone.

"What the hell was that?" said Luke, flopping down on the bed. His shirt went up, enough for me to see the fine line of his abs. Ah, how great was it to be this guy's girlfriend… when he wasn't acting like a knuckle-headed macho and wasn't jealous of every boy I spoke to.

"Get used to it. Moods around here aren't at all stable," I replied, sighing. I hated how right I was. "I'll go get socks and shoes in my room; there are leather jackets in the closet if you want."

Luke lifted his head up and gave me a weird look. "You're kiddin' me, right?

I shook my head. "Jackets, shoes, boots and equipment under the bed."

He rolled to the side of the bed and lifted the drape. There was indeed the equipment box set I had found under my bed. He jumped to his feet and checked the closet. He took a jacket from it and slipped it on. It fit him like a custom glove.

"My room's right next to yours," I added. "If you don't want to get lost, wait for me."

There wasn't really much to wait for. All I had to put on were my socks, shoes and jacket. Deciding to do like Luke, I opened the closet. There were five leather jackets in all, three for men and two for women. I took one for woman and looked at it. It was one of those that ended at the waist. I had always wanted one of those.

I considered wearing my old jacket and then decided to wear the leather one. It wasn't as if I couldn't borrow anything. I was a *'guest'* here, not a prisoner.

I sat on the bed to slip on my socks and shoes. I looked at my feet and then closed my eyes. Now that I was there on the bed, I felt like there was a thousand pounds on my shoulders. I laid back and put my hands on my eyes.

I thought of all the things I had to do. There was Mary I had to see, to make sure she was all right. Jane's disappearance, the why my home had been attacked and who I was… There were just too many to make sense of them in one minute.

Pushing myself up, I got off the bed. When I opened the door, Luke was already waiting for me. He was leaning against my door. So, when I opened it, Luke kind of fell backward, bringing me down with him. My head hit the cushioned floor but it didn't hurt *too* much. What really hurt was the weight of Luke. He was no light guy.

"Luke!" I managed to say. If he didn't get off me soon, I was done for. "Get off me!"

It didn't take Luke a lot of time to prop himself on one shoulder, giving me a chance to breath. He looked down at me with a kind of amusement in his eyes.

"Oh, you think this is funny?" I asked, sitting up with, of course, a smile on my face. "I don't have a death wish."

He started laughing. Not a low kind of chuckling you heard guys do when they were trying to reel a girl in, the kind of laughing you heard from a little kid having the time of his life. That's what made Luke so special. He was attractive by just being himself.

Once he was done, Luke jumped up and lent me a hand to help me up. "You know this isn't the first time this has happened."

Luke shook his head, a smile still on his face. "You know that time doesn't count."

"Uh, yes it does. You pushed me in the pool and then Britt pushed you…" I remembered that day neatly. Brittany's parents had brought Britt, Kait, Luke and me to the water park. Luke had wanted to pull a prank on me by pushing me in the water with my clothes on. Fortunately for me, Britt had my back and she pushed Luke in after me. There was also those other times when we had played tag and Luke had been running too fast and he ended up tackling me… Yeah, those were the moments I remembered most of my childhood.

"Wish things could go back to normal, huh?" he asked, his head tilted toward mine.

Looking at him, I shrugged. Another thing I loved about Luke, we thought the same way. "We should go."

Luke drew back and nodded. "Where's the garage?"

"Come, I'll show you."

It didn't take long for us to reach the garage. It was a little past the main entrance. When we entered, I found myself staring at six Ghosts, two SUVs and three motorcycles.

Gabe was putting on fingerless gloves and Shane was putting oil in one of the motorcycles. I walked to a Ghost and sat on it. I looked at the beauty in front of me, a black Yamaha YZF-R1. The night we had been attacked, I hadn't really taken the time to check out the bike I had been riding on because of the swelling in my neck *and* the evil ghouls chasing us.

I wondered if these were real… I got up and got a better look at the bike. It looked real to me.

"How much d'you pay for these?" I asked, not raising my head.

I wasn't surprised by the answer I got. "We stole them."

I looked up at Shane. He was done oiling the bike and was wiping his hands on a dirty white cloth. "Where d'you steal them?"

"We didn't steal them," said Gabe, giving Shane one of those sideway looks. "They were given to us by the Court."

"You know I still don't know what the hell the Court is, right?"

"You should read more," answered Shane, sourly. "Get your IQ to a higher level."

Out of nowhere, Luke stepped in front of me, blocking my view on Shane. "I'll show you higher IQ..."

Before this ended in a bloodbath, I got myself in front of Luke. I could have sworn I had heard him cracking his knuckles. "This won't lead to anything. Your stupid rivalry is really starting to be annoying," I said.

Nobody said anything for a while, until Shane got impatient. "Are we going to get some coffee or what?"

That pretty much slapped everyone out of a nonexistent trance. "All right, Luke and I will take a car, while Shane and Abby will ride on a bike. Does that sound good?"

"Why can't we all just ride in the SUV?" asked Luke, eyeing Shane.

"We take the SUV *and* the bike as a precaution. If we get followed, we can split up and lose them easily," explained Shane, giving Luke an I'm-better-than-you look.

"Can't three of us go in the SUV?" I asked. I was going to do everything in my power not to sit next to him. I didn't want to give Luke yet another reason to be jealous. He really didn't need one.

"Battle technique," said Gabe, shrugging on a coat. Funny how all of our jackets and coats were of leather. *Rich sponsors*, I thought to myself.

"Why don't you go with Shane?" said Luke.

"Unless he wants to pass as gay, Gabe will *not* sit with me on a bike. And neither will *you*," said Shane. "Abby is the only one who won't be criticized for having her arms wrapped around her boyfriend."

"I'm her boyfriend, you bastard and I'm going to be the one riding with her."

Shane gave him yet another devilish smile. "You don't have Nightrider training and I don't trust you one bit, so you won't be riding with her."

"Even without your stupid Nightrider training I'll whoop your a—"

Before Luke could do something he would regret later, I put a hand on his chest and said, "He's just trying to get to you. Anyway, *he's* the one who'll have his arms wrapped around *me*."

"What?" said Shane. "No way."

"You didn't expect me to let you drive, did you?"

"You don't even know how to drive a motorcycle. Now is not the time for lessons."

I turned to face him. I crossed my arms over my chest and leaned a hip on the Ghost I had sat on. "Lessons? Who said anything about lessons?"

Luke was grinning now. He had that sparkle in his eyes that made me smile. It was pride. "Haven't you figured it out yet?"

"Figured out what?" asked Gabe and Shane both at the same time.

"That I'm a pro when it comes to bikes? I won silver in the AMA Motocross Championship last year."

"You can't be serious," said Shane. "That's impossible!"

I glared at him. "Thanks," I said sourly. Deep down, I was happy. I had caught Shane off guard. Maybe he didn't know everything after all.

"You're *that* girl?" asked Gabe. "The one who almost …"

"Got paralyzed?" I interrupted. "Yeah, that's me." Not wanting to talk about it, I walked toward a shelf and took gloves and a helmet. I went to sit on the Yamaha I had been eyeing before and started the engine.

"Do you guys want coffee, or what?" I asked over the motor's sound. Gabe went in one of the SUVs and Luke followed him in. Through the glass window, Luke nodded to me, as if giving me permission. To do what, I didn't know. All I knew was that I was about to drive—a motorcycle.

This was a big deal for me. I hadn't driven since my accident in April. Jane hadn't wanted me near motorcycles ever since.

The garage door opened, letting in a fresh breeze. Gabe drove out, leaving me alone with Shane.

He straddled the bike, sitting behind me. It was awkward at first, for me, anyway. Shane placed his hands on my waist, which was only covered by my thin shirt, thanks to my fashion sense. I felt his body heat radiating near me.

"Got your helmet on?" I asked, receiving a light hit on the helmet as an answer. I pressed on the pedal and drove out of the garage. Shane pressed two buttons on the dashboard in front of me. "What was that for?"

"To open our speakers," answered Shane, "and to close the garage door."

Only then did I notice he had heard me when I hadn't been shouting. "I hear you voice perfectly fine," I said. "This must have cost a fortune."

"We stole them," answered Shane.

I grinned in my helmet. "Where we going?"

"Just follow Gabe."

"I think I lost ..." My voice trailed off when I saw the black SUV waiting for us to my left.

I revved the engine and followed Gabe, who had just started driving.

When I accelerated, Shane's hands lowered themselves to my hips. Again, I didn't know if I should punch him in the face or blush. I considered punching him in the face but then thought better when I remembered the look he had given me not so long ago.

"So ... you didn't tell me you were a pro," he said after a while.

"There was never a good time for me to tell you," I answered. "I mean, half the time I was knocked out of my mind and the other half, well, I was kind of being chased around. Besides, I'm not really qualified as a professional. Any bozo can win gold in motocross if they *really* put their minds to it."

"You're just saying that because you're good at it," reproached Shane.

"No, I'm not. Motocross isn't even a sport. It's just a thing that keeps your adrenaline pumping."

"Was it just for adrenaline that you almost got paralyzed?"

I stayed silent for a moment. I wasn't ready to reveal my side of the story, not yet. The media had asked me tons of questions and made up half a million stories on what had happened that day but only I knew what *really* had happened.

"It doesn't matter now," I finally said. "I quit a long time ago." *Quit?* The word slapped me in the face. Abigail Claire was no quitter but wasn't I that, after all that had happened? This was the first time I had taken a wheel (or bars) in months. Didn't that qualify as quitting?

Before I could question myself any longer, Shane said, "How long have you known ... Luke." The last word sounded more like a curse than a name.

"Since fourth grade. I actually met him through Brittany. They grew up together in New Jersey."

"I noticed that. With his accent and all, I wouldn't be surprised if he was a gay cowboy. Bet that's why he wanted to ride with me."

"Luke is *not* gay. You just wish he were gay. You're afraid that he might take all the attention the girls give you. *Not*, that you have any."

"Have you ever seen him kissing a girl before?"

"Shane... I've kissed him. I think I would know if my boyfriend was gay."

"I guess you're right."

"Do you think I could go back?" I asked. "To school, I mean."

Shane didn't answer right away. "It might be better for you to continue your studies at the academy. Mrs. Wildfire used to teach Gabe and I when we were younger."

"When you were younger!" I exclaimed, my voice mocking. "You're not that much older than me, you know."

"How old do think I am?"

"About eighteen?"

"Seventeen," corrected Shane. "A year older than you."

"My birthday's soon. I'm practically seventeen myself."

Wow. Seventeen. The number hit me like a boulder. Hadn't I been seven years old yesterday? It seemed that way. Time had passed so fast. What would I give to relive my life again and again? ...

Before I knew it, we were parked next to the SUV. Gabe and Luke were already inside.

"You drive pretty well, Claire," said Shane, grinning at me. "I'm impressed."

I stuck out my tongue at him and lightly elbowed him in the ribs.

"We should probably go in."

I nodded. I slid my gloves off, put them in my helmet and gave it to Shane so that he could put it in the box. While he was doing that, I looked at the building in front of us. The sign in front of me said 'Dunkin' Donuts.'

"You've got to be kidding me," I laughed. "*Dunkin' Donuts?*"

"Unless you like Starbucks coffee, you're welcome." Shane walked next to me. When I didn't make any move to advance, he rolled his eyes and opened the door for me. "After you, Angel."

It was my turn to roll my eyes. "Only because there's heating inside." I walked in the shop and mocked him by stepping on his foot.

"Hey," he fake whined. "That hurt."

I smiled at him. "Good." I scanned the room for Luke and Gabe. When he saw me, Luke made a gesture to catch my attention. They were sitting at the back of the shop, near the back exit.

I walked to them, Shane right on my heels. Once we reached the booth, Luke slid out the booth and let me get in. "Thanks," I said.

Seeing that no one had coffee or anything in front of them, I proposed to go get it.

"You don't have to." Shane was looking at his left. I turned and saw a tall blonde walking toward us with a tray in her hand. From afar, she looked good and from up front, she looked great, more than great. She could make just about any man drool. If only I was that gorgeous...

Her blue eyes bored into Shane's. He grinned.

"Here's your order, Shane baby," she said, putting the tray down in front of him. Not letting him have a chance to reach for his coffee, she added, "I have something for you in the staff room..."

Shane got up and followed her to a hallway, which probably led to the staff room. How fast had that been? He hadn't even notified us!

After staring at what had been Shane just seconds ago, I looked at Gabe. "Who was that?"

"Kana, an air fey," answered Gabe, taking a coffee and opening the lid. Well, could've fooled me. "This is a cappuccino." He pushed it toward me. "I don't want it."

"What did she want to show him?" I asked, putting the lid back on and reaching for the donut box. I took a napkin and took a strawberry one.

"Bet ya' she wanted to show him some skin," muttered Luke in his coffee. When I only glared at him, he gave me the most innocent look he had ever pulled off. "What? I'm surprised she didn't start making out with him right in front of us."

"I'm sure she wanted to," said Gabe, snorting in his cup, "but I doubt he would kiss her. God knows what she would turn him into."

"What do you mean?" I frowned and took a bite of my donut, my yummy, strawberry donut.

"When you kiss one of the fey, they have power over you. As in, they could make you think, hear, see, touch whatever they want you to. They can also make you act and look differently."

"So they're evil," I stated, licking my fingertips.

"Not necessarily. Not all are up to no good. Most of them would say *we're* up to no good."

"But aren't Nightriders part angel?" asked Luke, fingering the chocolate fudge brownie in front of him.

I wondered if this was all new to Luke as well. He only seemed to be expert in the shapeshifter domain, not anything else.

"Fey people are part angel but they're also part demon," said Gabe nonchalantly. "To them, the line between good and bad is very fine, to everyone else, in fact."

"So if I get this straight, any Nightrider could just go rogue."

"Of course," Gabe looked at Luke pointedly, "but that rogue would not go unpunished; he would be like a criminal going to jail. That is why I do not consider humans much different from us. They have the same way of thinking, the same way of adapting... The only real difference is that they are not exposed to the dangers we deal with every day."

Luke nodded. "It makes sense."

When I saw that no one was going to add anything on the matter, I said, "Did you get this for me and the coffee?"

"I knew you would hate it if Gabe took a black decaf for you, so I ordered for you instead," explained Luke, shrugging. "And I knew that if you didn't get your strawberry donut, your day would be a hundred times worse."

"Thanks," I said, just as Shane came back to his seat. He looked a little dazed, as if he still wasn't aware of reality yet. For a second, I was afraid the fey had kissed him and had sucked all his brain capacity out. Who knew?

Just when I was about to say something to make sure he wasn't a brain dead zombie, Gabe slapped him behind the head. Shane blinked several times before jabbing Gabe back in the ribs and saying, "What was that for?"

"I can't believe Kristen put you in charge," said Gabe. "I mean, look at you!"

"Kristen? Who's Kristen?" asked Luke.

"What?" I exclaimed. I looked at Shane. "*You're* in charge?"

"Oh, thanks for the confidence in me guys! Really encouraging," said Shane, looking straight into my eyes.

"Shane, I told you not to fool around with that fey," said Gabe, his voice low, like a father scolding his son.

"You also told me not to fool with that human and that shape-shifter and that Nightrider," said Shane, looking as if he might dismiss Gabe, like some kind of prince. He took the last cup on the tray and chugged down the liquid. I wondered how he could support coffee heat without wincing.

"And look where it got you," continued Gabe. "You're dumber than when you were still unconscious of women."

"And when exactly was that?" asked Shane.

"I honestly can't remember," admitted Gabe, looking blankly at his cup.

Shane tipped his cup toward Gabe. "There. This discussion is what I would qualify as useless."

When Gabe nor Shane said anything, I took my chance and asked, "Where's Kristen?"

Shane looked up at me, as if he had never seen me in his life but it was Gabe who answered. "She went to Eldoras with Damien. They both had to take care of business."

"What kind of business?" said Luke, sitting back, the muscles under his skin getting looser.

"Council business," said Shane before taking a sip from his still unfinished coffee. "It's kind of hard to explain."

"Please, do explain," I said, putting a lot more emphasis in my words than necessary. "We have all the time in the world."

Shane sighed. "The Council is constituted of seven royal families. All purebred Nightriders," he started. "They're the closest to royalty that we've known; some have even been kings and queens of different countries at one point but that doesn't really matter. What matters is that they form a council, a sort of senate, in a way."

"The Council members meet up every once in a while and debate things that are inflicted on them," continued Gabe. "And Kristen and Damien are part of royal families, the Wolfs and the Greenwhicks."

"They're royals?"

"Yep," acknowledged Shane. "You don't often see two royals of different families live together. Most of them are complete snobs but not Damien and Kristen. They fight for themselves, unlike the other royals, who hide behind their guardians."

"You don't like royals," I noted, taking in Shane's disgusted voice.

"It's not that I don't like them," clarified Shane. "It's just that I dislike people who can't fend for themselves."

"And you don't like shapeshifters," I added sourly, watching him finish the remnants of his cup.

Shane flashed a look at Luke, who glowered back. "It's not that I don't like shifters," he said. "It's just that I don't like your … *friend*."

"Her *boyfriend* has a name," growled Luke, "and her boyfriend really has an urge to kick your ass right this moment."

"Bring it on, mutt," said Shane. He half stood up and so did Luke, but before they could tear each other down, I got up, and suggested that we should leave.

Luke got up and said, "How 'bout I go with Abby."

"Not only do I not trust your sense of smell but I don't trust you at *all*," said Shane.

Before they could get into yet another brawl, Gabe nudged Shane out of the shop. I followed and so did Luke.

Once we were outside, Shane said, "I'm gonna' see Mrs. Wildfire with Abby."

Gabe nodded and got in the SUV.

Luke held me by the waist, pulling me close. I smiled as he brought his lips to mine and sighed when he deepened the kiss. I pulled back, aware that we were being watched. I gave him one last peck and moved toward Shane, who had been staring at us. He quickly looked away from me.

I watched as Luke got in the SUV and as it pulled away. I had this feeling in my stomach, something that told me that this was going to be one of our last kisses… I brushed it away when my heart squeezed so much it hurt.

ELEVEN

O nce the SUV was out of sight, I sighed and took the helmet Shane was handing me. "How about you drive this time," I said. "I don't feel like driving."

Shane nodded and got on the motorcycle. He put on his gloves and helmet and started the engine. He pressed the button to activate our headphones.

"Do you want to see Mary, yes or no?" he asked.

I nodded and slipped the helmet on. I sat down behind Shane and put my hands around him.

When we arrived in front of Mrs. Wildfire's old and out of place apartment, Shane parked the bike and said, "Do you think your sister's asleep?"

It was eleven o'clock in Boston, Massachusetts and Mary was definitely awake, even if she hadn't slept the entire night.

We put the things in the case and headed for the building. Before I could put my hand on the door handle, Shane put a hand up, gesturing me not to open it. "What?" I asked, pulling back.

"Demons." The two-syllable word sent a shiver up my spine. I thought of Mary, innocent little Mary, in front of a single demon. I pushed the thought away, shivering, and it wasn't from the cold.

"How can you be sure?" I asked slowly, my voice a little more than a whisper.

"It reeks," he simply said, wrinkling his nose.

I stayed silent. "I'm going to go in. If I don't come back in ten minutes, take the bike and tell Gabe to come. I don't want you to stay here, just in case they're here for you," explained Shane, shoving the keys in my hand.

He pushed the door open and went in. I stared at the door as it clicked shut. I looked at the keys and put them in my pocket. Clouds were now covering the sun. The darkness of them made me think it was going to rain.

I thought of Shane battling a demon with his bare hands. Surely he hadn't gone in without a weapon, right? If he hadn't brought anything useful with him, I was going to kick his ass when he got back. That is, *if* he ever got back.

I bit my lip, unsure what to do. I considered calling Gabe immediately from the emergency phone in the motorcycle's case but declined the thought. Hadn't I, not even fifteen hours ago, hated to be useless, a liability? Was this the time for me to step up to the plate? If I called Gabe right then, wasn't that defeat on my part? Did that mean I would be *quitting*? I couldn't quit. It just wasn't in my nature. I didn't want to think of myself as a deadbeat. Anyway, wasn't it my little sister up there, probably crying for me?

The thought of Mary crying was what tipped me off. I rushed to the bike and opened the case. I put on the extra pair of gloves and took what looked like a switchblade.

I went to the door and was about to open it—when it didn't open. I frowned and gave it another shove—nothing. After several more attempts, I gave up; it was no use. I backed up from the building and looked at the door, frustrated. I kicked it, as if it would magically break but no such luck. Shit, Shane had locked the door to make sure I wouldn't follow him. Damn him!

I looked at the outdoor stairwell that went all the way up to where Mrs. Wildfire's apartment was situated. I smiled to myself. Danger, here I come.

☙❧

SHANE

B *lood*, I thought, *blood everywhere.*

I was on the third floor and already I had found dead carcasses. Two of them, fortunately, had been demons. *Los demoninos del infierno.*

I walked quietly. To a human, it would have sounded like nothing but any Nightrealmer would definitely hear something. My hand strongly held a dagger, which had been washed with blessed water. There was also a Mark of Heaven on it, making it impossible for a demon to lay hands on it.

The lights were closed or rather, someone had cut the current. Until now, I hadn't seen or heard a living soul. All I had seen were the two dead demons; it had been obvious they had been put through horrid pain.

I slowly walked up the stairwell, taking note of broken glass and more blood. I looked around. The glass crunched under my weight. I winced but kept going. I could smell the faint smell of moisture coming from the corners of the floor and ceiling, I didn't like the way it gave my surroundings a rotten and dead feeling, as if there had been a decomposing corpse nearby.

Once I was at the top of the stairs, I put my ear to the heavy metal door and listened for anything out of the ordinary. Nothing—dead silence, too silent for my liking. There should be the sound of a child laughing or the sound of adults having a discussion. This was the place Mrs. Wildfire lived—and I heard nothing.

I tried the doorknob. It turned under my hand without any problem. I lightly pushed it open, the door giving out a loud creaking noise. Out of experience, I put myself on the side of the threshold, where no one inside the apartment would see me. I put my hand on one of my blades. I wasn't as good as Gabe was at this but I had no other option. I had left my gun at the academy and left the switchblade to Abby, in case she might need it.

Now, I was stuck there, with no other option but to use what I was least familiar with. I tightened my grip on the weapon and concentrated. I stopped breathing, to make sure I hadn't missed any sound from inside the apartment.

Exhaling, I moved fast, Nightrider speed. Expecting to see a demon jumping on me, I was surprised when I saw Abby, standing there, her face blank. I put the blade down but didn't put it back in my pocket.

I took the three strides it took for me to reach her. "They're gone," she whispered, staring into space, her face pale white, as if she had just seen a ghost.

I was about to put an arm around her waist, to get her out of her shock but then I stopped myself. Let her feel what every Nightrider had to feel daily, but she wasn't a Nightrider, at least not fully. Abby was an outsider.

Trying to take my mind off her sweet smell that was intoxicating me, I stepped back and looked around. The place was a mess. All the books that had once been on a shelf were on the floor, some ripped open and some upside-down. The kitchen that had once been so clean and inviting now looked like a tornado had passed by. I walked toward one of the bedrooms. I winced when I saw the kids' bedroom mattress ripped in two. The one I had slept in for so many years, when I had been younger. Spidey was ripped in two and so was Flash.

"Someone has definitely been here," I said, walking toward Abby. "And he was looking for something."

"It was looking for a Lost Element," said Abby, finally looking at me. My eyes bored into hers and saw nothing but fear in her eyes.

"How do you know that?' I asked.

Instead of telling me, she pointed to one of the walls that I hadn't seen before. There was a blade like mine anchored in the wall, dripping with blood. It was holding in place a white piece of paper with writing on it. I approached and read:

If you want to see your family alive and well,
Give up the Lost Element in your possession.
You have until the end of this week, or else…
I shall not hesitate to inflict pain upon those you love,
I surely won't think twice upon killing them if need be.
You have been warned.

I reread the letter twice but in vain. I didn't know to whom the writing belonged. I tried to smell out the writer but failed again.

I drew back and looked at Abby. She was on her knees, tears streaming down her face. "If only I'd come sooner, none of this would have happened," she croaked.

I hesitated for a few seconds, then went on one knee in front of her. I put my hand to her chin and made her look in my eyes. "If you'd come here sooner, they'd have taken you with them and you wouldn't have been able to help us."

The look she gave me then was more than I could handle. It was one of pure pain and sorrow. It was like watching the end of the world in her eyes. I cleared my throat and stood up. "We should go."

Abby got up and nodded. Then I noticed the blood leaking down her shirt.

છ∾ન્જ

ABBY

"I hurt myself when I got in," I briefly explained.

"You hurt yourself while going in the building," said Shane.

"That's what I just told you," I pointed out the broken window. I had kicked it open and had slipped inside, accidentally slicing my abdomen in the process, because the window wasn't very large. I was so shocked with what I had found coming in here, that I had also forgotten the pain.

Just as if someone had turned on a switch, I doubled over and gritted my teeth, making sure not to let out more than a loud intake of air. Tears were still streaming down my cheeks. I was hurting in every sense of the word. I had lost my whole family... and this stupid body of mine wasn't helping me one bloody bit!

This is so stupid, I thought. *Why am I freaking out over a small cut?*

"You should lie down," suggested Shane. When all I did was close my eyes and put my hands to my head, he sighed and scooped me up in his arms. My eyes shot open, surprised by how he hadn't just left me there, crying myself to death. I *wanted* to cry myself to death.

Shane brought me to the only comfortable place left in the apartment, the couch. "I ought to have known you would get hurt doing something so stupid," he muttered, placing me down carefully.

"Hey!" I protested.

Ignoring my protests, Shane kneeled next to me and took the hem of my shirt. My eyes widened as fast as my hands flew up to my shirt.

"I just want to see the wound, jeez," Shane said, making me let go. He lifted my shirt up, stopping short at my ribs. He winced.

"What is it?" I asked, lifting my head up to see. When I saw, I didn't need his answer. There were deep scratch marks that went up to my waist and there were some bits and pieces of glass shards stuck into my flesh. How couldn't I have felt it? Blood leaked down on the couch. I instantly made a move to get up but was stopped by Shane's hand. "I'm going to stain Mrs. Wildfire's couch!"

"I don't think she'll mind," Shane replied simply, as he started to rise. He looked around and went to the laundry room.

I exhaled deeply. Why hadn't I been the one to be taken? Like Shane had said, they needed me. *Need me, my ass*, I thought.

I moved up on my elbows and placed myself more comfortably. I could feel a light weight resting on my collarbone. It stuck to my skin like a damp cloth and I hated the sensation. I grabbed it with the hand that wasn't holding onto my wound.

Bringing the object to my eyes, I saw that it was my wind talisman. I barely remembered having it around my neck... I had kept it throughout everything that had happened. I closed my eyes and put both my hands around the necklace, as if in prayer. To whom, I didn't know. God? I wasn't even sure if there had even been one. All I did was pray. Pray for everything to get better, to find Mary, Mrs. Wildfire and Jane. I could also have prayed for world peace but I had to find peace in my own heart before wishing for that. I pressed the talisman to my stomach, where I felt no gash.

I don't know what to do, I mentally said. *I want to see the ones I love. I want to hold Mary in my arms again. I want to hear Mrs. Wildfire's chuckling and I want to see Jane smile again. I want to see my Mom smile again. I'm so scared of what could happen to them... I also want Shane to look at me as his equal, not as a delicate little doll. I want to be useful, for once in my life.*

The air around me shifted, a fresh breeze kissed my skin, like a moth's wing. My mind seemed to empty of all worry and sorrow; I only thought of the inner peace that was installing itself in me. The scratches that had been hurting me became numb. The hole in my chest also became numb, leaving me the feeling of being light, free of a ragged body. I fell into an angelic sleep.

∽∽

I gently woke up with a smile on my face. The cloth around me was silk and fluffy like what I thought to be a cloud. Everything around me was beautiful and white. I wasn't hurting anymore. Still smiling, I rose and slipped off the cloud. Actually, it felt more like cotton candy. I was tempted to take a bite but then thought otherwise.

The ground under my bare feet felt soothing and warm, just like my mood. I delicately moved my head to look around. Everything around me looked like it had been brought back from ancient Greece. The columns around the room were made of milk-colored marble. In the middle of the room was a fountain, with crystal clear water flowing down the Greek woman's chalice.

On the other side of the columns was the sky, letting place to the setting sun. The clouds were slowly turning light pink, making me think of cotton candy again. I was tempted to touch one of them, but stopped myself when a movement at the corner of my eye caught my attention.

I turned and saw what looked like a throne. On it was an old man. His beard was long and ended at the middle of his chest. He had long white hair covering his ears and part of his elbows. The wrinkles on his face showed wisdom and his grey-blue eyes showed generosity and pride. He was wearing what looked like a Greek general's clothes. His armor was silver, like his gladiator shoes.

Strangely, I felt an urge to bow before him, as if he were a god. I succumbed to the urge and went to my knees, my nose touching the floor. How strange that I knew the exact position of a servant's bow.

"Rise, child," I heard the elder man say.

I got to my feet and patted my white robe, which I hadn't noticed I had been wearing and said, "Where am I?"

The man got up and smiled. What a warm smile he had. I wouldn't have minded to watch him smile day and night. No matter how creepy that sounded, that's how I felt—mesmerized. "You are in my palace," he answered, his voice filled with pride. "Caana."

"Your palace is beautiful," I complimented, my eyes wandering to the fruit basket that was placed on what looked like an ancient and well kept, gold coffee table. The fruits looked juicy and perfect, not too ripe but not too green either.

Seeing that I had been eyeing the basket with envy, the man said, "Would you want one? A prune, perhaps?"

The way he said it, made it sound like he knew prunes were my favorite. I slightly nodded. "Who are you?" I asked.

"Why, I am Cairo, the wind god." As he said the words, the prune I had been eyeing for a while lifted into the air and slowly came toward me. It paused in front of my face.

My mouth dropped open. "Y-You're a wind god?" I asked. My hands started trembling. What the hell was this? A god? I had expected a prophet or a poem laureate but not a *god*! Then again, what happened every time I expected something? *Right*.

"You have no need to fret, dearest," assured Cairo. "I mean you no harm. You have my word."

That barely stopped me from trembling.

I gave the prune a final look and took it from the void where it had been.

"Please have a seat," said the god of wind, gesturing the fountain. I took the several steps it took to reach the center of the room and sat on the smooth edge of the circular perimeter of the fountain.

The god sat in front of me, two feet away. "Eat. The fruits here are best known as exquisite."

I didn't even acknowledge the presence of the prune in my hands. "What am I doing here?"

"You prayed to me while holding the wind talisman. It automatically teleported your soul here."

"And where exactly is here?" I asked, daring to talk boldly with the god.

He smiled, the wrinkles around his eyes and mouth getting more pronounced. "At the moment, we are over Mount Ararat, in Armenia."

I was a nerd when it came to geography and I knew that Mount Ararat wasn't in Armenia. "Isn't Mount Ararat in Turkey?"

"To humans, yes. To me, no. Don't you know what happened less than a hundred years ago?"

I shook my head. He sighed. "The Armenian genocide happened, that's what."

I stayed silent for a while. Cold-blooded murder wasn't a topic I wanted to discuss at the moment, especially after what I had just discovered in Mrs. Wildfire's apartment. "Why am I here?"

"Have you ever heard of the *Eleutheria* legend?" he asked, passing a hand in the water, making ripples that shined under the fading sunlight.

"No," I answered truthfully.

"Has anyone taught you anything about Nightrealm history?" said the god.

"Not really. I just got a grimoire. I haven't read much, though."

"Would you believe me if I were to tell it to you now?" The god leaned over, pressing his front-arms right above his knees. "Not many would in your position."

I took a deep breath, trying as hard as I possibly could not to let a tear escape. "I've just lost my entire family. If you can tell me something helpful, I guess I'll be more capable of understanding... I would listen for hours if it'll help me find them."

The Wind god smiled gently at me and nodded.

"Thousands of years ago, when the earth wasn't full of sinners and when peace ruled everywhere, angels lived among humans. Gods were born, then, angels that were more powerful and skilled. That's when things started to go wrong. Some of the gods wanted more; they wanted to be *The* God, the one and only. A lot of people died, angels as well as humans. The gods who wanted more power did cruel things. They killed men, strangled children and raped women. The half-human, half-god children were as evil and twisted as their god-parent was. Only, they didn't inherit their good looks. Instead, they looked as ugly as their intentions. Nowadays, they're called demons.

"Looking as that evil was growing stronger and stronger; the rest of the gods formed an alliance, to try to destroy what was tainting the world. That's how the Lost Elements were invented. In good hands, it could save the world from the dark forces. In the wrong hands... no one would be likely to survive. Everything would end in fire and death.

"Seeing that what they had built was more dangerous than protective, the gods gave them to the angels' descendants, the Nightriders, so that they could protect them from the evil forces while the angels and the gods retired to someplace safer."

"So you're saying that the gods cowered away from the demons?" I said. This was not how I had thought gods reacted to trouble.

"We did not cower away, Abigail," insisted the god. "If we had stayed on Earth, there would've been much more carnage coming from the lesser gods and their demons. They would've fought us on Earth and when we fight, Abigail, we cause great damage. While our descendants cause much less..."

"So you have your battles fought by Nightriders? Isn't that... *cowardly*?"

"We did so because we have no *choice*. Half of the Earth's population would be wiped off if we merely had *one* battle!" He paused and took a deep breath. "But that is not the question. A little more than a hundred years ago, there was an oracle who predicted the stealing of the Lost Elements. He also predicted that a hybrid would find one of the Elements and occupy himself in finding the other ones, engaging himself in a dangerous quest. It is said that the only way to make sure he is the one, he has to eat a fruit only an immortal could eat. You must eat the prune, Abigail."

I stayed unmoving and unblinking. "*The* One has to eat the fruit. Not me."

"You haven't figured it out yet?" he asked, a grin building up on his face. "You are the One, Abigail. How do you think you coming here is possible if it hadn't been for the wind talisman?"

"The necklace is an Element?" I asked, my voice echoing through the sky, to the clouds in the distance. I could almost feel the talisman getting heavier with meaning... This was what my sister and Mrs. Wildfire's kidnapper wanted? A *necklace*?

"Yes. If you eat the fruit and live through it, you will legitimately be *the* One."

"Wait a sec," I said, trying to get my bearings back. "You just threw me three bombshells here! The necklace I have, the one Mr. Porter gave me as a *birthday* present, is a Lost Element? I'm the One from a hundred year old prophecy? And if I *live* through it? Are you saying that I might not make it?"

He shrugged. "Unless you want to stay here forever, you must eat the fruit."

"So I can't leave this place unless I eat it and live?"

The god nodded.

I looked at the prune. Now I understood the legendary quote: '*Damned if you do, damned if you don't.*' I didn't want to stay here. There were too many things I had to do back home. I couldn't chicken out. I had to do it for Mary, Mrs. Wildfire and Jane. I couldn't let them down, I just *couldn't*. All my life, I'd acted proud and unafraid; now wasn't time to go against my convictions.

I looked at the wind god and felt nothing but trust. It was weird to have such a strong feeling for someone I had just met, putting my life entirely in his hands. Either I was incredibly gullible or there was no other option. Funny how my trust was always in demand these days. A day didn't go by without it being tested.

I hesitated for a while, focused on the prune and bit into it. What followed next changed the course of my life forever, once again. I looked in the eyes of the god, who was smiling, nodding. I wasn't sure if the burning pain was a good sign...

TWELVE

SHANE

When I came back from getting a cloth in the laundry room, I had found Abby, sleeping on the couch. She had seemed so peaceful and beautiful, that I hadn't dared to wake her. So, I had sat down and stared at her breathing evenly, some strands of hair covering her face. I kept my face emotionless as my eyes lingered over her.

God only knew how much I wanted to feel her skin under my fingertips. Of course, I had already touched her, but I had never really had time to think of it. Her sweet fragrance was sometimes too much to bare but I was a Nightrider and self-control was something I had learned to master.

Taking a chance, I leaned toward her and made a gesture to push the strands of hair away from her face, when I was stopped. At first, I didn't know by what, but as I forced my hand toward her face, I saw the air surrounding her. I pulled back and listened. I heard the sound of the winding breeze making the dry autumn leaves rustle, which was strange because there were no dry leaves nearby.

This was not normal, not at all. I looked at Abby more closely. Her hair was slightly moving and so were her clothes. She was in a *wind* bubble. I tried passing through again but in vain.

"Abby," I said, hoping she would wake up. She didn't. "Abby!" I repeated, this time louder—nothing.

There was nothing I could do. I couldn't shake her to wake her up and she couldn't hear me… God only knew what was happening. I didn't understand it and I hated it. Not knowing what I was up against was one of the things I hated most.

I knew I should've called Gabe; maybe he knew what was happening but I didn't. I just stared at Abby, feeling entirely helpless.

After five minutes, I was getting restless. *What if she was never going to wake up?* I thought wildly. I would never forgive myself if that were the case. If I hadn't left her alone, maybe things would have been different, but it was too late now. All I could do was wait.

I closed my eyes and sat down on the coffee table. What had she gotten herself into this time?

When I opened my eyes, I noticed a change in the air. The wind around Abby was quickening and it was lifting her up in the air.

I extended an arm to stop her from going any higher but the wind around Abby was so strong, that it literally hit me, with *a lot* of strength. The wind was howling and lifting every light object in the room, sending them flying.

I cursed and watched as Abby went up and up and up… She reached the ceiling and then abruptly stopped. She slowly came back down after a minute. I saw an expression of pain on her face, tears streaming down her cheeks. The rushing wind was so loud I couldn't hear her sobs but I sure as hell saw them.

Everything that had been flying in the room was now around Abby, into what looked like an endless dance. A few objects ripped at me, a pencil scratching my face and picture frames almost knocking the lights out of me.

With determination, I didn't know I had in me; I sliced through the wind and reached for Abby. I enveloped my arms around her stiff body, cradling her like a little baby. It was a miracle that I didn't fly away myself but she was safe now. I bent my head to try to protect myself from the flying objects.

ॐॐ

ABBY

The pain was agonizing. This was worse than the poison bite I had suffered from the ghoul. My almost-death hadn't been this painful. Heck, I hated it.

I felt tears rolling down my cheeks. I sobbed when another gut wrenching feeling took over me. I was going to die, for real this time. There was no one who could save me, not even Shane... Only I could save myself. This all depended on whether I was the one from the prophecy. If I was, I would survive this and if I wasn't... it would be the end of me.

I wasn't the type to cry when I broke a nail or skinned my knee but I did cry when I broke bones or was sad. Mostly, I didn't scream. So, I was very surprised when a scream ripped out of my throat, threatening to destroy my ears permanently.

Then everything stopped. All the pain, the moans, the sobs ... and mostly the black void I had been in, ceased to exist. The flames around me faded and I opened my eyes.

I blinked away tears and saw Shane. How beautiful he was now, looking down at me with worry in his eyes and something else I couldn't quite put my finger on. His royal blue eyes were shining and he had cuts on his face.

I suddenly had an urge to cry. Nothing was right and I didn't want to be alone, not now, not after living through all this crazy stuff.

"Abby, are you all right?" asked Shane, his voice barely above a whisper.

Tears welled up in my eyes. I flung my arms around Shane's neck and sobbed. Right then, he was the only thing that kept me from falling. I tightened my arms around him and brought my knees to my chest. Shane put his arms around me and bowed his head closer to put it against mine. I was desperately seeking warmth and he was offering it to my open-heartedly. I was a bit taken aback at how open he was in comforting me but didn't question it.

I could feel my throat constrict whenever I thought of Mary. I felt rage boil inside of me whenever I thought of the letter. Deep down, under all these mixed emotions, I was terrified—terrified of what could happen to my little sister and terrified at the thought of losing her if I did not hold my end of the bargain.

As all these uncertainties spiraled inside my head, Shane held me, strong enough not to let me atrophy into myself. For fifteen minutes, we stayed like this, until my tears had dried and all my emotions were washed away, leaving behind an empty body, indifferent to what could happen to it.

"Thank you," I croaked, unlatching my hands from his neck. His shirt was damp at the spot where I had laid my head. I brushed it away. "I'm sorry about that."

"What the hell happened Abby?" he asked harshly, looking at me with his piercing blue eyes. "You were flying!"

"I was flying?" I asked, dumbstruck. What was he talking about?

"Yes, you were, well, kinda. You were inside this wind bubble..." I stared at him, making him understand that I thought he was talking crazy. "I swear. You were unconscious and then there started to be wind... It was *protecting* you and you were floating. Then you started crying and then you screamed. That's when I grabbed you and everything stopped."

"Are you serious?"

He nodded, all sign of amusement nonexistent. You couldn't get more serious than that. "Abby, what happened?"

I sighed, resting my head on his shoulder once more. I was drained, both physically and emotionally. "You wouldn't believe me if I told you."

"Try me," said Shane.

He laid back on the couch and placed me more comfortably on him. I didn't care that I was in another man's arms at the moment. I didn't care if Luke got jealous over this. Right now, all I needed was this man's comfort. He would understand more than Luke would.

"I met up with the Wind god, Cairo, in his ..."

I explained to him in great detail my encounter with the wind god. I told him about everything the god had said, about me being the one from the prophecy, as well as the Lost Element. Throughout my entire monologue, Shane didn't say anything. He was as silent as a stone.

He let it all sink in for a while, staring off into thin air. I let him stay this way for a moment, hoping he didn't think I had gone mad.

"And where is the Lost Element now?" asked Shane, looking at my neck.

I frowned and reached for the talisman but found it missing. I looked down, panicking. Only the silver chain that had been holding the Element was there, hanging around my neck. Where could it possibly be? I scrambled off Shane and scanned the couch.

"It's gone," I whispered, panic gripping my heart. My head was spinning. It had been right there... How could it possibly have disappeared? I patted the corners of the cushions and only felt a stray toy—nothing.

Shane got up and stared at me. "Are you telling me you lost one of the *Lost Elements*?"

"Shane! I'm not saying I lost it... I just... can't seem to find it."

He threw his arms up in the air and let out a forced laugh. "Abby, our entire *survival* rests in that Element. It's not time to play dumb, not when so many people are concerned."

I fisted my hands and glared at him. "You think I don't know that Shane? I'm the last person who would play dumb now. My little sister's life is in play here." I could feel myself shaking with anger. How could he? ... "Don't you *dare* say I don't take this seriously."

Shane looked down, ashamed. "You're right and I'm sorry."

I snorted, still angry with him. "I thought you Nightriders were never sorry. That saying you're sorry is just a way of being polite."

"Are you making me swallow back my words?" asked Shane, frowning at me. He had taken a step back to put distance between us.

I looked into his eyes. I saw no emotion in them. He was good at switching his emotions off, very good, in fact. "Maybe I—"

I stopped short and put a hand to my stomach. I could feel my bloodied shirt stuck to my skin … and I felt no wound. I frowned. This is strange…

"Abby, are you all right?" said Shane, getting closer, a look of concern spreading over his face. When he saw me holding my abdomen, he groaned lightly. "I completely forgot about your wounds. Let me take a look at them."

How is this possible? I had been bleeding… Facts trump reason. Still confused, I slowly lifted the hem of my shirt, expecting to see a gaping wound, infected, with blood oozing out. *What the…?*

Shane took in a deep breath, while I just stared. My mind had gone blank. All I could do was stare… I quickly walked to the mirror in the bathroom, stumbling over several objects on my way there. I lifted my shirt once more up to my ribs and took a good, long look.

In front of me, I saw a girl, with long black hair and light purple eyes. She looked tired, agitated but most of all, she looked scared. Her hand was on her stomach, over black designs. The designs stretched from her left hip all the way to the tail of her sternum. That girl was none other than me.

I saw Shane come in from behind me, also looking at my mark. "So this is where the Lost Element went…"

My mind froze momentarily and then I snapped. "What do you mean?"

"I thought it was only a myth but I guess I was wrong."

I let go of my shirt, suddenly feeling very weak. I turned to look at him and my knees buckled. Shane caught me before I hit the floor. My head was spinning and I could feel a slight burning coming from where my mark was located.

"I don't really feel so good all of a sudden," I mumbled into his shoulder while he was carrying me back to the couch.

"It's probably post-traumatic pain. You were in too much shock to feel it at first and only now is it hitting you," explained Shane, laying me on my back and sitting beside me. "When we go back to the academy, I'll ask Gabe to make you something to alleviate the pain … and I'll make an herb fire to soothe your mind."

I put my hand to my forehead, trying as hard as I could not to lose consciousness. "What did you mean when you said you thought it was just a myth?" I asked weakly, my voice cracking at the end of my sentence.

Shane sighed. "There's an old myth, concerning the Elements, that says that when one of them makes contact with blood, it'll become one with that person to heal them. Of course, that person can't have an ounce of demon blood in him."

It took me a while to process what he had just said. At first, I kept my eyes shut but as the information he had just given me started to sink in, my eyes opened and I stared at him.

"Are you telling me that the wind element is *inside of me*?"

Shane grinned, scratching the back of his head. "I guess you can also put it that way. It's not really... inside of you. It's become *part* of you."

I groaned, frustrated at myself for not being able to think clearly. "Shane, are you telling me that not only am I the one from the prophecy but that I've also *become* a Lost Element?"

Shane looked down at me, with no trace of amusement on his face. "I'd be lying if I said no."

THIRTEEN

LUKE

I was pacing back and forth in the academy's kitchen. What was taking them so long? Had something happened? Or had the Nightrider just taken Abby somewhere? … I pushed the thought away. I didn't have to worry more than necessary. This was *Abby*, my girl-friend. She would never do something like that to me, but I didn't put it past that *dog*.

"I'm sure everything's fine," said Gabe, for the millionth time in the past ten minutes. "Maybe they just wanted to stay with Mary a little bit longer."

"Then why isn't Abby answering her cellphone?"

Gabe didn't answer right away. "That's because she left her cell-phone back at her house. I doubt she had time to grab it on the night of the attack." He put his knife back to the piece he had been working on since we had come back.

"Watcha doing?" I asked, deciding to finally sit down. I had to admit, my legs were kinda sore.

"A stake," said Gabe, slicing the wood, so that its end was sharp.

"Don't you have tons upstairs?" I said, remembering the room Abby had shown me before we had left for coffee.

146

"Yeah… When I have nothing else to do, I just start sharpening things. Making sure they'll work fine when the time comes."

I stayed silent for a while. What did I do when I had free time? If I was at home, I cleaned up the apartment. If I was at school … Well I never had free time at school and that was about it. Apart from Porter's, I didn't go anywhere else that often.

What could I do now? Nothing, and it was driving me crazy.

"So… Shane says you're blessed."

I turned to look at the Nightrider. "I don't know what you're talking about."

"Sure you don't."

"I'm serious! All this crap about Elements is completely stupid."

"Is it still stupid if it can kill thousands of lives?" asked Gabe, looking up from his stake. "If it falls in the wrong hands, that is, and we don't want that to happen now, do we?"

"I guess you're right but I have never touched one of these things. I was kept away from the Nightrealm all my life until last night."

"You were always part of the Nightrealm. You are what is called a Nightrealmer."

"You can say that," I admitted, "but I don't remember touching one of those…" I stopped. What if I had touched one of those? What if they didn't look like anything I thought they did? Now that I thought of it, the Elements could look like anything.

Just then, the phone rang. Gabe put his knife and his stake down on the isle and walked to get a cordless phone. He picked it up and put it to his ear.

"The Night Academy of Boston." Pause. "All right, we'll be waiting for you." He hung up, only to open it again. He dialed a phone number.

While he was waiting for the other line to pick up, I said, "Who you calling?"

"Shane," said Gabe simply. "Shane, are you… ?" "Okay, yeah." He hung up for what seemed like the last time.

"What is it?" I asked, following Gabe out of the kitchen.

"The Nightriders from Eldoras are coming earlier than planned."

"And... ?"

"And we need some planning," answered Gabe, opening the door that led to the garage.

Abby and the mutt were already there, putting the helmets and gloves back on the shelf. They were silent, too silent for my liking.

I walked to Abby and took her by the shoulders, to see her face. "Are you all right?"

"Yeah, I'm fine," she said, her voice weak. She looked over my shoulder. "Shane, can you make me the—"

Before she could finish her sentence, the Nightrider said, "Yeah, sure, no problem. Let me just talk to Gabe for a sec."

I turned around only to see Gabe and the other one exit the garage. I turned back to Abby, who was now shivering.

"Hey, what's up?" I asked, putting both my arms around her to keep her warm. I was worried. I didn't like the way she was ghost white. She looked even more fragile than usual.

"Luke ... th-they took Mary and Mrs. Wildfire."

"What?" I exclaimed, my voice echoing in the room.

How couldn't I have seen that one coming? Obviously bad people wanted something from Abby and her little sister was an easy target. Any sane person would have known that her family would affect her and that she would do anything for them. How could the Nightriders not have seen it? Stupid, stupid, stupid! I was going to have to talk to Gabe. If I had to, I would even talk to the *other* one.

"There was a note... Oh Luke, I should have known this was coming," she said, before burying her head on my shoulder.

I held her tighter, wishing for her to stop being sad but she couldn't help but feel depressed, since everything was only bringing her down, right? If only I could do something to cheer her up...

Suddenly, I had an idea. I was brilliant! Why hadn't I thought of that earlier? Abby would have said it was because I was simply a boy. I chuckled aloud, thinking of how smart I could be at times.

Abby looked up, her eyes glittering with unshed tears under the garage's light. "What is it?"

I stammered my sudden boost of energy and stopped smiling altogether. This was not a good time. "Nothing." Suddenly, the air seemed to have gotten colder and I saw that she was clasping her hands together to keep them warm. "We should get you inside."

She nodded, letting me lead her out of the garage. I was about to go in the kitchen when I smelled something was burning. Protecting her from a possible explosion, I got in front of Abby and looked in the steel door's rectangular window.

Gabe was making something at the stove, putting funny looking ingredients in a cup. The other one was ... not there. Seeing that there was nothing out of the ordinary in there, I turned around and behind Abby, saw some kind of living room, with sofas, a plasma screen TV and a fireplace. The Nightrider was there, building a fire.

"Don't you know how a fire is done?" I asked sourly. "It doesn't usually smell this bad."

The Nightrider didn't bother to look up; he just kept putting some herbs in the fire, making it thicker and higher. "These will help Abby recover," he said.

"Recover from what?" I asked, feeling like I was about to punch the guy any second now because he didn't even look up!

"She didn't tell you?" The Nightrider looked up this time. He looked at Abby. "You didn't tell him yet?"

I turned to look at Abby, who was now looking at me, a sad look in her eyes. "Luke ... there's something else you need to know."

∻—∻

ABBY

Luke didn't take the news the way I had thought he would. He looked calm and controlled—exactly what a ticking bomb looked like. I had told him what had happened at Mrs. Wildfire's, about the wind god and about my new '*destiny*,' which was pretty ironic because I had always believed in making *my own* destiny.

When I explained it all to him in detail—except when Shane had touched me and held me in his arms, there was no need to make him even more jealous, over nothing—it all seemed like a dream, as if I was telling the story of someone else.

I was sitting on a loveseat, alone, with Luke at my left and Shane at my right. Gabe was the only one of the three who seemed the most composed, unlike Shane and Luke, who looked like they wanted to kill each other whenever they looked in each other's direction. I could almost swear I had seen smoke coming out of Luke's ears.

I wasn't cold anymore, thanks to Gabe's special concoction of herbs and what's-the-name? *Akhor.* That's what he had called it.

"And there's something else …" added Gabe, his voice strong and loud, so that all of us could hear him clearly.

"Shoot," replied Luke, sitting back and putting his hands behind his head. "What can be worst, right?"

"You're going to have to drink a potion."

Luke jumped up from the sofa. "What?" When he saw Gabe wasn't kidding, he said, "No way am I drinkin' one of your … whatever they are."

"The Nightriders who were supposed to come in two days are coming tonight," said Gabe.

"So? Let them come; if it's room you're worried about, I can just go to my house, no big deal. I'm not drinking your hocus pocus stuff, no way."

"You're staying here, whether you like it or not, dog. And you're drinking the potion to hide your smell," said Shane getting up.

"Are you saying I smell?" asked Luke, stepping dangerously closer to Shane.

"Of course you do. You reek of pest."

Before this could get out of hand, I put both hands straight and put them in the form of a T. "Time-out! You two are acting like kids—again."

Luke must have seen how annoyed I was because he stepped back and sat down. Only Shane stood, looking at me daringly.

"*Que realmente puede ser una polla a veces,*" said Gabe, slightly shaking his head.

"*Bésame mi culo,*" replied Shane, grinning and sitting back down.

"Are you done?" I asked. One of the things you should know about me, I didn't like not understanding. Spanish was something I wasn't really good at in school.

"Sure," muttered Shane before his voice got higher, as if he were taking charge of the discussion. "New Nightrider recruits are coming in. They should be here tonight and we don't want them to know that you've," he turned to look at Luke "had a connection with one of the Lost Elements. And that you," he looked at me "are the one from the quest."

"Why?" I asked. Shane hadn't said anything about me having to hide the fact of who I was and he hadn't even told me completely why they had to make Luke drink a potion. "Aren't Nightriders on our side?"

"Yeah but at the same time, no."

"You know that doesn't really make sense, right?"

"What does?"

I stayed silent. Sometimes, I hated it when he was right. "Why don't you want them to know?" I said slowly. "Don't they have to be informed? Doesn't the Council have to know about this?"

"Sure they do but we won't tell them." When I only kept staring at him, he sighed. "I don't think any of you want to be treated as lab rats. They're not going to let the shapeshifter—"

"The name's Luke you son of a—" cut in Luke, his voice sounding angry.

"—out of their sight and Abby ... you'd be in danger," finished Shane.

I asked the question that seemed to rule my life, "Why?"

"No demon wants someone with a chance of vanquishing them to live," answered Gabe. He looked at me and then at Shane, "Do you think that's why she was attacked by ghouls at her house?"

"You saying that someone already knew she was the One?" said Shane, crossing his arms over his chest.

"Why else would they have tried to kill me?" I was getting tenser by the minute. A horrible thought erupted. What if it wasn't me who had been meant to be killed? "What if they wanted Jane ... or Mary?"

"I doubt it," said Shane, shaking his head.

"Okay, let's say I am what the ghouls were after and that I'm the one of the quest and Luke is touched or whatever you call it…"

"Blessed," corrected Luke, grinning sheepishly at me.

"*Blessed*," I said. "What are we going to do about it?"

"Your aura doesn't give up anything unusual, except that you're a hybrid, so all you have to do is not show your marks on your stomach. In other words, all you have to do is not get naked in front of them," said Shane, matter-of-factly.

At the corner of my eye, I saw Luke balling his fists. Before he could make a comment, I said, "What about Luke?"

"That's the problem," said Gabe, "We don't know."

"What do you mean '*We don't know*'?"

"We don't know how to hide the fact that he's blessed," answered Gabe, "and the fact that he's a shifter. Unless we're authorized to, we can't let anyone except Nightriders in. And only a witch or a warlock knows the ingredients to the potion Luke needs to drink."

"Uh … I can just leave," said Luke, looking as if he thought they were stupid for not thinking of that beforehand. He turned his head toward Shane. "I thought you wanted to hand me in to the Council."

"Things change," admitted Shane. As soon as he said it, he seemed to regret it. His voice had been low and careful, which seemed unnatural of him. I looked in his direction and found him looking at me. He looked away.

"But you shouldn't leave," quickly added Gabe. "We might need you."

"All right but what happens if I do stay?"

Gabe stayed silent. So did Shane.

When everyone stayed silent for a minute, looking for an answer, I took the word. "Don't you have a warlock or a witch you could consult?"

Shane seemed to consider the idea but then dismissed it. "The closest witch we know lives in the Maine and the closest warlock lives in Manhattan."

"Then why don't we go see the warlock?" I asked.

"Because he wants our heads cut off," said Gabe, as if the question's answer was obvious.

"What about the witch?"

"She wants to cut *his* head off," said Gabe, inclining his head toward Shane. "And other parts of his body I will not mention."

"I'm not surprised," scoffed Luke under his breath. I couldn't help but laugh at the expression on his face. Luke always made me laugh, even when the world was crashing down on me.

Shane cleared his throat, as though he didn't like being made fun of. "Melinda always says she wants to kill me."

"She's not the only one who always wants to kill you," commented Gabe, which made Shane grin.

"I guess you're right on that one," said Shane.

"I'm always right," bragged Gabe, giving himself a fake superior look.

"So, how are we going to get there?" I asked. "Maine is a good hour and a half away."

"Make that two hours. We're going to Portland," put in Shane.

"We're going by car?" asked Gabe, looking confused.

Shane shook his head. "I was thinking about using Ghosts. We won't make it back in time otherwise."

Gabe checked his watch. "Let's go then, we have no time to lose."

❦❧

SHANE

I was in the weapon room stuffing a charged gun in a duffel bag. Abby, Gabe and the dog were waiting for me in the garage. All I needed were some weapons. You never knew what could happen with a witch, especially when the witch was Melinda Reese.

Two years ago, I'd met her in a Nightrealmer party. We'd flirted and I had eventually kissed her. I hadn't been looking for a long lasting relationship; I never had but Melinda hadn't known that. The morning after the party, she had already been making plans of *marrying*! I, a fifteen year old at the time, had been terrified and had run away, leaving her fuming. Witches weren't the type to accept being turned down gently. She'd sent me several exploding gifts the first couple of months but then they had stopped. She'd met someone else and tortured him as well. I had unfortunately been the first one who had made her fall, so she would never fully forgive me.

Once I was done packing weapons, I slung the bag over my shoulder and went flying down the stairs to the garage. This time, because of the bag I was holding, I decided to slide down the banister; it wasn't as fast as jumping down but it was much faster than walking it.

When I arrived, Gabe was sitting on one of the Ghosts, showing Abby and the shapeshifter how to drive a Ghost. He was showing them the basics, which were easy, but when Gabe started getting into details, the shapeshifter's face grew more and more confused. Abby, on the other hand, was composed and cool; she looked like she'd known how to drive a Ghost all her life, as if it was no big deal. When she saw me, I looked away and went to another Ghost, the one I was going to ride.

I straddled it and looked at myself in one of the mirrors that were on the sides of each Ghost. Yes, even in airways, you had to know what was going on behind you.

To be truthful, I wasn't really looking forward to seeing Mel. She'd caused me enough trouble already… but what other choice did I have? If the Council found out we had been hiding knowledge from them, we would all be in big trouble. Our titles would be taken away from us. We wouldn't be able to claim ourselves Nightriders anymore. The shapeshifter would have his brain open (literally) to the Council, so that they could look in his deepest memories to see where he had had contact with the Element. I'd heard from people who had lived through it that it had been the most painful experience in their whole lives. Even the dog didn't deserve such treatment. Abby would be in more danger than she already was. The whole Nightrealm would know who she was and then demons would overhear… It could also come down to provoking the gods and that was the last thing everyone wanted to do.

"This isn't technology of today," said a voice in back of me. I didn't have to look up to know who it was.

"We have resources with knowledge more advanced than humans," I explained matter-of-factly.

"What kind of resources?" asked Abby, sitting next to me, her thigh touching mine.

"Aren't you supposed to learn how to ride a Ghost?" I said, trying to make her go away. I didn't want her this close to me, for personal reasons.

She didn't go away; instead, she just stayed there and said, "It's the same as riding a bike. They're just some things that are different but the basics are still there. What are your resources?"

"Uh ... smart people?"

"Don't play dumb with me," snapped Abby.

I looked up into her eyes. They were so beautiful... I'd seen so many pretty eyes throughout my short life, but these were by far the prettiest. I wasn't even sure pretty could apply to her light purple eyes... I mentally slapped myself. What was I thinking? Had I actually been daydreaming about the *color of her eyes*? This was crazy, insane.

"Who's the engineer?" she asked, more gently this time.

I sighed. She wouldn't leave unless I told her the truth. "Remember what I said about royals having extra powers?" Abby gave me a nod. "Well, there is one family of royals who is specialized in sciences, math and technology... They're the ones who built these Ghosts. Nightriders have always been twenty to fifty years ahead of humans technology-wise ... and other stuff."

Abby rolled her eyes. "Boys," she said before getting up and stretching. She raised her arms as high as she could; she even went on her tiptoes to do so. Being a boy, my eyes could only linger down her body, where I saw her shirt lift a couple of inches. I could see the navy blue lines on her back and abdomen. I'd only seen a few inches of her new-found marks and could only think of how much it must have hurt to have them burned into her skin. These were the marks she had because of the Lost Element.

All of it was really just confusing and we both knew it.

She must've seen me looking because Abby drew back and just contented herself by stretching her triceps. She slightly winced by doing so.

"Does it hurt?" I asked, watching her intently.

Abby shrugged. "I guess I feel kinda sore," she admitted.

I nodded. "Gabe's concoction?"

"I think … but it's no big deal."

I let it slide and looked at Gabe. The shapeshifter seemed to have grasped the concept and was already starting the engine. I got up, took the duffel bag from the ceramic floor, put my hand under the seat of the Ghost and opened the trunk. I stuffed the bag inside and took ski glasses from one of the side pockets. I handed one to Abby.

She simply looked at it confused. "What's that for?"

"It's to put around your head and shield your eyes from the wind?"

"Yes, but why are you giving it to me?"

"So that you can use them," I said, "and you might want to put a hat on, it might get windy."

"What are you talking about?" Abby put her hands on her hips, the glasses dangling from her wrist.

"They'll be useful when we're airborne. Ghosts can go really fast," I added.

"Oh." Abby's arms dropped. "Are you really going to give the wheel to Luke?"

I shook my head. "We're riding in pairs of two."

"I'm not sure Luke would like to look gay, or Gabe, or you for that matter."

Instead of telling her, I pressed a button on the left handle of the Ghost and slowly, an extra seat unfolded from the trunk. It was facing the opposite way of the driver, so if they would ever get attacked, there would be a shooter. Thus the definition of shotgun.

Abby looked more impressed than before. "Showoffs," she muttered.

FOURTEEN

ABBY

Shane was the one who drove. He obviously didn't trust me with the wheel. According to what he'd said, his excuse had been that I didn't know how to get to Portland. I had just scoffed. I knew how to get to Portland *and* I knew how to drive a Ghost.

Shane hadn't really meant it when he had given me the glasses and the old type of pilot hat. So, we finally wore helmets. At first, the view of Boston had been great, buildings I had never seen from above and big spots of green when we passed over parks and then we'd gone higher to not be seen. The view was ruined by the clouds.

I had always imagined what it would feel like to touch a cloud. I could sum it up in one word—wet.

Gabe had given me a heavier jacket for the road, because it would be colder than the average Boston weather up there. I had my hands clasped together, trying to heat them. I hunched over, so that my neck could be protected from the wind and moved my toes back and forth so that they wouldn't freeze. Shane and I were wearing the talking helmets, so I had no problem asking him when we would arrive.

"Another fifteen minutes," he'd said twenty minutes ago. After a while, I got tired of asking and just tried to enjoy the silence.

My thoughts went to the wind talisman. It was part of me, literally. Shane had told me that when the talisman made contact with my blood, it reacted in a sort of way that it diluted into me, healing me. Instead of moving on like an Element would usually do, the liquid— yes, liquid (the Elements had a mind of their own, therefore, were hard to predict)—stayed inside me, closing my wound behind it, so that it wouldn't leave. The only way for it to come out would be to cut my waist open. First, I didn't want to be sliced open and second, the liquid wouldn't *completely* come out. So, that option was out of the question.

I was tempted to look down into the emptiness the Ghost was gliding on but I knew better. Among my fears, heights was probably in the top three. The temptation, unfortunately was one of my major flaws and so was curiosity, which pressed me to look down, and I did. After sixty-seven seconds of watching the void underneath me, I sat upright and closed my eyes. My heartbeat was getting slower and slower, up to a point I was sure it was going to get me killed. I felt light-headed, my head spinning.

"Abby!"

I jolted in my seat and got my bearings straight. Just then, I realized sweat was tickling down my forehead and that my hands were clammy.

"Is something wrong?" asked Shane, worry in his voice.

"Are we there yet," I said, my voice low.

"Two more minutes."

Three minutes later, the Ghost was parked on top of an eleven-floor building. I had asked Shane if humans could see us but he just said, "Ghosts have a protection device. Technically, no normal human should be able to see them, but we didn't take a chance of being spotted by a Nightrealmer by going just above the cloud line."

Gabe landed next to us, with a shaken Luke in the backseat. Once his seatbelt was off, he high-fived Gabe. Both of them had grins on their faces. "That was sick man! Where'd you learn to do that?"

"Natural skills, I guess," said Gabe nonchalantly, looking at his fingernails. Shane choked on air and Gabe gave him a scowl. I couldn't help but smile at the brotherly affection between them.

After a few moments of awkward silence, Shane pressed us toward a door, which, I thought, would lead us into the building. I was glad when the cold was replaced by hot and when my toes started functioning normally again.

As we got down the stairs, I noticed how well kept this place was. The walls were cream white and looked like they'd been painted not long ago. The floor (or in this case, the stairs) were covered with a royal blue rug, almost like the one in the academy. The doors we had seen were all covered with varnish.

We had seen no one as we went down. Shane stopped at the fifth floor and walked down the hallway. He stopped in front of a door and turned to look at Luke and me.

"Whatever you do," he said, "don't get on Melinda's bad side." He then looked at Gabe and nodded, who returned the gesture. Shane faced the door and knocked.

⁊ఞ

LUKE

It didn't take long for the door to open. Melinda did not look like what I had imagined. I had thought of her as an ugly witch with graying hair and a huge mole on her nose. I couldn't have been more wrong.

Melinda Reese had a beautiful heart-shaped face with hair so pale and fine it might have been white. Her striking blue eyes pierced through me like bullets. I kept my mouth tight, trying not to drool as my eyes ran over her hourglass figure. If all witches looked like that, I might as well be under a spell. Then I saw Abby looking at me and the spell lifted off of me and disappeared into nothingness. God, had I just been eyeing a *witch* when I had *Abby*? I slightly shook my head. Stupid, stupid, stupid.

The Nightrider, on the other hand, looked as though he was waiting for his death ... or worse. Gabe had a dreamy expression on his face but it faded just as quickly as it had come.

I looked back at Melinda and noticed that she had a cute little curved nose.

"Well, well, if it isn't Shane McKenna and Gabe Longshadow," she said, her voice ringing like wedding bells in my head. *Shit*, man! Get a grip, I thought to myself harshly. "What a pleasant surprise. And you've brought Abby and Luke as well."

Abby flashed a looked at the Nightrider, who just shrugged.

"Melinda," said the Nightrider, his voice as sharp as a dagger. I wondered how he could hate this beautiful thing that much. She looked so inoffensive and innocent. "You know why we're here."

Melinda sighed and moved aside so that Shane could go through the door. "Oh well…" She looked at the rest of us and smiled. "Shane Honey can sometimes be very serious, too serious for his young age."

"You're saying it as if you were older," noted Abby, putting her hands in her back pockets.

Melinda laughed. "Darling, I am much older than Shane. I might look like a nineteen year old, but I'm actually much older than that."

"You're immortal?" asked Abby, her eyebrows flashing upward.

The witch smiled. "Come now. A hallway is not an appropriate place to chat. Come in."

Gabe got in and was followed by Abby. I hesitated but when Melinda gave me a warm smile, I followed Gabe and Abby into the witch's lair.

❦❧

ABBY

I was struck by how Melinda's home looked. Everything looked new and polished. It smelled of apples, which was strange, because it smelled of *pure* apples. I let my gaze wander to the kitchen, which must have cost a fortune and saw that there was an apple's peeled skin on a heated oven. So, that's where the scent had come from…

The place was what you would see in one of those 'I'm rich and famous' type of places. I could feel that the wood under my feet was heated right through my sneakers. The panel windows, which gave view to the richest part of Portland, didn't have any trace of handprints or dirt.

I could only dream of ever living here. I would never be able to afford it and even if I could, I wouldn't, because then I would look like

I was trying to impress. After a few seconds of afterthoughts, I knew that I would never live in a place like this.

Behind me, I heard the door close. I made a gesture to take off my shoes but was stopped by a voice.

"Oh, you don't have to do that," I heard Melinda say from behind me. "I have to clean the floor today, anyway."

I was surprised that she hadn't said, "My maid will clean it up." I walked to where Melinda was gesturing us to sit. It was a set of couches surrounding a knee-high glass table. I sat down. It was the most beautiful thing my bottom had experienced that day. No couch could match the quality of this one.

I was about to tell Luke to sit next to me, when Melinda took the place instead. From the corner of my eye, I saw Shane tense. I looked back at Melinda and noticed her smiling. What was up with that?

"Would you like something to drink? Hot tea, perhaps?" asked Melinda, all smile. I wondered why Shane had broken up with her in the first place. She seemed to be very nice and certainly beautiful. I had seen the look on Luke's face, as well as Gabe's when we had first seen her at the door. No matter how much it pained me to say this, she was much more beautiful than I was and Luke's wandering eyes had proven it. I felt like a stone had been dropped in my stomach.

"Yes, I'd like that," I answered calmly.

"What about you?" said Melinda to the boys, who were now sitting down. All three refused. Melinda sighed, raised both arms and lightly clapped her hands. On the coffee table appeared two porcelain China cups and a glass teapot with a silver handle. Inside the teapot were hot water and a flower, blooming at the bottom.

I marveled at the flower. It was bright red with different shades of blue and purple and looked like what you would find in the jungle, in the prettiest of jungles, that is, if you didn't count the slimy insects and deadly spiders.

Melinda poured some tea in both of the cups, her movements delicate and precise. She gave one to me and took the other one for herself.

Shane cleared his throat. What was wrong with him? I thought, kind of annoyed. Why was he so urgent in getting done with business and getting out of here? To calm my nerves, I took a sip of the tea. The potion Gabe had given me earlier was nothing compared to this. It tasted of apples, cinnamon, honey, vanilla and green tea all at the same time, which was an odd combination but it tasted great. I gulped the tea until the last drop. Well, that had been refreshing.

The girl next to me turned to look at Shane. "I know why you have come and I am already taking care of it, at least, for Abby."

"What do you mean?" asked Luke, his voice low and careful.

"Notice how her aura is getting darker and darker," said Melinda. "It was too light for a Nightrider, so I dimmed it with the help of this tea." She motioned the teapot with her hand.

"You poisoned me?" I croaked, my eyes wide. *How could I have trusted a witch?* my mind thought frantically.

"I haven't poisoned you. I just took some light out of you. Gabe and Shane were used to seeing your light, so they didn't think it was wrong, but any other Nightrider would know with simply one look that you are not normal."

"And what about me?"

I looked at Luke, who was looking straight at Melinda, a look of wonder in his eyes. I bit the inside of my cheek. Then I looked at Shane, just to see if they had all been put under a spell but no, Shane looked disinterested in Melinda … because he was looking straight at me. Why couldn't my boyfriend be acting like Shane? I looked away.

Melinda leaned over the coffee table and handed her teacup to Luke. "Drink," she ordered, her voice still as light.

Luke looked at the liquid suspiciously. If it hadn't been for the importance of him drinking the tea, I might have laughed. Luke, the tough one, was holding a porcelain teacup. Who would have thought?

After inhaling the scent of the fluid several times, Luke, brought the cup to his lips and chugged the tea as fast as he could, probably burning his tongue in the process.

The sides of Melinda's lips twitched. "There you go. You won't smell of animal as much."

Luke didn't say anything.

Surprisingly, Shane took the word. "Thanks, Mel. I owe you one."

"You don't intend on leaving now, do you Shane?" said Melinda. She inclined her head to the right, toward me. "We have so many things to talk about…"

Shane's lips were tight. "There's nothing to talk about."

"I'm sure there are plenty of things to talk about." Melinda crossed her legs at the knees and folded her hands over her thighs. "Do you like stories, Abby?"

"I guess?" I didn't know what kind of stories Melinda intended to tell but I had a feeling that we didn't have a choice, but to listen to her if we didn't want Shane to lose his head and other things.

Shane made a face of disdain. "Mel, I really don't think—"

"Oh, Shane Honey, please. I was just going to tell her a bit of our past, that's all."

"*Our* past?"

"Don't be so self-centered Shane," said the witch, in what sounded like a mother's scolding voice. "I mean the Nightrealmer past."

"Abby already has a book about the matter. I prefer she read true facts, not twisted-truth fairytales."

"Ugh!" The witch frowned deeply. Then her face brightened. "Ah, I know. Why don't we play with the Faiths?" she said, her voice echoing through the luxurious apartment.

Gabe's eyes widened but he didn't say anything. Shane's jaw was tight. "No," he said, his tone impassive.

"You said you owed me one," replied Melinda, "and you know how I tend to get when I don't get what I want."

For a moment, there was a deadly silence. Shane looked like he would kill someone just by looking at them. When the witch didn't do as much as budge, Shane gave in.

"Great!" exclaimed Melinda. She clapped her hands and the cup in her hands disappeared, as did the rest of the tea set. They were replaced by what looked like tarot cards. Melinda, with one swift movement of the hand, swept the cards in a straight line.

"Pick three cards," she said. "Any cards."

I flashed a looked at Shane, who nodded. He was the first one to pick his cards. Shane handed them over to Melinda. She looked at the cards and placed them on the table, so that everyone could see.

"Hmm. ..." The witch was concentrating hard, all her focus on the cards Shane had picked. She put a finger on the first one. "The lovers. Not necessarily my favorite card."

I was surprised that Luke didn't say anything smart-ass-like. "The lovers aren't what they seem. They may both be different paths, one that you will have to choose. A struggle between both paths," explained Melinda. She looked at the second card. "You are the leader, the boss but this means that all the responsibilities and burdens are on your shoulders."

Everyone looked at the last card. "Ace of Cups. I'm sure you know what this means, right Shane?"

I looked at Shane. He didn't meet my eyes but he nodded at Melinda's question.

"Gabe, it's your turn," said Melinda.

Gabe shook his head. "I don't want to know," he answered, his voice tight and firm. Something told me that he had already had a bad experience with tarot cards.

"Luke?"

Luke looked at Melinda. "All right." He picked up three cards from the batch and handed them to the witch.

Melinda smiled. She deposited them on the coffee table and said, "Six of Cups, known joy. You feel nostalgia for something or someone. You long for someone." She put her index on the second card. "The Tower—a loss, a major turning point in your life." She grinned at the last card. "Five of Wands—more competition or just stronger competition will make it harder for you to obtain what you want."

The witch turned to look at me. Funny how someone who looked younger than I did knew more than I did. "Pick three cards, Abby."

FIFTEEN

Before we had left Melinda's apartment, the witch had invited us to a Nightrealmer party taking place in downtown Boston. She'd said one of her old vampire buddies was going to celebrate his five hundred sixty-seventh birthday. Shane had said we'd think about it.

Ya but who were 'we'? I had thought. He was the one who was gonna decide, right? We had no say in this? His kiss-my-ass attitude was really putting a toll on me, big time.

I wanted to drive the Ghost. At first I had been scared of height— and still was—but now I wanted to show Shane that he was *not* in control. He was only losing control. *Leader, my eye.*

"Okay," he said once we were in the air. I hadn't had difficulty starting the engine or getting it airborne. "You know how to fly but can you land?"

"I'll figure something out," I grumbled in my helmet, accelerating. I looked in the rearview mirrors and saw nothing but purplish smoke. I didn't really know where I was headed but Shane didn't say anything about that. I hoped we were headed toward Boston or somewhere in that area.

Yeah, I thought dryly. *They're geniuses but how can they navigate over clouds when they don't have a built-in compass?*

"So what else should I know about the royal families?" I asked. I wasn't in the mood to listen to nothing and I doubted that this Ghost had a built-in radio system. Such great engineers they were!

"You don't want to mess with them. They're nasty," answered Shane, his voice a bit edgy. "One advantage humans have over us is that they don't really stick much to drastic traditions."

"Christmas is a tradition. You know, the day of the year when you receive *presents* from the big red man?"

"Christmas is a happy holiday passed down to new generations. What I meant by drastic traditions was that they still believe in what they believed over a thousand years ago."

"What's wrong about beliefs?" I asked into the speaker. "Christianity has been around for more than—"

"I know, I know," interrupted Shane, "but that's not what I meant. Abby, they still believe that the Old Ways are best."

"The Old Ways?"

"The penalty for infidelity toward a royal is death. An insult upon a royal might get your tongue cut off. Should I continue?"

"I think you've made your point." I lifted the hem of my coat and shirt and rubbed at my marks. They didn't hurt much anymore but they still felt itchy and sore (if that was even possible, considering it was my skin and not my muscles that were sore). "They still treat royals the way they did back in the Middle Ages?"

"Yeah. That's why I despise them, along with many others." Shane lowered his tone. "For the past hundred years, Nightriders have thought of rebellion more than ever, since the disappearance of the leading royal family, the Moiras."

"Why?"

"They were really a good royal family. Unlike the other royal families, who stayed in their big castles and behind their guards, the Moiras blended in with the average Nightrider and with every choice they took, they asked the Nightriders for council and suggestions, the same mentality as Kristen and Damien have. Turn a bit to your left—ten o'clock."

I did as he said. "I don't get why Kristen and Damien are how they are, so different than the others."

"Because, unlike the other royals, they were raised in the middle of the action, among other Nightriders. Their other siblings though, especially Damien's, are spoiled like you wouldn't believe."

There was a minute of silence. I only had one thing on my mind and it had nothing to do with the royal families.

"You know ... Mel's tarot cards aren't always accurate," said Shane, reading my exact thoughts. "Witches tend to go overboard sometimes with their predictions."

"I don't want to talk about it," I whispered, my voice so light I might as well not have spoken at all.

I had taken three cards. The Strength card.

"*You will have power; that is for certain,*" had said Melinda in a hushed voice, "*but whether you use that power for good or for evil is completely up to you.*"

The Star.

"*You may obtain fresh hope and renewal, healing of old wounds, a mental and physical broadening of horizons, a promise and fulfillment, an inspiration and an influence over others. Or you may obtain the unwillingness or inability to adapt to changing circumstances and accept the opportunities it may bring, lack of trust and self-doubt, obstacles to happiness and a diminished life.*"

Death.

"*The beginning of a new life and as a result of underlying circumstances transformation and change or it can also mean a change that is both painful and unpleasant, a refusal to face the fear of change oneself, agonizing periods of transition.*"

She had looked at me with a small smile on her face, an apologetic one. My gut had twisted in my stomach. This couldn't have been good.

"Why don't you let me take the wheel, huh?"

I shrugged. I might appear nonchalant to him but I really didn't want to do a *switcheroo* more than five hundred feet high in the air.

"All right, I want you to press the blue button at the top right of your screen."

I did as he said and all of a sudden, I was on the passenger side of the Ghost. Had I just teleported? I turned to look at Shane in disbelief.

He was also looking at me over his shoulder. I could see him grinning through the glass of his helmet.

"Advanced technology," he reminded me. I rolled my eyes but couldn't help but grin back.

It was already noon by the time we got to the academy. We parked in the garage and placed all of our equipment back at their places. While Luke went to make several phone calls in the living room and Shane went with Gabe to the kitchen to talk Nightrealm, I went to my bedroom and crashed on the thick covers of my bed.

I reached for the book on my nightstand and brought it to my face. I read the words '*Nightrealm*' written in what looked like gold. I opened the book and started reading the table of contents: Nightriders, Angels, Vampires, Nymphs, Fey, Werewolves, Shapeshifters, Demons, Gods, Lost Elements, Sins, Virtues ... which were all written in Latin, and how I could read them so easily was way past my comprehension.

I wanted to check out Gods and Sins. I opened the page of Gods and started reading. It explained in detail how a handful of angels became more powerful and how they turned out to each have a specific power. I read the list:

Thima, Goddess of Earth
Cairo, God of Wind
Laedin, God of Fire
Talana, Goddess of Water
Kaia, Goddess of Spirit
Kylun, God of War
Adron, God of Time
Cadalyn, Goddess of Love
Xanthius, God of Hatred
Izona, Goddess of Death
Zeric, God of Life

Twelve gods, all with different specialties. I wasn't really sure if I wanted to meet Izona and Xanthius. Laedin didn't seem too nice either. I flipped the pages to Sins.

What I saw was not what I had expected.

'*Sins are supernatural beings who take refuge in humans or even sometimes Nightrider bodies. The human or Nightrider who lodges a Sin is immediately affected. Although these sins live in every living being, the feeling and actions of the humans or Nightriders are intensified by a hundred. They are literally under the control of the Sin. The Sins change bodies whenever they choose to, but once gone from the human body, part of the sin remains and keeps its effect. Never do I wish someone to fall under the power of these following sins:*

Wrath
Sloth
Gluttony
Greed
Lust
Envy
Vanity

'*They are also called the seven deadly sins. Each and every one of them may one day kill you. You have been warned.*'

I closed the book, afraid that a Sin might jump out of it at any second.

ʘ•∽

I eventually fell asleep with my clothes still on, after opening the bathroom light. I had never really been scared of the dark for at least the past six years of my life but now, with all I had learned and seen, I knew better than not to be frightened.

It was a distant voice that woke me up. It was calling my name and telling me to wake up. At first I had thought it had been Mary's but as the mist of my sleep faded away, I noted that the tone was far too low for it to be my little sister's.

I opened my eyes and found myself looking at the silhouette of a boy, Luke's, to be more exact.

"Gabe told me to go wake you up," he said, his voice too loud for the half-darkness of the room. "The new Nightrider recruits just came in about five minutes ago."

"What?" I exclaimed, jumping up and accidentally hitting Luke's forehead with mine. "Sorry," I said, moving away from him and off the bed. "Did you see what they looked like?"

Luke nodded. "Almost all had something black on them, not Goth-kind of black but *black*." Right, like that made any more sense. "Apart from that, they looked normal. All of 'em had duffel bags."

I took a deep breath. What should I do? Go downstairs and greet everyone or stay here and wait for them to settle down? I didn't really want to see them right now... How would I ever remember all of their names? How many were they? Fifty? Hundred? Thousand? I wasn't sure I wanted to know.

"Were there a lot?" I asked.

"I'd say around thirty... I'm not completely sure, though," answered Luke.

Why hadn't I read about Nightriders instead? I thought. I don't know what to look out for...

❧ ❧

SHANE

I was waiting for them downstairs. The Nightriders had slowly gone to their assigned rooms. They went off in pairs of two and only four were left. Gabe, Dimitri, Connor and myself.

Dimitri was about three years older than I was. We had met at one of my old academies in Russia. We had been what I had once thought of as best friends, but when I had met Gabe, Damien and Kristen a few years later, my point of view had completely changed. Now I looked at the tall brown-haired Nightrider and could only nod. His green eyes pierced mine and I could tell that he had seen a lot since the last time we had seen each other. I faintly remembered how they used to shine with happiness and friendliness. They were all but friendly at the moment. He had every reason to be bitter. Since I had last seen him, he'd lost his hand in battle, and had recently lost his younger sister. His hand had been replaced by a metallic one, and his sister had been replaced with nothing but emptiness.

Connor was very different from Dimitri Petrovski. He had light brown hair and dull brown eyes. I could see right off the bat that he was nothing but trouble. He was lighter than Dimitri was and joked more, but I wasn't fooled. Connor was dangerous. He was a flirt.

"How was Montreal?" asked Gabe.

Dimitri shrugged. "The people there were very warm, nice people, aggressive drivers. Their English there is horrible. Their French is much too fast and pretty complicated too."

"We ate something quite good," added Connor, grinning and passing a hand through his hair. "I believe it was called *poutine...* I'm no' sure." He looked at Dimitri. "What's a '*roteux*'?"

"A hot-dog," answered Dimitri bluntly.

"Anyway," continued Connor, "where we stayed was verra nice. Everything was nice, except..."

"The bill," finished Dimitri. "So many taxes! But not as bad as France. "

"And Ukraine?" said Gabe, leaning on one of the sofas.

"Cold," said Connor at the same time as Dimitri said, "Warm."

Connor gave Dimitri a look. "Ye Russians are so ... cold-blooded."

"And you Scots are so annoying," replied Dimitri without hesitation.

Connor shot him a murderous look. "Ye talk another time insult of my country and I will cut off yer—" His eyes darted across the room behind my shoulder. He frowned and kept looking at what he was looking at.

I turned around and saw Abby and the dog opening the door from the stairs. My heart skipped a beat. What if Melinda had lied to us and had only given them normal tea? What if Connor and Dimitri sensed their abnormality?

Abby walked up next to me and gave me a nervous smile. It was clear that she had slept; there were still pillow marks on her left cheek but I didn't tell her anything about it. The dog had a smug look on his face and I couldn't help but notice it.

"Abby," said Gabe, smiling at her. *At least he didn't have a smug look on his face,* I thought sourly, *or I would have an urge to punch him too.* "This is Dimitri Petrovski." He gestured to the Russian with an inclination of the head. Dimitri nodded at her and she returned the gesture. Gabe turned toward Connor. "And this is—"

"Connor McFarlane," shot in the scot. He took Abby's hand in his, slightly bowed and slowly brought it to his lips. He looked up and smiled at her. "I was looking forward to meeting the latest Night recruit."

Abby smiled back, her cheeks slowly turning pink. Connor gently pulled back, still smiling. "And this is Luke," said Gabe.

Connor looked him up and down, as if sizing him up. Dimitri did the same, except he analyzed the air through his nostrils. If I hadn't been a Nightrider, I wouldn't have noticed the longer intake of air and the hint of narrowing eyes.

After fifteen seconds or so of silence, I asked if they had seen Kristen or Damien when they had stopped by Eldoras.

Connor nodded. "Damien wasna verra happy to see us."

"He was not happy to see you, that's all," corrected Dimitri, his face blank from any emotion. I had to admit that I admired him for that. Being able to conceal your feelings from others was important, for personal and professional reasons.

The scot grinned and scratched the back of his head. "I guess the lad has his reasons."

No one said anything. At the corner of my eye, I could see the dog shifting his weight and saw Abby wince when she touched her belly. When I turned to look at her, she gave me a forced smile.

The shifter moved closer to Abby and said, "Well, we'll let you guys settle down alone. You comin', Abs?"

She frowned but nodded. The shifter took her hand and slowly tugged her away from us and out of the door. What the hell had that been about? I muttered an excuse, got my jacket and followed them out.

They were already past the front gate when I caught up to them. "Where do you think you're going?"

Both turned to look at me. Abby still had the shadow of a frown on her forehead and the shifter seemed to be ready for a fight.

"Where we're going ain't your business," replied the dog. I could swear that I heard a challenge in his voice. I was about to take him up on his offer when of course…

"Guys, please calm down," said Abby, her voice weak. Although she had slept a long nap of at least five hours, she looked so tired. She was pale and her lower lip was lightly trembling.

"I really don't think it's a good idea," I insisted, more gently this time. "I don't like the idea of you like this, going out, at *night* on top of that."

"Shane… nothing can go wrong. I'm with Luke…"

"Abby, no," I said firmly. "It's not safe. It would be stupid to go out now and especially when you're obviously sick."

"I am not sick!" exclaimed Abby. I noticed the color returning to her cheeks. "I am perfectly fine and if you think you can tell me what to do and what not to do, well then you're wrong."

I had pissed her off. Good. Let her be pissed off. It was good for her mental state. It would also be better for me now that I'd seen her angry. Calm and soothing wasn't always good.

I sighed. I knew Abby wouldn't budge (God only knew how thick her head was) but I knew someone who would. Not really wanting to do this but doing it because I had to, I mentally reached out for the shifter's mind and said, *Where do you want to take her?*

I was looking intently at the shifter, whose eyes widened once I sent the message. He looked at me and made a snarling gesture.

Get the fuck outta my brain, Night, sent out the dog. *I don't want you messin' around with me.*

I rolled my eyes. *I just want to know where you guys are going.*

When the shifter realized that I wasn't going to let it go, he answered, *We're going to the mall. We're gonna meet up with Kait and Britt.*

Going to the mall? How creative of you.

Shut up. It ain't easy to get three girls someplace without one of them knowing what's goin' on. Girls like Abby are very hard to manage.

Tell me about it, I thought. *She can be very hard to convince. Almost as thickheaded as you.*

I can say the same for you, bug.

I wouldn't talk if I were you, dog.

We glared at each other. My fist was itching to punch the shifter in the face but that would only get Abby mad and God knew what she would do to me. I shoved my hands into my pockets and shrugged.

"You guys can go," I said frankly. Abby's face lit up and the dog's jaw relaxed. They almost looked *happy*. I was far too nice to let them look like that. "*If* I come with."

The shifter's jaw clenched again but Abby's good mood didn't seem to fade one bit. She almost jumped with joy. *Wow*, I thought, *it's easy to make* her *happy*.

"All right!" she exclaimed. I could almost see her happy glow affecting me. I found it pleasant until I found it strange. Hadn't she been death pale only minutes ago? Obviously, the shifter had noticed it too and exchanged a quick glance with me.

The shifter took Abby's arm in his and led her away. I followed them, letting them have several feet of distance. So they could feel less heard. *Less heard, my ass*, I thought. The only privacy they're gonna get is when I croak, in my case, when I get killed by a demon.

"Where are we going?" asked Abby, leaning a bit on the shapeshifter.

"You'll see," he answered. "It's a surprise."

"Is it a surprise that I'm gonna regret?"

"No. I think you'll quite enjoy it actually."

Abby shrugged and yawned. "Do you think we can get coffee on the way? I'm a bit tired."

Even from behind, I could see her happy glow slowly fading. It wasn't natural. Maybe it was Mel's potion that was giving her side effects. Instead of making a mental note to call her for that, I took my phone out of my pocket and dialed her number. I had used it so many times to tell her to stop sending me explosive teddy bears that I already knew it by heart.

She picked up at the third ring. Typical Melinda this. "Hello, Shane Honey," I heard her say. I tensed at the nickname she was giving me. I had told her so many times not to call me that. "Want to make out?"

I rolled my eyes. She would never change. "No."

"Oh, well… I suppose you're calling for information about the tea I gave Abby and Luke." Before I could say yes and ask about the side effects, Melinda continued, "Yes, they're what you call side effects. They should fade away in a few hours or so. I would even say now, considering it was several hours ago that they took it. Mood swings are what you should expect."

"Thanks, he muttered. "And Mel…"

"Hmm?"

I forced myself to say the words I had been wanting to say this afternoon. "I'm s—" But she had already hung up.

SIXTEEN

ABBY

"The mall?" I asked, surprised as we took the bus stop right in front of Cambridge Center.

Luke grinned. "Yup."

Shane was just behind us looking at the mall with what looked like pure disgust. When he saw me looking, he said, "Do we have to?"

I let out a laugh. *Guys*. So grossed out with the thought of entering a mall or having to look in a girl's purse, which, I thought with dread, was at my house, probably infected with demon plague or something.

"Why are we here?" I asked Luke, who was looking up at the top of the building, or rather at the big flashing sign that read: Cambridge Center. "You feel like buying yourself a new wardrobe?"

He shook his head and smiled. "You'll see," he answered.

Luke opened the glass door for me. I walked in and looked around. It was seven o'clock and the mall was still crowded. Not as much as on a Saturday but still considerably full. The nearest stores radiated different types of radio stations or CDs. From one side, I heard the song *'Morning After Dark'* from Timbaland and from the other side came *'Strip Me,'* from Natasha Bedingfield.

Last time I had come here was with Kaithlyn and Brittany, last summer. We had gone to this trendy new store for bathing suits. Brittany had bought a cute summer hat, Kaithlyn had bought me a hot pink bikini and I had gotten her *Dolce & Gabbana* glasses, which were probably fake 'cause they had cost me only ten bucks.

As we walked to where I didn't know, I noticed a group of girls who were eyeing Luke, who was on my right and Shane, who was on my left. They gave both boys dreamy looks and hateful looks to me. I felt protected with two, tough guys at my sides but I didn't feel safe from the girls. If they were to attack me right now, Luke would go get popcorn and Shane would be unsure what to do. I smiled to myself when I played the scene in my head.

I edged closer to Luke. "They're gonna kill me," I whispered.

His eyes widened and he tensed, but when he saw that I was talking about the girls, he eased back and grinned. "'S'called charm, Abs. Charm."

I rolled my eyes. He was far too proud. "Charm, my eye." He eyed me innocently and I *tsk*ed.

It was only a few minutes later that I noticed that we were heading for the food court. "Are you hungry?" I asked. "You brought me all the way to Cambridge to eat?"

"C'mon, I'm not that cheap," replied Luke. "On second thought, I am, so why don't you guys go get a table."

Before I could agree, Luke walked away. I sighed and turned to look at Shane, who was watching me intently. I frowned at him and headed toward a table for four. I sat down on a cushioned seat and looked at the little restaurants here and there; the neon signs flashed brightly. I looked up at the ceiling and then looked back down at Shane, who had sat down right in front of me.

"Are you okay?" he asked.

"Yeah, why wouldn't I be?" I answered. I gave him a smile to look more convincing. "What about you?"

He shrugged. "I'm not sure I like the idea of new Nightriders in the academy."

"You're afraid that they might find out about the Elements?"

"That, and you."

"Me?" I laughed. "What about me?"

"I still don't know what you are."

I stayed silent at that. After a while, I said, "I'm a cashier at Porter's?"

At that, he laughed. "Yeah, I suppose you are."

I grinned at him. It faded, thought, when I said, "Do you think we'll know what's going on with Mary and Mrs. Wildfire?"

Shane sighed. "The letter said that we had to hand in the Lost Element that we had but that would mean ..."

"That we'd have to give me in," I whispered, realizing that I was the object of trade. I was why Mary had been kidnapped... I was the reason for everything that was going. *Oh my God*, I thought. *They'll want to kill me.*

"Abby."

I looked up and locked eyes with Shane. I hadn't noticed it at first but now I felt the warmth of his hand on mine. My vision was getting blurry. The guilt and melancholy was ripping at me, but through my tears, I could see the meaningful look on his face, his eyes not leaving mine.

"I'm not going to let anything happen to you—never."

Before I could say anything, he let go of my hand and smiled at someone behind me. I turned around. My tears were hastily swallowed back and I jumped with joy.

My arms were around their necks in mere seconds. I squeezed them hard and laughed. Kaithlyn hugged me and so did Brittany. It was only when Kait said I was choking them that I let go.

"Wow," I said, sitting back down with Britt next to me and Kait next to Shane. "What a coincidence."

"Coincidence?" said Brittany, laughing. "Luke told us to come. He didn't say why."

"Luke?" I asked, frowning. I looked at Shane, who simply shrugged. "Luke told you guys to come?"

"Yeah. Where have you two been? *Alaska?*" said Kaithlyn, leaning back in her chair. "Probably heating each other up."

Brittany shook her head. "I think they would've been doing more than heating each other up Kait."

"You're right," admitted Kaithlyn, grinning at me foolishly. "So, anyway, where have you two been? And who are *you?*" she asked, looking at Shane.

He handed her his hand and she shook it. "Shane McKenna. I'm a friend of Abby's."

"Kaithlyn Porter but people just call me Kait," responded her friend, smiling at Shane. She was looking at him, his face, his chest... *Every girl's dream, or what?* I thought dryly.

"And I'm Brittany Hart. My friends call *me* Britt," said my other friend, handing her hand to Shane, who let go of Kait's hand to take Brittany's. She smiled.

I rolled my eyes. These girls were totally love struck. Like I'd once been for many guys but not Shane. I couldn't have been love struck with Shane... it was impossible. I was with Luke.

"Where'd you guys meet?" asked Kaithlyn, suddenly eyeing Shane suspiciously. I frowned. Hadn't she been love struck only seconds ago?

Shane looked at Abby. "Uh... at Porter's?"

I nodded. "Yeah. Shane was my customer."

"Are you guys dating?" asked Brittany, grinning at me. I rolled my eyes.

"No, we're not," answered Shane, his voice as thick and hard as what I imagined cement might sound like, that is, if it could talk. "We just found out that we're very distant cousins."

My eyes widened. I knew he had to make up a good excuse but that was just pushing it too far.

"Really?" said Brittany. "I thought Abby was an orphan."

Now it was Shane who was surprised by the new revelation. "Isn't Jane you mother?" he asked.

He had to be kidding, right? After all that had happened it had to be *impossible* for him not to know one of the most important things about me.

"She's my adoptive mother, not ... *mother-mother,*" I answered.

"Wow. You two really need to talk more often," noted Brittany, almost as surprised as me that Shane didn't know about me being an orphan.

I hadn't given being an orphan much thought before. I had all the love and support as any kid with parents. I loved Jane like a real mother and Mary like my real sister. I didn't need anyone else in my life … but now that I thought of it, my origins did twinkle my interest. I would have to talk about it with Shane sooner or later. Maybe we could find out a few things by looking in birth records or some other documentation that might be helpful.

"Abby," said Kaithlyn, "we haven't been able to contact you for the past four days. We called your house but it went straight to voicemail and so did your cell…"

I thought of a quick excuse and leaned on my right side, a little bit closer to Kaithlyn. "Jane brought Mary and me to New York for three days. It was a surprise, so I didn't get the chance to call you…"

"You went to *New York City* and you didn't tell us before?" squealed Kaithlyn. "What did you do?"

I gave Shane a quick look. "We went to take a walk in Central Park, we went to watch a movie, we uh… what else? We went window-shopping…"

"Did you buy anything?" asked Brittany, her eyes shining. Brittany, I remembered, had gone to New York City once, for three days and she hadn't stopped talking about it for a week. "Please tell me you got a cute cocktail dress. I am *sooooo* borrowing it from you."

I grinned and scratched the back of my head. How the hell was I going to get out of this one? "Uh, sure."

"Yessss!" exclaimed Brittany, who almost jumped out of her seat.

"Did you see any celebrities?" said Kaithlyn. "I heard Enrique Iglesias was in town."

"Really? I didn't get to see him. Bugger."

"Did you go to a club?"

"Heavy duty bouncers. No fake ID."

"Meet any cute guys?"

"As crazy as it seems, no."

"Did you get attacked?"

"Thankfully, no."

"Then what the hell did you do for three days?"

I heaved a sigh. This lie was costing me so much. Before I could answer that last question, Luke came with boxes of takeout Chinese food. He brought an empty chair with his foot and set it between Brittany and Kaithlyn.

"So ..." started Brittany when Luke was seated next to me, "how's life?"

"Oh, you know ... the usual," replied Luke, grinning at her. He shoved a box under her nose. "Your favorite."

"General Thai?" she asked.

He nodded.

"Isn't it General Tao?" I asked, accepting the box Luke slid across the table. "Thanks."

"Yeah, that's it," agreed Kaithlyn, opening her box. "Good thing I didn't eat. This smells delicious."

"Luke? Did you know that Abby went to New York-New York and didn't get mugged?" asked Brittany, playing a little bit with her food. Probably pushing the vegetables away, I thought.

Luke looked at me. "No, I didn't. When was that?"

"Last weekend." I opened the carton and let the steam make my fingertips wet. Yum, chow mein.

"Huh." Luke took chopsticks from the plastic bag he had carried the boxes with and brought them to his lips. Chop suey, I noted.

It was only when I was halfway through my box, that I noticed that Shane had nothing. I looked down at my food, my stomach satisfied with what I had eaten. I leaned across the table and put the rest of the chow mein right under his nose.

He looked up and raised his eyebrows. "I'm not hungry anymore," I said, grinning. "I ate all the veggies and noodles."

Shane took the box from my hand, "You left out the best part—meat."

I rolled my eyes. He laughed. My heart skipped a beat. Shane laughed so little, that when he did, my heart filled with joy, which was weird, 'cause I wasn't supposed to feel this way. I had a boyfriend for crying out loud!

"... have you been?" suddenly asked Brittany to Luke. "I haven't seen you anywhere at school today. You missed PE."

"PE is the least of my worries," said Luke, motioning to his upper body. Brittany rolled her eyes. "Ditched school. I had things to take care of at home."

҂๑ ๑҂

SHANE

I finished the remnants of Abby's chow mein. How could she have left all that meat? She was crazy for not liking stir-fried chicken, although I had to admit that I preferred beef. I had taken the plastic fork she had used because there was no other left. I was sure if I hadn't been Abby's 'cousin,' Kaithlyn Porter and Brittany Hart would have given me sideway looks. Dirty guy, they would have thought, which in some ways, I guess I was.

I unfolded the box, so that it was flat and threw it in the air. If I hadn't been a trained Nightrider, the box, or in this case, the flattened box, wouldn't have gone in the recycling bin. It went in, slicing through the air. *Score!*

"Do you want me to give you all the work you missed out on Monday?" asked Kaithlyn to Abby. She was a long-legged redhead a little taller than Abby. I got a weird vibe from her. She was probably one of those witches who stayed in the dark or something. I sure as hell wasn't going to be the one to get her out of her hole. I had enough people to worry about and one that counted for at least ten.

I saw the littlest hint of hesitation on Abby's part at the question but it lasted for only a millisecond. "Yeah, sure. Jane called the school to let them know I would miss a couple of days, but she forgot to ask for my homework." I grinned, proud of her quick thinking.

As Kaithlyn gave a long list of homework for Abby and Brittany gave a smaller list to the shifter, my eyes swept the perimeter. No demons here. That is, if you didn't count the mutt that was sitting only a mere two seats away from me.

I was about to loosen up when a strange smell caught my nostrils. I tensed all over and went on danger mode. Maybe I couldn't see those damn demons but I sure could smell their foul stench all the way over here.

I got up gently so I didn't worry anyone. "Abby, we have to go."

Abby read the alerted look I had on my face and she made up an excuse to her friends and followed me off the food court. The dog had a worried frown on his face, but he stayed back with the two girls not to have them worrying. When we were out of hearing range, she asked, "What's wrong?"

"Demons," I answered, "a whole bunch of them."

Her eyes grew more alert and she got closer to me. "Ghouls?"

"I'm not sure," I admitted. The scent could belong to any demon.

We speed-walked, passing shops fast. Everyone seemed to be looking at us, as though we were going to kill them. I had the feeling of being constantly watched, as if one false move would get us killed.

I had the cold and unwanted feeling in my stomach. This wasn't good, really not good. "Shit," I muttered under my breath. I put my arm around Abby and made us go inside a Sears. It should be easy to lose them in there.

Lose who? was the question that I kept asking myself. I sensed a demon aura from behind us and from our left. I motioned for Abby to duck into women's wear. I put a finger to my lips when she was about to say something.

We passed through the women's department and ran into the men's. When I was sure that we were far enough from whatever was chasing us, I crouched down and turned to look at Abby, who had done the same.

"You see that exit over there?" I whispered. Abby looked at where I was looking and nodded. "I want you to walk to it when I tell you to. Get out without looking too suspicious."

"What about you?" she whispered back, biting her lower lip afterward, probably trying to make the shaking of her lower lip stop.

"I'll have your back." I reached into the inner-pocket of my jacket. "Here." I handed her a dipped in silver dagger.

She took it in her hand and looked at it with what looked like terror and amazement. After staring at it for five seconds exactly, she slid the hilt into her sleeve; the blade had only an inch of visibility.

"Go," I said. Just before she got up, I added, "And Abby ... try not to get killed."

She flashed me a grin and left. I watched her go and scanned the surroundings. There was a large woman trying on shoes, a thirteen year old checking out bras and, bingo, a tall man dressed in a black duster and shades heading for Abby.

I was a bit more worried than before. This was no demon. This was a vampire and he was following Abby. This could *not* be good.

Abby didn't look at him and she kept on going as if nothing were wrong. I had to admit that she looked pretty convincing. When the man was fifteen feet away from her, I jumped up and gracefully, through the racks of clothes, got behind the man. Abby was now out of the store and so was the man. I followed them out.

It had started drizzling outside. The sky was pitch black and there weren't many lights illuminating the almost empty parking lot. Abby wove herself though the several cars here and there and kept going. She had probably seen the man by now and was maybe just making sure that she was being followed.

Yeah but the problem was that she was heading straight into a bad neighborhood, which most probably contained street gangs and rabid infected dogs. Ugh. Had I told her to go far? *No,* but she did it anyway... Ah man, this girl was going to be the death of me...

She made a turn left and then another left and then a right. I was still following them, downwind from the vamp, so he couldn't smell me. I had small but big enough to be significant, doubts that we might both make it alive. It's not that I couldn't take one demon on. On the contrary, I was sure I would be fine up against five and maybe even ten demons, but when I had been in the store, I had felt many demon auras and they had been strong.

I was about to yell to Abby to make a run for it and tackle the vamp, when I saw she was leading us straight into a dead end.

The demon had her cornered, or she had gotten herself cornered, whatever. This was bad. The hair at the back of my neck rose when I smelled a bunch of demons behind us.

In cases like these, I made fast mental lists of what had to be done before I most likely got executed:

Kill the demon that had started it all.

Get to Abby.

I tried to think of another one. *Nothing.* I could maybe throw her at the top of the building but then the demons would only jump after her... *Merda.*

I was already high on adrenaline, so I didn't have to push myself off hard to start. I was on the demon's back in merely a second. He was a little taller than I was, so I really had to kick myself off the ground hard, so that the demon could fall forward, probably ruining his face in the process. I had an arm around the demon's neck, squeezing the lights out of the guy. I reached for a switch-sword attached to my belt. I pressed the blue button on the hilt and a silver-and-gold blade flashed out.

The demon was struggling, very hard and with a strength that had me worrying. When I saw the flash of sharp, white teeth, I knew that he was about to bite me. Just when I was about to get thrown off by the vampire, with a fast and precise strike, I sliced the demon through the heart. The vamp's eyes widened and he let out a loud and ear-piercing shriek when he became nothing but dust.

Numero uno, check.

Not stopping to tap myself on the shoulder for my small victory, I got up on my feet and moved toward Abby. She was shaking from head to toe, staring at the other vamps behind us, who were staying a good twenty feet away from us. They knew we had no escape, so they took their time.

"Why'd you bring us here?" I asked through my teeth, my eyes not leaving the unwanted crowd about fifteen feet away from us now.

"There's a—"

She never got to finish her sentence. I heard a loud roar from behind the vampires that had been following us. If this was a monster and he was on the opposite side...

Think, Shane, *think.*

While the vamps turned to look at what had claimed their attention, I looked everywhere at once. There was a window and it was open. Twenty feet in the air and too close to the enemy, I thought, which were approximately twenty or so. There were dirty boxes behind us and a big trashcan, which Abby seemed to be desperate to move.

"What are you doing?" I hissed. "This is not the time to—"

"We have to move the trashcan." When I was about to ask why, she said, "Don't ask. Just do it!"

With one hand, I lifted the trashcan and threw it on empty boxes, which, lucky us, got the vamps' attentions. Four moved in on us, their faces very expressive. One showed bloodlust, the other reflected hunger, one was licking his lips and the other one seemed to be ogling Abby. Oh, that one was in *so* much trouble.

They were fast but so was I. I was actually much faster than the average Nightrider, so they were surprised when I reached them in the blink of an eye. I cut the closest one's throat and the head fell off, rolling awkwardly away. The body fell backward and I saw blood pouring out of the throat. The vamp had a black tattoo on his neck and it seemed familiar to me. Had I seen that design before? Before I could examine it more closely, the vamp's body disintegrated into dust.

The other three vamps were already ready for a fight when I faced them. One with red hair bared his teeth and lunged at me. I raised my sword quickly and since the vamp had been going fast toward me, the vamp sliced his hand. Blood poured out like a mini-stream but even a second after, I could see that the wound was already closing. Damn bloodsuckers.

The vamp cried out in rage and lunged again, not paying attention to his hand. This time he dodged the sword and hit my wrist so hard that the switch-sword slipped out if my grip. Before I could rapidly crouch down and get my weapon back, the vampire jumped on me, propelling both of us against a cement wall. My head hit the cement—*hard.* My vision got red for a second. I blinked several times and when I got my bearings back, I saw the angry vamp holding the collar of my shirt. Without thinking, I hit the demon's face with my forehead and before the vamp could recover, kneed him in between the legs. The vamp let go of me and doubled over. I punched him in the face with a force that surprised even me. The vamp fell backward. I took the opportunity and grabbed for my sword on the ground and pushed the weapon in the thing's heart. Eat my *dust*, I thought.

I zoomed in Abby's direction. Two vamps had her up against the wall. Her eyes were panicked but otherwise, the set of her jaw and body were calm. Why were all these vamps guys? I asked myself. It would have been so much easier if they had been girls... Not that I was sexist or anything... Okay. I was.

I stopped dead in my tracks when I saw Abby putting her arms around the vamp that had been checking her out. *Merda*, she was being compelled by that bloodsucking son of a bitch!

Vowing I was gonna stake that bastard if he took advantage of her, I ran forward to where they were, but the second vampire had heard me and showed me some teeth. I mentally showed the middle finger, crouched down and cut the very tall vamp's legs. He fell to his knees (or what was left, anyway) and said:

"You know that the girl won't live to see the next full moon, right?"

I hesitated before driving my switch-sword through his heart. I could have tortured him for answers but the beast roared and, God knew why, was killing the group of vamps. I still couldn't see it but I knew that it had to be powerful. Killing that many vamps one by one and still going on: that was a big feat. Then there was the untrained girl, named Abby...

Who had her face only inches away from the vamp. He had his hands all over her and she didn't seem to mind. I was frozen in place. I knew I should be kicking the guy's ass but I couldn't help staring.

When the guy would be kissing her, I would stake him from behind, taking him by surprise. I knew that was what an experienced Nightrider would do. It was a good technique, very good but I was Shane and she was Abby.

I braced myself to lunge, when Abby put both hands on either side of the bum's head ... and gave him a hard head-butt. The vamp stepped back and put both his hands to his forehead.

"You stupid bitch," he hissed, coiling his muscles to spring, "you're gonna regret that."

I took my chance and killed him. I had wanted to give him a long, slow and painful death but I didn't have the time or the luxury to do so. Dust was all that was left. I spit in it.

"Ow," muttered Abby, a hand to her forehead. "That hurt."

"Are you all right?" I asked, looking her up and down for any noticeable wound. I saw none. Before she could give me an answer, I said, "What the hell were you thinking? Are you nuts? You could have gotten killed!" I glanced down and saw that she had dropped her dagger. I picked it up and slipped it in my boot. "You could've used it, you know."

She was about to say something when I added, more calmly this time, "Do you have a plan?" I whipped up my head and looked at the decreasing number of vamps. They were still ten (and yes, there was a woman or two) and I could clearly see the beast now. It was a white tiger. Its fur was matted with vamp blood and street filth. I didn't look away. "What was up with the trashcan?"

Abby didn't answer me. I frowned when I saw that she was kneeling on the ground lifting a heavy sewer lid. I crouched next to her and together we pulled the lid off. The rim of the entrance to the sewer was golden and silver. She was a pure *genius*. Why hadn't I thought of that?

I heard rushing water from below. I would never have thought of that, I admitted to myself. Of course, I would never tell *her* that.

Instead of finishing off the last seven vamps, the tiger ran... straight toward us. I was about to push Abby into the hole if I had to, but the expression on her face stopped me.

"Luke," she whispered.

SEVENTEEN

ABBY

As the tiger ran closer and closer to us, I saw yellow eyes looking straight at me. I *knew* it was a shapeshifter, and I was sure that it was Luke. The feeling was strange but at the same time pleasant. Strange because it had never occurred before and pleasant because we might actually make it out of this *alive*.

Luke jumped into the air. Shane moved in front of me, as if protecting me from the lunging tiger. I closed my eyes when I thought Luke was going to land on Shane when ... nothing. I opened my eyes and saw Shane... with a bird right in front of his face, a little blue and green hummingbird. It flew around Shane's head and onto my shoulder.

Before I had time to say something to our savior, Shane took me beneath the shoulders and dropped me into the sewer. I was too surprised to scream. I landed neatly on my feet, which surprised me even more and moved out of the way so that Shane could easily slide inside and close the lid.

"That should slow 'em down," he breathed. I couldn't see him inside this dark, dirty sewer. "C'mon, let's move."

He started moving and so did I, only I fell to the ground. I saw the outline of his body facing mine and an extended hand. I took it.

"I can't see," I admitted.

"Good, 'cause then you'd be freaking out with all the rats in here."

"Rrrrattts?" I asked, getting closer to Shane.

"Yup. Big, fat, teethy, disgusting, bone-chewing rats."

"Shut up," I muttered. I hated rats more than snakes, spiders, horror movies and my sense of uselessness.

"Nice going, by the way," said Shane.

"Huh?"

"With the silver and golden covered sewer."

"Yeah, well... I had a dog once, when I was like eight or nine and I had wanted to take a walk with him somewhere new. Jane and I had gone to Cambridge Center but animals weren't allowed inside, so I proposed to stay outside with him while she went to get what she needed. She asked me to stay nearby and... I didn't. That's how my dog brought me to the sewer. It was open and I found it strange, the gold and silver there... It was also mentioned in the Nightbook that there were several all of these installed in the larger cities of the world, to be of use to the Nightriders."

"You find several of these in Boston, but only Nightrealmers can see them."

Shane seemed to be cruising us around pretty well. "I'm guessing you've been here before," I noted.

He shrugged. "There was once a cult of demon worshippers. They were hiding in here, so Gabe and I had to track 'em down. I also happen to have a very good photographic memory."

"Why do you think they were after us?" I asked.

He didn't say anything for a moment. "They weren't after *us*, Abby. They were after *you*." I didn't say anything. "And honestly, I don't know. There are so many reasons why you might be followed. It might have been in relation to the prophecy. Maybe they wanted to kill you for *that*. Or someone could have found out about our relation with the Lost Element... It might even have something to do with your unknown origins."

"I don't think my origins have that much importance."

190

"Oh but they do. You might be part nymph, although I think that's very unlikely and they might want to use your powers or you might be a long lost princess... Jeez, I don't know anymore and the blood samples we took from you were... unreadable."

"You took blood samples?" I asked. It shouldn't have surprised me.

"Of course. We had to know what you were. So if you suddenly grew fangs, we would be prepared."

"You say my blood was unreadable?"

Shane didn't answer right away. "It's not that they were unreadable. We found some human cells but that doesn't mean anything. Every Nightrealmer has human blood. The rest of the cells... well, they didn't correspond with vampire ones. That's all. We found some similarities in werewolf cells as well as shapeshifter... but that doesn't mean anything, again. It could just mean that you have the *potential* to shift. Into what, we really don't know."

"By 'we,' you mean you and ..."

"Gabe. He's a whiz with observation."

"You base your hypothesis on what he told you?"

"Yup. Entirely."

This was all so screwed up. I had so many things that were bad and that were concerning me. Heck, when I was being attacked, I didn't even know it was concerning what! There was only one thing I was sure of, the abduction of Mrs. Wildfire and Mary was concerning the Lost Element I had in my possession. I had *in* me! We didn't even know *how*, *where* and to *whom* we had to give me up.

The knot in my stomach I got when I thought of Mary was hurting me so much. What could I do? What could I do? There was no way we could trace whomever had taken them. What was there to do? I swallowed hard—nothing. There was *nothing* we could do.

I tried to get my mind off them. I looked at Shane, who was still holding my hand to keep me from falling.

"I don't get why you broke up with Melinda," I said. This was the best thing I could come up with to take my mind off things. "She looked nice."

"She is," admitted Shane. His voice echoed in the dark and humid enclosed space. "I guess I didn't really know what 'my type' meant back then. She was good-looking and very smart. I was probably just amazed with the fact that she was a beautiful and powerful witch."

"But..."

"But then she started to talk about the future she wanted with me..."

"Ahhh... you got scared."

I heard him snort. "Yeah, I did."

I stifled a chuckle. Shane, afraid of the future he could have had with a (I had to admit) hot witch, but ready to take on an army of demons by himself if he had to.

I almost jumped out of my skin when I felt something warm against my leg. Oh God, there was a rat against my leg. I froze in place. It was clawing at my jeans. When I thought I felt teeth against my leg, I squeaked and wrapped my arms around Shane's shoulders and got my legs around him as well. He almost fell forward in the process but got his balance back pretty quickly. Luke flew off my shoulder, putting himself directly in front of my face, as though making sure I was all right.

"I hate rats." The last words were a whisper coming from my mouth. I didn't let go of Shane until he suggested I go on Luke's back. I was about to protest, saying a tiny bird couldn't possibly carry me when I saw the white tiger from before; this time, its fur was clean black on white. I hadn't noticed him leaving my side to shift.

"We still have a good half hour before we get to the sewer right next to the academy; we can't afford to stop every five minutes for a small rat incident," explained Shane, "and I doubt you'd want to get those nice shoes dirty."

I looked down at my already dirty sneakers. "We're going to have to walk in the water, Abby," he added, and that took care of my decision. I walked to the beautiful feline and caressed its fur. Luke closed his eyes and waggled his tail left to right, in a slow, curve-like manner.

I swung a leg on my boyfriend (which you would feel pretty weird doing if you were in my position. I had already gone on him, piggyback but this felt so much different. He was a freaking tiger for crying out loud!) and passed my fingers through his fur, clutching at it when he started walking.

"What happened back there with the vamp?" asked Shane after a few moments of silence.

"You mean the one that I knocked out with my head?"

"Not really but yeah."

I sighed. "When you got into a brawl with that red-headed vampire, the two left walked in on me. They had me up against the wall and I couldn't get down and pull the lid off the sewer without them seeing me. I thought they were going to kill me..." my voice croaked, "but then I heard this voice in my head... It was telling me to do stuff like seduce him or something. I didn't feel compelled to do it; on the contrary, I wanted to punch him in the face. Then I saw that both vamps frowned when I didn't do what they told me to. So, I did... but thank God, it didn't go that far. I saw you and decided it was a good time to redeem myself. You know ... not being so useless."

Shane didn't say a thing and neither did Luke. I almost laughed. Of course, he couldn't talk. He was a freaking tiger at the moment! "Why can't you change back into your good ol' human self?" I asked the tiger.

"Sure he can, but I don't think he would want to walk around naked and freeze his ass off," answered Shane.

"Oh." I was glad Shane and Luke couldn't see my face, because I was sure I was blushing. "How'd you know that?"

"Angel... I'm a *Nightrider*, not some hooligan on the street! I'm supposed to know this kind of stuff."

"Stuff like how to get a vampire out of his clothes?"

"Yeah. All you have to do is stake 'em through the heart with wood or silver."

"You think you have an answer to everything; am I right?"

"I *have* an answer to everything."

I rolled my eyes. "Sure you do," I muttered under my breath.

"Damn it," said Shane. "They're following us."

He started running, and so did Luke. I tightened my grip on the white tiger's fur and suddenly ducked when a metal bar was gonna hit me on the head. Nice warning, Shane, I thought sourly.

Riding on a tiger was definitely one of the top things I like to do. It almost beat riding a motorcycle at a hundred and fifty miles an hour, if a bike like that even existed.

The half hour turned out to be less than ten minutes. Shane stopped at an old, rusted ladder and climbed up. I heard heavy metal straining against cement. I saw the faint lines of Shane's face.

"Come on up!"

I slid off Luke and watched as he shifted into a little chameleon. He walked on the wet cement and crawled up my jeans. I took him in my hands and placed him on my shoulder. His wet minuscule paws pressed against my skin, tickling me in the process.

I walked to the metal bars and put my hands on two of them. I climbed up after Shane and saw the golden glint on the edge of the sewer's entrance. Shane held out a hand and pulled me out the rest of the way. He lifted the lid and installed it back in its place. There was no one in the street, like usual.

"Let's go inside. Stay hidden," he said to Luke. I felt the little paws creep under the base of my ponytail, which I undid so that he could easily hide under my thick mass of hair.

We got in without being spotted. Instead of taking the stairs, we took the elevator. Shane leaned back and closed his eyes. He looked so worn out it was almost depressing. His jaw was loose and the purple circles under his eyes more prominent than before. His skin was bone-white under the bright light of the elevator. I almost felt sorry for him but I knew he would hate that, so I didn't say anything.

The doors opened with a ding and I walked out with Shane on my heels. We walked down the hallway, passing two or three small groups of Nightriders, who nodded when we passed. I returned the nods.

I stopped at Luke's door (number 102) and opened it. I settled him on his bed. "I'll let you ... do your thing. I'm gonna wash all this dirt off."

Luke nodded or at least what looked like a nod and I left him alone. As I closed the door behind me, I saw Shane sway on his feet.

He put his fingers to his eyes, rubbing his eyelids. "Man, I gotta go to sleep."

"When was the last time you slept?" I asked, leaning against Luke's door.

"Forty-four hours ago? I *think*."

My eyes widened. I had once stayed awake for thirty hours and I hadn't been able to keep myself upright a third of the time. "You really *should* go to sleep."

He gave a short, bitter laugh. "Care to join me?"

My heart skipped a beat. Then I saw the sloppy, half-hearted grin across his face. "It's the lack of sleep talking, right?"

Shane nodded, his eyelids dropping. It seemed to be impossible to open them again. "See ya' t'morrow, whenever that is."

I watched as he walked away, ready to go catch him (or at least try to) if he fell. Older sister instinct, I thought to myself. I walked to my own door and pushed it open. I locked the door behind me and looked at the inviting darkness. The bed looked inviting as well but I didn't really feel like sleeping. It was just my body that was tired.

I felt my way through the darkness and to my bathroom. When I flipped on the lights, I quickly slipped out of my dirty clothes and went under the hot water of the shower. My muscles relaxed and I closed my eyes.

"Ugh."

I had read so many books, with girls, tough ones, breaking down often because of 'troubling events.' I, Abby Claire, had never really understood or cared for those parts because I couldn't relate to them. I had never lost a member of my family because there were very few to lose. That was why I had much more place in my heart for each and every one of them. That was why my equilibrium had been taken away from me when I had found the note at Mrs. Wildfire's home. They were all I had, my base. How could I keep on living without them to depend on?

Of course, there was Luke who was there, Kaithlyn, Brittany, but what if the bad guys (whoever they were) decided that they wanted more bargaining chips? What would I do if I were to lose completely *everything*?

The question made me wonder who could have known about the Lost Element, before I ever knew that *I* had it and how I could get my family back. The questions kept piling up and piling up...

I washed the filth of the night off my hands and hair, also trying to wash away all my worries but not succeeding. I shut off the water and dried my hair until it was humid. It was only when I had my bath towel wrapped around me and was standing in front of my bed that one last question popped up. What the hell was I going to wear?

ھ∞ۍ

After ten minutes of searching, I found a pair of cargo pants for men, two sizes too big—no elastic. All there was were leather belts in the closet, hanging from a ramp of belts. I decided to wear the tank top I had worn before, since it was really just my jeans that were unwearable.

I used the hairdryer in the bathroom and just when I was about to unlock my door, saw that I wasn't wearing socks. *Bugger*, I thought, *Luke probably doesn't have any spares...*

My door opened. Luke was there, grinning when he saw I was barefoot. He too, didn't have any socks.

"They have everything except socks," he said. He looked down at my pants. "Nice pants. You ditched the jeans?"

"Yeah," I answered, smirking at him. "There were holes everywhere. Now, how did that happen, I wonder? ..."

Luke laughed at my expression. "Can I come in?"

"Sure. I was about to go see you, anyway."

He got in my room and I closed the door behind me. I flipped the lights I had turned off and flopped on the bed next to Luke. He had, in his hands, the book that Shane had given me.

"Did you learn anything interesting?" he asked, opening a random page. "… Nightriders can be sometimes very abusive and have several power trips a day. Not all are smart like shapeshifters."

I lightly slapped his shoulder. "Hey, I might be part Nightrider, so shut it."

"How'd you know you're part Night?"

I shrugged. "I said I *might* be part Nightrider. I'm still not sure what I am."

"You're you."

I looked at him. The almost too serious look on his face made me laugh.

"What's wrong?" he asked. "Do I have something between my teeth?"

"No." I sighed. "I guess it doesn't really matter what I am, right? I mean, it's not as if I can change forms like a shapeshifter or be lightning fast like a vamp or cast spells like a witch. I'm just a human who can see what she's not supposed to see."

"And you know what?" said Luke.

"What?"

"I wish I were you."

"Why? There's nothing special about me… I mean, all I can do is worry about what's going to happen to Mary or Mrs. Wildfire or Jane… and there's nothing I can do about it."

"Sure there's something you can do about it! You can ask Gabe or one of the other Nights to help with your fighting. There are plenty of people you can ask. Then you wouldn't be so 'useless' afterward."

The idea was *brilliant*! Why hadn't I thought of that sooner? Oh yeah, because I was *useless*.

"Abby, before you do that…"

"Yessss?" I turned toward him and was surprised with how close we were. I looked away from him and he leaned back.

He let out a short laugh, bitter and insincere. "I talked with Gabe some."

"Oh, yeah?" I said, sitting up. "About what?"

Luke didn't answer right away. "He said maybe I should consider joining a shapeshifter pack."

"Oh…" I bit my lip. It wasn't until after thirty seconds of awkward silence that I said, "Would you want that?"

"I don't see why not," he said, scratching the back of his neck, touching his mark. "I mean, my family doesn't care about me and I feel like I could learn to master my powers. To be honest," Luke looked at me, "I feel out of place here. I don't belong here."

I could not believe he was saying this. "Is this because of Shane?"

"That guy has nothing to do with it." The words that came out of Luke's mouth were sharp, almost ripping through me like blades. He had never raised his voice at me—never.

"You would leave me," I said in a small voice.

Luke's expression softened and he brought a hand to caress my cheek. "I've given this some thought, Abby. I think, once this is over, that we should … take some distance."

My heart skipped a beat and my jaw dropped. "You can't mean that…"

"Abby… I think it would be best if we did take a step back, so we could clear things up a bit—"

"Have I done something or not done something to—"

"It's not you, Abby. It's me."

That was it. He had said it. The 'it's not you, it's me' excuse. My throat constricted but my eyes were dry. I could not cry. I would not cry… but *why* was he leaving me? When I needed him most!

I just wanted him to leave, so that I could cry. He was my anchor, the one person who was supposed to be there for me…

Luke jerked back when there was a knock at the door. He got up and opened the door. "Is Abby here?" asked a husky voice.

I got up and walked around Luke, trying as best I could not to touch him. It was Dimitri, the Russian we had met earlier. I swallowed and hoped my voice wouldn't sound too hoarse. "Hello, Dimitri. Can I help you with something?"

"Yes. Gabriel has sent me to fetch you. He wishes to speak to you."

"Oh, okay." I didn't even look in Luke's direction. I didn't think twice of walking barefoot in the hallway. I just wanted to put as much distance between us as I possibly could.

I looked at Dimitri who motioned toward the stairs with his hand, his metallic hand.

EIGHTEEN

"How did it happen?" I asked once we were in the weapons' room. There was no one there, which was surprising with the number of Nightriders that were in the academy.

"My hand?" said Dimitri, raising his arm so that we could both see the hand-shaped metal. He moved his fingers, which moved perfectly, like a human's.

I nodded.

"My hand got cut off by a rogue shapeshifter four years ago. I'd rather spare you the crude details."

I sat on a stool next to an isle covered with arrows. The tips were half-gold and half-silver. "Couldn't they ... *glue* your hand back on?"

"I didn't want the Healers to. I wanted more useful fingers." I watched as Dimitri flicked his wrist and razor-sharp metal nails appeared.

"Wow," I said, my voice a bit shaky. I sure as hell didn't want to get on his bad side. "You must be ... *happy*."

Dimitri gave a short, bitter laugh. "You have no idea."

I was about to add something more when he moved toward me—fast. Before I even knew it, he had me up against the wall, both of his hands on either side of my head. This was *so* déjà vu.

"What are you?" The words echoed through my head like ripples. Each wave made me mentally reel, as if there was someone trying to enter my brain… It was the worst feeling. It was like when the vampire had tried to compel me not long ago…

I forced myself not to look away from his eyes. I said shakily, "I'm a student at—"

Dimitri punched the wall next to my head, taking some of my hair with it, and the sound… "I won't put up with that crap. Tell me what you are." His metallic hand moved to my throat. I swallowed hard.

"I don't—"

"Let go of her, Petrovski."

I looked up a little dazed. My vision was a bit blurry but I squinted and I could distinguish the lines of a guy. Shane? I thought hopefully, but no, he was asleep… Luke?

I saw light brown hair, too light to be Shane's and too dark to be Luke's. It was Connor and he looked deadly and charming at the same time. His expression was impassable.

"You may go, McFarlane. I have this under control," answered Dimitri through his teeth.

"I said let the lass *go* and that's an order."

Dimitri looked at me straight in the eyes. "This isn't over," he muttered. He let go of me and I took in a long breath.

Connor didn't look him in the eyes as Dimitri passed him; he simply stared into thin air. It was only when I heard the click of the door closing that he moved.

"Are ye all right?" he asked, moving toward me, human speed.

I shook my head and put my hand to my neck. "I don't feel too hot."

"Do ye need help?"

I shook my head again. "A bit scared but just a little headache, that's all." I forced a smile out of me. "Thanks." I took a step forward … and fell into his arms.

"Wow, ye don't seem okay t'me." He put his arms around me and led me to one of the Ghosts, making me sit next to him.

"Ye want me to get ye somethin'?" he asked. I shook my head. "Water, perhaps?"

"No…" I mumbled. "My head just hurts…"

"I'm verra sorry Dimitri acted that way. It's no' like him to do so. He's been a wee bit unstable lately. He lost his little sister two months ago; he's been destabilized since then."

"Oh…" I was still a bit shaken by what had just happened but I understood more. I knew what it was like to lose a younger sister. I just hoped I didn't turn out like him. "How did his sister die?"

"She caught a rare disease when she went to the tropics for an assignment. There was just no cure that could save her," said Connor.

Before I could ask anything else, I heard the weapons' room door click again. Gabe stood there looking from Connor to me. He seemed tired and unsurprised to see us. I read no expressive emotion as he talked. "Abby, I need to talk to you—alone."

"Sure." I gave a small smile to Connor as I walked away. When I got close enough to Gabe, I could see his eyes and how older he looked since the last time I had seen him even though it had only been a few hours earlier.

"See ye soon, Abby," I heard Connor say.

I didn't answer and just followed Gabe outside the weapons' room.

Gabe waited for the door to click shut behind me before talking. "Where did you guys go earlier?"

I held back from scratching the back of my head and grinned sheepishly. "Now, how can I put this in words?"

৵৽

"**D**o you know where Shane is?" asked Gabe after I had told him everything with the vamps and Luke. He listened to me with a lot of attention, nodding sometimes or just staying completely silent. We were sitting in one of the many living halls (which were almost the same thing as living rooms except they were in a hall and not a room).

"Last time I saw him, he was literally falling asleep in the hallway," I said, remembering the way he almost fell face first on the floor.

"Poor guy, he's worn out." Gabe shook his head. "Shane doesn't know his own limits. He thinks he can go on forever without resting."

"He's stubborn," I said. "Shane's as thick-headed as a mule."

"I've always admired him for that."

I looked at him. What had he just admitted to? "You admire him?"

"Yeah. He's always stood for what he believed in and he's always there for the people he cares about."

"Thick-headedness," I muttered to myself. I crossed my arms over my chest.

"We'll have to go to Mrs. Wildfire's to investigate." His voice was a tad lower than usual as he said so. Why, I didn't know.

Going to Mrs. Wildfire's and looking for clues didn't sound good. Last time I had gone there hadn't been great. It would only make me sad and make me feel even guiltier. I would think of Mary and everything I had lost in the matter of a day...

"What do you want to investigate?" I asked.

"I want to look for some clues of who might be behind Mary and Mrs. Wildfire's abduction."

"What would you see that Shane didn't?"

"This time we'll have a Seeker with us. He's a Night specialized in searching and digging up information. It's Connor McFarlane; you know him already."

"Of course I've met him." I paused for a while, looking at his eyes. He too didn't look like he had gotten much sleep. "You should go rest. You look tired."

He let out a small laugh. "I sort of had to deal with all the recruits and I had to go grocery shopping while you guys were gone."

"Oh..."

"Thank God I didn't have to cook!" He didn't say anything for a while and then, "Oh, before I forget." He fished something out of his pocket and handed it to me. "Here, put those on, they have a tracking device in them. If you're ever in trouble, you just have to break the beads and it is going to send us a signal that you are in danger. Shane and I have a GPS installed in both our cellphones that are linked to the earrings. So, if ever you have a problem, we'll receive the signal and we'll be able to localize you easily in order to come and help you."

I held the little earrings in my hands. They were little black beads that reflected my face. I didn't have any earrings on, so I slipped them on right away.

"You couldn't give these to me earlier?" I asked, smiling.

∽∾

"There was definitely a fight in here."

Connor skimmed his fingers over the little nightstand in Mrs. Wildfire's bedroom. The bed was flipped over and ripped to its core. Its springs had scratched the wooden floor and gotten a frame painting to fall off the wall. I leaned down to look at it. It was the portrait of an elegant man whose features were angular and beautiful. There was something in his emerald eyes that puzzled me. He seemed familiar… His eyes reminded me of someone I knew I should know. I read what was scribbled at the bottom right corner of the painting: Camellia DiCaprios.

"If you look at the floor, you can see dirty footsteps. Man, according to the length and width." Connor crouched down and looked at the floor more closely. "And the lines here," he pointed at them, "are the feet of someone being dragged off. It must have been an adult, for a child's weight wouldna be this apparent."

"Why would they flip the mattress over and rip it?" I asked, moving toward him, looking at the bed.

"That's what I'm goin' t'find out."

He walked out of the bedroom and I followed him. Connor went in Mrs. Wildfire's tiny kitchen. It was the same as Shane and I had left it—half-destroyed. "It was in the morning. There was coffee brewin' in the coffee machine, burnt toast in the toaster, burned eggs in the pan and milk in a cup. All smell two days old."

"They were having breakfast…" I whispered. While I had been at Dunkin' Donuts, my family was being taken away from me.

"Yes. Was it a rainy day?" asked Connor, crossing his arms over his chest. He leaned a bit over the counter, examining every inch of it.

"Yeah."

"So, it could have been vamps. Our list of suspects has no' gotten shorter."

"Do you suspect vampires?" I asked, putting my hands in my pockets.

Connor looked in my eyes. "I doona know. What do ye think?"

I could tell that he knew that I was keeping a part of the story from him. He was suspecting me of not telling the whole truth. I bit my tongue.

He sighed. "I know ye have no' known me for long... but ye should learn to trust me."

I didn't reply. What could I say? That I was bound to die one way or another? That I *was* a Lost Element? There were so many things I didn't know and I couldn't tell him until I was sure of what was going on.

Connor gave me one last look before walking out of the kitchenette and into the living room. I followed him and saw him leaning over a box next to the TV. He lifted it up and put it on the coffee table. He sat down on the couch (which, thank God, Shane had bothered to wash after I had bled and flipped the cushions over, just to be sure) and opened the box. I sat next to him and saw piles of old letters. I reached for one. There was a string around it, keeping it from opening. The paper felt old and used under my fingertips.

Connor got up, went into the kitchen and came back with a Wal-Mart plastic bag. "We'll look through these later." He took the letter from my hands and slipped it into the bag. He took all the other ones and dumped them in. I was surprised to find VCR recording tapes. I took one and read the label: 07/02/92.

"What do you think these are?" I asked, handing the tape to Connor.

"Probably security tapes or something. We'll look at these too."

When he was about to put it in the plastic bag, I said, "We should just bring the whole thing, don't you think?"

He nodded, placed the plastic bag into the box and closed it. "I still have things to check."

Around an hour later, Connor had swiped the apartment at least ten times and we were both in the van with at least three boxes in the trunk.

"I noticed one or two pictures of ye in the apartment," said Connor after two minutes of driving. "Ye know the lady, right?"

I nodded. "We were close." I felt a clump of sorrow form in the back of my throat. I swallowed it back. I still hadn't gotten over the fact that Mrs. Wildfire and Mary were taken away from me *because* of me and not to mention Jane… my mommy.

"I suppose ye do not wish to talk about it."

I shook my head and stared at the red light in front of us. "I'm going to see them soon," I said, as I thought of the note Shane and I had found the day before. I squinted as the sun made its appearance through the high buildings of Boston. Gabe had wanted us to go early in the morning instead of late at night. We were less likely to get attacked, he had said.

Connor pressed on the gas when the light turned green and dangerously weaved the SUV between honking cars and cursing pedestrians. I held my breath until we were at the next red light, only to have Connor burn it and have more cars honking at us. My hands gripped my seat as if it were a lifejacket.

"Where did you learn to drive?" I asked, through clenched teeth. "New York?"

"Nay." I heard a siren coming from behind us, God! Way to go on going unnoticed. "Paris."

I looked in my rearview mirror. I saw the flash of red and blue. Well, this wasn't good. "Do you have your driver's license?"

"No, why?"

I turned around to see the police car following us. "'Cause I think you're gonna need it."

"Doona' worry." Connor revved the engine and burned another red light. "Everythin' is under control." A red Mustang missed the SUV by an inch. Connor hit the honker once and did a dry turn on a one-side lane. Of course, we were going the wrong way.

We were on a residential street but he didn't slow down one bit. I almost let out a shriek when he zoomed past a few kids running on the sidewalk. Connor rapidly parked into an empty parking lot and told me to duck. I let go of the breath I had been holding when we heard the siren (sirens now) passing us.

"You should try to stay under the radar," I let out, sitting up and giving Connor a sly smile. "It won't hurt not to get noticed."

"Sweetheart, I was born to be noticed," answered Connor, grinning at me.

I gave him a sideway look. "You're overconfident; you know that, right?"

"Yur the first person to tell me that," he noted, leaning back in his seat. I watched as his chest rose and got back down again. His respiration was slow and rhythmic, evening mine.

"Huh, I'm surprised."

Connor smiled at me. He was somehow calmer than before and seemed at peace with himself. I was surprised; I would've been on edge if I had been driving like that.

The police was gone by now but Connor didn't reach for the keys, which were dangling from the ignition. He stared into space, expressionless.

"Ye remind me of someone." His voice was low and I heard a tingle of what sounded like deep, deep sorrow. I looked at him. His expression was pained and for a second, I saw through his eyes a wounded soul, maybe even dead.

"Who?" I lowered my tone to his, afraid of breaking what might be a sacred silence.

"A girl, around your age, I loved. She died no' long ago."

I sucked in a breath through my nostrils. "I'm sorry. I shouldn't have asked. Unless you want to… *talk* about it." My last sentence was more of a question than a proposition but Connor didn't seem to notice.

He slowly nodded, as if unsure if he could rely on me. "I have no' told this to anyone."

Taking the words he had used earlier on me, I said, "I know you've only known me for a little while but you could learn to trust me. One of the reasons people lay it all out on me is because I don't go around repeating it and I respect their opinions even though they are not mine." I could not believe I was saying this. Why was I going all Obi Won Kenobi on him was way past me.

Connor gave me a slight smile. He inhaled deeply. "She had the most beautiful eyes. When ye made her laugh, their color intensified, making the deepest and warmest of green and when ye got her mad, they suddenly became verra pale and dangerous." He laughed. "Thank goodness I didn't see them pale much.

"She was verra stubborn, much more than I've seen of ye I might add. And let me tell you, from seeing you talk, I can tell ye are verra, no but *verra* stubborn…"

For what might have been half an hour, Connor spoke of his love. How she dressed and how she reacted to all the strange and bizarre situations he had gotten into. She had been merely mortal but Connor had broken the rules and told her about the Nightrealm anyway. She hadn't fled or screamed in terror when he told her; she just gave him an almost knowing smile. Then he told me of how her life had been taken away by a demon when he had been gone for only a few days. He had found her house torn apart and a pool of blood with no body. For months, he searched for her but no sign of his love.

"I have done many things I regret up to now and I felt like I was redeeming myself by being with her. She brought light into my life. She would make me laugh like no other."

I found his story romantic and at the same time very sad. Connor described his emotions so well and clear that I found myself holding back tears. I wasn't really the type of person who cried while listening to stories. Heck, I hadn't even cried when I had watched Titanic, but then again this wasn't my best week, so bawling wasn't something new at the moment.

"What was her name," I whispered. I had brought my knees to my chin, gazing at Connor and watching as dozen of emotions crossed his face.

"Katalina, that was her name."

Knowing that I should slowly start to change the subject, which I knew would do Connor some good, I said, "Before you came here … where were you?"

Connor focused on me. "You mean with the other Nights?" I nodded. "When I first started bein' a nomad Nightrider, a Night who travels from academy to academy, I was 'bout twelve, the youngest of the group. My mom had died a week earlier, so I had three options: live with my dad in Eldoras, live in an academy somewhere in Thailand or travel around the world with other Nights. Livin' with my father was out of the question and Thailand was not very interesting for the young lad I was, so travelin' all over the world with no parent was what I chose. My father was no' verra happy with my decision, but I was and nothin' could make me change my mind."

"You were just a kid," I said, thinking of Mary. "You couldn't live like that."

Connor shrugged. "That didna' stop me from achieving what I most wanted in my life. I traveled everywhere with friends I made and new enemies, always livin' on the edge and feelin' free. I've gone to the colorful city of Prague, cold Russia, exotic and crowded India, historical France, cultural Italy… Have ye ever seen Vancouver in February? Beautiful!"

"Have you been in Brazil?"

He nodded and then grinned. "I'd like to go back, actually. You should really go to Rio de Janeiro. 'Tis verra nice. Place's crawlin' with demons."

I laughed. "I'd love to go, that is, when I get some training." My tone lowered a bit as I said the last word. Blast it, I had no freaking' training and I was part (or at least we all thought) Nightrealmer.

"Trainin' for what?" asked Connor.

"Well … let's just say I need to be able to protect myself."

Connor's eyebrows shot up. "Ye mean ye're a Night and ye have no' been trained?"

I nodded, trying to hide my embarrassment when he stared at me. Before he could ask why, I said, "It's complicated," and averted my eyes from his.

"Do ye have a trainer?" he asked. When I said no, Connor offered to do the job.

"You'd do it?" I asked, surprised.

"Why no'? It's been a long time since I've trained someone and anyway…" He trailed a finger down my nose, teasingly. "I'd love to see ye suffer."

I laughed. If only he knew how much I had suffered lately… "When do we start?"

☙ ❧

Luke had joined us. I didn't look in his direction, scared that I might erupt into tears. Luke had managed to find some clothes in his closet and brought me too big jogging pants.

When we were both on the sixth story (training level), Connor set diverse weapons in front of us. He too had changed and he just looked *too* attractive for his own good. No wonder Katalina had fallen for him. Heck, a complete prude would've fallen for him.

"Ye see these?" he asked, gesturing at the deadly looking things. Luke and I nodded. "Ye won't be touchin' them for a while."

"What?" I exclaimed. "Didn't you want to train us?"

"Of course, but I doubt yur body is in good enough shape."

My eyebrows shot up. "Are you saying I'm *fat?*" I turned to another Nightrider who had joined us to get some training himself. His name was Chi, from Mongolia. "Do I look fat to you?" He shook his head and I returned my eyes on Connor. "I don't know where you got the idea that I was—"

"I never said that," said Connor, defending himself. "You misunderstood me. Yur body is not… *qualified* for Nightrider training."

"I know it's not. That's why I asked you if you could help me fling a sword around. You know, just so I can be *qualified*."

Connor shook his head. "I'm afraid being able to fling a sword left and right is not enough. Yur body has to be able to run long distances without stopping; ye have to be able to climb a tree as easily as breathing. Ye have to be able to swim across torrid waves in the ocean, ye have to—"

"Okay, okay, I get it; I suck. Can we start with the training now?" I just wanted to get this over with. A few pushups here and there and I would be fine, right?

ॐ ॐ

Yeah. The pushups here and there theory was so wrong. Connor made me sweat like a freaking animal! Luke wasn't even flustered. My legs were aching and the clean, tight knot in my hair I had redone not even an hour ago was falling apart. My arms were sore and my breaths were quick and sharp.

I had lost count of how many times I had run around the room or how many times he had made me drop and do thirty. The nice and sad Connor from before was gone and all I had in mind was a way to kill him so that he could let me get a bit of rest. Every time he told me to do something that I didn't like, I shot him a murderous glare and without a word, did it. The weapons on the floor looked very tempting.

Other Nights had come and gone, to lift weights or practice sword fighting among themselves. I hadn't seen them looking but I could feel the eyes at the back of my neck. Connor had told Luke he could leave, since he was more *qualified* than I was, who 'needs much more training.' He had left, giving me a sympathetic look. I didn't return his smile. No words were necessary to express my anger toward him. That bastard was leaving me... I punched the punching bag as hard as I could.

At the time, much more training had sounded like 'a lap or two extra' but Connor had not been easy on me—again.

"It'll be all for t'day, lass. Ye can go now."

I didn't need to be told twice. I stumbled out of the room and headed for the elevator. Stairs were out of my league at the moment. I pressed the button and got in. Luke was probably still lifting heavy and impossible-to-lift weights, Gabe was somewhere and Shane was probably *still* sleeping.

I pushed the button of my floor and didn't have to wait long before the doors opened again. The hallway seemed to stretch in front of me, looking like an endless pit. Every step echoed in my brain. Oh God, I was going to blast Connor for it. Once in my room, I noted the box of VCR tape recordings. Maybe later, I thought as I got rid of my sweaty clothes. I had no PJs and that pissed me off. I scanned the room for something decent to wear. Finally opting for the red tank top I had worn about a day or two ago (my notion of time was completely screwed up) and my underwear, I slipped into bed and turned the light off.

Just before I fell into the comfort of sleep, I remembered that I had not locked the door. *Oh what the hell*, I thought, too tired to get up and fell asleep.

☙❧

A few hours or so later, I woke up, my muscles no better than they were before. Mentally feeling less tired, I randomly took a tape from the box and slipped it in the VCR reader and turned on the plasma screen TV I hadn't used yet. After taking the remote control, I crashed on my bed, only to get back up to go put on my jogging pants because I was cold.

Once I was back on my bed, I waited as the tape loaded and saw static on the screen. It went on for thirty seconds or so and then I saw the shape of a boy. The camera focused on the shape and I saw dark brown, shoulder-length hair and glowing amber eyes. Well built like Luke and around six-two. His face was angular, like any Nightrealmer, reminding me of Gabe. He held something in his hands.

He was inside what looked like some sort of mental hospital room, the walls cushioned and completely white. The boy held onto an object as if it were a life vest. He was mumbling something against the object and he suddenly fell to his knees. A roar escaped from his mouth as his back moved in impossible directions. I saw his white shirt drenched with sweat turn red at his back. Blood tickled down his spine from two holes.

At first, I had thought they were bullet wounds, and when I saw things coming out of the holes, I almost fainted.

The boy was screaming in agony and I was forced to lower the volume or it would alert the others. The boy fell on his side and I watched as he mutated.

NINETEEN

SHANE

I woke up with a start. I glanced at my watch. 2:47pm. Oh man, I'd slept more than sixteen hours, and I had a major headache. I never had a headache with lack of sleep, but did whenever I slept *too* much. Pretty ironic if you asked me.

My hair must be a wreck, I thought. What the hell, *I'm* a wreck. When I reached out for the glass of water that I had left on the night-stand, my legs got tangled in the sheets and I fell face first on the floor. *Ouch.*

I groaned and kicked my legs out of the white mess and dragged my feet to the bathroom. I let the water in the sink cool my fingers and splashed my face. I passed a hand through my mop of hair. Kristen said the look was badass and that I should keep it. I didn't know why I just didn't chop it off or something. Like that I would feel less like a bum next to the other clean-cut Nightriders.

After taking a cold shower (it's the only way I could *properly* wake up) and putting on some clean clothes, I padded through the hallway barefoot. I had to go to the laundry room and get some socks. My sup-ply was gone; probably stolen from a Night.

When I walked by Abby's room, I stopped and leaned forward to listen, like the freaking stalker I was deep inside. I heard the VCR machine rolling and a strange moaning sound from the other side of the door. I pressed my fingers against the door and the knob gave out under my fingers. I slipped into the room without making a sound.

Abby was watching something pretty gruesome on TV. She was so engrossed that she hadn't noticed me coming in. I didn't make a sound, watching from the corner of the dark room what she was looking at.

A boy, no older than me, was writhing in pure agony on the floor. I was about to tell Abby to stop this thing or she would have nightmares, when before my eyes, I saw the guy grow *things* from his back. Blood erupted from the holes and then I saw *bones* coming out. At first, I thought it was his spine but the things just kept on growing and growing, until, before my eyes, there was a set of white feathered *wings*. The guy was coughing blood now and lying on his side. I could see the pain in his eyes and could actually feel it echoing in my own damn soul.

Then the guy just ... *died*. His chest stopped moving and an object he had been holding fell from his hands. I just had time to see what it was before the tape ended with static on the TV screen. I heard Abby let out a breath and saw her putting a hand to her stomach, where she was marked. She had this sick look on her face, as if she was going to run to the bathroom and puke. She got off the bed and almost screamed when she saw someone was in her room but didn't when she saw it was me.

"How long have you been here?" she asked, trying to lean on the wall. I saw her composing her face, as if the sick look had never been there. I saw her knees buckle and she fell back on the bed, as if she were too weak to keep herself upright. I smelled sweat on her and deodorant.

"What have you been doing?" I asked softly. Now wasn't a time to be harsh on my questioning; not after what she had just seen, even thought it was killing me not to know *what* we had just seen.

"I had Connor train me. Five hours *without* the ten minute break," answered Abby, grinning as she rubbed her thighs. I couldn't help but stare. She looked great in jogging pants, with her bellybutton almost peeking out. "Remind me never to do that again."

"What did you do?" I said, quickly bringing myself to look at her lovely face. Had she always looked this soft?

"He made me run, a lot I might add. It was mostly endurance stuff." She sighed. "Luke, on the other hand, is in freaking great shape."

So, she lacked endurance and Luke didn't. I looked away from her eyes to the little cute mole located near her left eye and then back to her eyes. "Is that it?"

"He made me lift some weights but not much. He didn't let me touch a weapon, not even a wooden stick." She shook her head as if it was the stupidest thing ever.

I snorted, liking the way her hair shifted around her naked shoulders. "Good. You don't deserve it."

"Thanks, I appreciate the compliment," she said half-sourly. Abby brought her eyes to the TV and then looked away, as if scared that the tape would start playing again.

"What were you watching?" It couldn't have been a movie. The emotions had been too raw and true and Abby's expression too terrified. My eyes drifted to a carton next to the furniture that held the TV. I walked toward it and took out a tape. I read the label: *L.E. Phenomenon.* "Where d'you get these?"

"We found them at Mrs. Wildfire's place when you were asleep." She walked toward me and took the tape from my hands and threw it carelessly back in the box.

"*We?*"

"Connor had to come. You know, with him being a Seeker and all."

I saw red for a mere second and then it was gone. Connor, I thought. Damn *Connor.*

"What do you think it was?" I asked.

"It was the wind talisman," she whispered, putting a hand back to where she had rested it before. "Or at least I think it was. I'm sure it was a Lost Element. Do you think it's going to happen to me?"

I could have told her no, that everything was going to be fine but I couldn't. She deserved the truth. "I'm not sure…" I paused, wondering what I could say to her; anything to get that sick look off her face. "You'd said that when you were in Cairo's realm, that he made you eat a prune and that determined whether you were the one from the prophecy or not, correct?" She nodded slowly. "Well, maybe this guy... maybe this guy was never in touch with Cairo and that's what happened. Maybe to use the wind talisman, you need some sort of *benediction* from the wind god himself. Maybe this guy, well, he didn't get it and that's why this happened to him."

Abby seemed to ponder my words for a moment. "How could this guy have known that it was a Lost Element?"

"I could also ask this question: how did *Mr. Porter* know? If he didn't, isn't it a big coincidence that he gave it to *you*, the one who's destined to gather all of them?" All this was too fishy. How was all of this possible? There were too many ends linking for all of this to be a coincidence. All her life, Abby hadn't even known about her heritage and within a week she'd received a Lost Element as a *birthday present*, she'd met the wind god, she'd discovered she was the *One* and to top things off, unknown enemies had abducted her loved ones? She'd seen more action in a week than I had in a *year!*

"I'm one hundred percent sure that Mr. Porter knew what he was giving you," I finally said, thinking back at the older man.

"Why would you say that?"

"Well for one, he's one of our only suppliers in Akhor in all of Boston. He's part nymph; he knows every story about every product in his shop... "

"Wait, wait, wait! What did you just say?" exclaimed Abby, putting her hands up in the air. Her eyes had widened and her expression showed that of astonishment. "Mr. Porter is a *what?*"

I paused. Damn it, I'd told her too much—again. "He's part nymph. Maybe that's how he knew that you were destined. Nymphs have a sharp sense of observation and intuition. He might've caught on to something about you that everyone else discarded as something normal..." I looked into her eyes for a moment, marveling at how surprisingly light they had gotten... That was it! "Abby! That's it! Your eyes!"

"My eyes?" she asked dumbstruck. She blinked several times and looked right back at me. "What about them?"

"Haven't you ever wondered why they were purple?"

"The doctors said it was maybe just some sort of mutation or something. Nothing to worry about."

I thought for a minute, trying to remember exactly what had been said in the prophecy (I'd read up on it when she'd been recovering from her ghoul poisoning). "The prophecy said something about a girl having raven hair and eyes lit like the sky at sunset… Why did I not think of that sooner? Those are dead giveaways that the girl from the prophecy is you!"

"Ah man, I'm in trouble."

"Someone must've been watching you for a while, to know who your loved ones were and where you would be when he would strike."

Abby balled her fist to her sides until her knuckles became white. I could see her biting the inside of her cheek and could actually feel tension radiating from her body. Her eyes welled with tears and she let out a whimper. I had never seen a girl break down in front of me, except for Melinda and she'd thrown spikes at me. Kristen was too strong a character to show any weakness, so I had never seen her shed a tear. Abby, on the other hand, I'd seen her fall apart before but this time was different. She didn't have emptiness in her eyes like she had last time. This time, her eyes were filled with boiling rage. Every tear that rolled down her cheeks was filled with hatred for the people who had taken her family away. Her whimper had been filled with desperation and that alone had made me want to punch the ones who had caused her sorrow.

I could've let her alone. I could've just left and gone to get some socks and go do something else. I could've turned my back and walked right out of her life without regret, but I didn't. I took the two steps it took to get to her and wrapped my arms around her. She clutched at my waist and held me tight. She dropped her head on my shoulder and cried. I could feel her tears wetting my shirt, as well as her fingers digging mercilessly into my skin. I didn't say anything or move away. I just stood there and let her do whatever it was that would make her feel a bit better. I stroked her hair, enjoying their softness. I didn't know for how long we stood there, nor did I care. I let her cry all of the tears she had in her body, until she slowly pulled back, her eyes dry but still sparkling. She looked straight at me and I felt all of my life starting to gravitate around those beautiful purple eyes.

I tucked a stray strand of hair behind her ear and gave her the best sympathetic smile I could pull off. "Has anyone ever told you how beautiful your eyes are when you cry?"

She let out a short laugh, wiping her nose on the sleeve of her jacket. "No."

"Well, I am. Your eyes are beautiful when you cry."

She smiled slightly. "Thank you, Shane, for letting me vent on you."

"Any time," I said, winking at her.

Abby nodded. Then suddenly, she smiled, too hard. "Do you want to go grab a bite? I'm starving."

Before I could answer, she had me outside her door. In less than two minutes, she was out, fresh and clean, her hair pulled back in a ponytail.

"Where are we going?" I was more than confused. Hadn't she been hurting and… Whatever. This was Abby and I knew that I never knew what to expect with her. This girl was full of surprises and it was fun to discover more of them every passing day.

"I don't want to stay here." Abby walked with me to my room so that I could go get my coat. When I came back, she smiled. It was maybe a bit too wide but I let it go. "I really want to get out of here."

I frowned. "Why?" Not that I wanted to stay here or anything but her sudden wave of happiness worried me. I looked at her in the eyes and when she looked away, I knew she was just pretending to be happy but she really did want to leave.

"I just … don't want to stay here, that's all."

I walked with her to the elevator without saying a word. When the doors opened and closed behind them, Abby said, "I want to have a normal afternoon. I would've gone with Luke but he's training and I don't want to bother him."

I knew that wasn't all, what with that look in her eyes but I didn't want to press her for more. "Do you have someplace in mind?"

"Not really, I was thinking you would know a good place."

"How 'bout pizza?"

I thought of grabbing my cellphone before leaving but then decided against it. I didn't want to get called back to the academy. I wanted to have a little time off, not only for me but for Abby as well.

Abby smiled and nodded eagerly. I smiled back and led her out of the academy, silently hoping Melinda had been right about the side-effects only lasting a couple of hours.

ৡৈ৯

ABBY

"The New York Pizza?" I said, looking up at the sign. The sun was shining brightly over our heads, warming my hair and my face in this cold weather. We had taken a nice, ten-minute walk. My body didn't feel so sore anymore for some reason and my spirits were rising up. I really hadn't wanted to stay in the academy for much longer and I really didn't want to run into Luke.

Shane opened the door for me and I got in. He got us to an empty table next to the window. I looked at the big menu on the wall in front of me next to the entry.

"What are you taking?" I asked.

I watched as he stood up and exhaled, looking at the menu. "I'm coming back." I waited for precisely four minutes and forty-seven seconds before Shane came back with a large pizza box and two bottles of water. He sat back down in front of me and twirled the pizza on the table so that when he opened it we could both see it.

He put a hand on the box to open it. "Ready?"

I rolled my eyes and nodded. My stomach had been growling since the scent of the pizza had come over me. Shane opened the box and my eyes widened. I had never seen such a beauty in all my life (stomach talking). The crust was thin and looked crunchy, the olive slices looked like delicious little ringlets, the feta cheese smelled just right, the pepperoni slices looked like they were going to melt in my mouth…

Taking a piece of heaven in my hands, I heard angels singing. I was about to take a bite when Shane stopped me. Damn him.

"Let's play a game," he said grinning at me when I groaned in frustration. "It's easy. You take a bite; you answer my question—nothing but the truth. Same goes for me."

I slightly nodded and took a bite, a burst of pure bliss invading my taste buds. Yeah, a question was definitely worth it.

"Shoot," I said after swallowing and before taking another one.

"Okay. When—" He stopped when he saw me. "You know that makes two, right?"

I gave him a does-it-look-like-I-care? look. Shane laughed. "When were you adopted?"

"When I was five. I can't remember anything before that," admitted Abby. "No matter how hard I try, I just can't bring myself to recall anything. The longest I can remember was ..." When? Oh yeah. "When Jane came to get me at the orphanage in Spain."

"You were born in Spain?" asked Shane.

"You know that counts as a question, right?" I shrugged. "Jane asked the ones who were responsible for me who I was and if they knew anything of my background. They said they had found me at their doorstep only a month earlier. A man had given me to them, they said. He had been dressed in black, his face covered by a hat. Once they had me firmly in their grip, he just left—no name, no nothing. Typical fairytale, right?"

Shane seemed to notice something. He leaned over the table and trailed a finger down my pinky.

"What's wrong?" I asked, looking at my pinky. "Do I have something on my finger?"

He shook his head, a faint smile on his face. "Your pinky's raised when you eat."

"Yeah, so?"

"Like a royal." He chuckled. "Cute."

I flushed slightly. I had never noticed it before. Weird. I saw that he had taken a bite from his pizza. "And you? Where were you born?"

"Good ol' America. I traveled a lot when I was younger. Almost all young Nightriders do," said Shane. "We have to travel from academy to academy until we find one that suits us and has an opening." He shrugged. "I guess I kinda came back to level one."

I took a bite and almost choked on it when Shane asked his next question:

"What happened last April?"

I set down my pizza and could hardly swallow what I had in the mouth. God it didn't taste good at the moment. Clearing my throat, I wiped my fingers on my leggings. Thank God, I had put on the black ones Kristen had given me.

"Umm, well…" My voice was quavering, so I cleared my throat once more.

Shane raised his hands, proclaiming himself innocent. "If you don't want…"

"No it's all right." I let out a long sigh. "Now that I think about it, it's not … that crazy." When he just kept on looking at me expectantly, I calmed down. His eyes were calming me. This was Shane; he would understand. "It was the national championship. I was in the finals and I had a pretty good chance of winning. I had come in second the year before and I was really confident." I really had been confident, too confident even. "The race started and before I knew it, I was in the lead. The racecourse was right next to the woods, so there was nothing separating us. I looked toward it, seeing if I was really in the lead and then I saw this… *monster* in the trees." I shivered just thinking about it. It had been as if time had stopped when I had stared in its big, black, bulgy eyes. Its skin had been slimy and grey. It had looked like a corpse, a huge monster's corpse. Ghouls looked like butterflies next to it. "I panicked and lost control of my bike. Next thing I knew, I was propelled into the woods… I fractured my collarbone, my leg and I cracked two ribs." I looked down at my hands.

Shane tilted his head, making me look back in his eyes. "It's okay to have reacted like that, Abby. Anyone in your situation would have done the same."

"That's the thing… I thought I had imagined it but then I thought, how could anyone think up something like that? So I just thought I was going crazy and the nightmares didn't help." I paused to take another shaky breath. "The media didn't make things any better. When I was in the hospital, sports reporters kept knocking at my door, asking questions… They had all kinds of stupid theories they had come up with of the how and why I had fallen.

"The other thing is that it had been my chance to go higher and maybe go to the international… and in the blink of the eye, my chance was gone. I think that was the other thing that really put me in a depressive mode. I didn't even touch my baby after that; that's how bad I felt. So Jane sold it eventually." I looked at the pizza and then back at him. "The monster thing is very believable now, so that's why I agreed to tell you about it, but it's the losing part that I'm really ashamed of."

"I'm sorry Abby that things had to end up like that for you. I really am… but it's the monster I'm more worried about."

"Why? They're everywhere."

"Yeah but it's not normal for one to actually show itself. Even less since it lives in the woods… Can you describe it?" I gave him the best description I could possibly muster. After some thinking, he said, "It was probably a greater wood ghoul. They chew on tree bark and don't usually show themselves. We don't have many problems with them. It was probably just curious about all the noise."

I nodded and took a bite of the pizza slice in my hand. It felt good to have told him. It hadn't been a huge deal but it had still bothered me for the past seven months.

"I want you to tell me about you when you were a kid," said Shane. He let out a small, nervous laugh, which was unusual of him. "I wasn't really brought up normally, so I don't know what it is to be … *normal.*"

I laughed. "You say that as if it was a disease."

"Who wants to be normal? So, tell me about yourself."

"Well what do you want to know?"

"Everything."

"Everything? Aren't you pushing it just a *wee* bit?" I made a fake, embarrassed face. I knew it would make Shane laugh and he did.

"When I was seven, I used to climb on Jane's marble counter in the kitchen to get to the cookie jar. I was young enough to love munching them secretly and big enough to actually be able to reach the counter."

"When I was seven," said Shane, "I was in… Syria, eating baklavas." I could not imagine Shane chewing on baklavas, much less him being seven years old. "We had an in-ground pool and I stayed in the water for hours. Got burnt more than once," I said, remembering those sunny days when the sun seemed to shine much more than it did these days. Actually, everything seemed brighter when I had been younger.

"First time I drove a car, I was ten." Shane didn't seem to care about the one-bite-one-answer rule, so I figured it was just talking for now. "I crashed into Damien. He didn't really get injured or anything. Just got scratched up and bruised."

"First time I drove a car, I did fine," I gloated, proud of myself.

"And when exactly was that?"

I frowned. "This summer."

Shane grinned at me. "That's what I thought."

I gave him a half-smile. Again, with his oh-Nights-are-better-than-humans theory, and fact. "Tell me something about you that isn't neat."

"I honestly don't know. Do you mean physically or mentally? 'Cause we both know that I'm physically perfect."

I rolled my eyes. Yeah, how could I not notice the panther-like way he walked or the way his eyes glittered with amusement whenever Gabe made him laugh or the way his strong jaw set when he was angry. I also saw the way his muscles moved under his skin; so fine and beautiful, yet strong, agile. Nobody could say he was cute. The guy was smoking hot and he knew it. I felt like slapping him.

We talked for a while. Shane was making me laugh, which earned me deadly glares from the customers around us. I completely ignored them because I was with Shane and with him, I somehow felt normal. Also, I wasn't going to let any strangers dictate the way I acted. It was as if he had put his Nightrider attitude and life away and was simply … *Shane.*

"What good books have you recently read?" asked Shane after what might have been his fourth slice.

I thought about it for a while. I had read *Pride and Prejudice* from Jane Austen. I hadn't really had time to read in between murder attempts on my case.

"*Pride and Prejudice,* uh…" I scratched my head a bit. It didn't really make sense but simply doing that somehow helped me. Yeah, I already knew I was crazy, so why pretend otherwise? "There was also *The Iron King* by Julie Kagawa…"

"Any vampire books?"

"I've read enough vampire books to last me for a lifetime, believe me."

"Don't you find it strange that they write stories of vamps and not stories of, I don't know, wizards?"

"Well they always have these waves, you know? Like almost a year ago, it was the vampire wave and now… looks like fey are surfing up." I took a bite. We had stopped playing the game because questions and answers just came and went. It was hard to keep track. "Why do you ask?"

"I don't know. I just noticed all those vampire novels teenage girls seem to adore, *Morganville Vampires, House of Night, Twilight, Vampire Academy…*"

"You're telling me that you know almost all of the vampire books there are on the market? Were you *that* bored?"

"No, I just have a good memory, unlike you know, *humans,* but why vamps and not wizards?"

"Well, first, wizards are old and have long, not so attractive beards and vamps, well they're—"

Shane shook his head, smiling to himself. "Wizards look like us, they grow up and eventually die, like anyone else who is part human. They only age very, very slowly. They can live up to be five hundred years old; that's one of the reasons why they're so knowledgeable."

"Oh…"

"So, like I said, why are there more books on vampires than there are on wizards?"

"Because… because girls are attracted to vampires."

"That's my question. Why are they attracted to vamps?"

"Vampires are drop-dead gorgeous. Well, at least that's what they say in the books."

"So? Wizards can be as 'drop-dead gorgeous' as any vamp."

"Yeah but wizards aren't physically stronger and faster than vampires."

"And? Why would girls like having a vampire boyfriend when he's a hundred times stronger than she is? What if he got mad and decided he wanted to have a little snack? She wouldn't be able to stop him."

"I guess they like living on the edge? They most probably like the phrase 'tame the beast'."

"I will never understand girls. So... *complicated* with all their emotions and periods and other blasphemous stuff. Let me tell you this, 'What bleeds for seven days every month and doesn't die *must* be evil'."

I let out a loud laugh, which made several other customers turn toward me, their expressions deadly. "You know you're talking to one right?"

"Yeah, it's time for us men to speak up!"

Our conversation ended in laughs and it was time to leave.

Together, we had finished all of the pizza and both of the water bottles when Shane decided it was time to leave. He kept the door opened for me when we stepped out into the late afternoon. I didn't know how much time had passed and I really didn't care.

Walking along the sidewalk, Shane cast weird looks at people we passed. I asked him about it and all he said was, "Instincts."

"Do you think I could go back to school?" I asked after a minute of silence. Days earlier, I wouldn't have asked; I would've just done it but now, after all that was going on, going back to school seemed like a bad idea. I had come to respect Shane and his actions.

"I don't think it's a good idea," replied Shane, looking at a hooded guy who was walking toward us. His face was covered. Shane sniffed the air as he had done with all the others we had passed, checking out if he was human. Once he was sure, he continued what he had started. "If you really want to excel in your studies, I'm sure we could find you a proper teacher among the Night recruits. Normally, it would have been Mrs. Wildfire but..."

I nodded. "But she had been kidnapped because of me."

"Look, Abby." When I didn't look at him and kept on walking, Shane took my hand and gently pulled me into an alley. There I stood against the bricked wall, the sun shining lightly on my face, heating it lightly, just the way I liked it, probably giving me a golden glow. "It wasn't you're fault. We should have been more careful and I'm sorry all of this had to happen to you and your family."

Tears stung my eyes. I wasn't going to cry… I couldn't be weak now, not when so many people counted on me. I missed my family, not only Mary and Mrs. Wildfire but Jane as well. My mom, the mom I had left when we were on bad terms…

I looked at Shane, his face in the shadows, his eyes glowing like… like *sapphires*. My heart was beating fast and my stomach did a back-flip. He had prided himself on his physical assets but he didn't seem to care at the moment. They say the eyes are windows to the soul, and so many times had I seen them guarded and careful of revealing any emotion. Now… there was nothing but raw emotions coming from him.

He leaned slowly toward me and my breath hitched. Shane slid a hand in my hair and it was over. I threw my hands around his neck and crushed my lips against his. Shane was taken aback for a moment but got over it when he circled my waist with his other arm. His lips were warm and inviting against mine and I wanted more. I felt strong emotions well up from inside me, like tidal waves that were threatening to drown me.

It felt so good and magical that I had forgotten to breath. I pulled slightly back, my forehead against his and gasped for air. I opened my eyes and saw Shane's beautiful face under the last rays of sunshine. His breathing was even with mine, quick and warm.

Shane suddenly pulled back, leaving me feeling cold and lonely. "I shouldn't have done that," he said, rigid. What I had seen earlier was gone and replaced with an impassable brick barrier.

"Why?" I was suddenly very angry at him. It might have been anger that had been building up inside me from the first day I had come to the academy but then again, it might have been my hormones. "Because I'm not Melinda?"

"What? This has *nothing* to do with her."

"Then please, do tell me, what is it?"

"It'll never work out, that's why," exploded Shane, throwing his hands in the air. "I don't know why you kissed me. All it will do is bring us both regret."

"Regret? You think I regret it? Of course! I wouldn't have regretted it if you hadn't pulled this off!" I was fuming and I knew my face was red all over. "And if you knew you would regret it so much, why did you kiss me back?"

Shane looked away, as if unable to hold my gaze. Then he looked back at me, his eyes burning. "Okay, maybe I did kiss you back, like I do with every other girl who throws her arms around me. I know it'll feel good for a moment and then I'll move on but I can't do that with you, 'cause you're always gonna be freaking there! You think I like to save your ass when you get in trouble? You think I like having to deal with you and your problems? Well think again because I don't."

With that, he left. I was too shocked to say anything or go after him. All this time, had he really thought of me as an obligation? Had spending the afternoon together been like a chore to him? My head was spinning, my knees buckled and I fell. I fought hard to keep the tears from escaping.

For the past week, Shane had been the bit of light in the night. Luke had been too, at the beginning but the night had changed him. Now, I was left with nothing. Mrs. Wildfire, Mary, Mom... they were gone.

TWENTY

SHANE

Ducking at the metal post I wouldn't have been able to avoid hadn't I been a Nightrider, I cursed myself over and over. Why had I done that? Kiss her? How stupid and irrational was that? I, of all people, should have known that getting mixed up with Abby was a bad idea but how could I have resisted, with her shining gold, her black hair turning coppery red and her eyes glowing like stars in the night? I raked a hand through my hair, exhaling loudly. And the Kiss! What a kiss that had been. It had taken all of my strength to just lean back and leaving her alone had taken so much more…

I hadn't meant what I had said. On the contrary, Abby wasn't a downside; she was my sun. No matter how much I had tried to stay unfazed by her wide, beautiful eyes, I knew I had fallen—hard and I had left her! She was my sun in the apocalypse and I had left her alone … at night. Then it hit me like a brick on the head.

I stopped dead. I had *left* her… I swirled back and started running like a madman. I'd left Abby alone. Shit! My mind was going frantic, driving me to analyze every single detail, my eyes moving around at the speed of light. Great job Shane, I thought sourly, almost pushing a little old lady from the sidewalk. She cried after me but I didn't do as much as look back.

I shouldn't have let my emotions blind me. It was my duty as a Nightrider to take care of Abby, maybe the only chance we had at finding the other Lost Elements. I had left her, for a reason now *I* didn't even understand. I had left to do something I might have to regret later but in doing so, I had done much worse...

It was now night in Boston and for some strange reason, there weren't many people lurking about. I would have questioned it more but for the moment, I was only grateful for the space I had to run. I took a sudden, dry turn and ran into a man. We both toppled over and I let out a *whoosh*.

I looked down and saw two white fangs popping out from the man. He hissed and pushed me off with such a force that I hit the cement wall five feet away. Before I could even fall to the ground, the vampire had a hand around my throat, looking feral. How ironic, I hadn't been in this position in years and just when Abby needed me, I got caught up in this.

"We have been expecting you, Shane McKenna," growled the vamp, pressing his dagger-sharp claws into my neck. As he spoke, I reached inside my sleeve, fingering the knife I always kept attached to my forearm. "Do you know what the penalty is for killing a vampire without him freely attacking you?"

I now had the dagger firmly in my grip. "Did you have any buddies?" I asked, through my clenched teeth. I stared into the vamp's black eyes and saw his pupils dilate. The bastard was trying to compel me!

"Did?" The vamp let out a bitter laugh, not letting his guard down. "Why did—"

The vampire let out a horse cry as I plunged my Gabe-made stake (made with silver, gold, bronze, iron and wood, deadly to all creatures) in the vamp's chest, right through his dead heart.

The carcass instantly disintegrated into dust and I started running again. I didn't know what vampire the vamp had been talking about, but that didn't matter at the moment. It didn't take long for me to reach the alley where I had left Abby.

There was no one there. I scanned the dark alley over and over again. No sign of a secret passage, no windows, no Abby.

A loud scream erupted from behind me, piercing the silence of the night. I swirled around and saw nothing.

"Shane!" Abby's voice made my heart stop beating. She was in danger and where the hell was she? I ran to the voice, circling a huge abandoned warehouse. I stopped in the middle of the deserted parking lot, looking around me—nothing.

Suddenly, a form wavered in front of me. I focused and saw two figures. I concentrated harder and could see Abby with a tall, dark man. *Dimitri.*

He had his hand around Abby's throat and waist, holding her in front of him. His metallic hand clenched tighter when she tried to pry his hands away. Abby had her hands around his hand. When she saw me, her eyes widened, in what I didn't know.

Dimitri had an evil grin across his face. "Shane, how nice of you to join us."

"What is it you want Dimitri?" I growled, my fists tightening around my stake. I had known this guy half of my life and how could I not have seen that one coming? I was a pretty good genius when it came to decrypting personalities and this was not the Dimitri Petrovski I had once known. His eyes were completely black, insect-like, like a demon's.

"What I want? Isn't it obvious?" The demon brought his mouth to Abby's cheek and caressed her skin with his. Abby tried to stay as expressionless as possible but her eyes betrayed her. "I want the Lost Element you have in your possession. Give it to me and Abby here," she whimpered when demon-Dimitri squeezed, "won't have to suffer the consequences."

"Let her go and I'll give it to you." I knew I was in no position to bargain but desperate times called for desperate measures. "She has nothing to do with this." Which was completely false, because she *was* the Lost Element.

"You see Shane, that's where you're wrong. She has everything to do with it. If I let her go, I lose my bargaining chip and we wound't want that, right?" He took a step to the side, dragging Abby with him. She dug her heels in the cement but Dimitri was stronger. I took a step like Dimitri, a strategic move that fighters pulled on each other—like lions just waiting for the right moment to strike. "And I know that you, Shane, have a feeble for this girl. You would do anything for her and that's why you'll bring me the Element."

Shane! Can you hear me?

It was Abby and heck, she was sending me a telepathic message. Perfectly!

Yeah. Got a plan?

A flash of relief crossed Abby's face. *I thought you wouldn't hear me.* Demon-Dimitri still had a smirk on his face, probably thinking he had won. *Tell him you won't do it.*

I was careful not to reveal any emotion but it was kinda hard with Abby thinking of going on a suicide mission. *What? Are you nuts? He'll kill you!*

All right, all right. Then buy us some time!

"What happened to you Dimitri?" I asked, doing as Abby had said. She had closed her eyes, deep in concentration. "Why are you doing this?"

"The Dimitri Petrovski you knew is no more," answered the demon. He didn't notice Abby's sudden silence and how she ceased fighting. "He died long ago. I killed his soul. All that is left is this, a body, strong and well recognized throughout the Nightriders, easy to get in without being questioned and access to everywhere."

"Then who are you truly?" Pulling off 'fancy' words with this guy seemed to take his mind off Abby and the wanted Element. Yeah, *truly*, to me, was considered a fancy word. I didn't used it very often.

"I am the most powerful of my kind, weakling. You should tremble in front of my greatness! I am Belvedem, your worst nightmare."

The smooth breeze that had been surrounding us picked up enough for the demon and me to notice. Abby still had her eyes closed but her brows weren't furrowed in concentration anymore; they were relaxed, as if she were sleeping.

"What is this?" demanded the creature, tightening his grip on Abby, whose hands were now hanging loosely to her sides. When she didn't respond, the demon took his hand off her throat and went for her chin, so that he could see her face… Before his hand could touch her face, he cried out in pain and released her completely. To our amazement, Abby floated in the air, in her wind cocoon. I took the chance and lunged.

∂∽∾

ABBY

I hadn't really known if it was going to work. I had prayed with all my might to the Wind god. The first time it had happened, Shane had told me of the wind that surrounded me. It shifted and created a barrier. The demon had every intention to kill me because he didn't know that I was what he wanted. Knowing Shane would do something we would both regret, I decided it was time to take things in my own hands. It was, in some way, a chance to step up to the plate.

Now I stood in front of the god, who was sitting on his throne. I still wore the same thing I had last time I had come here, the shimmering white Greek dress. Mortal clothes did not seem to suit him.

"Child, how nice of you to come," said the god, unsmiling. "This will be the last time you force yourself into my palace. Next time, you won't be so pleased." He stood from his seat and crossed his arms over his chest, "But since you are, in a way, my child, I suppose I could let this one slide."

"Your child?" I burst out, my mouth almost dropping open. "You're my father?"

"Well not your biological father, of course." When he saw the look of disappointment on my face, the man rolled his eyes. "Do you not bear my mark?"

"Yes…" I swiftly recovered and sighed, "but the mark, what does it do? All it does is bring me pain… You said I would become the one from the myth, that I was the one from the myth but how can I, when I have all my battles fought by someone else?" The god was about to say something but I was on a roll. "I hate being useless. I know I can learn to fight like every other Nightrider but how long is that going to take? Too long for me to be able to save my family."

"I suppose you have someone fighting your battle at the moment, correct?" I nodded. "And you can't do anything to help." I nodded again, feeling the weight of his gaze on my face but I refused to look at him. How could he stand to look at me when all I was was a failure? "Such a noble cause, you fight for, Abigail. I sometimes wonder if it's too good to be true," Before I could say anything, he continued, "but I have seen the good in you and throughout the millennia, I have seen thousands and thousands of humans whom have succumbed to power. That is why I hesitate in giving you what you want. Will you use it wisely? That is my question."

Once again, I was struck by how godly he had spoken, reminding me of how small and insignificant I was. The wind god looked at me with no emotion at all. The weight of the question pressed on my shoulders but I knew there was only one correct answer, for the god and for me.

I closed my eyes and inhaled the smell of sweet essence that hung around the room. I opened them and held Cairo's gaze. "I will."

The god nodded. "And you know that all power comes with a cost, of course?"

My eyebrows furrowed. "What price?"

"You did not expect me to give you power without you giving me something in return, did you?"

"All right, tell me what you want and then we'll see." I felt blood rush to my face. I was dealing with the devil, talking like that to a god, and we both knew it. I was actually surprised about the nerve I had, even when it was good ol' Cairo.

So apparently did the god, but the flash of surprise was gone as fast as it had come. "So be it." He motioned at something in the air. Nothing happened for a while but the air shimmered into something different. Slowly, I saw before me appear a glass ball. More like a crystal ball really and I suddenly thought that the wind god was going to grow a second head or something scary like that. Cairo reached out for the globe and I expected him to start waving his hand around the ball like a nut job, when with a slight graze of his index finger, the god made me see things...

I had wings! Freaking, flying wings! The crystal ball Abby was soaring high in the air, looking swift and unstoppable and free. She looked like she could do anything, beat down the nastiest creatures, save lives … and then the image shifted. She wasn't in the air anymore or had wings; she was normal again, her shoulders hunched low, shaking with silent sobs, tears flowing down her cheeks freely. I wondered what was wrong and then I myself felt like crying, or better, screaming with rage and helplessness. Mary's body lay in her arms, her lifeless hand limp on the floor.

The happiness and wonder I had felt when I had seen myself flying was completely gone and a feeling of raw and pure sorrow settled in me. I watched as Abby in the crystal ball cried and ended up crying myself.

Then it was over; the globe was gone. I had fallen to my knees in the same posture I had been in the crystal ball but sobs didn't come; only the tears didn't stop. I wiped at them several times, but seeing it did nothing to help, I slowly stood up, my legs shaking.

The wind god had his eyes glued on my face, his expression softer than before. I swallowed back strong and very persistent tears. My voice was a bit shaky when I spoke. "If my family has to die in order for me to get my powers, you can forget it. The goal of me getting my powers is to *save* my family, not *destroy* it."

"What I showed you were merely possibilities of your future. The best case scenario and the worst," explained the god, crossing his fingers over his thick leather armor, bringing my attention to how strong he was, not just god-wise but physically. It kind of creeped me out but I showed no emotion of that, for my fear for Mary was greater. "None of them would come true, of course, if I don't give you the powers you seek."

"So you mean there's still a chance of Mary… *dying*?" The last word almost refused to come out of my mouth but I knew better than not to finish my sentence in front of a god.

"It all depends on you," said the wind god, "which brings us back to my previous question: Will you use your powers wisely?"

"What is it you want in return?" I repeated, my voice barely over a whisper. I wouldn't have been surprised if the sound of the not-so-loud beat of my heart pounded over it.

"I ask only one favor in return. When I shall call upon you, you will come without question and do as I say." The god rose to his feet and added, "Oh, and one last thing, I'll be taking your color."

"My color?"

"Yes, your hair color. Does the contract suit you?"

The thought of losing the darkness in my hair, the one thing I had always prided myself with, was almost heartbreaking. All those years of brushing, taking care of... Mary was worth much more than hair and Cairo knew I wouldn't refuse. "Yes, but why do you want the color of my hair?"

"It gives a bad signal to others. Demons are attracted to the dark and I can't risk losing a favor." The wind god held out his hand toward me. "Power against a favor and your color, deal?"

Without a second's hesitation, I grabbed his hand and shook it; his old yet strong grip tightened before he let go and oblivion accepted me with open arms.

໐৵৵

SHANE

Both my daggers were locked with Dimitri's hand, which had miraculously turned into a sword. Sometimes, I didn't really appreciate Nightriders' advanced technology. This was one of them. I gritted my teeth and pulled at one of my daggers. I went for Dimitri's heart but the demon saw my move and blocked it. We both backed away, turning around and taking our breaths. Sweat trickled down my face and I had to blink to get it out of my eyes. Abby was still in her bubble, her face peaceful; I just hoped she wouldn't start screaming. Dimitri had let her go and that was what I had wanted.

"If it is not I who will kill you, it will be yourself," hissed Dimitri-demon. His face was clean from cuts and blood and not a bead of sweat in sight. He knew he was going to win, not expecting any upset. I saw it in his eyes and it made me sick. "When you die and missy wakes up, there'll be none but me. What will you do? Watch from above as I kill the bitch!"

I usually tended to ignore what my opponents said in battle. They only talked to intimidate and demon-Dimitri was no different. The old Dimitri, on the other hand, had always been dead silent, making his opponents nervous, another proof that this wasn't Dimitri.

"A high fine, they give for her," continued the demon. "Impressive, considering who she is."

Looking up, still crouching a defensive stance, I narrowed my eyes. "What do you mean?"

The demon grinned, knowing he had caught my attention. "Ugly bastards want her skin, alive if possible but not grave if dead. Every rogue has heard of Abby, the lost orphan, long black hair and purple eyes." Dimitri paused, swinging his metallic arm in front of him. "You wouldn't be interested, would you?"

"Who wants her?" I asked, not letting my guard down.

"Give me the Element." The demon lunged, swinging his hand in front of me, changing it into a double-edged sword. I had been ready and I threw my dagger straight at Dimitri's forehead. It zipped through the air and I heard a clang as the demon deflected it with the hilt of his sword (or base of his hand).

After several minutes of attempting to get past my defenses, the demon lost his temper and began to batter at me as if to pound me into the ground. The demon had expected a quick defeat and easy humiliation on my part, not an equal opponent.

I fell back into the rhythmic swordplay I had learned throughout the years; I parried and blocked several deadly blows Dimitri sent me. The wind, that had whizzed around Abby, howling and biting, became completely silent and the air rang with the sound of the singing blades and the hoarse rasp of our breathing. Dimitri was getting tired, to my advantage. I saw the hint of a frown on the demon's face and his skin getting wet.

From the corner of my eye, I looked for Abby. The wind had stopped rustling the leaves and I couldn't have Dimitri near her. When I didn't see her and tried to get my eyes away from the demon, Dimitri let out an angry cry and jumped at me. I barely had enough time to bring up my dagger and block. I almost scrambled away before Dimitri caught the hem of my jean. Jumping up, using the lever of my blade, before even thinking, I dove for the demon's neck.

"Wait!"

The tip of the dagger dragged a bead of blood out of Dimitri's throat. The demon took my moment of hesitation to drive his own sword through my skin, right into my forearm. I bit the inside of my cheek and tasted salty rust. Agh, that son of a … I was going to make him pay for that. This was going to leave a helluva scar. In one swift movement, I kept a hand around the demon's throat and I went blindly to cut the metallic hand off. Dimitri lost his grin and made a grab for my neck.

"Shane!"

I did the mistake to look up and received a hard blow to the jaw. My vision went blurry but only for a second. Pain made me concentrate somehow; it was a reminder that things had to be done *now*.

Dimitri had gotten up and I followed his quick lead. The cut sword/hand lay in a pool of black blood on the cement. The demon stared at it in disdain for a few seconds. He was weaponless. Before the demon could get to the blade on the ground, I snaked my hand between his deadly lashes and scraped at his eye. Dimitri howled in pain and brought his hand to his bleeding face but I was too pumped up to stop just then. I made a grab for the demon's shoulder and kicked his legs out.

I had him in a headlock and Dimitri had nowhere to go. Bringing one of my daggers to the demon's slightly cut throat, I looked for Abby. She was standing merely a few feet away, her fingers slightly shaking. Her face was frozen in something I couldn't quite put my finger on. Something between shock, horror, amazement, envy… God, reading her was not easy.

She took a step forward and Dimitri tried to jerk himself out of my grip. When she was only two feet away, the demon was thrashing wildly, desperate to get to her.

"You'll die bitch! You think I'm the only one? You'll be dead before the next moon!"

Abby held her ground, staring down at the demon, not looking away when he called her names I had never heard before. Her hands had stopped shaking and her facial expression was much cooler and controlled. She flickered her gaze to me, making me notice how her purple eyes seemed lighter and her pupils like those of a cat, like the eyes of a predator.

"Who sent you?" she said, her eyes looking down at Dimitri, who hadn't stopped shouting curses and insults and fighting to get out, which was more like struggling. I gripped him tighter, not letting go.

The demon spat at her. "Does it really matter? You're already dead."

I was getting tired of this and Abby didn't seem very tolerant either of Dimitri's words. She narrowed her eyes and they seemed to glow bright white. Then it was gone and Dimitri had stopped moving; his eyes were fixed on Abby. For a second, I thought he was dead and almost made a grab for his pulse when I remembered that demons had no heartbeat, or heart for that matter.

"Who sent you?" Abby's voice was harsh and disturbed me for some reason.

"A very powerful man," answered the demon, his voice emotionless.

"Why did you want to kill me?"

"There's a bounty over your head, a bounty that's not worth missing."

I exchanged a look with Abby. I could read it in her eyes. *Help?*

"Once you'd captured Abby, what would you have done?" I asked.

Dimitri didn't look in my direction when he said, "I would have hunted down the Element you have possession of and I would have to burn one of her hairs and a drop of her blood."

"What would that do?" said Abby. The demon blinked once and then twice, his black eyes catching no light. "They would come and claim her and pay the ransom they had promised."

Abby seemed satisfied with the information he had given and was about to let him go when I decided he had one more question to answer.

"When were you going to do that?"

"It is already done; they are here."

TWENTY ONE

ABBY

"**S**hit!"

I blinked several times. The demon who had once been Dimitri started thrashing again the second I broke the psychic connection. I didn't know how I had done it or how I had known it would work but it was over now and I had gotten the information we had needed.

"You bitch!" hissed the demon, knocking the air out of Shane when he elbowed him in the stomach. He hadn't been expecting the demon to hit him and he hadn't been on guard.

I heard a loud crack and Shane fell backward, the demon on him. They started beating at each other again, much more intensely than before. I jumped to my feet and was about to head into the fray when I thought better of it. What was I going to do? I had no training and I didn't fully trust my newfound powers. I tried breaking into the demon's mind as I had done before but I couldn't because I didn't know how I had done it.

Oh, this was even more frustrating, because I knew I could do something about it but I didn't know how! My blood boiled with rage. It rushed to my face and my fists clenched and unclenched, my nails digging into my skin, drawing blood.

The demon roared and my ears almost popped. Shane too seemed a bit startled and that was all it took for Dimitri to bringing his fist to Shane's face, punching the lights out of him. Shane let out a low moan before collapsing on his back. His blade fell a few inches away from his hand. He lay motionless on the ground, his body limp.

I had let out a faint cry when he didn't get back up. Dimitri-demon grinned viciously and I actually saw his eyes flicker red but only for a second. When he blinked, they were back to their pit-black color. They gleamed with bloodlust and I ran. He was after me and if I got him away from Shane, he wouldn't get hurt. Anyway, I did not want to stay next to Dimitri-demon. He scared the bejeezus out of me.

Every step I took brought me away from Shane and as my feet hit the ground, I could hear his voice in my head, saying *Run.* ...

I didn't wait a moment longer and ran as fast as I could, my mind-set on reaching the streets, where hopefully I could find a pay phone or something and call Luke or if not, Gabe. Why did my cellphone have to stay back at my demon-infested house?

My mind flickered to Shane, his limp body crumpled on the floor and I felt tears prickle my eyes. I didn't know if my anger toward the wind god was bigger than the emptiness I felt toward Shane. I had asked for powers, dammit! Powers to protect... I cursed under my breath and kept going. Once I was back on the streets, my eyes raced over my environment, looking for demons as well as a place I could call. There was nothing open! It was only early evening and everything was closed?! Not a person in sight.

I saw a flash of red to my right. Maybe it was too good to be true but I was in too much of a rush to really care. *Open.* It blinked several times and then shut down, only to restart a few seconds later.

Running for my life, I pushed the glass door open making a tiny bell ring atop me, like at Mr. Porter's shop. It was a little bistro. There were maybe two or three customers drinking coffee in their own corner, reading the newspaper or a book. Two looked up at my sudden entrance, giving me empty looks. They were sending bad vibes but I didn't wait long. I speed-walked straight to the counter, where a barmaid smiled at me, showing off her straight white teeth. Her brown hair was pulled tight in a ponytail, no stray strands left aside. Her skin was pearl white and I felt that freckles were missing on her face.

"Hello, how can I—"

"Do you have a phone I could use?" I asked in a rush. When the girl didn't react and just stared at me as if I were crazy, I exhaled loudly. "Now!"

"I'm sorry but I need to register your name in order to let you use the phone. Bistro's policy," said the barmaid very calmly, almost smiling when she said it. Without even looking, she pulled out a pen and notebook from behind the counter. "Your name?"

"Victoria Fletcher," I answered, saying the first name that came to my mind. Why I said my arch-nemesis' name, I didn't know. I just didn't trust anyone with my name right now.

The barmaid looked up and slightly squinted in my direction, arching a perfectly shaped eyebrow, but she didn't say anything. When I stayed composed, she looked back down and wrote it down. She muttered something I didn't quite catch and then gave me a forced, warm smile.

"Just turn to your right and there's a telephone cabinet you can use," said the barmaid, motioning. "You don't have to pay."

"Thanks," I muttered, not waiting a second more. I walked to where the barmaid had told me to go. When I didn't see the cabinet the girl had talked about, I ventured further into the hallway.

I stopped short when I arrived at the end of the hallway, where I found no phone, no doors and a trap. The hair on my back raised, chills racing everywhere in my body. Every inch of me was on alert, pumping with adrenaline, one change and I would jump.

Before anything could catch me from behind, I whirled around and screamed in terror. The barmaid was there with the two 'customers' who had been drinking 'coffee.' They were snarling at me, like animals ready to pounce and, oh yeah, they had mean-looking fangs.

Their nails had grown to be sharp and deadly and I remembered too clearly my last encounter with what were starting to be my least favorite creatures of the night.

ತಾ⊸⥂

DIMITRI

I was a man of justice, a man of respect and most of all, a man of honor, but what I was doing was anything but honorable. Well, at least what my body was doing, what the demon that possessed me was doing—Belvedem, that *fucking* traitor. I had traded my soul for my sister's life. My little Yulia… she was only ten years of age and the demon had killed her, with my own two hands.

Two months, I had been in my own body, without having power over it. For two months, I had witnessed what this *mudak*, ruining other people's lives, had done. For two months, he had been using the title I had made for myself against other Nightriders. Nightriders like Abigail, who had never done anything to deserve the faith she got.

"Nice job," said the demon inside me to the vampire woman named Rita. She and one of the two other vampires were holding Abigail, bringing her closer to us. We looked at her and Belvedem caressed her cheek with my hand. The one he had not lost in battle. "Tie her up and get her in the truck."

He picked up the boy at his feet, my old friend, Shane. He had grown up and was much stronger than the last time I had seen him. I had beaten him so many times when we had lived together in Moscow but now, I was not sure if I could have beaten him as easily. I remembered the good times we had had in the academy, always together, as two brothers. He was unconscious at my feet, now. Things should not have been this way.

Abigail … she too had suffered at my hands. We had taken her younger sister as well as her grandmother and put them in a prison cell. We had sent the ghouls to go get her and when they had failed, we sent the vampires the same day we 'arrived' with the other Nightriders. No one except my good friend Connor had noticed my arrival in the group. He had not said anything… We had even taken one of Abigail's blood samples in the laboratory, a strand of her hair and a summoning amulet to burn them, to summon the Fire god himself.

Belvedem had told him to meet us in an abandoned warehouse, forty minutes south of Boston. We were going there right now.

"Ah, little Nightrider," said Belvedem to a very much unconscious Shane. "You will regret not telling me where the Lost Element is."

This demon was powerful; there was no doubt about that. He *knew* things… He knew that Shane knew where the Lost Element was located when he had never even seen Shane before last night. He knew that Abigail had been the one from the prophecy without ever laying eyes on her. He knew that the fire god, himself wanted her, to kill her with his own two hands, so that the Lost Elements would never be found by the savior of humankind. He even knew *why* the god wanted her dead. The god didn't want the Elements to be found by the savior so that they could be found by demons and then 'the world would end in blood and *fire.*'

Belvedem threw Shane in the truck the vampires had stolen and went to the driver's seat, waiting for the vamps to finish tying Abigail and to come.

The demon was either a madman or a genius. He would give Abigail in and claim the bounty on her head and force Shane to tell him where the Element was by threatening Abigail's life, even when she would already be in the god's grasp. Belvedem had been planning this for a month now. He had coordinated his and everyone's every move in a perfect, deadly synchronized dance.

You see, Dimitri, thought Belvedem to me. *I always obtain what I want.* *Even if it means killing innocent people?* I responded sharply.

He chuckled. Especially *if it means killing innocent people.*

ॐॐ

ABBY

I woke up in the dark and cold. I wasn't aware of anything except my brain for at least a minute. I wished I could say that this wouldn't happen often, but I doubted that the future would be that nice.

First thing I had to establish was some sort of plan. I wasn't the most battle-strategic person ever. I had no experience and I didn't know what crap I had gotten into this time. I could barely remember the last time I had been conscious. I knew I had gone into a cafe, then there had been a trap, the vampires and then there was a blur. Okay, so one thing was for sure, I was in waist-high shit.

Once I did get the feeling of my toes and feet back, I tried kicking. Of course, no such luck. They were bound and so were my arms, and it *hurt*, as if someone was slapping your sunburnt skin. No, there wasn't any aloe vera to alleviate the pain (unfortunately).

I rolled over on my stomach and got on my knees, only to fall back on my face. Second thing I had established, I was on a truck or something like that. I had just started noticing the rocking feeling.

Fine, so I couldn't get up and I was in a truck. What else? I had to know if there was anything that could come in handy. I had nothing to lose. So, that's how I ended up rolling around in the truck, hurting myself whenever the vehicle did a harsh turn. After several (four) painful hits, I rolled on top of something, or rather someone. I stopped short, my back against the warm body. My breath caught and my heart went racing.

The person didn't move and in fact, I wasn't even sure he was breathing. I got on my knees to see who it was and I almost fainted.

It was dark in the truck but I could see very well Shane's pale skin.

"Shane," I croaked out. I swallowed hard when he didn't respond. I wanted to shake him awake but my hands were tied behind my back and there was no way I could get out of them. "Shane, please wake up."

After a minute of staring at him, trying to nudge him with my knees, I was sure he wasn't going to wake up anytime soon. He was still breathing but barely. I put my head on his chest and listened to his heart beating. I felt safer now because he was here with me and I wasn't alone anymore.

I said to myself, he won't be able to protect us when our abductors come to get us. I went back up on my knees and groaned. If anyone was going to save us, it had to be me. What could I do? I had nothing to cut the binds or burn them...

I fell back on my side and cuddled next to Shane. I was getting cold and my determination to free us left me. There was nothing I could do that would help us. Shane was bleeding, barely breathing and I felt completely lost. The surge of power I had when I had taken over Dimitri's mind was gone; there was only emptiness.

I stayed like this for what might have been an hour or just five minutes. I listened to Shane's steady, slow heartbeat.

I'm sorry Shane, I sent out to him. I hoped he could hear me and better yet, answer me, but there was no response. *I didn't mean for you to get hurt. … It's because of me you're hurt and you don't know how much I wish I had jumped in there to try and help you. It's all my fault and I take full responsibility for it.*

Still nothing. I sighed and closed my eyes. Might as well say everything that was on my mind since he was unconscious. *Thanks for tonight, by the way. For the pizza, I mean. I appreciate what you do for me, even though sometimes you do tend to get on my nerves. I know for you it's nothing but a babysitting job and that you're responsible for me but for me… well, before tonight, I thought… Well, I thought you felt the need to protect me, like I feel the need to protect Mary but I guess I was wrong.*

My situation was so… pitiful. I'd never thought I'd be this brought down ever in my life. I was supposed to be a fighter, not some random, crying, useless girl… Now, of all times…

I felt a slight itching at the back of my throat and swallowed. I was nothing better than a love struck fool and that I was falling for this guy and … God, why was my throat itching like that?

When the retched itching didn't go away, I cleared my throat and felt me eyes water. The strange odor that came out of my mouth stung my eyes and I shut my trap right away.

I'm supposed to be more than this. I should've figured out a way to get us out by now. I shouldn't be listening to his heartbeat like a…

Then I started coughing, slightly at first, until it became gut wrenching. I bent in half and rolled off Shane. I started shaking heavily and my throat was killing me. I felt my saliva rolling down my chin and got on my knees so it didn't go up my cheeks.

What was wrong with me? As far as I was concerned, I wasn't sick…

The truck made a dry turn and I fell against the wall. Tears were running freely down my face and a sob escaped my lips. I coughed more and more until I could barely breathe. It went on like this for at least a minute.

I suddenly felt arms around me and I didn't react. I was in too much pain to care.

"Abby!" exclaimed Shane next to me, shaking me. I wanted to cry out because his shaking was hurting me but my coughing didn't allow me to. When he saw that I couldn't do anything about it, Shane took my chin and tried to see into my face. I fell into his arms and he hugged me tightly to his chest. He rocked me back and forth and when the coughing stopped, I fainted for the zillionth time this week.

᠅

SHANE

I had just been stabbed in the arm and I was feeling perfectly fine. There was no pain, no feelings, just this retching sound at the back of my mind. At first, I could tune it out to think about ... *nothing*, really. Then it got stronger and more forced. I heard a sob and that's when my eyes flew open. It was Abby.

The pain in my arm immediately came but all I could think of was getting to Abby. I half stood up, only to be pushed back down by an invisible force. It was only then that I noticed my surroundings. I was in a dark compartment (a truck, I later found out) and Abby was against one of the sides, coughing what might have been blood. I was at her side and put my arms around her. She was shaking like a leaf and every cough vibrated through her.

I tried shaking her out of it and called out her name. Maybe she had inhaled some dust, but the blood covering her suggested otherwise. When I saw that shaking her only made her face contort in more pain, I stopped and held her as tight to me as possible. She was with me now and I wasn't going to let anything hurt her... except that thing inside her that was killing her.

I could see her shoulders were hurting her because she always tried to bring her arms forward. They were bound, something I had failed to notice in this circumstance. I stretched for the blade hidden in my shoe, careful not to move her much and sliced away the rope around her wrists and ankles.

Abby cuddled into my chest. She brought her hands to her chest as she continued coughing. At that moment, I wanted to be a doctor, to try to help her ... but I wasn't a doctor and there was nothing else I could do but rub her back and wipe her forehead of sweat. I leaned against the side of the truck and closed my eyes.

What if she was going to bleed out on me? What if she... I couldn't bring myself to think but I knew that that prospect wasn't impossible.

Her coughs finally decreased and became less forced and my pressure dropped slightly. Once they stopped completely, I opened my eyes and made a grab for her wrist, which was limp on her lap, to check for a pulse. It was slow but steady. She had fainted and she would definitely live. So, she hadn't bled out on me... Then, what was all this muck on me?

I considered the possibility that it might have been something she had eaten and possibility that it *had* been blood, until I saw her, *really* saw her. Oh Lord...

This was turning out to be a shitty night out.

TWENTY TWO

ABBY

I woke up in Shane's arms. I didn't need to open my eyes to know it was him. I could recognize his natural fragrance anywhere. Wow, I was *really* going nuts. He was carrying me, to where, I didn't know and I didn't open my eyes to find out. My throat throbbed a bit but that was nothing compared to before.

I let my head fall to the side, right into the crook of Shane's neck. I cuddled next to him and smiled inwardly. His skin was so soft ... I could stay like this forever.

Abby.

I groaned. *Leave me alone.*

You've been asleep for two hours now. It's time to wake up.

I don't want to.

Fine. Pretend to sleep but let me tell you this; we're waist high in shit.

Your waist or mine?

I felt his groan vibrate through his chest. *My waist.*

Ew. That's not good.

No. It isn't.

Where are we?

I don't know but all those guns say we're not welcome.

Have they said anything? I asked.

No. They covered my head with a sack so I couldn't see anything when we got out of the truck.

Did you get a good look at them?

Yeah, he answered. *No one I know of, except Dimitri.*

I didn't say (think, you get what I mean) anything for a while and neither did he. I concentrated on the sounds around me. I heard footsteps against hard floor, their echoes from one ear and Shane's heartbeat against my other ear.

Shane suddenly stopped walking and I felt his grip tighten around me. I heard what might have been a knock on a door.

"Come in!" exclaimed a voice behind that door.

Shane's grip tightened even more and I bit the inside of my cheek not to let out a sound. The door clicked open.

Abby, open your eyes and when I let go of you, cry.

Cry? I asked after opening my eyes. We stood in front of the office and I gulped. We were surrounded by armed men (with guns) and they looked mean and ready to kill. Shane was tense next to me and his arms stayed around my waist when he let me on my feet.

Yes. Cry!

Why?

Look innocent and we might make it out alive.

Okay, but I won't stoop as low as to cry.

Yeah, like you've never cried before.

He pressed against me, making me step forward. We walked into the office, where I saw Dimitri, staring at me as if I'd grown a second head.

Once we were all in the room (armed guys included), the door closed behind us. The floor was carpeted red and there were countless shelves holding old looking books. The room was well lit but not *too* lit. There were brown leather couches facing a large desk.

I was pressed up against Shane, trying to look as innocent as possible. I lowered my gaze to the ground and shuffled my feet.

"Hello, Miss Fletcher."

I looked up at the person or rather the back of the big black chair who had spoken.

"You do know why you are here, right?" It was a man. He could have been in his mid-forties or mid-thirties. I would've been able to tell if the guy had the decency to *look* at me.

When I didn't answer (playing innocent), the person sighed. "Word has it that you are the one from a long forgotten prophecy." He paused. "The one who is supposed to gather the Lost Elements and bring salvation on Earth."

"What makes you think she's the one from the prophecy? She's just this girl I met on the streets. She has nothing to do with this," said Shane, his voice firm and convincing.

"Why, my dear Belvedem, is this insolent boy here?"

I held on to Shane's hand and squeezed it. Dimitri, or Belvedem, grinned at us. "I was asking myself the same question." He walked toward us. Shane got in front of me, blocking Belvedem's view of me. "Let's go have a talk."

Shane hesitated before leaving the room. *Keep me updated.* I nodded before he left. The door shut behind them. I was on my own now.

He had told me to play innocent, so I would play innocent. "Why have you brought me here?" I said in a small voice. Inside, I wanted to make him look at me and make him tell all of his secrets that could help me find my family again. Yeah, like that would ever happen.

"Because you, my dear girl, have something that no rightful demon would want to be unleashed," he said, his voice calm and blank of all emotion.

"I'm not who you're talking about. I just want to get out of here and go to this party at my friend's house." Shane had said to play as innocent as possible. Well, I hoped as hell I sounded innocent! "I got her this cutest bag in the entire city of Boston! She is going to *flip*! Why the fuck am I still here?"

I heard a dark chuckle emanating from the turned seat. It made me feel all jittery and scared. I didn't know what I was up against and that wasn't really the best of things. "Girls these days are so naive and entirely blind. They are incapable of seeing through their bubble world. And I don't like shallowness, especially from people with great importance in the development of events."

I didn't say anything, not because this guy scared the bejesus out of me even though I hadn't yet seen him but because his words leaked with disdain and superiority, which could only mean one thing. He wouldn't hesitate to kill a little bug like me.

"Why, if you are innocent, was that Nightrider with you?" he asked. It was goddamn frustrating not to be able to see his face.

I tried to answer as quickly as possible, so he would hear no hesitation coming from me. "I just met this guy on the street last night, at this party..." Wow, I sounded like a real party-animal, which wasn't exactly the case. "I wanted to hook up with him tonight, so I told him to meet me at the little café, where I got fucking *ambushed* by this crazy bitch and two other psychos..." I stopped and caught my breath. "I really wanna get out of here. You guys give me the creeps!"

The man didn't say anything for a while. So, I took the opportunity to contact Shane.

Shane, are you all right?

A few seconds passed before he answered me. *I could be better. Have you learned anything?*

Nothing worth mentioning. Should I ask about Mary and Mrs. Wildfire?

No, definitely not, that would blow our cover. Remember, innocent and pretend not to know me. They haven't talked things though with Dimitri, so this guy doesn't know anything about you having anything to do with the Lost Elements or your missing family or anything. He just knows you're the girl from the prophecy.

Thank you, Shane.

And Abby...

Yes?

The earrings that Gabe gave you? Break one of them if anything bad happens okay?

Okay. Be care—

The connection had been broken. I tried prying in his mind again but it was impossible. I gulped. I was *really* on my own now.

∞∽

SHANE

I gritted my teeth as I received another hard blow from Belvedem. Bastard was a word I would rather use to call this fucking traitor. He betrayed his own kind; he betrayed the Nightrealm and that was something that didn't sit well with me.

Two guards (two demons in human form, to be exact) held both of my arms as Dimitri kept punching me in the gut. I had tried to keep the pain out of my voice as I 'spoke' to Abby and as far as I knew, it had worked. If I could spare her any pain, physically or mentally, then I would do it. She had gone through enough within the past week; she didn't need to worry about me.

I *almost* let out a whimper as Dimitri knocked my—most probably broken—rib. I wouldn't give him the satisfaction of hearing my pain.

"Well, little Nightrider, are you willing to tell me where the Element is?" asked the demon, hissing like the vicious snake he truly was.

He let me breath for about ten seconds. Getting beaten could really be tiring. I panted, feeling a bit light-headed. "Up your ass, bastard."

I lifted my chin to watch as his face contorted in an ugly grimace. He wasn't the happiest person around the block; that much was evident.

"Well then." Belvedem stood up straighter and looked over my guards. "I have to speak with the big boss. Don't let him do so much as move a finger. I don't feel like adding two heads to my collection."

I felt the guards' grip tighten, but they were underestimating my strength. I could easily get free if I wanted to, even with a damn broken rib and a severed ligament. Thank God for all those painful hours of work with Kristen to get myself free...

I received a hard blow on the jaw, making me bite my tongue in the process. I tasted blood in my mouth and I could see the light spinning of stars around my head, even though my logic told me it wasn't real.

Dimitri smiled at me and all I wanted to do was punch the lights out of him. God only knew how much he deserved it. He turned around and walked to the sleek wooden door that led to the office, his steps echoing in the large empty hallway of the warehouse. Once the door closed behind him, I spit out blood.

〜〜

ABBY

I held my breath as the velvet chair slowly turned toward me. My heart was beating like a jackhammer, my head felt like it was going to explode and my stomach was contracting like there was no freaking tomorrow.

He wore a nice black tux, which fit his body like an elegant businessman. He was an older man, around his fifties or sixties. His shallow wrinkles travelled all over his face and his eyes were blue. They weren't a rich, nice blue like Shane's eyes; they were pale, so pale that they could be mistaken for white. His sleek black hair was greying but not in an ugly manner. He was all class … and dangerous. I could see it in his eyes, the way he looked around as if he wanted to enflame things and watch as they burned.

My description of him was not exaggerated. He was a monster in a tux—a demon.

When he laid eyes on me, it was as if I was being pierced by a spear. Then he laid eyes on my face and all his cool expression faded. He looked at me with a surprised expression and then an angry one. Just at that moment, the door behind me opened. I knew right away it was Dimitri because my skin started to crawl.

"Belvedem!" exclaimed the man, his face contorting with anger. "What is this?"

Dimitri/Belvedem looked at me with disdain and turned toward the man, who was now standing up. "Why, it is the girl you have asked for, my lord."

"It is clearly said in the prophecy that she is to have purple eyes and *black* hair," bellowed the demon, his face bright red.

"Yes, about that…" Belvedem cleared his throat and gestured toward my head. "There is this new invention that humans have, that permits taking away the color in one's hair. I believe that she has bleached her hair so that she didn't fit the description of the prophecy. When I first saw her at the academy, she had black hair."

The demon didn't even look fazed. "Do humans *bleach* their eyebrows?"

"No, my lord but like I said—"

"I do not care what you have said, filthy *assnik!*" said the demon. "You have brought me here for nothing. This girl," he gestured me with an accusing finger, "is a simple case of albinism." I jumped when he kicked the huge desk toward the other end of the room, as if it were nothing more than a soccer ball. "You have brought me here for an albino!"

"But my lord, I have *seen* her with black hair—"

"Filth like you never tend to tell the truth. All you wanted was the bounty on her head," replied the man, who looked at me once more, "which you do not deserve. I will have to talk with my brother about what we shall do with you."

"But master, Rita and the vamps have seen her with black hair as well; otherwise, they wouldn't have brought her—"

"I don't want to hear another word of this, assnik. You have brought me here for nothing and that is all." He sighed in frustration. "We shall see of your punishment." He looked toward me and then back to Belvedem. "Erase her memory. Don't kill her; we need easy kills like her in the world." He walked out of the room, slamming the door shut behind him.

Dimitri turned toward me, his face red with anger. "Stay here or I'll kill your family," he barked out. He too left, again slamming the door.

I stood frozen on my feet, my heart having difficulty beating. Did he have my family? My legs felt like they might give out. I stumbled my way to the closest couch and crashed down. This wasn't good. This *really* wasn't good.

Abby?

I jumped up, startled. *Shane, we are in deep shit.*

What happened?

Nothing good.

Hmm. Okay… Do you know why we're here? Is it for the Element or…

It looked as if the guy in the tux only cared about the prophecy and not the fact that we possessed a Lost Element.

Hmm… Maybe Dimitri didn't have the time to tell him? suggested Shane.

I doubt it. It's not a small deal that you can just forget.

You're right. Maybe Dimitri only wanted to hand you in for the bounty on your head.

I have a bounty on my head?

A pretty big one if you ask me.

The man in the tux said I didn't fit the bill.

Yeah, about that… How the hell did you pull it off?

Pull what off?

Your hair.

My hair?

There was a pause and then, *Take a look at your hair.*

I tugged at my ponytail until my hair came loose around my shoulders. At first, I didn't believe what I saw but when it finally did sink in, I gasped. No. This couldn't be real. Oh God, help me…

I had seen people turn into dust and people shift into animals but nothing could have prepared me for this. My hair, which I had spent so much time taking care of…

I have freaking white hair, Shane.

Then I remembered. It had been in the deal I had made with the wind god. He had said he would take away my color because it attracted darkness.

That contract had most probably just saved my life… Oh yes, the god had helped me alright. I looked at my hair again. There were much worse things in life, much worse.

I took a shaky breath and did my best to clear my mind. I closed my eyes and tried to visualize a happy place… only I couldn't find a happy place anymore. Damn it to hell, these stupid mental tricks!

When Dimitri's gonna erase your memory, act as if he did.

It took me a few seconds to answer. *What if he really does erase my memory?* I asked, panicked by the thought.

He won't be able to... Look, the vampire couldn't control you.

But Dimitri knows more than the man in the tux. He must know that I can't be controlled or have my memories erased... I think he knows where my family is, Shane.

Maybe, but we're not in the best of situations now, so don't try to question him. I don't want you to get caught.

But what happens to you? They know they can't control you...

As soon as you get out of here, break one of the earrings.

But what about you?

He didn't answer right away and I knew that he wasn't planning on leaving. *Shane, you can't stay, God only knows what they'll do to you...*

I'm a warrior Abby; there's nothing to worry about.

Shane...

He was already gone.

Damn him! I ripped one of my earrings out of its hole and threw it on the floor. I got up and stepped on it, putting in much more strength than was needed. The glass shattered and I prayed that this would work.

TWENTY THREE

SHANE

Well this is it, I thought when I broke the connection with Abby. I wasn't sure if both of us coming out of here alive was possible... probably not.

I watched as Belvedem spoke with the man in the tux rather hotly. It was obvious that he was pleading his case to the man. I wondered why Belvedem was so afraid of this man. Hadn't he been the one bragging about how powerful he was not so long ago? Then again, demons always boasted their true strength... but this... Belvedem really *was* afraid of the man. No matter how strong a demon was, they were rarely afraid of anything, much less another demon.

"Do not try to plead your case with me, assnik. I am the Fire God and I don't have time to waste with filth like you."

My mind reeled. *What*? This guy was the Fire God? What would the Fire god want with Abby? Whatever it was he wanted with her, it couldn't be good.

"But my lord—"

"Enough!" bellowed the god. His face was red with anger and I saw his fists turning bright red. "I was a fool to send out a public announcement for this job. Any fool could summon me without actually having the girl!"

"But she is the girl, my lord. I have seen her with my own two eye—"

"Eyes you won't have if you do not stop talking right now. I will be lenient and leave you with one fair warning," growled the god. "And this."

The god's hands were now in flames and with one swift movement, he took Belvedem by the neck. The demon hissed out a cry and waited for the god to take his hand off. The god smiled to himself, satisfied to see the demon writhing in pain.

"Think twice next time you call on me, *assnik*. Next time, I will burn you whole." With that, the god vanished in flames.

Belvedem fell to the ground and held his neck with both hands.

"Not so tough now, eh?" I said, a sly smile on my face.

The demon was up on his feet within seconds. He grabbed me by the hair and brought my face close to his.

"You know, Shane," he hissed. "I may just have lost the biggest deal of my life and I'm not really happy. But you know what?" He paused and smiled slowly. "I won't take it out on *you*."

My blood ran cold. "You—"

My guards kicked me to my knees and then to my stomach. I had been unprepared, damn it!

I heard the door clicking open and looked up. Abby poked her head out. Her white hair hung loosely around her shoulders and she was looking around. When her eyes found me, she shut the door behind her.

"Ah, Abby, we were just talking about you." Belvedem walked toward her and she took a step back, bumping against the door. "I don't know how you pulled that little trick of yours. It was really... *amazing*. You'll have to teach it to me someday."

She didn't say anything, just stared at me.

"You could have warned me beforehand, so that I could have avoided being burnt." Again, she said nothing. "I believe you owe me an apology."

Abby looked at him, a sneer on her face. "I don't need to apologize to *you*."

"Oh but I think that you do." He looked in my guards' direction. "Get him up."

They did as he said and got me to my feet. I could get out of their grip but decided against it because Belvedem was too close to Abby.

Belvedem got something out of his coat. It was a non-blessed katara. Abby looked at it, clearly remembering what I had told her about it. *The Indians used it for sacrificial rituals.* It was as if he had known the conversation we had had. "You see, Abby, I'm not in a very good mood and this dagger here is *very* sharp. Don't think of pulling that little trick you played on me earlier. If they see that you are compelling me, these guards will kill him and it will all be *your* fault."

Abby's eyes darted in my direction and then back to Belvedem.

"Now that this is settled, tell me where the Lost Element is, Shane or I will pierce her pretty little heart with this." He raised the katara and gave me the evilest grin I had ever seen. *Damned if you do,* I thought. *Damned if you don't.*

෨ঙ

ABBY

The guards will kill him and it will *all be your fault.*" The last words stuck to my mind like leeches on skin. He knew exactly where to hit the spot. I balled my fists and looked in Shane's direction, who was now standing upright. I could not let anything be *my* fault anymore. It was *my* fault that Mary and Mrs. Wildfire had been kidnapped. It was *my* fault that Shane was here… It was all *my* fault. I could *not* let this be my fault. I couldn't.

Shane didn't say anything but he saw the look in my eyes and he slightly shook his head. *Don't do it Abby.*

"Shane doesn't have it," I said slowly. I turned to look at Belvedem. "I do."

Belvedem snorted, clearly not believing me. "Where is it then?"

I let out a long breath. "I—"

"Shut up Abby. Don't you dare say it!" shouted Shane, straining against the two guards. "Abby, he'll—"

"*I* am the Lost Element," I exclaimed, to stop Shane from saying anything else. The four men stared at me. The two guards had horror written all over their faces and Belvedem had an amused look in his eyes. Shane looked like I had just killed his reason for living. I looked away from him, feeling the heaviness of his look on me. I felt like I had betrayed him.

"Is this a joke?" asked Belvedem, laughing. "The Lost Element is *a girl?*"

I nodded.

"Prove it to me then, because I really don't believe you."

How could I show him that I was the Lost Element? How?

"She's on crack, Belvedem! Don't listen to what she—" Shane grunted when one of the guards punched him in the gut. I bit my lower lip.

I closed my eyes and concentrated. I couldn't go back to Cairo's palace, because then Belvedem would kill Shane and the god would kill *me*. I placed my hands on my abdomen, where most of my marks were situated. Make the wind blow, I thought, concentrating. Make the wind blow so hard that chairs fly off the ground. I opened my eyes and saw that my hair was starting to lift up in the air. *Make the wind blow!*

Then it was as if the wind suddenly decided to listen to my every word. The guards tightened their grips on Shane and distanced their feet to stay balanced. Belvedem was laughing now, looking at me in awe. He was still laughing when I told the wind to calm down.

"Ha! That's wonderful, Abby." He took my face in one hand and kissed my forehead. I let him, knowing that if I objected, he would threaten Shane again.

"So you'll let Shane go if I surrender myself to you?" I asked in a small voice.

"Of course, but I think we both know you are already mine, so it's my turn to hold my part of the deal." He looked in Shane's direction, all smiles. I didn't like it. "Guards, let him go."

The vamps did as he said and stepped back. Shane was looking at me, sadness written all over his face. "Abby—"

"Shane, leave now," I whispered. I had given myself to the demon now and there was no chance for me to get out of this alive *with* Shane. It was him or me and at this point, I'd rather it be him.

"I won't leave you," he said firmly. My heart suddenly welled up with love. My eyes prickled with tears.

"Isn't this heartbreaking," mocked Belvedem. "Shane, I didn't know you were in love with *my* Abigail." Rage flashed in Shane's eyes. "Don't worry though. She'll come see you soon enough."

With one quick movement of the hand, Belvedem threw the katara toward Shane. He was too surprised to do anything and just stood there.

"NO!" I screamed. I did the first thing that came to my mind and with my hands, gestured toward me, away from Shane. Wind to me! A sudden surge of wind came in the room and the dagger was swept away from Shane and toward me. I let out a small whimper as it entered my stomach. I looked down at the katara, with its hilt sticking out.

I fell to my knees just as the windows around us shattered. My ears were ringing with every shatter and every shout. I looked up just in time to see Nightriders entering the building with swords and guns. I saw several faces I had already seen before. There was Gabe, Connor, Chi— I looked for Shane but I couldn't see him through my blurring vision. Where was he? I fell to the cold ground and felt the blade inside me shift. I yelped and pulled it out, using every ounce of force I had left. It clattered to the floor. Everyone was running around me, leaving me on the cement floor. It was so cold. My eyes closed slowly. I was all alone. He too had left me…

⧶•⧷

SHANE

I thought I would die for real this time. I had been trained all my life to move away from a dagger when one was thrown at me but this time, I had stayed frozen in place. I couldn't bear the thought of losing Abby to a dirty demon like Belvedem. No matter how much it pained me to admit it, the demon was right. I did love her… The realization hit me exactly when I heard Abby scream. I knew I would at least die with her voice in my head. I knew Belvedem would never let me walk out of this alive, he was a demon after all; they never kept their end of deals. So, when the dagger came flying toward me, I let it. I thought I would die... until the dagger wasn't there anymore. There was a sudden gust of wind and it was gone.

I saw an opportunity and took it. I lunged for Belvedem, who was still frowning. I tackled him to the floor and heard glass shattering around us. I didn't have to look up to know it was reinforcements.

"I told you that you weren't so tough," I grunted as I punched him in the gut. He doubled in half and let out an *oof.* "You thought you would keep her for yourself? Eh?" I hooked him on the nose. "Your cell is going to be so deep in the earth that you won't even be able to *dream* about seeing sunlight again." I was so angry at this guy; the rage was eating me, making my hits harder. Belvedem barely fought back; he knew he had lost. I only stopped when I was pulled up by Connor and another Nightrider I didn't know.

"Shane," said the Scot. "Get a grip, will ya?"

My heartbeat slowed down and I looked around. There were about ten Nightriders in the room and about five more in the office. The two vamps were being taken away and Connor and the other Night were on Belvedem.

"Ye'll be taken into questioning at the academy," said Connor. "You try to fight, we put ye to sleep. Understood?"

Just before his hands were completely tied up, Belvedem looked behind him and then back at me. He smiled. "If I can't keep her, then neither can you."

"Come on!" exclaimed Connor, shoving Belvedem forward. They walked away toward the exit. I didn't look back to see if they were out or not. My eyes were glued to Gabe in front of me. With every step I took, the words the demon had just said sank into me further. *If I can't keep her, neither can you.*

"No..." I fell to my knees. My hands were shaking and my entire body went cold.

"Shane, get a grip. We have to get her to the academy right away!"

I couldn't register the words he had just told me. I just stared. Her pale hair was around her head like a halo around an angel. Her lips were rosy pink against her pale skin and her eyelashes looked even longer than they usually did. Her pants were stained with her hair color and her shirt was stained with blood. I saw the bloodied katara on the floor. This couldn't be happening.

"Shane!" shouted Gabe, shoving me in the head. "If we don't get her outta here fast, she's going to die. Do you hear me? She is going to DIE!"

That snapped me out of it. I looked at her sweet face. My hands were shaking as I reached for her face to tuck a strand of her hair behind her ear. I slowly put my hands to her neck, to feel for her pulse. It was much slower than it should be. It was decreasing. … I looked at Gabe and read an urgency in his eyes. He'd always been there to unnerve me and right now, he was urging me to save her life. I gripped my resolve and balled my fists. I was not going to let Abby die on me. I slipped Abby's frail body onto my arms and I took her under the knees and waist and lifted her up, her body limp in my arms. "Where are the Ghosts?" I asked sharply to Gabe.

"There right to the left when you go out."

I was out before I knew it. I jogged to the nearest Ghost, strapped Abby in the backseat and made sure the cloth Gabe had been holding against her wound held. I put her helmet on and started the engine. I flew us straight to the academy. Oh please, let her live through this… A part of me would die if she didn't.

ॐॐ

LUKE

I was pacing the front lobby over and over again. My mind was racing in all kinds of different directions, and my stomach churned every time it ventured into negative scenarios. Around an hour ago, Gabe's phone had started ringing loudly, in an awful distress call. He had jumped from his seat and gone running to the weapons' room, barking orders at the Nightriders that were on his way. I hadn't known what was happening, and Gabe panicking didn't help my blood pressure. I had followed him all the way to where the weapons were stored and asked him what the hell was going on.

"Abby's in danger," was all he said, and that sent my mind reeling. He even refused to bring me with them after I insisted. "You don't have the proper training." That was worse than receiving a punch to the jaw. He was basically telling me that I was useless. That all my abilities were worthless in saving the girl I loved. I'd bitten down on my cheek and dug my nails into my palms. He and ten other Nightriders had left on Ghosts, and I was left behind, to freaking academy-sit.

An hour later, my blood pressure had risen dramatically, and my nerves were on edge. All I could do was wait, and that by itself was more than I could handle. I thought I was going to loose it, when I heard the upstairs garage door open. My heart skipped a beat, and I ran up the stairs to the weapons' room.

My heart tightened inside my chest as soon as I saw who had come in. It was Shane, and he was holding an unconscious Abby in his arms. The smell of blood hit me before I saw it. The Nightrider was tightly holding a cloth to her gash, and I could see worry written all over his features.

"Instead of just standing there like a complete idiot, make yourself darned useful and go get Greta," barked out Shane, his voice echoing through the large room. I could see more Ghosts nearing the academy, and without asking any questions, I did as I was told. I didn't like being ordered around by anyone, much less this mutt, but Abby's life was at stake, and there was nothing more important than making sure she was alright.

As I quickly went down the stairs, to go to the main level, my mind stayed on the thought of Abby. She'd been hurt, badly, and I vowed to myself that I would kill the person who had done it. I felt a deep and consuming rage take over me, as I came to the realization that Abby might not make it through the night. It wasn't anger, and it wasn't even rage. It was wrath, and the one who had caused this to my love would feel it full swing. I was in a murderous mood.

I found Greta, an older Healer from India. She came with me as soon as I said she was needed. We made our way to the infirmary, where Shane had most probably taken Abby.

The Nightrider had laid Abby on one of the beds, and had gone in an adjacent room to get morphine, and a sterilized medical equipment kit. Gabe was there, and he was cutting open Abby's shirt with scissors, careful to not move her too much.

Greta went to wash her hands, and as soon as she had gloves on, she got to work. None of us had to tell us what had happened; she just knew what to do.

Gabe stayed on the opposite side of the bed, ready to help the Healer as soon as she might need it. He too had scrubbed. And all I could do was watch. I slouched down on a chair across from where Abby was taken care of. I simply watched as they worked on her pale body, until Shane tapped me on the back.

I looked up, and I couldn't even muster up anger towards him as I usually could; I was too devastated for that.

"You should come with me. There's nothing we can do in here," he said calmly, almost sympathetically.

I grunted, and felt my throat constrict. I had a nagging sense that all of this was my fault. That somehow, I was the one who had pushed Abby to leave the academy in the first place.

"Feeling sorry for yourself won't make things any better Luke." At the mention of my name, I stiffened. Not once had he called me by my name. "But I know one thing that will make you feel better."

I accorded him a second glance, and he continued: "We have the one who did this to her."

I saw red for a moment, and I swiftly got up. I only had one thing on my mind, and that was blood. I looked one last time at Abby's inanimate figure and made a silent prayer in her stead. All I hoped was that after what I was going to do, I would still have a shred of humanity left in me. Although all I felt in the moment was an animalistic urge to kill the one who had caused Abby pain.

I followed Shane all the way to the basement, where I had first been kept on the night Abby had come to see me at my apartment.

This place was one of the only areas kept unclean in all of the academy. It was bellow ground level, and therefor always had a strong scent of moisture. The walls were partially wet due to the constant humidity, and the bars were thick, unbreakable. There were two longs rows of cells that stretched on for a good two hundred feet. The cells were barren of anything, it was just big enough so that an average size man could comfortably lie down. There was a good three feet of cement between each cell, and the bars were incrusted in gold, silver and steel, as to not allow any Nightrealmer to be able to escape.

There were several Nightriders already there, and they were all around one particular cell. I recognized them all by face, but I only knew the Scot's name, Connor. He was the one that had the most murderous look on his face. His jaw was tight as he spoke, and his knuckles white as he held on tightly to his sword.

Shane and I walked up to them, and only then was I capable of seeing who, or more like what, was in the cell. It was Dimitri. Or at least, what looked like Dimitri. His eyes were black like coals, and his metallic arm had been cut off. He wasn't even bleeding, and payed no attention to his stump.

"You bloody bastard, ye thought ye could get away with this?"

"I did!" Dimitri answered in a superior voice. "You silly Nightriders never suspected anything! I was capable of infiltrating your troops without you even questioning me. I had easy access to just about everything in the academy, and you were never even able to figure out that the one who had trespassed that old woman's apartment was me! And you call yourself a Seeker. Pff! There was nothing easier than fooling all of you, and I did it!"

The Nightriders standing there looked a bit uncomfortable due to the fact that the demon had infiltrated their troops, and they had been incapable of discovering his true identity. There was only Connor and Shane who were entirely unfazed and that kept their murderous stares.

Shane stepped up to Connor, and gave him a questioning look. The Scot nodded, and Shane pressed the cell door open and walked in.

The demon was in chains and didn't try to break out of them: it would have been useless. The chains were covered in those Holy marks, as well as in gold and silver. These cells were made to keep even the worst of Nightrealmer criminals at bay, and no one was afraid this one would be able to escape.

Shane crouched low next to the demon, and stared into his eyes. "Where are they?" he asked, every single word ringing with measured, deadly anger.

"I won't die. You can torture me all you want, but I won't die. This body will, but not I, Belvedem. You won't get anything out of me."

He was right. Once this body would die, he would only come back, in a different body. For as long as the body was alive, the demon had a refuge.

"I know you won't tell me a thing. But Dimitri will."

The demon gave Shane a cocky grin. "That fool is long gone. He won't answer you."

Without another word, the Nightriders closed their eyes, and all had concentrated frowns on their faces.

The demon laughed. "Dumb, dumb fools, you think that you could overpower me? I am Belvedem, and you will never..." He stopped speaking, and a look of pain spread over his face.

It was only when he started screaming that I understood what was happening. They were doing that mental communication thingie, all at the same time. I wondered if they were trying to pry the information from him, but when his eyes turned back to their human form, it all clicked. They were trying to reach the real Dimitri.

Within twenty minutes, it was over, and the demon was back, laying still on the ground.

"I'll go fetch them," said Connor. He walked away.

Shane looked at the remaining Nightriders. "You can leave us."

They solemnly nodded and followed after Connor, not saying a word. All of them had tired expressions on their faces. Shane beckoned me to come closer. I could feel my muscles tensing, and I knew this would be my revenge.

Shane's face was tight, as he roughly brought the demon to his knees. He held his head up high, so that we could look into his coal black eyes.

I cracked my knuckles. What happened next was beyond what I had thought I could ever do to another living thing. I expulsed all of my animalistic rage upon him. I didn't kill him: that would be letting him off easy.

We left him bloodied on the floor of his cell, and we went our separate ways. I went up to my room. I stepped into the bathroom and flipped the lights on. I could barely recognize myself in the mirror.

I walked inside the infirmary, and almost did a double-take. Different emotions swarmed inside of me. Anger. Jealousy. Bittersweet happiness. Shane was at Abby's bedside, holding her hand. He had fallen asleep onto his chair, leaning on the bed's metallic contour.

My feet stayed glued to the floor as I watched Abby's sweet face enveloped in the bliss of somnolency. There was a growing ball that was forming itself at the back of my throat. The realization that she didn't belong to me anymore was slowly hitting me; it was making itself inside of my head as painfully as a knife seeking its way through flesh. She was his now. From the moment she had become the Element, she had been his. I'd noticed the way she'd look at him. It wasn't anything much, but it'd been enough for me to get the hint. I'd given breaking things off with her much thought, because things had gone so well for months... But the cards had changed. She'd unknowingly fallen for another guy, and I, on the other hand, had found a path that might make me feel... as though I belonged. Sure, I had friends like Brittany, Wesley, Kait and Abby. But let's face it, they couldn't exactly understand the things I had to go though. Abby now understood what it was like to see things you'd rather not see, but she still couldn't understand certain things only shapeshifters could understand and relate to. I had to find someplace where people would be able to help me through the difficulties of the Nightrealm. And I couldn't do this with Abby, because we wouldn't see each other as much, or maybe at all, and I didn't want to have to put her through that... especially when there was this Night that wasn't uninterested in her.

I shifted my weight, and was about to leave, when I saw Shane lift his head. He glanced towards me, then at Abby, and got up. He walked in my direction, and ushered me out of the room.

"I know," I said bluntly. I looked directly into his eyes, and he didn't look away. "I know that she's fallen in love with you." He was about to say something, but I kept going. "I still love her, but I decided to end things with her, because I've made a decision. I'm going to join a shapeshifter pack as soon as things with the Lost Elements are settled. I'll stay here for as long as Abby'll need me, and for as long as my help is needed. Gabe has informed me about some of the packs I could join not too far from here, so I won't be too far. There is only one thing I want to warn you of: if you hurt her, in anyway, I will hurt you. Take good care of her. She's yours now."

Shane's eyes didn't wander away from mine. "She belongs to no one. She's too strong-willed to stoop to the level of someone's belonging."

I grinned. I couldn't have said better myself. "Just take care of her. I'll be here for a while, but not forever. And she'll need all the support she can get with all the obstacles that will come her way."

The Nightrider nodded solemnly. "I know."

And with that, I did what I had never thought I would ever do in my life. I extended my hand as to offer my tolerance. Not my friendship, I was too proud for that yet, but my tolerance. He took my hand, and we shook on it, for our sake as well as Abby's.

EPILOGUE

ABBY

I woke up with a nagging pain at the back of my head. Why did I always wake up like this? It was starting to be annoying. My body was all sweaty and I felt that if I didn't get out soon, I would lose my mind.

I opened my eyes and saw nothing but white for a moment. I took in a deep breath. The scent of antiseptic overcame me. *Ugh.* I was in a hospital, or something very similar to it. I moved my arms from under the thick covers to get that damn humid cloth off my forehead. Why did everyone think I needed a *damn* damp cloth to keep me alive!

I sat up and felt a sharp pain stab my stomach. I was wearing a hospital gown, so I didn't dare look underneath, from fright of seeing stitches. I didn't like stitches.

I looked up and saw Shane sitting right next to me, sleeping peacefully, his head resting against the corner of my bed. Wow, he needed a thick skull to be able to sleep like that. I smiled to myself. His hair looked really soft under this light. I had always wanted to touch it to see how it would feel against my fingertips.

I bit my lip as I ran my hand through his hair and he sat up abruptly, ready to attack the person who had *dared* touch his hair. He looked up at me and I smiled. He looked so … out of place, sitting here at my bedside, waiting for me to wake up.

"Abby …" He seemed at a loss for words. "I don't—"

"Before you start telling how much you hate saving my ass and shit like that, let me tell you something." I paused. My abdomen hurt whenever I heaved too much air out. I would have to be more careful. "I saved you today, Shane or whenever it is that I saved you. I didn't just save your ass; I saved your *life with my own!* So, you can't hold it against me anymore—and something else; I love you! I've given it much thought in my dreams or whatever it was. No matter how much I hate to admit it, I do love you. That's why I kept on fighting these past few days; that's why I haven't fallen into a depression. It's because of you! You showed me strength I didn't have and I envied you for it. I wanted to show you that I too could be strong." He was about to say something but I stopped him. "Wait, let me finish. I love you and there's nothing I can do about it. I've completely fallen for you without realizing it, and if you don't feel the same, that's f—"

Shane put a finger to my lips. "I love you too, Abby. I have since the very first day I looked into those purple eyes of yours." He smiled at me. "And I love saving your ass. It's what makes my life so much more exciting."

"But you said—"

"Screw what I said. I was afraid of what I was feeling for you. I had never felt that way before. Now, after having spent four full days in this godforsaken place, I have come to the realization that I should not run away from my fears. I should embrace them." He paused and brought his hand to my cheek. "I thought I would lose you that night. I wasn't afraid of my feelings anymore; I was afraid of losing what caused them."

My throat constricted and I felt tears stinging my eyes. He saw them and sat back. "Wow, I'm sorry if my declaration was horrible but it's the best I could come up with."

I shook my head and laughed. "It's the most beautiful thing anyone has ever said to me."

He let out a nervous laugh and scratched the side of his head. "Well, I'm happy you liked it." He smiled and brought his face closer to mine. "I love you, Abigail Claire."

"And I love *you*, Shane McKenna."

"I thought no one would ever say that," he said, bringing his forehead to mine. I wrapped my arms around his neck and laughed as he brought his lips to mine. It was the sweetest of all kisses and it was making me lightheaded.

"Get a room you two, will you?"

I looked up and saw Luke standing at the clinic's threshold, grinning at us. My heart skipped a beat. Last time we had really seen each other, he had broken up with me. I looked deeply into his eyes, to see if there was any hurt or betrayal in them. To my surprise and great relief, there was none. He actually seemed genuinely... *happy* for me. It was as though a huge weight had been taken off my shoulders.

"So does this mean you two are going out?" asked Luke, grinning at the both of us.

Shane raised our intertwined fingers and grinned foolishly. It was the first time, I noted, that the two of them didn't start a fight or look at each other with anger in their eyes. I don't think I had ever seen Shane this happy before. "Yup."

"Well, I'm happy for the two of you."

"Well, there's more good news to come," exclaimed Shane. I looked at him. I still had difficulty wrapping my mind around the fact that we were *together*. What more good news could he give me?

"What is it?" I asked, leaning into him.

"Belvedem was questioned and we found his lair. Abby, we found ... Mrs. Wildfire and Mary. They're alive and well."

I froze, my mind– glazing over. I couldn't believe my ears. Had I heard him right? "What?"

"They're not here right now; they're at Mrs. Wildfire's house."

"You're not kidding," I said in a doubtful voice. Were they playing with me? Because if they were, it *really* wasn't funny. I was going to blow their asses off to Canada—literally.

Luke shook his head, with a widespread smile on his face. "We're not kidding."

I jumped out of bed and almost fell face forward but thankfully, Shane was there to catch me. He held me at the waist and pressed me tightly against him. I felt butterflies tingling in my stomach when he pressed his lips once more to mine. I licked his lips and he groaned. "Ugh, once I've tasted those pink lips of yours, it's hard to stop."

"Okay guys, I know I might have made a mistake in letting Abby go but come on, Shane, you know it's wrong to rub it in!"

Shane smiled against my lips. "I think it's the best mistake he's ever made."

I laughed. "Are you going to let me go see them?"

Shane scooped me in his arms and hugged me tightly to his chest, careful not to hurt my abdomen. "I'm even going to let *you* drive."

I still had to find my mother; I still had to find the other Lost Elements and I still had to fight the demons who would stand in my way. I still had to learn how to fight; I still had to learn a lot from life. I had all these things to do but at that moment, I couldn't care. I was in love and everyone, or almost, that I loved was here for me.

I looked into Shane's eyes and all my worries faded. He would be here for me. I loved him and I wasn't going to let him go anytime soon...